HOLD DOWN A SHADOW

The time is 1995. The place, Lesotho, a tiny land-locked African state, famous for its soaring cliffs and awesome snow-covered peaks. The occasion is the opening ceremony of the key Katse Dam.

Gathered to celebrate the opening will be dignitaries from nations worldwide. But one man – the sinister Maluti Rider from the 'mountains of death' – is seeking revenge for the loss of his family, the loss of his land. He determines to destroy the dam and release a killer flood. Helping him fulfil his vengeance-lust are four of the world's most wanted men – the Chunnel Gang.

Key to their plan is the golden Eagle of Time, a horological masterpiece crafted by the beautiful Grania Yeats. Grania becomes an unwilling pawn in the deadly plan as does Sholto Banks, a brilliant young barrister, known as the Riverman, because of his prowess as a canoe racer.

In *Hold Down A Shadow*, Geoffrey Jenkins has written a spell-binding, high-speed adventure thriller which grips the reader to the very last page.

HOLD DOWN
A SHADOW

GEOFFREY JENKINS

COLLINS
8 Grafton Street, London W1
1989

William Collins Sons & Co. Ltd
London · Glasgow · Sydney · Auckland
Toronto · Johannesburg

BRITISH LIBRARY CATALOGUING IN PUBLICATION DATA

Jenkins, Geoffrey, *1920*–
Hold down a shadow.
I. Title
823 [F]

ISBN 0–00–223379–7

First published 1989
© Geoffrey Jenkins 1989
Maps by Leslie Robinson
Photoset in Linotron Plantin at
The Spartan Press Ltd,
Lymington, Hants
Printed and bound in Great Britain by
William Collins Sons & Co. Ltd, Glasgow

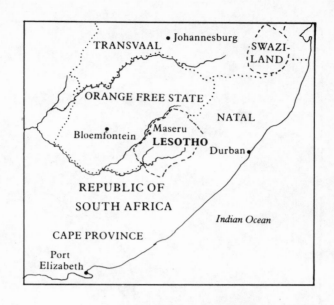

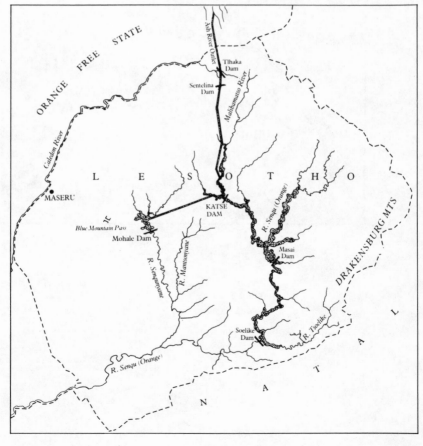

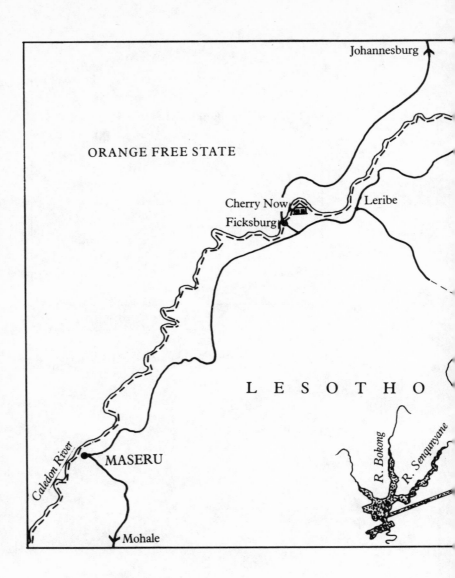

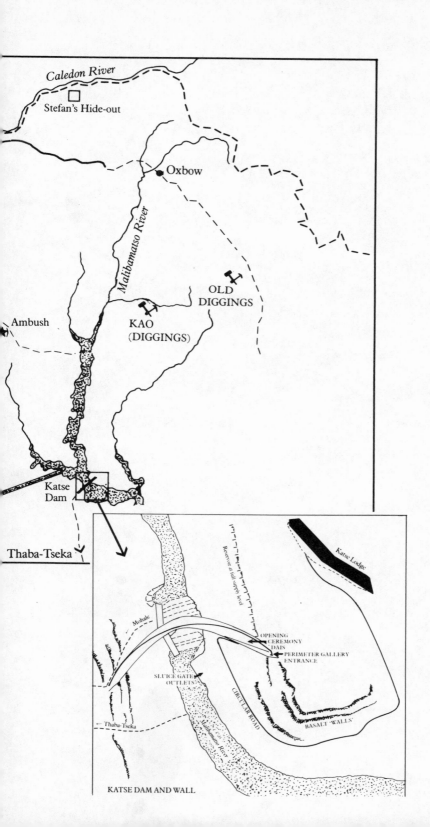

PROLOGUE

Forty degrees. The watcher shivered. Ten degrees to go to optimum firing angle.

His tremor was not fear or bitter cold which struck up from the rocks among which he lay at the top of the pass: it was anticipation, joyful anticipation.

Fifty degrees. He'd calculated that fatal angle when he had staked out the place. That would blast the van driver and his cab-mates full frontal. Like the other raids, there must be no survivors, no one to recall that just before the fusillade there had lurked a blanketed figure among the ice-bound rocks . . .

The approaching headlights narrowed the firing angle. The diesel stomped up the pass. The growing illumination picked out a line of white snow which deckle-edged the black basalt boulders flanking the rough gravel road.

The ambusher reached under the blanket he wore like a poncho. A separate strip of the same pattern enveloped his head, something like a flattened old-time tricorn hat. It masked his face and eyes so that in the faint light there was only an emptiness of the eye-sockets, like a dead man's.

Swiftness and control were in his movements. From under the poncho's folds he whipped a Kalashnikov AK-47. The way he put the barrel against his cheek for a quick second could have been a kiss or a temperature check. He reached again inside the poncho. His fingers felt for the old-fashioned German carbine hook on his belt and automatically unclipped two grenades. He laid them beside him on the rock. The casings were as wrinkled and black as the grooved rock itself.

The AK-47 rifle had a wooden stock; the man ran a cupped hand under it as if he were stroking a favourite dog's chin. Along the smooth wood, his fingers encountered a different texture, that of paper, tiny serrated paper squares. He smiled grimly and counted – yes, eight. Eight postage stamps. He had stuck them

I

on the way frontiersmen of the Old West made nicks in their gun-butts to record the number of their victims. These Lesotho postage stamps depicted the traditional Basuto straw hat, the conical shape of which is the country's emblem.

The blanket he wore was traditional also. The Basuto have developed a blanket culture as no other nation has. The ambusher made sure that his poncho's stripes ran vertically and not horizontally – horizontal brings bad luck. He deliberately wore a type – named the Seana Marena – which was widely popular. A more exclusive sort would make him more easily identifiable if he were spotted.

Eight stamps. Eight ambushes. Eight burning, blazing trucks – how many bodies? Over twenty, he guessed. The wrecks lay scattered about the Mountains of Death. Tonight's shoot-up – only minutes away now – would make the tally nine, and probably his last. Somehow, he could have wished for ten, for the sake of a round number. But he'd have to be content with nine. The grand opening ceremony was only a little more than a fortnight away; he'd be crazy to risk another in that time. Police and troops would be out like a stirred-up hornets' nest.

Here it was! The van accelerated up the summit, headlights blazing, right into his line of fire.

He snapped the AK-47 to his shoulder. It bucked and jerked and recoiled against his cheek, shouting death in a blasting voice across the rocks at its victim.

The windscreen dissolved under the hail of 7.62mm slugs. So did the driver's face. The ambusher had a split-second glimpse of horror and terror in the face next to the driver before it, too, disintegrated.

But the third man in the cab had life still. The ambusher could not nail him through the remnants of the granulated windscreen. He cut his fire. The survivor flung open his door, jumped. The van careered backwards down the steep incline.

In seconds the escaper would be protected either by the vehicle slewing to a halt against the roadside rocks or by the boulders themselves. *There must be no survivors!*

The blanketed man leapt to his feet, held his sights on the figure dodging and plunging among the wet rocks like a cockroach scuttling and twisting breakneck to safety from a boot. The AK-47 again intoned its requiem of death. Limbs and body went still among the rocks.

The vehicle lay canted drunkenly. The ambusher picked up a grenade, pulled the pin, waited a brief moment, then pitched it. The van responded to the detonation as if it was about to leap over the cliff to the river far below. Then it settled, fuel pouring from a ruptured tank.

The ambusher again waited a few moments while the fuel splashed a pool under the stricken vehicle. Then he took the second grenade, hurled it. The van stirred like a living being absorbing a death-blow. Then it threw its own counter-punch – a blinding rocket of flame leapt into the darkness. Almost simultaneously, a concussion stunned the ears.

The blanketed figure turned away, doubled to the rear of the rock battlement from where he had opened fire to a spot between two other high rocks. A saddled mountain pony jerked uneasily at its tether, and the glare of the fire was red in its eyes.

The blanketed killer slipped the AK-47 into a saddle holster, unhitched the horse, mounted, and vanished into the night.

CHAPTER ONE

The scream of a police siren sent a ripple through the crowd. An involuntary reflex action by one of a group of four men who stood together in the street sent his gunhand to his empty shoulder holster where his pistol was normally concealed. He checked the movement, dropped his hand, and flicked a half-embarrassed glance at his neighbour to see if the movement had been observed. However, the shortish dark man, who seemed to have an unconscious air of authority over the quartet, had not spotted it. His attention was concentrated on a posse of motor-cycle police heading a green security van travelling down the main street towards the building outside which the crowd waited on the pavement. It was no ordinary building; it was shaped like a hat, and no ordinary hat at that: conical, thatched, topping a two-storeyed circular structure raised on concrete pillars.

This was the Basuto Hat craft and exhibition centre, in the heart of Maseru, the capital of Lesotho (formerly British Basutoland), the small landlocked black kingdom in the south-eastern corner of South Africa. Lesotho, only one-and-a-half times the size of Wales, boasts the most spectacular scenery in Africa within its small confines. Over forty of its great mountain peaks soar to a height of over 3000 metres; the highest touches nearly 3500 metres, or over 11000 feet. In winter, all are snow-blanketed. Lesotho takes for its national emblem not its great peaks but the conical grass hat with its curious four-piece woven topknot which is to be seen everywhere, capping blanketed tribesmen riding wild ponies in the mountains, or topping ordinary town dwellers.

The posse slowed, the sirens receded to a gurgling growl. The man whose reflexes tried to outrun his commonsense drew a little closer to his three companions, as if the police presence bugged him and he needed protection. He was young, with a

5

pale blotchy skin and sandy eyebrows. The dark leader's face was inscrutable as he watched the posse fan out round the security van, now pulling in to the kerbside. The other two of the foursome were in sharp physical contrast: one seemed slightly older than the others (none of whose ages could have been more than thirty) and looked as heavy as an English butcher with a matching heavy sense of grievance; the fourth, in faded jeans and a sloppy bomber jacket, one could pass anywhere in any street – until you saw his eyes. You could trust a primed grenade more.

The security van halted. The motor-cycle escort, like a well-drilled *corps de ballet*, slid into double row formation to the door facing one another, gripping ugly little sub-machine-guns. Two security men, in dark green uniforms, dropped from the cab and stood at the ready by the van's big sliding side door. Each held a heavy .38 Service revolver. The driver came round from his side and slid open the door.

If the crowd of several hundred had expected to view the spectacle for which they had assembled they were disappointed. All the interior held was two more security men – they wore Bank of Switzerland light blue uniforms – and a grey steel box like that used to transport gold bullion. It was rectangular, with rope carrying handles, and a little over a metre tall.

The driver nodded, and the two Swiss hefted the box out of the van, and carried it through the double row of guards to the entrance.

The leader of the foursome, whose name was Jules Bonnay, said out of the corner of his mouth, 'Very neat. Very professional.'

The sloppily-dressed man, called Burt Hayward, replied, watching the Swiss guards passing through the door and the armed men closing rank behind them, 'Makes you think, doesn't it?'

Bonnay glanced at him sharply. It wasn't the meaning, but the inference behind the words, which provoked his return fire. 'Then don't think.'

The door was still open. The interior of the Basuto Hat – ordinarily a landmark craft centre specialising in anything from woven grasswork to tapestries, but now converted to a top security display area – was brilliantly lit by floodlights. From where he stood in sunlight, Bonnay could see the probing eye of closed-circuit TV cameras moving restlessly on their axes and, at the far end, a raised dais where a group of well-dressed people were gathered. In front of them was a small rostrum, on which stood a glass case.

The Swiss guards with their burden were heading for this via a roped-off gangway, which continued on past the rostrum and back again to the entrance, as if intended to guide queues.

Then the doors closed on the crowd. However, they could still view the proceedings inside on big TV screens at the door.

Formal clothes and comfortable years made the group on the dais look security-safe. The generation gap cleaved the party in half and isolated two – a young woman and man – who clearly did not belong to the diplomat-dignitary class. She had short black hair cut in a modern style back above her ears and wore a champagne-coloured, severely-tailored suit. The TV lights, tracking the Swiss guards as they neared the rostrum, threw back the red-yellow translucency of her fashioned carnelian earrings which otherwise might have been missed because of their smallness. The man who stood next to her filled his suit – its cut might have been that of a barrister's suit – with wide shoulders and a rangy, above-average height body. The TV cameras were incapable of defining the slight cast forward of his right shoulder, or the powerful muscles running from shoulders to neck. Yet they did reveal his tan, in contrast to the indoor paleness of the rest.

However, the unkind light of the TV did pick up how crumpled the Swiss uniforms were – the guards had slept in them next to the bullion box on the non-stop flight from Zurich.

Now, the guards reached the rostrum. The group seemed to tense. The rangy man threw his companion a brief smile with a special-delivery stamp for her alone. Her face remained withdrawn, however, even remote. The only sign that she shared the tension — she had more reason than anyone present to be uptight – was that her right fingers reached involuntarily for the carnelian in her right ear-lobe, and then checked, as if she were conscious of the giveaway habit.

7

The guards set down the box and handed the key to a dignitary who came forward – he was, in fact, the Lesotho Minister of Water, Energy and Mining. He took it, and turned to the group.

'Dr Hans Poortman.'

A well-dressed man, with a banker's figure and flyaway eyebrows, took the key with a slight bow and put it, under the guards' guidance, into the bullion-box lock. The two guards then unfolded the container into four panels – padded on the inside – to reveal its contents.

The hard light spotlighted it; the group gave a gasp. So did those outside the building, who had the benefit of a TV close-up.

It was a tiny thing – not more than eighteen centimetres high – from which light struck off the jewels and goldwork. It was clearly a clock: its delicate hands and perpetual calendar were to be seen in one of the sixteen side-panels or modules, each containing exquisite miniature works of art, the subject and symbolism of which still required detailed explanation to the onlookers.

Even without explanation, however, the overall effect was stunning.

They were looking at the world's greatest horological masterpiece.

But if the sixteen modules, not to mention a gold module containing a carillon of tiny bells to strike the hours, left the spectators breathless, it was the pediment topping the time-piece (on which a spotlight was focused) which was the ultimate eye-catcher.

It was in the form of a bird of prey, sculpted in gold, gripping in its talons a thunderbolt, its wings still folded, but poised for flight at any moment. If it could have flown, one would have felt it would have launched itself with its angry eyes in protest against the gawping crowd, so life-like was it. The golden wings were fashioned with a delicacy and fineness which indeed made them look capable of flight.

Dr Poortman announced, 'I give you the Eagle of Time.'

CHAPTER TWO

It was, in fact, not an eagle, but only half an eagle. The other half was a vulture. The two birds meet in nature in the form of a lammergeyer – a mighty, near-extinct bird with a wingspan of up to three metres, whose glorious black and orange gold plumage is to be seen (if one is lucky) against the purple-violet crags of Lesotho's mountains. Its golden mane as it soars with an eagle's grace is a never-to-be-forgotten spectacle; a lammergeyer has even been sighted above Mount Everest. The vulture in the lammergeyer's make-up emerges in its carrion diet; it seldom attacks living creatures. However, because farmers have claimed that it kills their small stock, it has been ruthlessly exterminated throughout the world; the very name – 'lamb-vulture' – embodies the prejudice. The lammergeyer still survives in the mountain fastnesses of Lesotho, where the breeding colonies are protected against further extinction.

The Lesotho Minister spoke into the microphone. 'We are privileged to have with us today Dr Poortman, who heads the Swiss banking consortium which has been responsible for investing so many millions in our country and whose idea it was to symbolise the great enterprise we have undertaken – in collaboration with South Africa – over the past nine years and which is now at the point of realisation. We are happy to have with us also today the South African diplomatic representatives and officials who have been involved with us – ' the Minister made a gesture towards the group behind him ' – but our task at this moment is to pay tribute to the person responsible for this unique and magnificent timepiece. However, I will leave Dr Poortman to perform the introduction.'

The Minister drew Dr Poortman to the microphone. The Swiss banker did not speak immediately. Instead, he turned and led the young woman in the champagne suit to the rostrum. 'I now give you the artist responsible for this – ' he indicated the golden lammergeyer on the pediment ' – Grania Yeats.'

The group burst into spontaneous hand-clapping; had the main doors not been closed, the VIPs would also have heard the applause of the crowd outside. All were clapping except Bonnay and the other three standing together. Bonnay, by contrast, seemed to be memorising every detail of Dr Poortman's face as the cameras zoomed in on him and Grania Yeats; Burt Hayward was concentrating on the Eagle of Time.

Hayward remarked, 'Must be worth a lot of green.'

A woman bystander next to him thought the remark was addressed to her. 'Millions, I'd say. Look at all those jewels. And that bird on top – solid gold.'

'Aye, solid gold,' echoed Hayward.

It was Bonnay who again silenced him with a tight note in his voice. 'Aye, solid gold – not negotiable, is it?'

The cameras held on Grania's face. She did not look like the conventional image of an artist, let alone an artist-goldsmith capable of executing the pediment. She might have been any well-dressed young woman, except for the eyes below the casual curls on her forehead and well-defined eyebrows, slightly lighter in colour than the hair. The cameras were not capable of portraying their withdrawn air, faraway, some might even say, mystic. Nor did they focus on the hands which fashioned the masterpiece, the slender bones and wrists of a master craftsman. The complete absence of any jewellery, even a dress ring, on her fingers seemed to deny her deep involvement with her craft. Except, on the strap of her gold wristwatch, there was a stylised engraved face which looked Oriental.

However, the cameras could not avoid relaying something indefinable – it could have been shock or tragedy – which had engraved a degree of maturity on the youthful laughter muscles of her twenty-eight-year-old face. Now, however, that vanished as she gave a warm smile and said into the microphone, 'Thank you, thank you very much. You are too generous.'

She started to back away, but Dr Poortman restrained her.

'You all know that the Eagle of Time has been fashioned to commemorate, here in Lesotho, the greatest civil engineering project ever undertaken anywhere in the world, and Grania Yeats' contribution has proved worthy of the faith I and my banking consortium have in it. Our interests have, during the years of hard preliminary work, been equally worthily looked after by– 'he indicated the rangy man in the barrister's suit ' –the person we call our ombudsman, Mr Sholto Banks . . .'

The year was 1995. Eight years previously, Lesotho and South Africa had signed a treaty in the terms of which virtually the whole of Lesotho was to be turned into a gigantic reservoir by the construction of a series of vast dams, interconnecting tunnels, hydrostations and pumping stations which would supply water-starved South Africa's needs well into the next century.

It was known as the Lesotho Highlands Water Project.

As Dr Poortman had said, it was the biggest and most imaginative civil engineering scheme ever attempted anywhere in the world. It was scheduled to cost over R4 billion. It was due to be completed in the year 2019.

Sholto Banks hung back, but the man with him, a Basuto with a proud face (he was of royal blood), ushered him forward to join Grania Yeats and Dr Poortman. His name was Jonathan, a royal name in Lesotho.

Sholto Banks stood very erect, taller than the other two at the microphone. The couple of strides which had brought him forward were long and easy–a mountaineer and sportsman's gait. His long, dark brown hair fell somewhat untidily over his forehead, despite the formality of the occasion, and the cameras did not miss the square, strong jaw and easy half-smile which tugged slightly leftwards.

'You all know Sholto Banks from his picture, at least,' Dr Poortman was saying. 'He has brought fame and distinction to Lesotho in the competitive sphere of canoe marathons and now again, in a different context, with this imaginative Highlands Project where he has piloted Swiss banking interests with such success . . .'

The crowd applauded, not as loudly as for Grania.

Outside, Hayward looked round for somewhere to spit, but he was too closely hemmed in.

Instead, he muttered, 'Slap my back and I'll slap yours.'

The butcher-contoured heavy man, whose name was John Kennet, added taciturnly, 'That's the way it goes, in Lesotho, anywhere.'

The blotchy-faced fourth member of the party – he was Paul Pestiaux – said, 'Like you said, you see his picture all the time in the papers and on TV. Orange River marathon, 1000 kilometres, or something.'

'Keep watching, anyway,' cautioned Bonnay.

Dr Poortman handed over the microphone again to the Lesotho Minister.

'The VIP party will now withdraw for an official reception to mark this auspicious occasion, and the hall will then be thrown open to the general public,' he announced. 'However, our Lesotho Chief of Security here, General Makoanyane – ' he indicated a uniformed man with an uncompromising face among the VIP group ' – has asked me to state that the strictest security measures will be in force. This will apply to the next twelve days also while the Eagle of Time is on view until the official opening of the Lesotho Highlands Project at Katse Dam, which is the key storage centre of the whole great project, and the first to be completed.

'However, to enable the construction workers at Katse to participate in the triumph which belongs to them also, the Eagle will be taken to Katse four days from now and be on view there for the day. There will, as a result, be no showing at the Basuto Hat that particular day.

'This afternoon, the VIP party will fly to Katse for a preview of the dam. The public will now be allowed in in small groups at a time, and must pass the rostrum in single file . . .'

Bonnay led in his foursome among the first-comers as flashes from press cameras lit up the rostrum. What he had not noticed through the open door was a table which had now been brought forward and at which stood a pair of uniformed security men. On it was one of those electric metal-check devices through which handbags, briefcases and the like are channelled.

Pestiaux said in an agonised whisper to Bonnay, 'My shoulder holster!'

12

'Keep going!' snapped back Bonnay. 'It's not metal, it won't show. Don't give yourself away. If they ask, it's for self-protection.'

The tiny muscles in his temples were beating; it seemed hot in the place; the TV monitors were pointed at the first-comers. He hardly took in the display of blown-up photographs, maps and plans – even a scale model – of the giant water scheme which would turn the north-south spine of Lesotho into one huge lake over 160 kilometres long. At the heart of it lay the first key dam, Katse, whose wall would soar 168 metres and from which an eighty-kilometre double underground tunnel would feed water to South Africa.

Hayward, on Bonnay's heels, muttered, 'Camera monitors give me the shits – ever since.'

The guard asked formally, 'No parcels, sir? Briefcases? Handbags?'

Pestiaux shook his head, walked on. The camera monitor watched through its beady, suspicious eye. He kept going with a tight face. Bonnay, who likewise passed through the check, joined him, and they waited a moment for Hayward and Kennet to catch up. Bonnay knew there was a patina of sweat on his face, but he would wait until later before finding his handkerchief and wiping it off. Security men could be bastards about picking up any tiny giveaway.

The four men walked to the timepiece, now safe under a glass case.

As they reached it, the clear, almost ethereal chimes of the six-bell carillon brought silence to the queue. All that could be heard underplaying it was the soft whirr of the TV-eye controls. The chimes came from one of the sixteen modules or panels of the clock. On this module had been recreated in gold a miniature of Picasso's masterpiece depicting the town of Guernica being destroyed by German bombers during the Spanish Civil War.

The art was lost on the quartet, but not the stunning overall impact. It was not for nothing that it had been called the world's most complex clock. It had taken 10,000 man-hours by master-craftsmen of a leading Swiss house to work, fashion, chase and chisel its 9000 pieces. The clock had thirty-two separate functions, ranging from the indication of conventional time to the movement of the stars over Lesotho, New York, Berne and Sydney. The Signs of the Zodiac were picked out in semi-precious stones, and a perpetual calendar had been set to conclude its functions in the year the Highlands Water Project would be complete in all its phases.

Each module – the whole timepiece was only eighteen centimetres by nine – was a triumph of miniaturised art and had as its individual contribution an elemental or continental theme. The chronometer had as its theme Time and the Memory of Man; Africa was depicted by the Goddess Nimba.

These subtleties were lost on the four now staring at the timepiece; their eyes were riveted, as were all onlookers', on the exquisite pediment above the clock and its gold lammergeyer. The wings were folded now; what almost superhuman mechanism would make them spread twelve days hence to signal the grand ceremonial opening of the Highlands Project? No one could guess, any more than they could guess what miniature works of art were still to be revealed – again, Grania's own goldsmithing craft – in a secret capsule concealed beneath the pediment behind an opaque viewing window.

The momentum of the queue behind edged the four men forward.

'I've seen enough – let's get out,' said Hayward.

Bonnay said emphatically, 'You – all of us – will not get out – yet. We will look at the models, the photographs, all of them, just like the other spectators are doing.'

'Jeez . . .' Hayward started to protest.

Bonnay said through his teeth, '*You will stay, see?* What would you do, even if you were a dumb cop monitoring the TV of this crowd, if you saw four men scuttle in and then scuttle out again without giving a damn for the one thing that really matters? You'd say, they were interested only in the treasure! Pull yourself together man. We stay!'

They did. They read with unseeing eyes the overwhelming barrage of facts and figures of the mighty Project, and of the immediate colossus, the Katse Dam. Finally, Bonnay gave the all clear and they made their way uneasily again past the security check with the TV cameras which, they all felt, were boring into their backs.

Even Bonnay was now in a hurry to get out. So much so that, as he emerged from the door, he collided with a man entering. He was bumped hard off the shoulder like a Rugby hand-off. The man, of stocky, medium build, was striding in with such concentration that he did not even seem to notice the collision. The timepiece might have been a light luring a moth. The guards, too, noted his absorption – but he stared past them, his eyes riveted on the Eagle of Time.

Then the group was outside, clear of the exhibition hall.

Hayward said, 'My oath, I need a drink! And I intend to have it!'

Kennet made one of his rare utterances, 'It's not yet ten in the morning.'

'Dumb monitors, my arse!' Hayward retorted. 'I felt all the time I was inside there like I did in the foyer at Marseilles . . .'

But TV monitors are dumb. If they hadn't been, they would not have let pass the world's four most wanted men.

They styled themselves the Chunnel Gang.

CHAPTER THREE

There is notoriety in killing one prime minister, but the Chunnel Gang had aimed for two leaders – a premier and a president.

Nearly two years before, in mid-1993, the Channel Tunnel, the R21-billion undersea link between Britain and France, was ceremonially opened by the British Prime Minister and French President. Like the Lesotho Highlands Project, the Eurotunnel, as it was called, caught the imagination of the world; it was the culmination of over a century of off-on negotiation between Britain and France. Such an undersea tunnel had first been proposed by Napoleon. The scheme had finally received the go-ahead in 1986 from Mrs Margaret Thatcher on the British side, and President François Mitterand on the French. However, critics on both sides of the Channel – local opposition in Kent and Calais was as high as ninety per cent – accused the two statesmen of political opportunism, of seeking to put their names to one of the world's most glamorous and impressive engineering feats.

Local opposition crystallised itself in the form of a body of mainly unemployed stop-at-nothing extremists in France calling themselves *Les Patriots de Calais*, and in Britain, The Men of Kent. The Frenchmen asserted that the Chunnel would kill their city, already reeling under the highest unemployment rate in France; the British argued that the new transport links would ruin the environment and destroy long-established local landownings going back centuries. Both sides maintained that the two statesmen had bulldozed the project through without proper consideration.

The Men of Kent had gathered under the banner of John Kennet, a bitter, dispossessed widower and landowner whose generations-old farm had been swept away by a new highway. Kennet had also suffered great personal sorrow in the Channel itself – his only son had been drowned in the *Herald of Free Enterprise* cross-Channel ferry disaster of 1987. His paranoia, a sense of bitter grievance of having been singled out by an uncompromising fate at the age of twenty-eight, manifested itself in an implacable hatred of anything connected with the Channel.

Jules Bonnay was one of those men of great leadership ability which a situation like the Calais ferment against the Eurotunnel throws up, who batten on to a lost cause to find themselves. His past and identity were probably lost amongst the French police files, and at twenty-nine, he was the oldest member of the Chunnel Gang.

Bonnay with his Calais *Patriots* and Kennet with his Men of Kent were bound to meet up. They did. Between them, they fabricated an assassination plot which was calculated to stun the world and at the same time wreck the Eurotunnel forever.

It was as simple as it was grand in concept: the Chunnel Gang, using the sophisticated services of a former IRA explosives expert, Burt Hayward, would detonate a bomb at the Chunnel opening which would kill the British and French leaders, let in the sea and flood the Chunnel, thus effectively wrecking it forever. The thought of assassinating the British prime minister had instant appeal for Hayward, one of the IRA's top men; the bottom line of Bonnay and Kennet's dossiers at Scotland Yard read, 'ultra-left wing Trotskyites pledged to assassinate Western statesmen.'

Perhaps Scotland Yard knew more than it admitted, perhaps it was tipped off by a squealer. Whatever it was, the Yard, working with the French police, unearthed the plot on the eve of the opening. However, the Chunnel Gang slipped through the subsequent dragnet, thrown Europe-wide by the combined forces of Scotland Yard, the French police and Interpol.

Bonnay's cool nerve and skilled leadership qualities surfaced through the welter of public anger, media outrage and police traps. He and the gang realised that their life-expectancy in Europe was extremely limited. They needed money – lots of money – to escape abroad.

He struck at the biggest bank in southern France, in

Marseilles, which also harboured the largest number of private strongboxes in France. These held fortunes in jewels, coin and scrip. The four men braved the bank's monitoring TV cameras to hold the bank staff to ransom at gunpoint for over twelve hours, in the face of a siege by hundreds of armed police. When the police finally rushed the place they found it empty. The Chunnel Gang had escaped via an unknown sewer running beneath the bank vaults.

Where to escape abroad, even with plenty of money and the faked passports that it could buy? Bonnay had a brother who was a lay worker at a French Protestant mission in Lesotho – French missionaries had done pioneering work in the country for over 150 years.

Interpol was hot on the gang's heels – Hayward had been identified from one of the videos in the bank's foyer. Once again Bonnay outwitted the authorities, and the four men found themselves in Maseru, capital of Lesotho – safe, unknown, beyond the reach of extradition proceedings.

That was nearly two years ago.

Now the four men walked down Kingsway, Maseru's main thoroughfare, and turned down towards the Caledon River, the international boundary with South Africa, near which their hotel, the Croupier's Arms, was situated. The place took its name from the fact that it was half-hotel, half-casino.

They made for the casino bar. It was empty, except for an early-bird whore.

Bonnay selected a table out of earshot of the barman, whose name was Umberto.

Umberto looked across interrogatively at the quartet. 'Usual?' Bonnay nodded.

'Even at this time of day, whiskey is best,' observed Hayward.

'What is that supposed to mean?' asked Bonnay.

'Anything you care to make it mean,' replied Hayward.

'If you drank real whisky, spelt without an "e", and not your dog-piss,' said Kennet morosely. 'Anyway, beer is best.'

They waited in silence until Umberto put down the drinks.

'What the hell is wrong with you guys?' demanded Bonnay.

'I'm allergic to TV monitors after Marseilles,' responded

Hayward. 'That bloody thing back there in the hall felt like an X-ray punching between my shoulder-blades.'

'Well, it was you Interpol identified from the bank videos,' remarked Pestiaux. The stuff he was drinking looked like raspberry and smelt like alcohol fuel.

'Is that meant to be funny?' demanded Hayward.

'I had the creeps myself,' replied Pestiaux sympathetically. 'Someone might still have those bank videos and see us on today's pictures . . .'

Hayward swallowed the rest of his bog-whiskey at a gulp. 'I thought it was tickets, once we were trapped inside that bank.'

'Why all the backtracking into the past?' demanded Bonnay.

'You know the reason,' answered Hayward. 'The Eagle. I keep asking myself, what would have happened . . .'

'Nothing did happen,' replied Bonnay tightly. 'Except the way we wanted it to happen. Remember that. We got all the money and freedom we wanted.'

'Call this freedom?' demanded Hayward. 'Nearly two years of it – same bloody dump, same bloody faces, same bloody one-armed bandits, same bloody whores . . .'

He made a gesture towards the tart leaning against the bar. She took it for a signal, and swung across to their table.

'Buzz off,' snapped Hayward.

She looked inquiringly round the rest of the group. 'Too early,' added Bonnay.

'It's never too early, I say.'

'Can't a man even have a drink in peace without sex rearing its ugly head?' said Hayward. 'I said, buzz off, push off – '

'Okay, don't say the word for the next time round,' the girl answered. 'I know it.'

'I'll bet you do.'

'I'll be around, if wanted.' She reversed course and returned to the bar.

'That's what I mean,' continued Hayward. 'Bored. She's been around here for two years, and after two years you lose the taste for it. This place gives me a pain in the backside. We daren't even cross the border and have ourselves a thrash among the bright lights of South Africa for fear of being caught.'

Kennet drained his beer and asked, 'What's that thing worth?'

There was no need for the other three to ask what he was talking about.

'I told the lady in the crowd – plenty of green,' answered Hayward.

'Just the sort of green we need,' added Pestiaux. 'Broke – or damn near broke. The Marseilles loot is just about used up, eh?'

Bonnay shrugged expressively in reply.

Pestiaux said, 'Let's all have another drink.'

'We can drink the last of it away, whore it away, or any other way, except get out of this dump,' went on Hayward. 'Hell, for a little action . . .'

Umberto came with the drinks and they fell silent until he was out of earshot again.

Hayward said softly, 'It'd be a crazy thing to do!'

Bonnay said, 'So was Marseilles.' He gave a short, brittle laugh. 'Hell, how you three stank after that sewer!'

Pestiaux was infected with reminiscence. 'I thought that kilometre and a half of sewer would never end – all dark and slimy and shitty . . .'

'And to think the police hadn't a clue about it,' added Hayward.

Kennet said, 'From what the papers said afterwards, nor had the bank. How'd you find it, Jules?'

'This calls for another drink,' said Bonnay. He gave the necessary signal to Umberto. The whore watched the four men with their heads together. She would never understand men's priorities.

Bonnay was on his mettle in his reply. 'It was that giveaway toilet in the vault. All toilets lead somewhere.'

'Fancy anyone wanting to crap down there!' said Hayward.

'Anyone could be taken short,' said Kennet heavily.

'I'd have been, in sight of so much green,' said Pestiaux.

'You weren't, if I remember,' replied Bonnay. 'You took your whack of loot along with the rest of us, without one small heave of the bowels.'

The four men laughed uproariously. The tart eyed them

speculatively. A changed mood could mean a change in business prospects.

Hayward burst out, 'Action – my oath, for some action! Any tiny bit of action! Every time I hear of someone setting off a bomb, I find myself praying to be there!'

'You've been blowing bombs ever since you were a kid in Ireland,' said Bonnay. 'You've got a taste for it, that's what, Burt.'

'I've got a taste for a lot of other things which I don't find where I'm stuck right now,' retorted Hayward. 'One of them is money. It won't be long, like Paul says, until the Marseilles goodies are all used up – then what?'

'Negative talk . . .' began Bonnay.

'Aye, that's right,' went on Hayward. 'Negative. Negative money – broke. That's us.'

Kennet answered Hayward's question. 'They'll kick us out of Lesotho. We're only here because we can pay the protection money – in cash. That's the way it's been, right from the start. Your pal in the administration . . .' He looked accusingly at Bonnay.

'He's expensive, protection money is always expensive,' responded Bonnay. 'They've left us completely alone so far.'

'And when the money is finished?'

'Nothing to panic about yet,' replied Bonnay defensively.

'That's because everyone is playing it soft because of the Highlands Project,' Hayward said. 'They're sucking up to the tourists so that they'll all come along for the grand opening. But that's only a fortnight away; after that, the administration will clamp down on foreigners, mark my words. That means us – right?'

'What do you want me to do about it?' Bonnay's voice grated.

'You're the leader, the think tank. Put something in the tank, and think,' sneered Hayward.

Bonnay looked round his companions. 'Is this a mutiny?'

'We can't afford a mutiny,' answered Kennet, and the others nodded. 'We're simply making a statement of fact. We're nearly on our uppers – broke. When our present cash runs out, we'll be run out of Lesotho – simple as that.'

21

'Where to?' asked Pestiaux.

'They usually deport undesirables to their country of origin,' answered Hayward.

'You know the way it works, I see,' said Bonnay.

'I don't like the way you're saying it, Jules, but I know that's the way it works – a French jail for you two, a British jail for John and me,' said Hayward. 'Attempted assassination of two heads of state. Life imprisonment. How the media will go for it!'

'You're jumping the gun,' said Bonnay roughly.

'What gun?' Kennet was deliberately obtuse. 'I've still got mine, and I don't give that up easily.'

'That's the first bit of guts I've witnessed from any of you today,' Bonnay tongue-lashed them.

Pestiaux was silent.

'Paul,' said Kennet. 'Do you go along with our point?'

'I'm thinking,' replied the Frenchman. 'We could soon be in trouble – a lot of trouble – unless we do something about it.'

'Magnificent! A masterly summing-up of what we've been trying to say for the past hour!' jeered Kennet.

'I don't like a crack like that, John,' retorted Pestiaux. 'I've shot people for less.'

'Cut it out, all of you!' snapped Bonnay. 'Don't waste your brains and energy on cutting one another down to size – keep them for something constructive.'

'Meaning?' asked Hayward.

'You know what I mean,' rejoined Bonnay. 'Something which is going to bring us in a lot of money – quick.'

CHAPTER FOUR

The gang's argumentative mood, fuelled by three quick drinks, was stopped in its tracks by something none of them could really account for. Perhaps some dark vibe entered the casino's tawdry interior along with the man who came in at that moment.

It was the short, stocky man who had shouldered Bonnay at the entrance to the exhibition centre.

Whatever it was, a silence shadowed across the gang.

The newcomer walked across to the bar. 'Two bottles brandy.' His accent was clipped, harsh.

Umberto found them, set them on the bar. The man put down money without asking for the price, as if he already knew. Umberto handed back change, in silence. The man walked out, tucking one bottle under an arm, holding the other in a tough fist. He did not even cast a glance at the Chunnel Gang.

Bonnay signalled Umberto and the whore with one gesture. She came over to the table, expectantly. Liquor is a girl's best friend.

'Who is that guy?' Bonnay demanded.

'Dunno – I'm a working girl,' she replied, as if the two were connected. They were, in her mind.

Bonnay also got the connection and put down a small note.

'Name, Stefan du Preez.'

'That all?'

She scooped up the note. 'Nothing for nothing, and precious little for R2.'

Bonnay put a larger denomination note on the table.

'That's better,' she said.

Hayward said, 'She's bloody rapacious.'

'That's my trouble – I rape easy,' she rejoined. 'Good-hearted. Weakness for men in my big loving heart.'

'It isn't your heart . . .' Hayward began, but Bonnay snapped at her. 'What else?'

'Comes from over the border. Nearby. I dunno where. Often. Eyes the colour of piss.' She shuddered. 'Drinks alone.'

'What did he tell you about himself?' Bonnay went on.

'*Him*? No women for that guy! Looks at a girl as if he'd screw her hormones one by one, but that doesn't make him take the plunge. *Not him!*'

'Why do you say *him* like that?' asked Pestiaux, himself a fancier of female flesh. 'You make him sound like he's got AIDS.'

'Not AIDS; that guy's sickness is in the mind,' the girl said darkly. 'I dunno what it is, I don't know. It burns him up, eats into him. No man drinks alone like that if he's got something to go home to. Brandy. Always brandy. You saw.'

'Two bottles isn't much, if you've got problems,' said Hayward, starting on the next drink which Umberto had brought.

'Oh, he's no alkie, if that's what you mean,' she answered. 'You should see those hands. Strong. No shakes.' She tapped her forehead. 'Brandy is for what's inside him, here.'

'Maybe sometimes it's worse than others . . .' Hayward started to commiserate, but Bonnay snapped again at the tart. 'Anything more to tell me?'

'I don't like the way you said that.'

'Anything more?'

'Naw.' She backed away. 'Men! But that one's strange, I'm telling you. Strange . . .'

Hayward waited until the woman had returned to her pitch at the bar and then, deliberately excluding Bonnay, said to Kennet and Pestiaux, 'What'd you think of the security – John? Paul?'

The thing which had been in their minds surfaced again under the thrust of the drinks and the departure of the tart. They all knew tacitly what they were talking about. Bonnay remained silent, scowling slightly.

'Professional. Well drilled,' Kennet answered. Pestiaux nodded agreement.

'That they were,' agreed Hayward. 'But could they be beaten when the chips were down? That's what security is all about.'

Hayward said, obliquely, 'It would be suicide, of course, to take it right under the lights and TV monitors . . .'

'*And* the guards,' added Kennet, picking up the unspoken theme. 'It'd mean a straight shoot-out, getaway car, high-speed chase, all that jazz. They'd have the border tight shut before we could even get there – it's only five kays from the exhibition centre. Yeah, it would be suicide. Nice stuff for the media, but not on – for me.'

'The bank would be a cinch, I reckon,' said Hayward.

Bonnay regarded his three companions, letting them talk the idea out of their systems. He joined the discussion as a ploy.

'Why the bank?'

'Well they'll move the thing backwards and forwards every day – before the show in the morning, back again in the late afternoon. I'd say that after a few days the security on the run between the bank and the centre would slack off . . . but I'd still go for the bank strongroom.'

Pestiaux said chauvinistically, 'As a Frenchman, I'd say their bank strongroom isn't up to anything we had against us in Marseilles.'

'You wouldn't think he was a Calais *Patriot*,' Hayward mocked.

'It's worth a lot of dollars,' Pestiaux went on. 'Must be.'

'Millions, I reckon,' added Kennet. 'Priceless. You can't put a value on a thing like that.'

Bonnay cut in incisively. 'See here, when I plan a heist, I like to have everything clear-cut, organised. No side-issues, no unspoken hints which blow up in your face when the action hots up. Are you guys planning to heist the Eagle of Time? Instead of the target we've already agreed on? I ask you, straight from the shoulder.'

'Could be,' replied Hayward. 'We are sort of sniffing around the bait because the other looks so bloody impossible. Haven't decided yet one way or the other.'

'Keep your voices down!' ordered Bonnay. He glanced round the room, still empty except for the barman and the tart. He went on, again stringing along with the others. 'Okay then, we snatch it . . .'

'Where?' demanded Hayward. 'Not from under those bloody TV cameras!'

'The bank, then,' responded Bonnay. 'We do it the way we've always worked – quietly. We take it from the bank strongroom one night, then we have the whole night ahead of us before they discover the next day that it's gone, but by that time we've got clear . . .'

It could have been the raspberry or alcohol fuel which made Pestiaux repetitive. 'I say again, the bank strongroom is for me . . .'

'Yeah, yeah, I know,' retorted Bonnay. 'Anything which Maseru has, Marseilles has better. We beat 'em once, we can beat 'em again, that's what you're saying?'

'This is the sort of talk I like to hear!' exclaimed Hayward.

'You're not going to when I tell you you are all talking the biggest lot of crap outside a French sewer – listen to me! We snatch this clock, or timepiece, or Eagle of Time or whatever fancy name they give it. We have a lot of fun. Bank strongroom? Or shoot up security guards? Whatever, we heist it. I like to know what a thing is worth, before I stick my neck out.'

'Millions,' said Hayward. 'All those jewels, all that gold!'

'Priceless – as a bloody museum piece,' retorted Bonnay. 'We don't need a museum piece, we need hard cash.'

'The gold . . .' interrupted Kennet.

'Ah yes, the gold!' sneered Bonnay. 'Did you look at it, study it, the way I did? Gold, yes, but it's thinner than cigarette paper. I'm talking about that bird's wings – not an eagle, a . . .'

'Lammergeyer,' supplied Kennet. 'It's a Lesotho bird, they said. Very rare.'

'Precisely!' rejoined Bonnay. 'So bloody rare that after our heist, every art dealer in the world would be on the alert for it! Go back a little in time – you want to snatch it from the bank strongroom one night – to have the whole night to drive clear – where?'

'Over the border, of course,' said Hayward.

'And there, waiting for us – he hasn't yet heard the general alert because it's too soon – is a buyer waiting for us for one of the world's great art masterpieces?'

Kennet backed Hayward, who seemed deflated by Bonnay's scalpel-edged analysis.

26

'We'd have to do our homework first, of course,' he said. 'There are a lot of wide guys in Johannesburg . . .'

'Do you really imagine any of them would handle anything as hot as the Eagle of Time?' went on Bonnay, pushing home his advantage. 'You couldn't get rid of it any place, even if you wanted to.'

'I've got it!' exclaimed Hayward triumphantly. 'We'd melt it down!'

'Aye, that's it, melt it down!' echoed Pestiaux.

'All that gold!' Hayward went on. 'We could smuggle the gold out of Lesotho via one of the tens of thousands of Basuto mineworkers who commute to South Africa . . .'

Bonnay interrupted sarcastically. 'Use your nut, man! Remember that bird's wings – delicate as an angel's! How much gold d'ye think you'd get out of them – a couple of ounces? At a current price of – what? A thousand dollars an ounce?'

Hayward was against the ropes, and he knew it. But he fought back. 'There's not only the gold – there's all the rest . . .'

Pestiaux said, 'A few thousand dollars! I see your point, Jules. We need a million.'

'I'm glad someone else does,' replied Bonnay caustically. 'You wouldn't think I'd brought you bastards safely through all the hassles we had after the Chunnel balls-up.'

Bonnay's remark seemed to touch a sore point in Hayward. He replied hotly, 'Today the Eurotunnel would be filled with seawater instead of cars and trains if we'd only stuck to the original plan! You made me improvise on the detonating switch – and that's what gave the game away to Scotland Yard!'

'The change of plan wasn't my fault, or any of our faults,' answered Bonnay. 'It was just one of those things.'

'We had the perfect firing mechanism right under the noses of the two blasted leaders of Britain and France. It would have sent them to kingdom come the moment they touched it. Seeing the Eagle of Time there today brought it all back.'

'This conversation is getting us nowhere fast,' said Bonnay. 'It's not what did or didn't happen two years ago that counts, but what we do today. We're in trouble – deep trouble.'

'Fair enough,' retorted Hayward. 'But don't buck the blame for the Chunnel shimozzle off on me, see? I say again, put something in your think tank.'

Bonnay's voice was quiet, but filled with purposeful menace. 'That's just what I have done . . .'

The other three put down their drinks at his tone and started to stare at him, when a mechanical voice came from the TV screen over the bar:

'Lesotho Television is privileged to present to you the first showing at the Basuto Hat earlier this morning of the fabulous Eagle of Time, which will be the centrepiece of the ceremonial opening of the first stage of the great Lesotho Highlands Water Project at Katse Dam in twelve days' time.

'During the gala ceremony at Katse the Eagle of Time will have the place of honour on the opening dais on the wall of Katse Dam. When the two heads of state, of Lesotho and South Africa, jointly press a switch to open the dam's sluices for the first time, the public will witness an almost uncanny exhibition of timing: at that precise moment, the lammergeyer which forms the pediment will spread its wings and reveal underneath a secret gold capsule in which are lodged three miniature works of art epitomising Lesotho. No one has yet seen these masterpieces, or knows their subjects.'

The TV cameras proceeded to track round the interior of the Basuto Hat, showing the platform with the VIPs at one end, and the street entrance at the other.

'This is the moment we have all been waiting for,' said the announcer. The cameras focused on the security van arriving at the entrance and the Eagle of Time being conveyed into the centre by the Swiss guards. *'The timepiece will be on display every day from nine in the morning until four in the afternoon,'* the announcer went on. *'However, in four days' time, it will be transported to Katse Dam to give construction workers there the opportunity of viewing it, since they have played a major role in making the initial stage of the Highlands Project possible.'*

The gang watched in silence as the Eagle of Time was taken to the viewing rostrum – they had witnessed all this before. When, however, Dr Poortman came forward to receive the key to open the padded box, Bonnay hissed, 'Keep your eyes on him! Everything about him! That's our man!'

Hayward muttered, 'It won't work, I tell you!'

'Shut up – watch him!' retorted Bonnay.

The announcer said, '*You are now viewing Dr Hans Poortman, the noted Swiss banker, and with him Miss Grania Yeats, the artist responsible for sculpting the Eagle of Time pediment above the clock. It was through Dr Poortman's initiative orginally that the services of this brilliant young artist-craftsman were secured for the Eagle of Time. Dr Poortman will hold financial discussions in Maseru before flying to Johannesburg in four days' time for further consultations with the South African monetary authorities. He will, however, return to Lesotho to be present at the Katse Dam opening ceremony. Also in Dr Poortman's company with Miss Yeats is the Swiss consortium's ombudsman in Lesotho, Mr Sholto Banks . . .*'

'That's the guy who wins all the canoe marathons . . .' began Pestiaux.

'*Keep your eyes on Poortman!*' rapped Bonnay.

The four watched the rest of the ceremony in silence, except for the occasion when the doors opened and the crowd moved in; they saw themselves bunched together, all looking uncomfortable, Hayward scowling and hanging his head.

'I look as bloody allergic to those TV monitors as I felt at the time,' sniffed Hayward. 'Let's get out of here.'

'Wait,' said Bonnay, gesturing at the screen.

'*Here is an important announcement,*' said the commentator. '*Police Headquarters has released the Identikit we are now about to show you of the man who is wanted in connection with a series of attacks during the past few years on vehicles transporting materials and supplies to the Highlands Project. He has also terrorised tribesmen in the remote northern mountain regions of the country and has been responsible for a number of deaths.*

'*A reward of R25,000 is being offered for information leading to the arrest and conviction of this man, who has gained notoriety under the nickname of the Maluti Rider. This name is due to the fact that he is known to operate on horseback.*

'*The latest attack took place three days ago when all three occupants of a van conveying sound equipment for the Katse opening ceremony were gunned down and the vehicle destroyed by fire, along with all the equipment.*

'*During his attacks on innocent victims, the Maluti Rider has always been concealed in a typical Basuto blanket, which he also drapes round his head like a turban. It is not known whether the killer is black or white.*

'*After the latest attack, a quantity of Russian-made AK-47 shell cases were found at the scene of the attack, and grenade shrapnel has been analysed and also found to be Soviet-manufactured.*'

An Identikit close-up flashed on the screen. The police artist had obviously taken refuge in the hazy description. The face was almost invisible under a turban-like wrapping round the head; the eyes were similarly lost in its shadow.

'That could be anyone,' commented Pestiaux.

Bonnay said, with a note of concealed admiration in his voice which made the other three eye him, 'That guy has a lot of guts – he's been shooting 'em up for years now and getting away with it. Must have a secret hide-out somewhere where the fuzz can't nail him.' Bonnay looked round the group and asked ambiguously, 'If you passed him in the street right now, could you identify him?'

'From that Identikit?' Hayward asked derisively.

'I'm not talking about the Maluti Rider, I'm talking about Dr Poortman. What would a million dollars be to one of the world's richest men?'

Hayward shrugged. 'We've been into all this before. It simply won't work, Jules, and you know it. Not even for a million.'

Bonnay's eyes went round his companions, and then to the TV screen, which was fading.

'Pity I need the assistance of you dumb bastards, but I can't manage it myself.' He indicated the screen. 'I know now how to make it work – all the way.'

'I need another drink,' said Kennet.

'No more drinks. We're getting out of here to our quarters. We've got a lot to thrash out – behind closed doors.' He glanced at his watch. 'We've got to act fast – we've only four days. The stake on the table is a million dollars.'

CHAPTER FIVE

'It won't work, I tell you!' asserted Hayward, getting up from his chair and pacing up and down. 'I'm not saying the kidnap won't come off – that's relatively easy. But it's what to do with Dr Poortman afterwards that bugs me – while we're putting out our ransom claim for a million.'

'Dollars or Rands?' There was a scarcely concealed note of cynicism in Kennet's jibe.

'Dollars,' replied Bonnay. He seemed relaxed, in comparison with his previous tense air. 'The exchange rate is in our favour. It'll jack up the value to us to nearly twice a million in local terms.'

The gang had withdrawn to Bonnay's room. It was pleasant enough, facing out across a lawn and trees towards the Caledon River in the far background. To Bonnay, however, it had become a living prison.

The gang seemed to have split in two – Hayward vocalising his objections and Kennet backing him; Pestiaux aligning himself, as faithful gun-dog, with Bonnay.

Hayward went on, 'Who will you demand the ransom from? That's the first question even before we consider the logistics of the snatch.'

'Anyone at bloody-all,' retorted Bonnay. 'The Swiss consortium – Dr Poortman's own capitalist buddies sitting back there in Switzerland with their bums in butter. Plus the Lesotho authorities. And South Africa – all three together. They couldn't risk the scandal of a VIP kidnap on the eve of the opening of what they've proclaimed is the world's most prestigious civil engineering feat . . .'

'More so than the Chunnel?' interrupted Hayward.

'It's grown to be that,' answered Bonnay. 'Yeah, I know the Highlands Project had a low-profile beginning, but it's picked up steam over the years. You can judge that from the media coverage the opening is getting – pressmen and TV from every major country in the world.'

'And you intend kidnapping the key figure – just like that?' asked Hayward. 'One thing you can be sure of is a lot of exposure.'

'Don't keep saying "you" as if the rest of you aren't in on this,' said Bonnay. 'You are.'

Hayward shook his head and Kennet acquiesced in disagreement. 'Not yet. In principle, yes. We could use that million dollars and a safe passage out of this dump. But I want to be sure that we are alive and free to enjoy the safe passage. Snatching Poortman the way you say just isn't on, in my book. You can count me out, I say. I know when the odds are hopeless. And they're hopeless in this instance.'

Bonnay lit another cigarette and eyed the others through the smoke. Kennet was contributing to the fug from a pipe; he looked like a Basset hound masquerading as Sherlock Holmes.

'What do you others think of the idea of kidnapping Dr Poortman?'

'We've all got guns,' Kennet replied. 'I guess the security round Poortman isn't so hot. In the exhibition centre today I didn't see anyone who looked like a plain-clothes man guarding him – or anyone else, for that matter.'

'Does that mean you agree?' demanded Bonnay.

'In principle yes; in practice, no. Listen, Jules, we're back to square one. We snatch Poortman – okay. But what the hell do we do with him afterwards? Bring him back here to the hotel and set up a siege? Run with him into the mountains – where?'

'Aye,' agreed Hayward. 'Hotel siege – the police and army are very much on the alert after the Maluti Rider's attacks. They'd storm in, shooting from the hip. They might even call in the South Africans. How would you fancy a helicopter drop on the roof?'

'That isn't the way it works,' replied Bonnay. 'We'd say, come close and we'll shoot the guy.'

'Would you?' asked Hayward. 'Would you? That's the kicker. In that kind of game you can only bluff so far. We'd be caught like rats in a trap.'

32

'As for the mountains, we – and Poortman – would die in the snow like lapdogs thrown out of doors,' added Kennet.

Hayward went on, 'Maseru is a small place – even if we didn't go for the hotel, we'd be trapped if they carried out a house-to-house search. We've been through all this before, Jules. The Poortman kidnap isn't on – even for a million dollars. We'd be forced into surrender after a couple of days. Then, once our international reputation came to light – ' He made a throat-slitting gesture. 'What we need to make it work – you said it yourself, Jules – is a safe house, somewhere where we can stash Poortman away after the snatch, from which we could conduct negotiations and stand up to a siege.'

'It's impossible – it won't work,' asserted Kennet. 'That's what got us talking bull about heisting the Eagle of Time instead.'

'Poortman off, eh? The Eagle off, eh?' Bonnay eyed them. He added, as a throwaway line, 'They're taking the Eagle up to Katse for a special showing – right? They'll have to transport it the day before, won't they? It's the best part of 160 kilometres from here. That would be the time to strike, wouldn't it?'

Hayward responded angrily. 'One moment you're talking about kidnapping Poortman for a million dollars, and the next heisting the Eagle of Time when you've already persuaded us that it's so hot as an art treasure that no one would handle it, and worth peanuts if we melted down the gold . . .'

'I'm not talking about us, I'm talking about the Maluti Rider,' answered Bonnay enigmatically.

'What the hell *are* you talking about then?' demanded Hayward, and the others nodded agreement. 'What the Maluti Rider does or doesn't do is no concern of ours.'

'It is, if he's on our side,' responded Bonnay.

The others looked their disbelief and waited for him to resume.

Bonnay said slowly, 'For years, the Maluti Rider has shot 'em up, blown 'em up, and they've never nailed him. Why?' He paused a little histrionically. 'I'll tell you why – he's got a safe hide-out somewhere. Deep in the mountains, I'd guess. Just the sort of place we need to stash Poortman away after the kidnap.'

'Do you know the guy, Jules?' asked Hayward sarcastically. 'The guy the police are offering R25,000 for? If you do, you could pick up some cash the easy way. Or do you intend giving him a buzz on the phone and saying, come, fellah, we need your secret hide-out. For a consideration, I suppose?'

'We'd have to cut him in on the million, of course, and each of us would lose a little as a result.'

'I'm pretty easy about parting with easy money . . .' went on Hayward in the same tone.

'Don't be an idiot,' snapped Bonnay. 'I'm serious. This is where my master plan comes into operation. The key is the Maluti Rider.'

'I enjoy fantasy, being Irish myself,' sneered Hayward.

Bonnay ignored the crack. 'We ambush the Maluti Rider.'

Kennet said derisively, 'You mean, he ambushes us. It's his speciality, don't forget.'

'Either way, it doesn't matter,' replied Bonnay. 'Either way, we get our hands on him and force him to give us the use of his hide-out for Poortman.'

'Go on, it's marvellous stuff – for the TV serials,' retorted Hayward. Pestiaux remained silent.

Bonnay kept his cool. 'We need the Maluti Rider's hide-out, wherever it might be, and I intend to get it. Take a look at the Maluti Rider's track record – he's done everything he can to harass the Highlands Project. But he could still make his biggest gesture.'

Hayward changed his previous tone. 'What would that be?'

'The Eagle of Time.'

'He'd be crazy . . . '

'No, he wouldn't, only very daring. I'm trying to project myself into the Maluti Rider's thinking, what I'd do if I were in his shoes. The Eagle will be the centrepiece of the opening ceremony. Smash the Eagle, and you've gone for the jugular. The only bigger prize would be to knock down Katse Dam wall.'

Hayward shook his head disbelievingly; the other two remained silent.

'If I were the Maluti Rider, I'd go for the Eagle of Time when it's being transported to Katse for the display there. That's what

I meant when I said the TV announcement had given me the key. It's the Maluti Rider's golden opportunity, the last golden opportunity he'll have to strike at the very heart of the Highlands Project.'

He gave his words time to sink in, and added, 'If I were him, I'd ambush the security van taking the Eagle to Katse.'

Kennet made a curious whistling noise via the stem of his pipe. 'And where do we come into it?'

'We have our own security van. A decoy. The same – exactly the same – as the real one. We trail our coat. We allow the Maluti Rider to ambush us. Then we ambush him, grab him, put the heat on him to give us the use of his hide-out for Poortman. We also sugar the pill – we offer to cut him in on the ransom money.'

'And if he doesn't go along with us?' Hayward seemed to be softening.

Bonnay shrugged. 'We turn him in. We'd be public heroes. It'd also be an easy way of picking up R25,000 reward.'

'Twenty-five grand – that's peanuts!' Pestiaux broke in.

'I know, I know,' replied Bonnay impatiently. 'It wouldn't help you to escape to Brazil to all those lovely señoritas showing their tits on the beach. It's only our last resort. I'm going for the jackpot – a million ransom for Poortman.'

'I don't know where you intend to lay your hands on a security van, or any of the finer points of this scheme,' said Hayward carefully. 'Remember, the Maluti Rider isn't an ordinary hillside bandit, Jules. This is a real bastard – he knows guns, he knows explosives. He doesn't give a stuff for human life – look at the way he's shot up those tribal villages – first an incendiary grenade or two into the huts while they're sleeping and then mowing 'em down with automatic rifles as they came out screaming.'

Bonnay also sensed that the gang was coming round to his scheme.

'And you guys are made of the stuff which made you stand up to a siege for thirty-six hours inside a Marseilles bank while the police threw the lot at us – far more sophisticated weapons than the Maluti Rider can muster. But we made it, didn't we?'

'Ambush,' mused Kennet, sucking his pipe. 'Security van. What kind of security van will stand up to automatic fire?'

35

'They've got armoured glass and I expect armoured panels all round inside,' answered Bonnay. 'No problem.'

'It means we've got to take his fire,' Kennet pointed out. 'Then we open up . . .'

'You don't, I do,' replied Bonnay. 'I drive. He'll go for the driver first. I face up to whatever flak he throws at the van. You three don't try and shoot back. You will bale out of the van. There's no question of killing or wounding our man – you've got to bring him back alive, see? Alive!'

'The whole thing sounds one hell of a gamble,' said Hayward. 'It's full of loose ends which I need to have tidied up before I agree.'

'It's a gamble, I'm not saying it isn't,' replied Bonnay. 'But we can pull it off, if we play our cards right. What happens to us if we don't go for broke on the Maluti Rider and Poortman?'

'We go for broke,' retorted Hayward facetiously.

'What comes first – the Rider ambush or the Poortman kidnap?' Kennet asked dubiously.

'The ambush,' replied Bonnay. 'Unless we grab the Maluti Rider, the kidnap is off.'

'I don't go along with that,' said Kennet. 'If we're going for the kidnap, let us go for it – boots and all. There must be an alternative plan.'

'We'll put that on ice for the moment,' answered Bonnay. 'However, whatever we decide, we have got to work fast. You heard the announcement – Poortman flies out to South Africa in four days' time. The Eagle goes on show at Katse in four days' time. We're locked into four days.'

'That's a mighty short time, Jules,' said Kennet.

'We act, and we act quickly – today,' he replied.

'What do you mean?' asked Hayward.

'I've already taken some preliminary steps – just in case,' answered Bonnay with a slight grin. 'Just in case you guys agreed. Just in case I found a solution to the hide-out problem. Now I need your approval to stake the rest of what we've got left in the kitty in order to win more on the table. I know the price already. I've done the groundwork. It will nearly clean us out.'

'What are you talking about?' asked Hayward.

'I'm flying to Katse this afternoon – in a couple of hours – with the VIP party.'

Kennet said heavily, 'I'd like to see your official invitation.'

'That's what will just about clean us out,' replied Bonnay. 'Our faceless protector in high places in the administration who has looked after us so well ever since we arrived in Lesotho has agreed – for a consideration – to get me a Pony Pass for Katse . . .'

'What in hell is a Pony Pass?' demanded Hayward.

'It's a special little disc about the size of a Rand piece which has the emblem of a Basuto pony embossed on it,' explained Bonnay. 'VIPs and other top brass connected with the Highlands Project have been issued with them. It's a free pass, no questions asked, anywhere, anytime, in Lesotho. I've already fixed one, like I said. All I have to do now is walk up the street and collect it.'

'And pay,' added Kennet.

'It's a question of staking what we have left in order to win more, in gambling terms,' Bonnay replied.

'What do you intend to do at Katse?' asked Hayward.

'There's the VIP village there called Katse Lodge – Poortman will probably be staying there until he leaves for South Africa. I'll stake out the place. In fact, I'll stake out the whole set-up – it may provide the alternative we're looking for, if the ambush doesn't come off. Right?'

'How do you expect to get away with posing as a VIP?' asked Hayward.

Bonnay grinned. 'That's my problem. I'll be what I really am – French. I'll speak only French, no English. No one will know who I am – there are a lot of odd foreign high-ups around with the opening in the offing. With the Pony Pass, no one will dare cross-examine me on my bona fides. I'll trail along – keep my eyes and ears wide open. Find out the lay-out, check the security arrangements, all the rest of what we need to know.'

'And us – what happens to us?' asked Pestiaux, his first incursion into the discussion.

'You take our car and the three of you get up to Katse by road. Meet me there. Your job is to case the highway for likely ambush sites. I'll break away from the VIP party and return to Maseru with you. We can put our heads together about what we find.'

'If Poortman is staying at Katse Lodge, it puts a different complexion on things – we might be able to pick him up there,' said Kennet. 'There may also be some place there where we could hole up.'

'It's something you can be sure I'll check,' said Bonnay. He looked round the gang. 'All agreed about the Pony Pass? Fine. I'll get on down to our protector right away, before he closes his office for an early lunch . . .'

However, Hayward objected. 'There are still too many loose ends to this whole business. I feel I'm being crowded into a situation I can't see the end of. The ambush, as a start – how do we get hold of a decoy security van? You talk as if there was one just for the taking.'

Bonnay grinned. 'Taking is the right word. We take one. We also need security uniforms. We take them too.' He glanced at his watch. 'I'll talk fast. Here is my plan . . .'

CHAPTER SIX

'Blue Mountain Pass,' announced the girl courier in the VIP aircraft. She was wearing a long-sleeved white T-shirt on which was emblazoned the word *Study* and white Basuto earrings which emphasised the darkness of her skin. She held the microphone like a disco singer; she was attractive enough to have filled the role without difficulty.

She repeated the words in German and French, and added, 'Look there, just close to the top of the pass, see? That peak is called Thaba Putsoa – in our language it means blue-grey mountain.'

'That's just what it is,' agreed Grania Yeats, craning to see. She turned to Sholto Banks next to her. 'It's wonderful; the view is stupendous.'

Sholto smiled at her enthusiasm. 'In Lesotho, you need a plane to appreciate the grandness of it all.'

The vista from the executive jet flying the VIP party to Katse was truly oceanic. It was one of three aircraft which had taken off that afternoon and was now soaring above a mountain spine which bisected the country east to west. The passengers could make out a road fighting a way up the Blue Mountain Pass, one of the country's staggering scenic routes. The VIP party had been divided into three to fit into the small planes which had to be used for the restricted airfield at Katse, about 110 kilometres on an airline from Maseru. With Grania and Sholto in their aircraft was Dr Poortman; Lesotho's Security chief, General Makoanyane; and others; at the rear was Bonnay, wearing his Pony Pass in his lapel.

He nodded appreciatively when the Basuto girl spoke French – not bad French either, he reckoned.

The girl was saying, 'If you now look out away to your left on the other side from the Blue Mountain Pass you will see a great river coming down from far in the north. It is the Sengunyane, one of the Orange River's biggest tributaries. Almost below our aircraft now is the site of another of the Highland Project's big dams which will be built only in the next phase of the scheme . . .'

Grania and Sholto could not miss the great riverway which cleft through the mountains; to their left, or westward, the longer light of afternoon showed range upon range of the Malutis. But it was to the right, where a glittering augustness reared out of the east opposite the declining sun, crag upon crag, gorge upon gorge, blue and purples and muted reds fluctuating on the horizon, that Sholto's eyes were fixed.

He said softly to Grania, 'Lammergeyer Land!'

For a moment, it seemed to him, her eyes were intense and unseeing, and then they focused on the time-honoured monarchs of Lesotho's mountain kingdoms, bound in lavish blues and purples.

Neither of them heard the facts the courier was disgorging about the Highlands Project.

She replied equally softly, 'That's where it was, was it?'

His muscles held his return smile a little in reserve. 'There's weather coming – the mountains don't get all dressed up like that for nothing.'

'Lammergeyer Land!' she echoed, gesturing with her left hand.

As she made the movement, Sholto's eyes fell on her gold watch strap. On it was a tiny engraved face. She had told him on her first visit that it was the face of an ancient Japanese good luck god named Hotei. The words which she had used then – reinforced now by eighteen months of doubt on his part – hit him like a landslide: 'I have had so much bad luck that I feel I need something to placate the gods' anger with me.' They had carried an odd prophetic chill of foreboding.

It hadn't been that way at all, at the beginning. He liked to think of it as the Golden Time. He had thought then that she considered it the same – until the cold had descended with the long silent months she had spent in isolation in Switzerland sculpting the Eagle of Time pediment.

It had not always been known as the Eagle of Time. The

timepiece had originally been designed to mark the opening of the Chunnel Project two years previously, in 1993. As the Highlands Project had now captured the imagination of the world as the biggest civil engineering task ever undertaken anywhere, so had the Chunnel then. The clock had been conceived – and largely executed – as the 'Rose of Time'. All but the pediment which topped the sixteen modules which made up the standard, or base, of the timepiece had been hand-crafted, awaiting the golden rose whose petals were to unfold at the hour of the Chunnel opening ceremony. The concept was backed by the same Swiss banking consortium which had played so large a role in the Lesotho Highlands Project, being also heavily involved in the Chunnel financing.

Involved, too, was Sholto Banks, to whom the consortium's attention had been drawn as a brilliant young barrister who had been responsible for the intricate documentation and legalities of the Eurotunnel. Sholto had had much to do with ironing out the early troubled stages of the Eurotunnel. Hence his appointment by the Swiss banks as their ombudsman in Lesotho once the Highlands Project took off.

Now, as Sholto's eyes held on her hands for a moment, she seemed to sense something, and a smile glimmered across her lips.

The consortium's judgement had been dead on target in choosing those beautiful, sensitive hands to fashion the golden masterpiece on the pediment, although at the time it had seemed a major risk to have selected a young unknown artist studying at the Tokyo University of Art. But Grania had had the accolade of the legendary maestro of artistic goldsmithing, Yasuki Hiramatsu. Sholto remembered the agony in the banker's voice – it must have been towards the end of 1992 – when Dr Poortman had telephoned him to say that the man who was crafting the pediment of the then Rose of Time, Elie Kiefer, had died of cancer. At that stage, the Chunnel opening was a little more than six months away. There was no one else known of the calibre of Kiefer, who had an international reputation.

One of the consortium's bankers had suggested that the Rose of Time should be completed by another craftsman – but by

41

whom? Dr Poortman himself had proposed Grania, the daughter of a Swiss banking friend of his.

Grania had been approached post-haste. She refused the commission. She had maintained, Dr Poortman was later to tell Sholto, that the Rose of Time could not be completed within the scheduled time limit of six months.

Sholto had had the second, more important, reason from Grania herself on the first day of their Golden Time, when he had gone to meet her, at the consortium's request, at the Golden Gate National Park, which adjoins Lesotho on its northern boundary. He had not known what to expect – probably a long-haired temperamental artist, he was to tell her laughingly later. In autumn there are few places lovelier than the Golden Gate, a place of ochre-hued sandstone cliffs and hills, golden Lombardy poplars and crystal-clear willow-lined rivers and streams, backdropped by the stupendous mountains of Lesotho.

The day and the place were casting their golden shadows ahead on the days which followed. He had driven up to the long, Swiss chalet-like main building called Brandwag (Sentry), named after a huge ochre-coloured cliff nearby. He had had no prior description of Grania; all his briefing had been was to meet the consortium's choice and conduct the artist where she wished to go in Lesotho – 'for inspiration'.

Sholto had walked into the reception area. A dark-haired girl, wearing a skier's anorak and slacks against the autumn chill, was waiting in the foyer. Somehow, there had hardly been any need for them to know they each had the right person.

'Grania Yeats?'

Three things had impressed themselves on him at that moment: how young she looked – and yet the face had something stamped on it which was not youthfulness – and the fine-boned, slender hand she held out to shake his. The other was the fire which had risen up in the hazel-opal eyes when he went on, 'Dr Poortman tells me you are looking for inspiration to complete the Rose of Time.'

'Then both you and Dr Poortman have got it wrong,' she replied. 'It is exactly why I turned down the consortium's offer

42

the first time. They wanted me to complete the Rose of Time pediment. I'm afraid I don't just tag along behind another artist and finish what he began, however brilliant Elie Kiefer might have been. I am myself, and anything I do must reflect myself, not anyone else. That's why I'm here. I want to get the feel of Lesotho, and a theme for a completely new pediment. Nothing to do with a rose.'

'I see,' he said, although he didn't. He added, rather lamely, 'Where do you want to go?'

'That's why you're here, isn't it? They said you knew the remote mountains and rivers better than anyone else.'

'It's a big place . . .'

Her smile was full of warmth and amusement. 'Then I must have come to the wrong place. They told me it wasn't much bigger than Wales.'

He smiled back. 'The mountains make it seem bigger than it is.'

She said, 'Why are we standing here in an artificially heated foyer when there's that magnificent view from the terrace?'

They went out.

'There's so much gold everywhere that it fits the concept of gold for the pediment,' she said.

'Can you be more specific about what you want to see in Lesotho for your inspiration?' he asked.

'I don't use the word inspiration,' she said. 'I need a symbol which equates with me, the inner me.'

'I don't know much about the inner you – yet.'

For a moment, a blind seemed to have been drawn across her eyes, and she replied levelly, 'Given the right theme, something valid floats up, is released, from my unconscious. That's about the nearest I can describe it.'

'You're making it very tough for me to know where to take you. Flowers – is that what you want to see?'

'Not necessarily. I saw a very beautiful protea at the Chelsea Show and it had a wonderful heart which spread wide when the bud opened – *protea magnifica*.'

Sholto found himself disappointed. He had expected something more original when she had spoken of a creative impulse

43

from her inner self. A protea – even the one named *magnifica* – was very much a derivative of the Rose of Time theme.

He said, with a flat note in his voice, '*Protea magnifica* doesn't grow in the Lesotho mountains; it comes from the Cape.'

'Haven't you got proteas in these mountains, then?'

'Yes. We have about five species, and I'd reckon that one called *roupelliae* is the best. It has big bright red flowers. We could find them at an altitude of about 1800 metres.'

'Let's go and look then.'

'There are many more beautiful wild flowers in Lesotho than proteas.'

'The same sort of cup-shape which could open and reveal the secret capsule underneath.'

'Secret capsule?'

'Don't you know about it? When the subject of the pediment opens – it must have a shape which can open, to link up with the clock's mechanism – it will reveal this secret capsule in which there will be several miniature art treasures . . .'

'What are they?'

'I don't know – yet. I'm responsible for them also. That's why I want to *look*.'

'If you want to view the proteas, remember it's autumn and the going could get rough if there's an early snowstorm. It's not a difficult climb, however . . .'

'That's okay with me. I've climbed in the Swiss Alps. It would be rather fun to do the same here.'

'There won't be any rockwork to the proteas. In fact, it could be quite tame.'

She stood and faced him, smiling. 'You're not really sold on the proteas, are you?'

He replied defensively, 'My brief is to take you to see what you wish to see.'

'But you'd love a bit of rockwork hanging on by your eyelids instead; Dr Poortman said you had a formidable reputation as a climber. Not to mention all sorts of canoeing awards.'

'When would you like to start?' he asked.

'Now.'

'Just like that?'

'Why not?'

'We'll have to pick up a couple of climbing tents and some supplies first – that means you'll have to come back with me to "Cherry Now".'

'What a glorious name. "Cherry Now" – what is it?' Here was her well-remembered warmth and enthusiasm.

'My farm – it's outside a town called Ficksburg, which is about 120 kilometres from here southwards.'

'But "Cherry Now" – where'd the name come from?'

'My father gave it the name – a line of poetry. Something to do with the cherries: "loveliest of trees, the cherry now."'

'It's a cherry farm, then?'

'Yes. When the hail doesn't wreck the crop. This border area on the edge of Lesotho is one of the worst hail areas in Southern Africa. Shortly after I returned from London after my father's death – it was before I was offered the ombudsman's job – I lost my whole crop for three springs in succession. The farm really took a knock.'

'Is your climbing gear there too?'

'Most of it. But I keep a supply of gear and iron rations stashed away in a secret place – ' he gestured widely towards the high mountains ' – in a kayak up there in the headwaters of the Malibamatso River – that's the river which has been dammed to form Katse.'

'Is it safe to leave things out without protection?'

She liked the way his wide smile seemed to take off from among the strong muscles of his neck.

'It's very, very remote – it's high, too – some of the mountains round about have never been explored.'

'Except by you.'

He grinned. 'Some of them – not even by me.'

'Can't we go there?'

'It's nowhere near the proteas. They're much lower down. I said, they are only a hike, not a climb.'

'Couldn't we deviate?'

'My brief from the consortium was to take you where you wished to go, but I didn't expect this.'

'It could be fun,' she replied spontaneously.

45

The ancient sentry of Brandwag loosed an isolated spear of light which struck gold into her opalescent eyes.

'It could be fun,' she repeated.

Sholto dated the Golden Time from that moment.

CHAPTER SEVEN

Had the Golden Time depended on the proteas, it would have fallen on its face right at the outset. When Sholto led Grania to a mountain slope on which grew a number of small trees whose leaves were covered in woolly down, she was surprised – she had not expected trees. When she saw the bright red, saucer-shaped flowers about ten centimetres across with a centre of tight flowers flanked by clusters of spoon-shaped bracts on the perimeter, she said to Sholto:

'You were right. This is not what I want.'

Sholto shared her let-down. It was the first time that day her voice had lost its vibrant interest in everything around her. From the moment of their snap decision to set out, her artist's eye had revelled in the countryside he drove her through to reach 'Cherry Now'. It was the border route, on the South African side, and took them via fertile valleys, weird sandstone hills and contorted ravines. She had asked him to stop several times to admire the gold and dusty-pink hills, which seemed to be mere wavelets in the great ocean of the Maluti Mountains to the east. Harmless and benign they looked in the clear light reflected from the pastel-coloured farmlands shouldering the mock sandstone castles, fortresses and cathedrals; yet these same Malutis bore the title, 'The Mountains of Death'. But there was nothing vicious or malicious about them now.

The holiday air made Grania's meeting with Sholto's mother, Mary Banks, an instant success.

'Grania!' she had exclaimed. 'That's an unusual name.'

'Irish,' Grania had told her. 'So is Yeats, to go with it. Yeats is my mother's name – my real surname is Guedal. Dr Guedal, Swiss banker. But where would one get in artistic circles with a name like Grania Guedel? So I use my mother's name instead.'

They had laughed together, and Sholto had collected scarlet pup tents, backpacks, sleeping-bags and supplies.

'We're not going high,' Sholto had said. 'And the weather's holding. We could probably do without tents – I prefer to sleep under the stars, when I can. But we'll take 'em along, just to be sure. We're not doing anything adventurous . . .'

The let-down of the proteas forced the adventure upon them.

'What now?' asked Sholto when Grania stood looking disappointedly at them.

'What about going higher? We may happen on something.'

Sholto noticed that her disappointment revealed something he had not noticed about her face before while she was animated: there were two distinct halves to it. The right side reflected something which made it graver, maturer, than the left.

'To look for what?'

'I don't know. Myself, perhaps.'

They loaded up their gear. Sholto led, taking her above the soft protea slopes towards the high places which flashed forth the penetrating light in new and exciting colours from the basic grey-blue in whose matrix rested the fossilised bones of prehistoric creatures, including dinosaurs. The heaviness of the air began to fall behind them, and they had their first taste of the clear upland atmosphere.

They had their heads down, so they did not see the big bird pulling out of its dive; all they were aware of was the brittle rattle of splintering bones on a group of rocks ahead of them. It was the only sound in the vastness.

Sholto threw back his head. 'Grania! Look!'

Sunlight flickered like a golden snake along the length of the huge bird hanging high above the rock which was its chopping-block. It touched the tapering wings and disproportionately long diamond-shaped tail. In that clean, clear sky the white head stood out against the blue of the atmosphere, contrasting with wings and tail as black as the thunderclouds which roll up so unexpectedly among the peaks.

However, it was the regal throat and neck which the sun stage-lighted so that the ruff appeared like a golden mane afloat on the winds: it was pure, pure gold, enriched by a tincture of

48

orange as the great bird – its wingspan must have been every bit of three metres – banked and swung resentfully above his rock towards which the humans were headed.

'Lammergeyer!' exclaimed Sholto. 'A lammergeyer! It is one of the rarest of all birds!'

Grania slipped the backpack off her shoulders to see better.

'It's gold, pure, pure gold, look, he's turning ! What are those feathers under his beak?'

The lammergeyer was riding an updraught; there seemed to be a flash of red from the eyes.

'They're not feathers – they're bristles,' said Sholto.

'Look at the glorious way he flies!' enthused Grania.

'They say he's a cross between an eagle and a vulture – the flight of an eagle, and the carrion habits of a vulture.'

'What was that noise we first heard? He seems to be watching us very closely.'

'We're lucky, lucky!' exclaimed Sholto. He indicated a rock ahead on their upward path. They made out a number of smashed bones on and around its flat surface. 'It's a legend going back to Ancient Greece that the lammergeyer drops the bones of its carrion onto a favourite rock to break them open for the marrow. He always uses the same rock. Again, it's something I've heard and read about, but never seen.'

'We have got to look!' exclaimed Grania excitedly. Without her backpack, she sprinted ahead of Sholto to the rock. A number of bone fragments, fetid with the smell of old death, lay about.

When he joined her, she said, 'It looks like a sacrificial altar to the black spirits.'

They sensed, rather than saw, the lightning-fast descent like an air-to-ground missile; there was only a susurrus of disturbed air from the swoop as the great bird passed low over their heads.

'We must get away from this rock!' exclaimed Sholto. 'That run-in was a warning. He'll come for us, next time – lammergeyers have been known to attack lone climbers. First I must have a quick look at these bones and see what he was eating – farmers have tried to exterminate the lammergeyer because they say it takes lambs – hence the name.'

49

He went forward quickly. Grania, however, remained, with her head tilted to the sky.

Sholto called, 'As I thought – these are rock hyrax – we call 'em dassies. Nothing lamb about them.'

She didn't seem to hear him. She was fixated on the great bird's soaring flight.

'Come!' called Sholto urgently. 'We must get safely outside the range of his rock – Grania!'

She responded automatically, but her attention remained on the bird. In less than a minute the lammergeyer started his dive-bombing run.

Gold trailed from his ruff and leg-feathers like vapour trails; he pulled out about ten metres above his slaughter-site, and then came into land, wings outspread, eyes red with suspicion at the near-presence of humans.

'See how he lands! Look at those wings, Sholto! It's the most beautiful thing I've ever seen!'

The lammergeyer attacked the bones, watching the climbers warily.

Grania refused to duck down. 'I've got to *see*! It's a once-in-a-lifetime experience!'

The bird was nervous. It stalked about the surface of the rock like a captain pacing a quarterdeck; then suddenly it spread its wings, ran forward lumberingly, and took off.

Grania ran out into the open to follow its line of flight. In seconds, it seemed, the lammergeyer was one with the high peaks.

She stood staring after it. 'Sholto, it was so short! It was too short! It gave me what I wanted, but it took it away again before I was ready!'

'What are you saying, Grania?'

She spread her arms wide. 'It's it, it's it! I see it! I have it now! There, atop the pediment! A golden lammergeyer – spreads its wings at the critical moment, had them folded beforehand – underneath is the secret capsule – then the wings reveal it . . .'

'A golden lammergeyer – Lesotho's own special bird!' echoed Sholto.

She stood in front of him. Her eyes were full of herself – and he liked what he saw. 'Wonderful! Thanks to you, Sholto! You've brought me the symbol I was looking for . . .' She laughed delightedly. 'Protea – alongside *that*!'

He was much taller than she was, and he looked down into her animated face.

She went on, 'You've given me the most wonderful gift that one person could give another. The moment I saw him – there, high in the sky, all golden and wonderful, I knew he was what I was looking for. We'll call the timepiece the Eagle of Time from now on! Gold – pure light and dark gold, up there in the clouds. I don't have to look any further for my theme.'

'I'm so glad the proteas were a sell-out,' he said simply.

'You thought so right from the start, Sholto!' Her mood switched. 'It was all so brief, though, I didn't even have time to sketch him – and I must see him again like that, coming in to land like that, with his wings outstretched, and record the action . . .'

'His landing-flaps down, and ready for a quick take-off again, in case he didn't like the look of us,' grinned Sholto.

'Where can we see it all again? Will he come back? Sholto, I must – I have to!'

'He won't return while we remain around here. You saw how nervous he was.'

'Where can I find him again?' she demanded. 'In my mind's eye I can see him poised on the pediment, but I've got to draw him, get him on paper, for the physical detail and the poise.'

He asked, at a tangent, 'How well can you climb?'

'Why do you ask?'

'If you're prepared – and able – to hang at the end of a sixty metre length of rope over a cliff-edge, and squeeze yourself flat on a rock ledge about half a metre wide and a couple of metres long, I can take you to see another lammergeyer.'

'Close?'

'Yes. I know the location of a lammergeyer eyrie – but it's high, it's tough, and the view of the drop over the precipice leaves your stomach hanging in mid-air. All you'll have between you and certain death is your nerve and a couple of pitons.'

'That goes for you, too,' she replied.

'It's on,' said Sholto. 'The trip will take a couple of days. It's far, it's tough.'

'It's on,' she repeated.

They climbed. They deviated and collected extra climbing gear and supplies from Sholto's kayak, which was hidden in a remote spot on the bank of a tributary of the Malibamatso River named the Tsehlanyane. They climbed, on a new course which headed them towards the high sanctuary of Lesotho's mountains – the source of four of Southern Africa's great rivers. As the altitude grew, they felt the faint prick at their lungs of a dagger-like wind, only a sly little reminder at that stage of the destroyer it could become when it rode on the back of snow and sleet.

At sunset the first night they stopped to camp, and watched in wonderment as the light exploded against a constellation of peaks which brooded like enormous Klu Klux Klan creatures on the opposite horizon; the great stars hung over them that night, when the only life in the silence encircling their red nylon tents was the sharp ice-blue point of gas flame on which Sholto cooked supper.

On the third day, they reached the area of the lammergeyer's eyrie.

It must have been what athletes call an 'endorphin high' – the brain's secretion to block the sensation of pain and so force the body's muscles to unprecedented feats – which sent Grania sixty metres on a rope's end over a breath-catching precipice to a narrow ledge less than a metre wide, from which she could look across a gap between crags to the lammergeyer's eyrie opposite. The bird's hide-out was on a shelf even narrower than the one Sholto and Grania occupied, but the bird's had an overhang which made it safer against the weather.

Grania, Sholto noticed, was very reserved as he drove pitons into the rock above the abseil point. She was pale, too, and he wondered whether the first sight of the precipice and the lammergeyer's eyrie far below – the crags seemed to fall away to the base of the world – had been too much for her. Nevertheless, she roped up without hesitation and went over first, Sholto paying out the rope and monitoring her carefully. She landed on the ledge, and gave him the signal to join her.

She was already sketching, using a pocket-sized block and pencil, when he reached her. The bird was nervous and flew off as Sholto came down. However, it clearly had something in its nest – a chick, perhaps? – but they could see only bits of sheep's wool, sticks and animal skin from where they were. The lammergeyer held a watching vigil; Sholto moved Grania back out of its direct vision behind a shoulder of rock, round which the ledge narrowed to half its previous width. Grania stood with her back thrust hard against it to steady herself. So high were they that the ground itself was hazed, as if with a light mist.

The bird returned, coming in to land with wings out-stretched, just as dramatically as they had witnessed at the slaughter-site. Grania inched forward to see better round the shoulder of rock, using pencil and block. She craned further outward for a still better view.

It happened so quickly, that afterwards Sholto credited his reflexes, not his brain.

Grania lost her balance, her body tilted sideways, outwards. Both hands were occupied with block and pencil. Even if they had not been there was nothing to grab hold of. She jerked her head half towards Sholto. The fear of a death-drop of over 500 metres hit them. Sholto's arm moved quicker than the death-strike of a black mamba. He was not standing, but was half-crouched on the narrow platform, in order to give Grania the best vantage point. As she pitched sideways to the drop his right arm took the strain of her falling dead-weight; at the same time he clamped himself with knees and shoulder against the rock.

For a moment, it was gravity versus Sholto's strength.

Grania hung like a rag doll, doubled over across his arm and elbow. His muscles won. He pulled her in – both her feet and head were already hanging in space – asprawl over his own body. He then made room for her as he shoved her hard against the floor of the ledge.

After a while, she said in a small voice, 'I've still got my sketching-pad and pencil, Sholto.'

'I'm glad, Grania.'

They lay like that, unspeaking, for what seemed hours, although it was not more than a minute or two. Then she felt the reaction start to kick in his hand muscles.

'I'm safe now. You can let me go, Sholto.'

'When you turn, face inward, against the rock. Sit up, to start with.'

She did as he said, and he, too, swivelled on his own axis to sit beside her.

She said, 'We didn't even break the point of my pencil.'

'Have a breather, and then we'll get out again on the rope.'

'No,' she said. 'There are a couple more angles of the bird I must have first. Only then will I go.'

'This time I'll hold you while you work.'

He did, grasping her round her hips while she craned round the shoulder of rock considering the great bird. She went on for a time, then he felt a muscle ripple spread from her stomach towards her groin.

She said abruptly, 'Enough. Sholto – I think I'm going to pass out.'

But she didn't, and the spasm passed as he half-carried, half-led her to the rope and fixed it to her climbing belt. They sat a long time in silence on the broader part of the ledge until she had recovered sufficiently to be able to make the ascent.

That night, looking into the blue-white diamond star of the tiny flame with its matching constellations wheeling about in the heavens, she tried to thank him, but he stopped her. 'It was a reflex action,' he said. 'Nothing premeditated about it.'

She replied gravely, 'Sholto, twice in my life I have been in the presence of death. The first time I was completely alone. Today I had you.'

She did not elaborate, but only sat staring into the flame. Later, when Sholto went to his tent, she still sat looking into its blue heart; hours later, when the flame was gone, Sholto woke and found her still sitting, alone with the stars and the peaks.

The Golden Time returned next day, however, when they struck back homewards from what she had named Lammergeyer Land. She was fired up about the sketches she had made; she discussed with Sholto possible themes for the

54

miniature artworks which would be contained in the secret capsule below the pediment. He told her about Lesotho's famous fossil beds; when he mentioned that a minute dinosaur embryo (one of the few in the world, and about the size of a baby lizard) had been discovered in a fossilised egg near the Golden Gate, she became almost as excited as when she had first seen the lammergeyer. 'What a find for the secret capsule!' she exclaimed.

By chance also he had told her the legend of how the spirit of the Basuto nation was supposed to inhabit a strange, red-coloured dune atop the impregnable stronghold where was buried the founder of the Basuto nation, Moshoeshoe. She demanded to be taken to the place, called Thaba Bosiho. 'Wonderful, wonderful!' she had exclaimed. 'You've given me the second subject for my miniatures! How can I ever thank you enough?'

He had thought she meant it enough to accept the suggestion he made a fortnight later that she should stay on at 'Cherry Now' and sculpt her golden lammergeyer. He noted the hesitation in her refusal on the ground that she had to work in her own studio in Switzerland among familiar things. She also stressed that only there would she have access to the necessary gold.

Sholto thought the Golden Time would go on forever: he told her he would write, telephone, even go to see her in Switzerland when there on consortium business. In retrospect, he thought it must have died when she turned away to catch the plane home from Maseru airport. He heard nothing from her; when he had telephoned, he found himself hurt at her coolness. When, after several months, he had the opportunity of going to Switzerland on consortium business, she somewhat reluctantly agreed to see him. She hid behind the excuse of being totally immersed in the lammergeyer sculpting – 'and it inhibits my creativity to discuss my work until it is finished.' All Sholto's attempts to spark her memories of their climb to Lammergeyer Land and its magic (which she had made no secret of previously) failed. Finally, he cut short his visit and returned, deeply despondent. Grania in Switzerland was simply not the girl he had met at the Golden Gate.

There remained about six or eight months after that until the grand opening of the Highlands Project was due: he did not attempt to get in touch with her again. What mystery lay behind her studied silence? He asked himself that many times; what also had been behind her cryptic remark the night of the near-tragedy at the eyrie that once she had faced death alone? Sholto found no answer.

Rather formally, and with little hope of her accepting, he had invited her when she came to Lesotho for the gala opening to stay at 'Cherry Now'. To his astonishment, she had responded at once: she would be happy to come. He had met her at the airport, the Grania he remembered.

Now they were together, heading towards Katse. Sholto eyed the good-luck symbol on her watch strap. What secrets of Grania's did that ancient stylised face conceal?

CHAPTER EIGHT

'Katse Dam!'

The Basuto girl courier cut into her torrent of facts and figures about the Highlands Project.

'We will be overhead shortly, and the pilot will circle the construction site to give us a full view of this key dam in the entire Project,' she said.

Grania remarked to Sholto, 'You've seen it all before, but I find it very exciting.'

'Never from the air,' he replied. 'It has a vastness you miss from the ground.'

At the rear of the plane, Bonnay tensed. What he observed now would determine the gang's strategy for the Poortman kidnap. It seemed ironical that the very man they were after was sitting only a few seats ahead of him. So was the big man they called General Mak, head of Lesotho's Security. He alone seemed totally disinterested in Katse.

The plane passed over the dam wall. The curved, boomerang-shaped structure which bulged towards the north, or upstream direction, of the Malibamatso River, appeared grey against the shale-blue of the crags on either side into which it was anchored. Excavation cuts stood out like unhealed scars against the cliffs, through which the river's course formed a natural L-shape which engineers had blocked to create the highest dam wall in Africa.

The passengers had a glimpse, too, of the litter of construction below the wall: orange and yellow dumper-trucks, low-level loaders; sections of steel liners of the water penstocks four times the height of a man; a covered gantry like a giant roller coaster, which was used to transport stone aggregate to the massive concrete-mixing platform; bits of redundant water intake orifices five metres high. There was also a cofferdam and a spade-shaped object in the river bed below the wall which was

57

the terminus of a water tunnel used to divert the river's flow during building. Almost next to it were two bell-mouthed discharge outlets from the dam proper. The dam itself was half full of water; below the wall, the river bed was dry – the sluices were shut. Men in yellow shirts and blue hardhats were everywhere.

'That was too quick,' remarked Grania.

'We'll see it all from close up on our tour this afternoon,' Sholto said.

The pilot pulled up hard over the eastern, or far, cliff and banked so that the VIPs could see the 35 kilometre vista of the great dam.

Grania pointed. 'Look, there's another river. I thought Katse dammed only one.'

About two kilometres above the wall another river flowed in from their left.

'Bokong,' Sholto told her. 'It doesn't look much, but it was a thorn in the side to the road engineers. It cut the main road from Maseru here in a flash flood a while back and carried away a magnificent new bridge. They've laid down a temporary causeway in its place.'

Beware the Bokong Crossing, Grania. Beware the Bokong Crossing, Bonnay.

'Look at the colour of the water upstream; if a dinosaur's tongue was pink, I'd say it was the same colour,' said Grania.

Sholto laughed at her comparison and said, 'One day, when that 160 kilometre lake down the centre of Lesotho is a reality, I'm going to canoe the length of it. I've promised my sidekick Jonathan to take him along.'

'Why him?'

'The Highlands Project is as dear to Jonathan's heart as anything could be to a man. He's of royal blood, you know. He sees the scheme as a way of bringing his nation to greatness again.'

'Why didn't he come today?'

'This is a VIP party. He's only an assistant ombudsman. He's a great guy though, and I am very fond of him.' The plane started to bank again and Sholto said, 'Look there – away to the

58

southeast. Storm clouds. Snow. I hope we don't get trapped here at Katse. The systems move very quickly.'

'What's that village we're passing on the cliff?' Grania asked, as the plane banked again.

It was a collection of what appeared to be typical Basuto thatched huts, all in traditional style, grouped about a stone central complex. The place had obviously been sited to command a splendid view.

'Katse Lodge,' replied Sholto. 'That's the VIP village for the opening. Dr Poortman's going to stay there until he leaves for South Africa.' He added quietly. 'It's where I thought you might have been staying too – you're a VIP, you know.'

She did not meet his eyes. She had not missed the hurt in his voice.

'I know,' she replied. 'But I chose "Cherry Now".'

He leaned forward and seemed to her about to take her arm in his strong hand, but then he eased back again in his seat.

Instead, he said, 'Your welcome at the farm tonight includes the famous cherry pie.'

The Basuto courier's voice interrupted her response.

'We shall be landing shortly, and you will notice that the airfield is some way away from Katse itself. This reflects our problem in Lesotho – there is so little flat land. The valley below the dam is one of the few places where it is flat enough to grow crops. If you look over to the left, you will observe a settlement in the distance. This is a tribe which was displaced from its traditional home in the northern mountains by the outfall works and hydropower stations of the Highlands Project. The tribe has been relocated here about fifteen kilometres below the dam, where they will have arable land and regular irrigation water which they never enjoyed in their mountain home . . .'

'About nine hundred of them,' Sholto told Grania in a low voice. 'Their removal caused a public uproar. The tribe had no wish to move. They are mountain people, and love it up there – sometimes a little beyond the law, I might add. There are always cross-border raids and cattle rustling. I've experienced them myself on "Cherry Now". No chance for that kind of diversion where they've been dumped at Katse. The mountain people are great haters. They have blood feuds going back generations. Some of their revenges are pretty blood-chilling.'

CHAPTER NINE

Grania shivered and indicated the mouth of the tunnel. 'Like descending into the dark unconscious,' she said. 'I feel a little scared of something – I don't know what.'

Sholto noticed her serious face and preoccupation. 'You'll find it all brilliantly lit by electric light,' he jollied her. 'Nothing dark about it. In fact, the naked bulbs worry one's eyes after a while.'

The VIP group – augmented by those from the other two planes – stood at the entrance to the perimeter gallery of the dam wall where it joined the cliff. There were about thirty men and women. They had been brought by minibus from the airfield. Some of them sported bright blue construction workers' hardhats. The party was scheduled to go deep down – below water-level – on a conducted tour of the outlet control chamber as well as the adjoining hydropower chamber.

This the VIPs already knew. But a new courier added to the information and sent a ripple of expectancy through the party.

'Your visit this afternoon has been scheduled to coincide with the first real test-run of the sluice-gates,' the guide told them. 'It is, therefore, a privileged occasion. We shall all proceed beyond the control chamber to the low-level discharge channels on the river bank itself – you probably saw those huge spade-shape concrete objects from the plane. There they are now, down there.'

About 250 metres below in the river bed, the group could see their objective.

A woman asked in a doubtful voice, 'Is it safe? I mean, all that water and this is the first test . . .'

The guide gave a well-schooled PRO laugh. 'Safe as . . . the Katse wall itself.' He gave them a confidential grin. 'We wouldn't be risking all you VIPs if it wasn't one hundred per cent safe.

'Now, before we go down, I would like to draw your attention to something else. A little way along the wall from where we are standing now the opening of the Highlands Project will take place jointly by the heads of state of Lesotho and South Africa. There will be a special ceremonial dais, the details of which are being kept a secret until the great day. Many of you here will be on the dais on the great day – it is really quite special.'

The guide's eyes scanned the group and stopped at Grania. 'We are privileged to have here with us the artist whose masterpiece will figure prominently at the opening – Miss Grania Yeats.'

Sholto saw Grania's face close and she gave a stiff half-smile at a burst of hand-clapping.

'You all saw the Eagle of Time at the unveiling today – picture it here on the great day, with a spotlight on it and its wings ready to unfold . . .' He laughed self-deprecatingly. 'I am anticipating. In the control chamber, I will show you how the signal will be received from up here on the dais when the Eagle spreads its wings and how the sluices will open simultaneously . . .'

Grania and Sholto found themselves among the first to start down the sloping ramp of the shaft which gave access to the twin control chambers far below. They descended via a concrete-lined shaft; after about ninety metres it made a ninety-degree turn towards the river to form a dog-leg. Here the guide stopped, waiting for the rest to catch up.

Sholto indicated the naked electric bulbs. 'Dark unconscious still?' he asked Grania.

'Maybe my chill was the first breath of the storm,' she replied. 'It smells wet down here, Sholto.'

It should have been: the guide announced that they were now below the normal operating level of the water dammed only a few metres away outside. Billions of litres of it, he said playfully. 'If anything happened to the dam wall . . .' He shrugged expressively.

They reached the hydropower chamber first. Bonnay moved up among the front-runners. His eyes did a quick calculation of the size of the place – roughly ten metres square. There was only one way anyone could enter, and that was through the relatively narrow shaft through which the party had come. There was only one way anyone could get out, and that was the way they were going. The shaft's concrete skin would stand up to an artillery shell. Tear gas was another consideration. With both entrance and exit sealed off, there seemed no place through which besiegers could pump in gas and overwhelm the kidnappers and their hostage inside.

Bonnay was as disinterested in the two giant 52-ton generating turbines as the remainder of the party was fascinated. The giant spiral casing looked unobtrusive set into the solid concrete floor so that it seemed impossible they could generate the kind of power the guide claimed.

Workmen were putting the finishing touches to one of the turbines; Bonnay stared into the spiralling steel-and-concrete depths. Could a commando unit use this as a sally-port to break an otherwise impregnable hostage siege? He doubted it – no one could squeeze past the turbine blades. But he must bear in mind that tear gas could possibly be pumped through the orifices.

The hydropower chamber offered distinct possibilities as an alternative to the Maluti Rider ambush plan. Yet, in his heart, Bonnay fancied the ambush.

Via a small doorway – no door, Bonnay noted – the concrete shaft continued for another twenty metres to a smaller chamber.

As they entered it, the PRO announced, 'This is the control centre from which the giant sluices are operated – hydraulically, of course. This is really the nerve centre of Katse, because from here the water downstream is controlled and regulated in times of flood so that the dam wall cannot be endangered.'

The concrete chamber which they went into was only about half the size of the hydropower centre. Like a business executive controlling an invisible empire, the place had only one small console – about the size of a big office desk – in the middle. On this stood a couple of telephones and a number of coloured switches. A middle-aged man, wearing a white coat and jovial complexion, occupied the single chair.

Grania looked taken aback. 'Is that all?' she asked Sholto softly. 'I was expecting something much more dramatic.'

'It's a bit of a let-down, isn't it?' he replied.

'It's so small – it doesn't seem possible for such sluices to be controlled by a couple of desk switches . . .'

The PRO overheard her last remark, and addressed the group as a whole. 'It's just like the human brain. We have one of the smallest brains in the animal kingdom, and yet look what we do with them!'

Bonnay's own brain was firing on all cylinders. This small place would be much better than the hydropower chamber in which to sweat out a siege. Anyone trying to rush the place would risk severe losses, especially from automatic fire.

'It's all a matter of remote control – and knowing the right button to punch,' he added. 'Frank here knows the right buttons. He'll press it on the day of the gala opening when the signal comes through from the opening dais.' He indicated a couple of workmen busy on an instrument near a wall clock. 'That's a special signal buzzer which will indicate that the Eagle of Time has just started to spread its wings. The outrush of water will follow simultaneously. It only takes a minute or two for the first water to start to flow, but in five minutes the sluices will be open to their normal operating level.'

The PRO picked up a small two-way transmitter from Frank's console. 'We are now going to a point close to the outlets and you will be privileged, as I said before, to witness the very first water ever to flow from Katse Dam. When I signal Frank, he will press the button and release the water.'

Frank indicated a radio receiver on the console. 'Ready whenever you are.'

It took, in fact, nearly ten minutes for the group to be mustered at their vantage point. It was a narrow concrete ledge with a steel railing which formed part of the outlet tunnel wall itself. It was about four or five metres high and sloped downwards like the tunnel at its extremity. Therefore it meant that its outer end would only be a couple of metres above water-level. This was where Grania and Sholto found themselves. Further on, the group could make out the river bed itself at the terminal end of the tunnel.

Bonnay logged the fact with satisfaction that a steel door

blocked off the control chamber from the outlet tunnel – no siege-breaking route that way!

The PRO said into his transmitter, 'Frank! Frank!'

The party heard the disembodied reply: *'Roger. All set.'*

'Then shoot!'

The crowd made out the rumble from deep inside long before they spotted the first sign of water. Then it appeared, muddy-brown. It seemed to feel its way in a shallow trickle over the rough man-made surface towards the river bed.

'I'd expected a great big roaring rush,' Grania confided to Sholto.

'Maybe it's to come,' he replied. 'Perhaps Frank is taking it easy to start off with.'

Seconds later, Grania got her roaring splash. Without warning, a brown torrent erupted down the tunnel. A wall of living water foamed past, licking at the new walls, licking right at the bottom edge of the VIP ledge itself.

Grania shrank back. The torrent was close enough for Sholto and her to have reached down and touched it. Foam and flecks reached for the head of the VIP party.

Sholto threw an anxious glance at the PRO.

'Please move back – higher up, please!' He had to shout above the roar of the water.

There was what seemed another surge of brown; suddenly foam lapped at the lowest edge of the ramp.

'Grania – run! Take off your shoes! Get back up there – quick!'

She slipped off her shoes and started up the rough surface. Sholto put his arm round her to steady her.

'Frank!' The PRO was yelling now into the radio. 'That's enough! You're flooding the whole tunnel!'

Sholto and Grania were among those nearest to the transmitter and heard the reply.

'Get your people out of there quick! Something's happened – stuck – sluices jammed wide open – '

The water seemed to hurl itself at them in ever-heightening steps of foaming brownness. One moment it was below the ramp, the next it was inches over it, chasing only a few metres behind the retreating VIPs.

'Keep going – quick! Keep going up in front there!' The PRO was shouting at the top of his voice.

Grania winced as her foot snagged in a projection in the rough surface, and grabbed the handrail to steady herself.

'We should have brought our climbing boots along, Sholto!'

The VIPs scuttled towards safety. The water kept coming, coming. It plucked at the ramp, but couldn't quite make it. Spray splashed across the concrete, making it slippery and slowing down those in front who kept on their shoes – and dignity.

Sholto and Grania hurried on with the rest. Then the tunnel kinked, the handrail ended, and they were clear of the outlets and into the main perimeter gallery shaft – and safety.

The PRO banged closed the steel door. Sholto and Grania were the last through.

Sholto regarded Grania. 'What price your premonition now?'

Half an hour later, the VIP group was soothing its nerves on tea – in some cases, something stronger – under the thatched dome of the central complex of Katse Lodge. The roof supports were of crude treated timber; the bar in the corner had its own little thatched top. It was a cosy, safe place; it would be cosier still when the snow came and the big metal stove (it was an Austrian model) cast its glow under the dark blond thatch. The Basuto traditional theme was everywhere – outside the building was a two-metre thatched replica of the traditional Basuto hat or mokorotlo. A Basuto crier, in a blanket daubed with bright ochre suns and also wearing his mokorotlo, helped put the shaken guests at ease by strumming a small tribal instrument. He had a drum, too, but did not resort to it.

Bonnay was delighted. Not with the tourist gimmicks, but with Katse Lodge. He nearly burst out laughing when the minibus which brought the party from the wall stopped at one of the huts on the cliff-side to unload Dr Poortman's suitcases. He knew now precisely where his victim was housed – in Number Fourteen. Moreover, the lay-out of Katse Lodge might have been tailored for a kidnap: it was all a grid-pattern of straight paths, a road in front, a mean little security gate, and a security fence – below the level of the cliff-top path. All that a determined intruder had to do was to climb up from the outside, go over, and land more or less at ground level on the side where his target lay among the huts. Which was Number Fourteen. An additional landmark to Dr Poortman's hut was a bigger thatched structure which, the PRO said while Dr Poortman's suitcases were being carried in, was a hut for storing ski gear.

Bonnay changed his mind about not having a drink when the party settled inside. A cinch like Katse Lodge deserved a whiskey, at least.

When it came, he breathed the word into his glass.

'*Spetsnaz!*'

CHAPTER TEN

───◆───

'*Spetsnaz!*' snapped Bonnay.

'Come again?' asked Kennet ponderously.

'My oath!' exclaimed Bonnay. 'If you don't know what *spetsnaz* means by now, you should go into retirement.'

'It's because I've been in forced retirement in this dump for a couple of years that I'm out of touch,' retorted Kennet sulkily.

'*Spetsnaz* – stealth, surprise, the cold-blooded surgical strike,' Bonnay amplified. 'That's what this kidnap is all about – and Katse is the place for just that. Tailor-made.'

The four members of the gang had just walked into the casino bar at Maseru. It was early evening. A short while before they had returned – by road – from Katse Dam, where they had collected Bonnay, who had broken away from the VIP tour. They had now taken up station at their favourite table in the corner.

Bonnay couldn't leave Kennet alone. The way he needled him was symptomatic of his inner tension and excitement, now that the Poortman kidnap had emerged from the realm of speculation into reality.

'What sort of Trotskyite are you that you've never heard of *spetsialnoye naznachenie* . . .'

'I said, I've been too long away – and who the hell among your Trotskyite pals has cared a damn for us all this time we've been marooned in this hole?' rejoined Kennet angrily.

'Oh, for Chrissake, leave it alone, you two!' broke in Hayward. 'I, for one, am damn glad to be here in this pub, snug and warm, out of the cold. It started to become perishing on the road back from Katse.'

'Snow coming,' said Pestiaux. 'That's what the forecast said.'

Hayward glanced round the bar. The place was full and there was a splurge of raised voices. None of the gang had succeeded in catching Umberto's eye; he was too busy fuelling the loud conversations.

'What's going on here tonight?' asked Hayward of nobody in particular.

He caught sight of the casino whore and signalled her across to the gang's table.

'Somebody's birthday?' he asked.

The woman looked at their faces. 'Why are you guys so down in the mouth? Can't you feel the vibes?'

'Too much bloody noise and too many people,' interjected Bonnay.

The woman gave them a superior look born of having known men and their ways for too long.

'The vibes – this is the way it always happens when there's something in the air. I remember it was like this years ago when the South African commandos broke in and shot up terrorists in Maseru. Something's cooking, mark my words.'

'What?' demanded Bonnay.

'The answer will cost you money, and you mayn't be as satisfied as if you had used my own personal services.'

Bonnay, in his uptight frame of mind, had been aware of the air of spurious *joie de vivre* in the place as soon as the gang had walked in. It had contributed to his uptight mood.

'I'll give you the price of your services without you having to work for it,' he said. 'Here.' He put down some notes on the table.

'Well, this is easier than having to entertain a dreary bastard like you seem to be tonight,' she returned. She whispered in Bonnay's ear, so that the others had to crane to overhear.

'They say something's going to happen out in the mountains. Big. A Happening.'

'Who's they?' demanded Bonnay.

'Friends I have in low places.'

'What is going to happen?'

She glanced furtively round and replied in a low voice, 'Even if I knew, I wouldn't tell you – not for a few mingy smackers.'

'Then push off,' rejoined Bonnay.

She flounced off.

'The smart touch, the feminine touch,' sneered Hayward. 'I'd say that story of a Happening was all a bluff, just to pocket some green without working for it.'

Kennet said heavily, 'There *is* an air about this place. I feel it.'

'You don't have to be psychic to sense that,' responded Bonnay. 'Out in the mountains,' he ruminated. 'What could be going on out in the mountains?'

'It could snow tonight,' said Pestiaux. 'Could be a good night for . . .' He glanced round. There were noisy men and women everywhere. 'You know who.'

Bonnay got up. 'We can't discuss anything between ourselves here . . .'

'Can't even get a drink,' added Hayward.

'We'll pick up ours at the bar and go to my room,' said Bonnay. 'What we have to discuss would add a lot to the vibes, if it was overheard.'

In his bedroom, Bonnay closed the door and locked it, as if to ensure the casino vibes did not enter.

Pestiaux said, as if still afraid to utter the bandit's name, '*He* always uses an AK-47, the papers say. Usually a grenade or two as well to finish off his operations.'

'Security vans have armour-plated glass all round and built-in armour-plating inside. They'll stand up to ordinary small-arms or automatic fire,' Bonnay said matter-of-factly. 'You can test out the proof of what I say for yourselves, once the Maluti Rider opens up on me. If I'm wrong – ' He shrugged. 'In the driver's seat, I'm the guy who'll collect the shit. But I reckon instead we'll nail him. I fancy that spot at the Bokong Crossing.'

'It's a natural. There wasn't anything to touch it all the rest of the fifty kays from Leribe to Katse,' said Hayward. 'All big new highway, no steep curves, no sunken culverts.'

Earlier, when Bonnay flew off with the VIP party to Katse, Hayward, Pestiaux and Kennet had reconnoitred the highway for possible ambush sites and had finally located Bonnay at Katse Lodge's security gate chatting to one of the guards, who was deferring to the Pony Pass in the Frenchman's buttonhole. The man had shaken hands with Bonnay when the gang's car drew up, and had wished him a pleasant return drive.

'Like taking jam from a kid,' Bonnay had told the gang once he was safely inside the car.

The gang had gone on to make a complete familiarisation tour by road of the dam site complex, and then had headed for home.

It was only when they had got well clear of Katse's environs that Bonnay put the question which had been uppermost in his mind.

'Ambush site?'

'An absolute sure-fire spot – about twenty kays from here,' Hayward had replied.

Bonnay had agreed, when he saw the washed-away bridge and replacement causeway over the Bokong River. The river flowed ankle-deep over the temporary structure, which had been built as a dogleg between two waterfalls, one on either side of the roadway. These splashed down from bush-cloaked cliffs which formed the narrow gorge into which the river had been compressed at this point. The higher of the two falls was about ten metres above causeway level; the second was shallower and noisier, tumbling over a drop of blue-grey shale. The causeway also by-passed one of the former bridge-pillars whose base still remained intact. Other concrete wreckage littered the stream-bed. Any of the chunks could provide safe cover from small-arms fire.

'The Maluti Rider has got the choice of half a dozen good vantage points here,' Hayward had observed.

Bonnay had looked about, assessing, projecting himself into the Maluti Rider's possible thinking. He dismissed as firing points the shattered concrete remains, all of which were scattered downstream from the causeway itself.

'On every job he's done, he has also always made a smart getaway,' Bonnay ruminated, eyeing the bush-clad slopes.

'The media says he has a horse, a superhorse,' added Pestiaux.

'Yeah, yeah. If you believe the media, he flies into his ambushes on its back and flies out again afterwards,' scoffed Bonnay. 'Here, he'll go for the side where the bushes are for cover for both himself and his horse. That's also where I want him to lie up.'

71

'You seem damn sure of yourself,' Kennet had commented.

Bonnay had gestured to a gully parallel with the waterfall whose head made a notch against the threatening sky.

'With a horse, that's his best route out,' he had replied. 'Up – and out.'

'You seem almost telepathic about second-guessing what he is and is not going to do,' Kennet had continued in the same doubting vein. 'He'll be here, he'll be there . . .'

'This isn't a hard-kill counter-strike on our part,' Bonnay had broken in. 'You three have got to bring him in alive. Remember that: however tough he reacts.'

He had again looked searchingly round the causeway site.

'It feels right,' he had told the others. 'I drive up in the van, and then play the fool as if the engine was giving trouble. I give him time to line up his sights on the cab – and me. I half turn and stop, about here.' He indicated a spot on the causeway. 'That means the body of the van will hide you three in the back when you bail out the door. He opens up on me. Out you go, into the bushes, and up the slope at him, still hidden. Okay?'

Hayward had asked, with admiration and a touch of awe in his voice, 'Aren't you pissing yourself about his AK-47 fire, Jules?'

Bonnay had replied matter-of-factly, 'I said before, all security vans are armour-plated. Windscreen and windows too. I guess they'll stand up to his fire. If they don't . . .' He shrugged.

'He might try a grenade or two when he sees he's not making an impression with the AK-47,' Kennet had said.

'No, not here – too much water,' Bonnay had answered. 'He'd never set the van on fire, as he has always done in the mountains.'

'This is damn close to the mountains,' Hayward had said. He had indicated the peaks blurring and drifting in the distance on their route home.

'The peaks are where he'll make for after the shoot-up – if we let him,' Bonnay had said. 'It's over to you three to handle that side of the operation once the van is trapped on the causeway. It's only by using a van with armour that we can turn the tables on the Maluti Rider. That means we've got to have an official security van.'

Now, back in the locked bedroom, Bonnay asked sharply, 'Did you check the Maseru van depot while I was away at Katse?'

'There wasn't time to case it carefully,' Kennet replied. 'The depot isn't far from here – less than two kilometres, I'd say – near the prison.'

'I hope that isn't an omen,' said Hayward with a grin.

Kennet ignored the Irishman's crack. 'Security fence all round, of course. About a dozen vans parked there. It's dead simple to find – up the main road past Moshoeshoe's statue. That's not the route we're using, though – we'll take a back way. Also, we take a back route out of town once we've grabbed the van.'

'Why?' asked Bonnay.

Kennet laughed ironically. 'There are *two* police stations close to one another on the main exit – *two!*'

Bonnay cut in incisively. 'All this talk is far too bitty-and-piecey for my liking. Let's get the whole picture completely clear before we start discussing detail logistics.'

'Hear, hear!' added Hayward.

'Good!' said Bonnay. 'Good! We ambush the Maluti Rider at sunset – just as it is getting dark – the day after tomorrow. We lay our ambush at the Bokong Crossing – agreed?'

The others nodded, but Hayward objected. 'We haven't yet got ourselves that security van.'

'We heist the van early in the morning – you already know that,' replied Bonnay. 'It has to be early, so that we can get clear of Maseru before the hunt is up.'

'And where do we spend the day with a piece of hot property on our hands like a stolen security van?' asked Kennet. 'What about road blocks?'

'I asked you to look out on the Katse highway for somewhere to stash away the van until ambush time,' Bonnay replied.

'We did,' answered Kennet. 'You can forget about anywhere along the highway. But I did spot a likely side-road leading off it beyond Leribe. The sign read, Kao Diggings. It didn't look more than a track – pretty grotty.'

Bonnay found a map. 'Kao Diggings are northward up the Malibamatso from Katse – there's a whole collection of diggings shown here. Some are marked "disused". We could lie up for the day somewhere along the track leading to them from Leribe and then double back in time for the ambush. That way, we could time our arrival precisely at the Bokong Crossing.'

'If the Maluti Rider doesn't show up, what then?' asked Pestiaux. He had taken almost no part in the discussion; he seemed willing to accept whatever Bonnay suggested.

Bonnay sensed the tension ease in the other two when he replied, 'We go on to Katse Lodge and snatch Dr Poortman from his hut.' He added, with a grin, 'I even know his number – fourteen.'

'That same night?' asked Pestiaux.

'That same night – whether we manage the Maluti Rider ambush or have to resort to our alternative plan of holing up in the dam's control centre. This is the way it will work: we take Poortman from his nice warm bed at the point of a pistol. We walk him to the control centre entrance – it's not far, just across the road. We hole up in the control centre. We also need supplies of food and water for a siege. That's easy. We help ourselves from the Katse Lodge kitchen, but we'll have to make sure that everyone has packed up for the night. That means a longer wait before going for Poortman.'

'You've done no more than mention that the control room and hydropower chambers are good places. What makes you so sure of them?' asked Hayward.

In reply, Bonnay outlined the lay-out of the perimeter gallery, its access point, how the two control centres were interconnected, and the single route out to the outlet tunnels.

'That doesn't sound good to me,' objected Hayward. 'They could rush us from the river bank via the outlet tunnels.'

'There's a steel door barring the way,' Bonnay answered.

'What makes you think that the security forces won't simply leave us to sweat it out until we run out of food and water?' asked Kennet.

'Because they'll be squeezed by time,' answered Bonnay.

'I don't follow.'

'Listen. Poortman is due to leave Maseru for South Africa in four days' time. That puts the squeeze on us to act soon. Either we snatch him before his departure date or we scrap the idea altogether – right?'

'That's our problem,' said Kennet. 'I'm talking about *them*.'

'The grand ceremonial opening of the Highlands Project is only twelve days away from today,' answered Bonnay. 'We kidnap Poortman on the night of Day Three. They won't discover he's missing until they find our ransom demand next morning, Day Four. Okay? That gives the authorities eight days to make up their minds to meet our demands – or else.'

'The two concrete chambers and the controls sound just the place for a bomb,' observed Hayward.

'You and your bloody bombs – always a bomb,' rejoined Bonnay ironically. 'We haven't got a bomb – but we could always threaten to blow the place up, nevertheless. It would be a good bluff to twist their arms.'

'The biggest bomb we could raise wouldn't even make a dent in the Katse wall,' Hayward answered. 'Just think – it took the RAF a whole damn-busting squadron of heavy bombers and specially invented bouncing bombs to breach the walls of the Moehne and Ede dams during the last world war . . .'

'Okay, okay, I know you're familiar with every noteworthy bomb that was ever planted,' said Bonnay impatiently. 'The point is, we haven't got so much as a grenade. Still, we can try the bluff.'

'Eight days?' said Kennet thoughtfully. 'You reckon the authorities will knuckle under by then?'

'Yes.' Bonnay's response was very sure. 'How could they go ahead with a ceremonial opening with a top VIP hostage being held in the control chamber just below where everything is due to take place? They couldn't so much as operate the controls, with us in possession. It would be an untenable situation for them. Think, man!'

'What about a bomb in the controls?' asked Hayward. 'That would fix 'em!'

'The control console for the dam sluices consists of one steel desk not much bigger than a business executive's and half a dozen switches. It could be done – but why?'

'Just for the hell of it,' replied Hayward.

'There are also a couple of telephones on the console which

75

would be useful to keep in touch with the outside world and put our demands,' went on Bonnay.

'What else?' Kennet was uneasy at Bonnay's apparent over-confidence.

'One big clock on the wall, and a buzzer which is to relay a signal from the opening dais on the big day,' replied Bonnay. 'Nothing else.'

'Sounds too good to be true,' commented Kennet.

'Surely they'll try and rush the place?' Pestiaux asked.

'If they are crazy enough to try, you will find plenty of employment for your Makarov and yourself,' Bonnay replied. 'They'd suffer heavy casualties in the confined space. Which reminds me, Hayward, Kennet – are your guns in order?'

'I'm taking the Colt,' said Hayward. 'It's been getting rusty lying around ever since Marseilles.'

'Get it cleaned, then,' ordered Bonnay. 'Kennet?'

'Scorpion,' he replied. 'But it's fairly low on ammo after the Marseilles affair.'

'Bring it,' said Bonnay. 'I'll have my Browning.'

Pestiaux said, as befitted his gundog status, 'I've cleaned my Makarov just like I clean my teeth. She's ready and willing, any time.'

'Plenty of firepower between the four of us,' observed Kennet.

Bonnay went on, 'I want you all to understand, this is not a shooting party – the more we do without it, the better our chances. It's what *spetsnaz* is all about – stealth, surprise, cold-blooded strike. No chance for the enemy to even reach for his gun. Total, clinical surprise.'

'What do we do with ourselves tomorrow?' asked Hayward. 'It looks like an off-day in our schedule.'

'Tomorrow we recce Maseru until we know the lay-out of our various targets and our escape route backwards. That is going to take time. Everything has to dovetail together so that we can slip away in our borrowed security van without anybody suspecting a thing.

'And we start early, see? That's the drill the next day also. Early. That means checking target times early tomorrow for the next day. We've got to find out what time our Number One opens its doors. Being the sort of outfit it is, it'll probably be seven, I reckon. Now, a laundry is the key to the entire ambush plan . . .'

CHAPTER ELEVEN

'Your premonition was spot-on target about something happening at Katse, wasn't it? It was a pretty scary moment when the sluice-gates stuck, wasn't it?'

Sholto and Grania were alone together in Sholto's study at 'Cherry Now'. It was after dinner. They had motored from Maseru to the farm after the VIP party had broken up. They had talked about superficial things on the hour-long journey: about the ominous storm clouds building up in the east, dramatically lit by the incendiary-burst sunset so that it was impossible to distinguish between storm-wrack and mountain peak; the ordered chaos of the new dam; the widespread acclaim for Grania's masterpiece; the opening ceremony in twelve days' time. By the time they had reached 'Cherry Now' the wind was icy, although there was no snow or sleet yet.

A fire in the study threw a snug glow off the ochre-coloured walls, built of blocks of sandstone quarried from the surrounding hills, and off the long curtains and shelves of books.

Grania took her glass from the tray between them, on which stood a bottle of Pierre Jourdan champagne.

She dodged his question. 'This champagne is exquisite. It was worthy to wet the head of your mother's famous cherry pie at dinner.'

'It's very rare and special. I had to have something special for you when you said you would come.'

Both Sholto and Grania had changed out of the formal clothes they had worn for the Katse visit. Now Grania had on a black and beige Ricci jumper with a bold fur trim pattern across her breast, and pants only a shade darker than the sandstone walls. Her only jewellery – apart from her carnelian earrings – was a triple-tier string of pearls. Sholto was wearing his khaki-coloured Fath bomber jacket with a cream trim, matching pants, and a ribbed V-neck jersey, the colour of fossil shale.

When she had first seen him at dinner Grania felt they showed off his sun-tanned face to perfection.

There was a pause. Outside, the wind had begun to pluck at the roof of 'Cherry Now'. All through dinner, as on the road back from Maseru, the conversation had been pitched in a low key; the air of constraint between them was surfacing now that they were alone. And, from the following day, they would be very much in their own company, since Sholto's mother was going to stay with friends in Natal until immediately before the opening ceremony.

Grania went on quickly, as if fearing what Sholto might ask next. 'Yes, it was scary. It could have been a tragedy. It all happened so quickly. But you're wrong about my premonition, as you call it, Sholto. It wasn't about the sluice-gates incident.'

He eyed her and sipped his champagne. She was, he told himself, beautiful. She didn't need the help of champagne and lovely clothes. She had been beautiful even up there in the peaks of Lammergeyer Land with a climber's anorak and faded work-shirt.

'What was it then?'

Her eyes slid away from his and she fingered her right earring in her characteristic way.

'I don't know. What I think I felt was much bigger, something much more sinister and evil than what we experienced.'

'Much more sinister and evil,' he repeated thoughtfully. 'There were enough dignitaries; if anything had happened to them . . . Yet you say your premonition did not apply . . .'

He stopped. She was looking at him the way he had seen her eyes, close-up, when he had grabbed her from pitching over the precipice near the lammergeyer's eyrie to certain death. It was more pain than anything else he could define. What he had to say he had to say now, or leave their relationship at the level it had been operating ever since her arrival.

He stood looking down at her sitting in his favourite leather chair.

'Why did you accept my invitation to come and stay at "Cherry Now", Grania?' he asked. 'You'd have been given the VIP treatment, like Dr Poortman, if you'd chosen Katse Lodge.'

She put down her champagne as if its taste had gone for her.

79

'Can you imagine my going to Katse Lodge and meeting you at the gala opening and saying, thanks, Sholto, for everything?'

'Everything? You didn't make it seem like that, all that time you were away in Switzerland . . .'

'Anything the Eagle of Time has, it owes to you,' she interrupted. 'You gave me the lammergeyer; I came to you with nothing in my creative head and you gave me things I can never hope to repay or will ever forget. That great golden bird – I sculpted only what you showed me. And the mountains – it was magic, there. I could have been alone with God. You gave me a new world of glory; just the two of us, you leading on the rope, hammering in the pitons. I nearly fell, but you were there. I owe you that, too, Sholto, never forget.'

'You transformed a lammergeyer into a masterpiece of art. That owes nothing to me.'

'It wasn't only the bird,' she answered. 'You gave me the dinosaur embryo as a theme for my secret capsule – nobody has seen it yet – and the red sand dune on top of Moshoeshoe's fortress where you told me his spirit moves with the blowing sand. It's all yours, Sholto – and I would not have it otherwise.'

'There are three, not two, miniature artworks in the capsule,' he said.

'The third one is my own . . .'

'You don't have to let me into the secret, Grania.'

She brushed aside his remark. 'It's a minute silver chalice, made of platinum. Water pours symbolically from a silver stream out of the chalice; it symbolizes Lesotho's water flowing to South Africa.'

'Then why – if what you say is true – were you the way you were towards me all those endless months in Switzerland?' he asked in a low, hurt voice. 'You never replied to my letters. I phoned you – remember? You were so distant, I couldn't believe it was you I was talking to.' His shoulders moved unhappily under the bomber jacket. 'And then when I came to see you in Zurich, it was a disaster. I don't believe you even wanted to see me. That's also the impression I had when I made my surprise phone call once I arrived. I was scared to phone in advance.'

'I didn't want anyone to see the Eagle before it was finished. That's the way my creativity works. It would have killed it in its tracks to have revealed it prematurely.'

'I asked to see *you*, not the Eagle. You all but refused.'

'They were synonymous at that stage.'

She was looking away from him, playing with her right earring. He wanted to kneel down and pull her face round to him to try and find out what was going on behind her eyes.

Instead, he said, 'I find that hard to accept.'

She replied, rather desperately, 'I wouldn't let you come because I wasn't ready for you – can you understand, Sholto?'

'You've said that already.'

'I said it in another context, my artwork wasn't ready. Nor was I . . .'

'But you are now, that's why you've come to "Cherry Now" – is that what you are saying, Grania?'

She moved forward so that her face caught the added illumination of the firelight and Sholto observed again the strange dichotomy which seemed to divide her face: when she was under stress, the one half was older than her years, and the other half younger.

Her words came out with a rush.

'Sholto, must we go on with this conversation? I looked out at those mountains from the plane today and they brought back one of the happiest times of my life. Couldn't we go there again – before the opening ceremony? Just you and me? We could fit it in – there's nearly a whole fortnight to go . . .'

'It wouldn't be the same a second time with all those eighteen months of silence lying between us, and all the questions which you still haven't answered. We started off before from the Golden Gate with the slate clean . . .'

'And wrote it with magic.'

'Grania, why – '

'"Time present and time past Are both perhaps present in time future, And time future contained in time past,"' she said enigmatically, making a strange gesture in the direction of the mountains beyond the big windows.

'That's a good quote,' he said bitterly, ' – to put on a plaque at the base of the Eagle of Time.'

'It's very meaningful in my context.' Her voice cracked slightly as she said it.

'If only I knew what your context was.'

There was a knock at the door. 'Yes?' asked Sholto.

It was Mary Banks. 'Sholto, it's Jonathan, from Maseru. He wants to speak to you urgently.'

It was a striking figure who entered and grasped Sholto's forearms for a moment, without saying a word. It was a gesture which revealed the extent of the relationship between the two men. He might have been someone coming in from the Tibetan snows: he wore a light fawn quilted snow jacket with large buttons, a shoulder-wide furry collar, and overlong sleeves. A bright yellow hat, which looked like a soft sawn-off top hat, added to his height, which was over six feet. He wore half-calf boots with red and yellow facings and yellow lacings down the sides. He might have been a comic figure in the strange rig, except that his presence brought with it power and authority.

His glance went to Grania and the champagne.

'I'm sorry – I see I intrude. But I had to see you, Sholto. A matter of importance. It won't take long.'

Grania had risen to go. 'I think we had more or less finished what we had to say.'

'The Eagle has been drawing crowds all day,' he told her. 'Congratulations on your superb artistry. Lèsotho is proud of you.'

Grania smiled appreciation and addressed Sholto. 'It's been a full day. See you in the morning. I can't wait for you to show me the farm.'

Without inflexion in his voice he said, 'Goodnight, Grania.'

Jonathan removed his high hat and moved to the fire. 'I've come unannounced like this because of some news I was given late this afternoon. I felt it was too important to wait. It's too private for the telephone.'

'Go on.'

'Sholto, you know how close the Highlands Project is to my heart.'

'Yes.'

'You see it as a technical and financial shot in the arm for Lesotho, but I regard it as the start of a process to bring greatness again to my country. It is because I have royal blood in my veins, and my first love is to my country – great and free, standing its own man again.'

'You've already proved your worth over the project, Jonathan. Look at the way you handled that strike at Katse about a year ago. It could have become very ugly and damaging, except for you.'

'This Project is my dream – it *has* to come true, Sholto.'

Sholto gestured towards the champagne bottle, but Jonathan shook his head.

'Where I am going tonight may need every bit of clear thinking I have.'

'You didn't come here to make a pretty speech to me, Jonathan.'

'This afternoon I was visited by a man. A terrified man,' he said gravely.

'How'd he get past my two Swiss secretaries?'

'It wasn't at the office. He came to my home. In secret. He left in secret, and more terrified still at what he had revealed to me.'

'Who was this – informer? What did he have to say?'

'I said, I am of royal blood. And for a Basuto, blood – especially royal blood – is thicker than . . . than . . .'

'Banknotes?'

'In this case, I think that is so. He came to tell me, because he believed that he knew of something which pointed a dagger at the heart of the Project.'

'*What!*'

'If it is correct, something deeply unsettling, and full of danger.'

'That's pretty nebulous. What did he actually *say*?'

'He gave me a hint only – as I said, he was terrified. He clammed up even as he told me. He demanded an indemnity, which of course I was in no position to give. But I am on my way tonight to find out for myself. It could be a wild goose chase.'

'Wait while I change into some field clothes, and we'll sort this out together. You look as if you're bound for the snows.'

83

'Reds and yellows always show up well in the snow, if they have to send out a search party for you.'

'That's a pretty pessimistic start to our venture.'

'Sorry, Sholto, but you're not coming.'

'Not coming! Of course I'm coming!'

'See here, Sholto, you speak Sesotho like one of us, and in the dark no one would know any different. But where I'm headed a white face could be your – our – death warrant. Do I make myself clear?'

'Clear enough to have me worried stiff about your own safety. *What did your man say, Jonathan?*'

'It was no more than a hint, a rumour.'

'I feel I should know even that.'

'No. It's the reason why I'm on my way tonight – to try and find out something concrete.'

'The more you say, the more I think I should tag along.'

'Sorry, Sholto.'

'Have you got a gun?'

The big man slapped his quilted pocket. 'This is a one-man operation, Sholto. Two of us might drive our man away.'

'Man? What man? You aren't on the trail of the Maluti Rider, are you, Jonathan?'

'I don't know – at this stage. I may know later tonight. I know how to look after myself, Sholto.'

'So do I. It was part of my ombudsman background – security, unarmed combat training, guns, all the rest of it.'

'I know this, and I would like you with me. Yet it must not be, I'm afraid.'

'You know more than you're admitting, Jonathan.'

The big man looked uncomfortable. He had few secrets from Sholto. 'I'll come back in the morning, and report to you what I find out.'

'Is that a promise?'

'Yes. We can take it from there, you and I, depending on how strong the information is.'

Sholto saw him to the door. Jonathan pulled on his yellow hat against the wind whose freezing sharpness needled the eyes. The last Sholto saw of him was when the hat dropped out of sight

84

suddenly like an over-accelerating stage moon as Jonathan slipped into the driving seat of his car.

It was, however, not a moon of any sort, artificial or natural, which jerked Sholto out of sleep in the early hours of the morning. It was the smell. A strange, frightening smell which was more in his brain than in his nostrils, with all the hideous sanction of the nightmare of which it was part. He had witnessed Jonathan lying in a cave on what seemed a bed of mountain grass. He was still dressed in his snow-clothes, but he appeared to have shrunk, so that in place of the strong features, beard and moustache there was only a smooth wizened wisp of a face. It was a criss-cross of purple veins which had erupted to the surface, like scummy weeds. It was a repellent mask, yet it was Jonathan.

A small fire was burning near the bed. Four figures, clad in long antelope-skin cloaks, tended it, and they rose from time to time to peer at the man on the bed. Sholto saw the face of one as he moved: it was ancient, saurian, and malicious – the face of a Bushman. That was borne out by the creature's lack of height as it crossed to Jonathan. It said something in a thin, desolate, clicking voice, and the man on the bed rolled away from the sound, as if terrified by its message . . .

Sholto felt nauseated by the scene; and more nauseated still by the repulsive, animalistic smell which he judged must come from the half-cured skins the four Bushmen wore against the cave's chill. However, it was unlike any carcass-smell he had ever smelt: it seemed to well out of primeval darkness. The figure on the bed tossed and whimpered, and Sholto knew that Jonathan smelt it also, and knew what it meant. Now he himself did too – it was the smell of death.

CHAPTER TWELVE

'I'm starting to get desperately worried about Jonathan, Grania. He promised to report back to me first thing this morning.'

Grania checked the time. The good-luck god on the watch strap eyed her mockingly.

'It isn't late yet – it's just gone ten.'

Sholto put down the flat metal box whose base was full of holes. It was made that way to accommodate cherries during the destoning process of the farm's crop in the spring. They were in the big cherry-packing store on 'Cherry Now' where he had been explaining to Grania how the cherries, which formed a substantial part of the farm's output, along with asparagus and wheat, were packed later in the year, about November.

Sholto played anxiously with a sharp steel instrument, almost six inches long, which was used for de-pipping the cherries. His mind was only half on what he was telling Grania: even the bright day with loose billows of cloud masking the sandstone hills further to the east in the direction of Lesotho, and the eternal mountains far beyond them, failed to dissipate the darkness of the nightmare and Jonathan's own half-expressed hints of danger. Nor had he been able to rid himself of the death-smell. Its awfulness seemed impervious to the fresh cold wind from the east and would not pass away. Telling Grania about the dream helped, but not enough.

Sholto pulled his attention back to the cherries.

'This is how it works,' he said, plunging the de-pipper's point into an imaginary cherry trapped in the steel box. 'It's got a specially hardened steel tip. The workers are remarkably skilful and quick. You should be here in the spring. You'd never forget the sight of the cherry blossom against the sandstone hills.'

'I've seen cherries in Japan,' Grania replied. 'But somehow they seem more sophisticated. This looks so . . .' she searched for a word ' . . . un-urbanised.'

They laughed and he added, 'Neither is spring here the fragile thing I imagine it to be in Japan. We're hot – and the hail – ' he shrugged. 'Hail is something I don't care for.'

'The mountains with a hint of snow remind me of home,' she said. 'I can even wear my favourite old clothes.' She paused a moment, and then said, 'You're very fond of Jonathan, aren't you, Sholto?'

'Yes. He had me worried last night. I still am.'

'Maybe he's only got caught in the snow and has been delayed.'

'No,' he answered. 'There probably was snow on the high peaks far in the east, but there was no general snowfall last night – that's what the weather report said this morning. It seems that there are two cold fronts hard on each other's heels, and the first – and smaller one – passed by last night. The real punch is yet to come.'

She leaned forward and held the cherry de-pipper which he was twisting round in his fingers. 'Can I have this as a keepsake?'

'Of course.'

For a moment, he forgot his anxieties about Jonathan. He had been delighted – and surprised – at Grania's identification with everything he had shown her on the farm that morning. Less than ever could he reconcile it with her chilling rejection of him in Switzerland. Was it, in fact, what she claimed – that her creativity needed total isolation? Somehow, he could not credit that. He was sure there was some other reason, something far deeper.

His suppressed feelings came to the surface.

'I see you don't wear any rings.'

She held up her fingers. 'In Japan they have a saying that a ring is suitable for a wedding or a funeral, but that it takes an artist to fashion a buckle for a kimono.'

'It's a good answer, but it's not the answer I was looking for, Grania.'

She went on, side-stepping his probe. 'I'm like a magpie with things that are special to me – I secrete them away in the satchel where I keep my goldsmithing tools. This de-pipper joins them.'

'You brought your tools with you?'

'Yes. They've been a part of me ever since Japan.'

'Japan really gave you something, didn't it, Grania?'

As he said it, he realised he had lost her mood. He was at a loss to know what provoked her flat answer. 'Yes, I owe it my identity. As a person, apart from an artist.'

'Grania . . .'

'You promised to show me your stonemason at work on the sandstone, remember?' She pulled the conversation away from the precipice towards which it seemed headed and gave a glimmer of a smile. 'As one artist to another.'

'Old Moho would be flattered to hear that.'

'Moho – that's an odd name.'

'It's a nickname, really. It's short for Mohokare, which is the Basuto name for the Caledon River.'

They could make out, a few kilometres away, the line of the river itself which was marked by its flanking willows and riverbank greenery. Beyond the procession of sandstone hills were the hazy summits of Lesotho's mountains, blurred by the approaching weather.

Grania indicated them as she climbed into Sholto's pick-up.

'Does that mean thunder?'

'No thunder at this time of year – and no hail, thank goodness.' He paused with his hand on the ignition switch. 'What made you create the lammergeyer gripping a thunderbolt? It was a master-stroke, but you didn't learn it here.'

'No, it's something of a derivation. The battle standard of the old Roman legions was an eagle gripping a thunderbolt in its talons. It's the way our lammergeyer grasped the bones that day when he dropped them on the rock.'

'It looks very dramatic.'

'The lammergeyer's feet were a hassle to me – you told me its talons were like those of a vulture and not striking like an eagle's. So I got round the difficulty by giving mine a thunderbolt to grip.'

Old Moho's pitch needed no signpost: generations of stonemasons had burrowed away at a fine hill which backed the homestead at a distance and had left a clutter of debris down the slope. At its foot, where activity seemed to be concentrated now, was a rough pole structure with a thatched topknot against the sun. Old Moho sat on a small stool; they heard the jink of steel against steel as he dressed a block of stone.

Sholto addressed the stonemason, who wore a dusty off-white overall with overlarge pockets, in Sesotho; an exchange followed, during which the old man kept glancing at Grania.

Finally, Sholto said, 'He asks, can he see your hands?'

'Why, yes.' She seemed half-embarrassed, and held them out.

'He says, you have very beautiful hands, but you can't have been in the business long, because they have no callouses.'

'Did you tell him I worked in gold?'

'He demanded to know all about you.'

Old Moho broke in and said something more to Sholto, gesturing again at Grania's hands.

'What does he say this time?'

'Do you really want to know?'

'Yes, of course.'

'He says, there must be a lot of stupid men in your world that no one has given you a beautiful ring for those fingers.'

She turned away from the two men; her eyes seemed as far away as the distant Malutis.

'What reply do I give him?' Sholto asked. 'I can't pass on the one you gave me about Japanese weddings and funerals.'

'Sholto . . .' Her voice was full of suppressed agony. 'Sholto, please!' Then she got a grip on herself and said flatly, 'Tell him, as one artist to another, I'd like to see him at work.'

Sholto cued in to her mood; he spoke quickly and impersonally.

'This could be very interesting. I'd hoped we might see the way he shatters the rock in its matrix in order to get the individual blocks for dressing. Old Moho certainly wouldn't do it to order, but by chance he is about to carry out the operation now himself. He employs a curious mixture of sugar, saltpetre and sulphur to make a kind of low-powered gunpowder. It is only powerful enough to crack the rock, without shattering it to fragments, as modern explosives would. It's a tradition which dates back a long time.'

'I'd love to see.'

When they reached a spot where the scarring in the rock was new, Old Moho pointed to a scrap of paper projecting from a hole in the rock.

'He first cuts a hole in the rock, or simply enlarges a crack – these sandstone hills are riddled with cracks,' Sholto explained. 'Then he puts in his gunpowder charge and tamps it closed with newspaper, as you see.'

Old Moho was grinning and handing Sholto a box of matches.

'He says, he would like you to light the fuse and then you will feel the joy of working stone, which he is sure is much more rewarding than gold.'

Old Moho busied himself with the paper, and then gestured to Grania.

Grania hesitated. 'Will we have time to get clear before it explodes?'

'It's very slow-burning.' Nevertheless, he questioned Old Moho. 'At least five minutes, he says.'

She lit the fuse and Old Moho took his time tamping the paper back into position.

'Won't the fuse go out through lack of air?' asked Grania.

'Not likely. Old Moho knows what he's doing.'

Old Moho led them to safety a little way off. He searched in his voluminous pockets and drew out a smallish glass container with grey-brown powder in it.

Sholto translated Old Moho's words. 'He wants you to have this container of gunpowder as a souvenir. He hopes that sometime you will show him how you blast gold out of the rock for your work.'

'What a wonderful gesture!' exclaimed Grania. 'This is my second keepsake this morning! It's going straight into my tool satchel with the cherry de-pipper . . .'

The explosion was more a muffled thud than a blast. They were near enough for it to obliterate the sound of a vehicle being driven hard and fast towards them; dust from its wheels as the driver slammed on his brakes mingled with the sandstone's.

A farmhand jumped out and sprinted to Sholto.

'Quick! Come quick!' he gasped. 'There's a dead man on the raft in the river!'

CHAPTER THIRTEEN

The body was Jonathan's.

Sholto had sensed it even before he spotted the quilted fawn snow jacket and boots with their fancy ribbons. All the hideousness and evil portent of the nightmare was back with him on the high-speed dash from Old Moho's pitch to the river. Grania hung on to a grab-handle as he threw the pick-up over the rough track. There was nothing to be said; he knew, she knew.

The pick-up finally banged to a standstill among reeds and riverine scrub. The raft's function was to suck up sand from the river bed and feed it ashore through a thick canvas hose to a dump. The sand was sold for building. The raft was a crude thing of planks and old empty fuel drums, on which was mounted an engine and pump.

Where the pick-up stopped gave them a vantage-point higher than the raft, so that they looked down on it. Sholto sat numbed for a moment at what he saw lying, face to the sky, on the raft's planks.

Then he got out and joined the group of workers standing silently on the bank. The yellow hat which lay alongside Jonathan's body might have been a plague-signal and the raft in quarantine, the way the group stood back. The quarantine was death.

Not death, but murder.

That is what Sholto found when he climbed from the little skiff – it held only Grania and himself – on to the rough planks.

Jonathan's clothing was not wet, so he could not have drowned. That was the first thought which flashed through Sholto's mind as he knelt and reached for one of the outsize wooden buttons of the snow jacket. As he started to undo it, he suddenly seemed to become aware of Grania next to him.

'Do you want to be here?' he asked in a thick, choked voice. 'It could be ugly.'

Jonathan's face wasn't pretty. The lips were drawn back, one eye was closed, but the other was staring; there was a tiny blue vein on the closed lid. Sholto shuddered. He recalled the stricken face in the cave with its weed-like veins and nightmare attendants.

'I'll stay,' Grania replied.

Sholto undid the buttons; there were no marks of violence on the shirt or throat, no tell-tale bullet hole.

Sholto gripped the dead man under the arms and hefted him over on his front.

Then they saw.

One knife-stroke had done it. From behind. Not the amateur's overhand thrust, but the up-and-under of the skilled professional who knew exactly where the heart lay in the broad landscape of the big man's back. It had power, too – the terrible power of one killing stroke, for the heft had snagged onto the gash which the blade had ripped on its fatal passage in and had torn loose some of the threads round its lips.

The blood. The shirt at the back was soaked down to the waist: the quilting had absorbed and masked the awfulness from the front.

There was hardly any need for Sholto to check Jonathan's heart; he had felt the awful fast-approaching rigor mortis in the shoulders when he had heaved him over. The blood was dry, too.

He said to Grania in a voice which she scarcely recognised, 'It must have happened quite soon after he left me. There is nothing we can do for him. This is a police matter.'

Grania was deadly pale. She was standing as he knelt. Her left hand grasped his shoulder meaningfully.

'I'll use this bit of tarpaulin over the engine to cover his face,' he said.

He started to roll the dead man again on to his back, and reached for the oil-soaked strip of tarpaulin which usually protected the engine overnight.

'Look at his finger, Sholto,' said Grania. 'It's covered in blood.'

Jonathan's right index finger was red up to the first joint.

'Strange. There's no sign of a cut.'

'There's no blood on the rest of the hand,' said Grania. 'Just on the finger.'

'Perhaps he tried to reach the wound – reflex action – '

'Sholto, there's a smear right round his shirt, too.'

'If he used his finger it means he must have deliberately tried to get at the wound from the back – the blade didn't emerge at the front – while he was dying.'

Sholto examined the shirt; he saw there were two roughly parallel blood trails leading out of the mouth of the wound.

'Sholto . . .' Grania began.

Sholto regarded her. 'We'd better go ashore before you pass out.'

'I'm all right,' she answered, although her shaky tone denied it. 'I'll get back to the farmhouse and phone the police, if you want me to.'

'Sure you're fit enough?'

'I'm okay.'

Sholto placed the oily engine cover over Jonathan's face. This seemed to help Grania.

'It's better if I stay here,' went on Sholto. He glanced across at the opposite bank of the river. 'This could provoke an awkward situation – the river is the international boundary. This side is South African, and that Lesotho. When you speak to the police, say that I request a senior officer to come. Tell them who Jonathan is, too, and his connection with the Highlands Project through me . . .'

'It depends on where he was killed,' said General Mak judicially. 'That will determine who will carry out the investigations – either ourselves or the South Africans. It's a matter of protocol. I think you realise that?'

'Jonathan's last words to me were that he was going into the mountains,' replied Sholto. 'That means Lesotho.'

Sholto and Grania were in the Lesotho security chief's office in Maseru that afternoon. It was situated in a new office block in the city centre. After the arrival of the South African police at the raft, plus an ambulance and a doctor, under a captain from Ficksburg, Sholto had phoned General Makoanyane and had asked to see him urgently.

The security chief had been easy and friendly – until he had heard Sholto's news about Jonathan and the intervention of the South African police. Then he had become cold and formal; Sholto knew that the old animosities provoked by cross-border raids and cattle rustling gangs in the past were flaring in the Security chief's mind, despite the years of close collaboration over the Highlands Project between the two countries.

'Why do you want to see me?' General Mak had asked him off-handedly over the phone. 'You surely must have made formal statements to your own police about the murder. It was on your property, and outside my jurisdiction, being across the border.'

'There are other things involved,' Sholto had answered.

'What things?' General Mak had been suspicious, distant.

'Things I can't discuss on the phone, things which are very close to your heart and mine.'

'Sholto,' General Mak had said, 'this is the kind of emotional appeal I don't care for – especially when murder is involved.'

Sholto had known from his modified tone that he had established a foothold, and he capitalised on it.

'Grania Yeats was with me when I found the body,' he had gone on. 'What I want to discuss with you involves her, too. I'd like to bring her along with me to see you.'

There had been an appreciable pause before General Mak had answered. 'Very well, then. But only on condition you don't drag in issues which could embarrass me.'

'Does the Eagle of Time embarrass you, General Mak?'

There was a still longer pause, and then General Mak had said briefly, 'Get here as quickly as you can. There'll be priority clearance at the door.'

Had Bonnay and the Chunnel Gang witnessed the smart way Sholto and Grania were ushered into the tower-block building, they would have been intrigued – and perhaps a little apprehensive. But they had finished working that part of the town in the morning, and were now busy, a mere kilometre or two away from General Mak's headquarters.

Now Sholto and Grania faced General Mak across a big desk. By way of introduction he said briefly, 'This conversation is being recorded.'

'Why?'

The security man regarded them narrowly. 'Because I like to listen afterwards to things like inflexions in people's voices, half-finished sentences – things like that.'

'We have nothing to hide,' replied Sholto and Grania indicated agreement. 'In fact, just the other way round.'

'Where did they find Jonathan's car? He'd been to see you, you say?'

'They haven't. My guess is that it's not on the South African side of the border but in Lesotho. In the mountains.'

'Or in the river,' snapped General Mak. 'What sort of car was it?'

'A white Toyota hatchback.'

'Anything to make it different from a hundred other white Toyota hatchbacks?'

'Yes. It had white upholstery. It was a piece of vanity – like Jonathan's fancy snow-boots with their coloured ribbons.'

'Huh. What did Jonathan have to tell you that made him rush off from Maseru to your farm on a freezing night and say he was going into the mountains?'

'It was more what he left unsaid.'

'That's the sort of statement I don't care for. Tell me something explicit – or else you're wasting my time.'

'He hinted that he had learned of something which was a threat to the Highlands Project. A hint, no more.'

'From whom?'

'He wouldn't say. The informer asked for an indemnity, and clammed up when Jonathan couldn't promise him one.'

'And so the unknown followed him to "Cherry Now" and put a knife in his back?'

Sholto leaned forward across the desk. 'You've got the wrong orientation, General Mak. Jonathan was gravely, deeply concerned about a threat to the Project. So was I, although he told

96

me no more than I am able to tell you. It was the *way* he came across. The Highlands Project was something very close to Jonathan's heart.'

'What sort of threat?' demanded the security man. 'A physical threat to the opening ceremony? To one of the VIPs?' He half-indicated Grania. 'Someone of Miss Yeats' status? It couldn't be the Katse Dam itself – that wouldn't be possible.'

'Jonathan didn't define the threat,' said Sholto.

'What was your impression, Miss Yeats? You were present?'

'No, I wasn't. Jonathan asked to see Sholto alone. He didn't stay long. But I had the feeling that he was deeply worried about something.'

General Mak banged the desk-top with his fist. 'Feelings! Inferences! The *way* he said it! Bah! Give me one hard fact!'

Sholto answered quietly, 'I believed him enough to have volunteered to go along with him – wherever he was heading last night.'

'Why didn't you?'

'He said, a white face could be my – our – death warrant.'

'His face didn't help him,' retorted General Mak roughly.

Sholto ignored the other man's abrasiveness. He realised that it sprang from a feeling of real frustration that he and his men were not handling the investigation.

'If you locate Jonathan's car in Lesotho, you can start your own inquiries,' said Sholto.

'I have to wait for a formal request from the South African side before I can act.'

'General – a man has been killed – knifed to death!'

'I don't get my knickers in a twist every time a man is knifed to death,' replied General Mak. 'A man was fished out of the Caledon on the outskirts of this town this morning – he'd been knifed to death. It happens all the time.'

'Who was he?' demanded Sholto. 'It could have an important bearing on Jonathan . . .'

General Mak held up a hand. 'You stick to being an ombudsman, Sholto, and I'll keep to police work. There's no connection. This guy was a layabout, a good-for-nothing. Some hobo stuck a knife into him for the price of a bottle of spirits. You don't have to tell me my job.'

'General Mak,' went on Sholto, emphasising his words. 'My belief is that Jonathan had uncovered some kind of threat to the Eagle of Time. By striking at it, whoever it was would bring the Highlands Project into discredit. He wouldn't have to go for VIPs or the Katse Dam. The Eagle epitomises the whole Project in total. To smash it would be to smash the Project, especially since the opening is so close.'

'What do you say to that, Miss Yeats? You were responsible for the masterpiece.'

'It would break my heart if anything happened to it.'

'Listen, Sholto, you're talking nonsense. The Eagle is guarded all day by armed guards while it is on view at the centre. At night it is safe in the bank's strongroom. Nothing can happen to it.'

'Except when it's not there,' said Sholto.

'What are you driving at?' General Mak leaned forward from his previous attitude of derisory lolling.

'On the day after tomorrow, the Eagle is to be on view at Katse Dam to the construction workers, isn't that so? Everyone knows that – it has been publicly announced and broadcast. That's the time – during its journey from Maseru to Katse, when there must of necessity be soft spots in the security arrangements.'

'It's travelling up to Katse by security van tomorrow afternoon,' General Mak interrupted. 'Four of my best men – all of them armed – are riding shotgun with it. They'll also guard it during the day it is on show at Katse. Nothing *can* happen!'

Sholto continued, 'What I came here to ask – only to request because the decision is wholly yours – is that you change the method of transporting the Eagle. Hold the Katse exhibition as planned. But transport the Eagle some other way. I ask that for Jonathan's sake.'

'How do you propose it should be conveyed?'

'In dead secrecy. By plane. Fly it up to Katse the same morning as it goes on show. You've then cut the security risk in half. More than in half.'

The security man's reply was gruff, but Sholto knew he had

won. 'The weather's closing down for flying. What if it's snowing?'

'It's worth the risk. We can't let anything happen to the Eagle.'

'I think you have a point. I'll fix it that way, Sholto.'

'Thank you, General Mak. Jonathan would be pleased.'

The uniformed figure shrugged and said, 'If we're going to tighten up in one direction, we might as well go the whole hog. I'll have all security arrangements tightened up – just in case. Does that satisfy you?'

'What about the VIPs?'

General Mak grinned. 'At the moment there are only two, and one of them – ' he indicated Grania ' – is in your charge anyway. I'll have a special bodyguard allocated to Dr Poortman as from this afternoon. He's here in Maseru now, isn't he?'

'Yes. At the Finance Ministry.'

'The Ministry's very close. I'll ask him to come over here to my office and tell him what it's all about.'

Five minutes later, when Dr Poortman was shown in, the banker's Faustian eyebrows quirked up to their most flyaway at the sight of Sholto and Grania with the security chief.

General Mak intercepted the banker's keen glance and said quickly, 'They're not on the mat – I wish I did have someone on the mat.'

'Trouble?' asked Dr Poortman. 'Nothing to do with the Eagle of Time, I hope?'

'Not yet,' answered Sholto. 'But it could come to that.'

'Sholto is putting two and two together and making five,' General Mak intervened. 'He has nothing to back up a statement like that. Now listen, Dr Poortman . . .' He gave a quick run-down of Jonathan's murder, and added, 'Sholto is convinced that Jonathan had found out something which constitutes a threat to the Eagle. That, in my view, is purely an assumption. However, he is so concerned about it that I have agreed – somewhat against my better judgement – to change the transport arrangements for the Eagle for its showing at Katse the day after tomorrow. It will now be flown there, instead of taken by security van with an armed guard, as was originally planned.'

'Good,' said Dr Poortman. 'Good. That's what I, too, would like to see. We don't want to lose anything more – Jonathan was a first-class man. You'll miss him, Sholto, and so will the consortium.'

'Yes,' Sholto replied briefly. 'I've a feeling that his murder is only the tip of the iceberg. I have a hunch that the Highlands Project itself is at risk somehow.'

'What makes you say that?' demanded Dr Poortman. 'My consortium has sunk scores of millions into it. Nothing must go wrong at this stage, with the opening just around the corner.' He addressed General Mak. 'What are you doing about the murder, General?'

'The body was found on South African soil – it is their affair. I cannot intervene unless I am requested. There's nothing to show that he was killed in Lesotho. I stand by that until I hear something – hard fact – to the contrary.'

Sholto directed his words to Dr Poortman. 'Jonathan told me – almost his last words – that he was going to the mountains. In my book, that means Lesotho.'

General Mak brushed aside further discussion. 'You ask, Dr Poortman, what am I doing? First, I am switching the Eagle arrangements. Second, I am tightening up on all security arrangements connected with the Project. That includes you, Dr Poortman.'

'What do you mean?'

'From the moment you leave this office, you will have a personal bodyguard. He'll go everywhere with you, all the time.'

'He won't!' retorted Dr Poortman. 'I will not be saddled with any gun-toting bodyguard! Not for anything! I've been in many tough spots in the world by virtue of my position as Swiss banker and I've never had a bodyguard before, and I don't intend to start now. That is final.'

'The guard won't intrude on your privacy. He's been groomed as one of the squad to guard VIPs for the opening ceremony. It's only a question of starting his duties now instead of later.'

'It's out!' snapped Dr Poortman. 'I've always opposed the suggestion of a bodyguard – and hasn't it paid off? I'm here, aren't I? Besides, I leave for South Africa the day after tomorrow. What do you think can happen in that time? I'll be here in Maseru tomorrow anyway for consultations with Sholto. I am all for your precautions about the Eagle of Time – but for myself, no. It's plain over-reaction. What about Grania? What goes for me also goes for her – even more so, since the Eagle is her brain-child.'

'She's staying with Sholto. He underwent a full course in unarmed combat and how to use a gun when he became ombudsman. I know, I arranged it. He is quite capable of looking after her. You are a different proposition.'

'The final answer is no.'

'Where are you and Sholto holding your discussions tomorrow?'

'At Sholto's office. I'm staying overnight at Katse Lodge, as you know. They'll fly me down in the morning for the meeting.'

'I'll compromise,' said General Mak slowly. 'For the moment, seeing you're in Lesotho for only one full day more, we'll skip the personal bodyguard. But there'll be two men guarding Sholto's office tomorrow – just in case. Right?'

Dr Poortman shrugged. 'So long as they don't cling too close to me. I don't mind them outside the door.'

General Mak got to his feet and glanced out the window. The evening was prematurely dark.

'You'd better get back to Katse before the storm if you're flying.'

As he extended his hand to shake the banker's, the phone rang. Sholto watched the security chief's face tighten as he listened to the call. It went on for a couple of minutes, and then he said, 'We'll talk about this further.'

General Mak put down the instrument. 'That was my deputy. He had just had a call from the Ficksburg border post. Jonathan passed through there shortly after nine last night, into Lesotho. He took the main highway to Katse.'

CHAPTER FOURTEEN

'Jonathan's informant – can't you remember anything, anything more, he said about him, Sholto? Something we could take to General Mak as a hard fact, now that he's involved in the investigations?'

Sholto shook his head. 'Nothing. General Mak's right. Everything I got from Jonathan was supposition, inference. It was his desperate concern which moved me, not facts.'

It was after dinner that night. Sholto and Grania were in the lounge at 'Cherry Now', the red of the fire reflecting from the ochre of the sandstone walls and drawn curtains. They needed the fire: there had been scurries of sleet on the road home from Maseru. Grania had dressed against the cold: she wore dark pants and a black full-sleeved jumper with gold braid and diamante studs, and a bold spiralling pattern across her breasts and upper arms. The dark colours complemented her hair and seemed to add a touch of charcoal to the shadows in her eyes.

'The only real facts I have about the informer was that he was terrified, and that he went to Jonathan out of loyalty to his royal blood.'

'Maybe he belonged to the same tribe, or clan . . .' Her voice trailed off, and the only sound was the lift of the wind outside and the soft collapse of a log in the grate.

'I didn't have that impression,' said Sholto. 'I felt rather it was someone beyond the law who wanted an indemnity from Jonathan so that he could emerge from an underground existence.'

'Who could it be?'

'There are quite a few doubtfuls around – ex-members of the Liberation Army, some men wanted for acts of terror across the border, cattle rustlers – and, of course, criminals.'

'Why did you link the body General Mak mentioned had been found in the Caledon at Maseru with Jonathan?'

'Only because he happened to have been knifed more or less at the same time and that his body was also in the river.'

'Couldn't you check? He might have been Jonathan's informer?'

'You saw General Mak's attitude. Leave police matters to the police. No, I daren't interfere. As it was, I went just about as far as I dared about getting the transport arrangements for the Eagle to Katse changed. If General Mak thought we were starting our own investigations into Jonathan's murder, it would be the end of his goodwill.'

'Where do you think Jonathan's car could be?'

'We know now that it passed through the Ficksburg Gate heading east towards Katse, on the highway. Some time before midnight, Jonathan was killed.'

'Why before midnight?'

'The police doctor said he had been dead for at least eight hours – most of the night. His body was brought to my dredging raft and dumped.'

'How could that be, Sholto? The killer couldn't have conveyed it back through the border gate. It would have been shut, anyway, at that time.'

'There are a score of secret routes across the border. Cattle thieves and thugs use them all the time. That in itself puts the killer in a particular category.'

Sholto got up and stood with his back to the fire.

'Grania, listen. About ten or twelve kilometres upstream from "Cherry Now" is one of those secret crossings. Don't ask me how I came to know about it, but I do. It's a place which raiders from inside Lesotho have used for generations for sorties into South Africa. Tomorrow, after I have had my meeting with Dr Poortman in Maseru, I want to go and look at it, because I think that it may be where Jonathan's body was taken after he was knifed – inside Lesotho.'

'How was it brought to "Cherry Now"? Ten or twelve kilometres is a long way to transport a dead man, Sholto.'

'By river. Boat. Kayak. The police say there was not the

slightest clue – no footprints, no tyre marks, on the river bank – to indicate how the body was conveyed to the dredger. The river's my answer.'

'It would fit the facts – except for one thing. How did the killer get the body to your secret crossing?'

'He used Jonathan's own car. The main north to south road inside Lesotho hugs the river for a section. From the road, it's only a short distance to the secret crossing, hence its usefulness. The killer could have left Jonathan's car hidden near his embarkation point and used it again as his getaway vehicle on his return from the raft.'

'How will you travel tomorrow?'

'By kayak.'

'Will you take me?'

'I was hoping you would ask that.'

'Wouldn't it be simpler to go by land and use the road you mention which runs parallel to the river?'

'No. I'd never find the spot – it's all cliffs and gorges. I know the landmarks from the river only.'

'Perhaps it will give us a concrete clue to take to General Mak.'

'I had one today, but I dared not produce it – not after the general's attitude. You may agree with him about it.'

'What are you talking about, Sholto?'

For an answer, Sholto pulled from his pocket a tiny, pinkish-crimson, mud-spattered flower set in a small matrix of hardened mud.

'That, I believe, is the key to Jonathan's killing.'

'Where did you get this?'

'From the instep of one of Jonathan's boots. I spotted it this morning while I was waiting for the police. It would mean nothing to them – or to General Mak in particular, I realised, when I saw his attitude. Or to most people, for that matter.'

'Just a flower . . .'

'Yes, Grania, but it is a flower with a difference. It's very rare. It's called the River Lily.'

'Go on.'

'There are two kinds of River Lily in Lesotho. One is this

pinkish-crimson type. The other – which is much more common
– is crimson. The pinkish one hardly ever occurs in the
mountains. I myself have encountered it only once or twice. This
one favours valleys, valleys at a much lower altitude.'

'What are you trying to tell me, Sholto?'

'Apart from a sheltered valley on the way to our lammergeyer
eyrie, this one confines itself to one valley on the road to Katse
dam from here. The Bokong River.

'The Bokong crosses the highway about twenty kilometres
before Katse. It came down in a flash flood recently and washed
away the new bridge. There's a temporary causeway there now.'

'You're sure about its being the River Lily, Sholto?'

'There's no doubt – the satin sheen on the leaves and the six
petals are proof.'

Grania turned the flower over in her hands. 'If only it could talk
and tell us!'

'It would have something horrible and nightmarish to tell,
Grania. Jonathan trod on this either as he was being killed, or
shortly before.'

'He didn't necessarily tread on it at the site of the murder.'

'Its very rarity and limited location makes it pretty certain he
did. Jonathan was using his car – there's no way he could have
reached the alternative site on the way to the lammergeyer eyrie
by car. Or in the time. It takes days on foot. He was alive when he
trod on the River Lily – it could not have become embedded in
mud the way it was without the weight of a living man to press
down on it.'

Grania put the muddy little flower away from her on a low table.

Sholto went on, 'After the killing, it would have been simple for
the murderer to have loaded the body into Jonathan's own car,
and then come back to the road along the river – and the secret
crossing.'

'It presupposes a canoe or a boat, doesn't it?'

'If the killer knew about the crossing, he knew how to use it,
and that means he had a means of crossing. A canoe, a kayak, a
boat of some sort. The river's over half a kilometre wide there.
The crossing's on my list to investigate, as well as the Bokong
causeway.'

Grania looked at him with something in her eyes he did not understand. 'I've never been more frightened in my life – except once – than now, Sholto. Can't you see the implications of what you've been saying, if your deductions are right?'

She shook her head so that her earrings threw back the firelight under her dark, short-cut hair.

'Jonathan's body was brought back deliberately to "Cherry Now" . . .'

'To confuse the hunt, of course.'

'No! No! For God's sake take care of yourself, Sholto! That body was dumped on your raft as a keep-off-the-grass warning – to *you*, Sholto!'

CHAPTER FIFTEEN

The laundry looked as if it were wrapped round in a fantasy spider's web of spun sugar. Steam from its appliances swirled above the roof and clashed with the icy, snow-particled air which scudded across Maseru's buildings on a wind which lowered the wind chill factor to well below zero. The Chunnel Gang's car headlights picked up the fog which air, ice and steam had confected out of the dismal morning.

Bonnay, who was driving, felt a throat-catching surge under his diaphragm at the sight of the gang's first target. He indicated it with a movement of his chin.

Hayward, who was sitting next to him, said, 'Spot on – seven o'clock on the dot!'

It was the next day. Maseru had not shaken off the night's darkness. It was only half-light under the impending storm which, during the night, had dumped some snow and sleet on the capital, although its main force was yet to come. The four men had left their hotel sooner than was really necessary to cover the one-and-a-half kilometres to the laundry which was situated not far (had they known it) from General Mak's headquarters. The short drive had not taken long in terms of the clock, but in terms of stress it was as long as a shot to the moon.

The laundry was the gang's first objective on the day's schedule to ambush the Maluti Rider.

'Ready?' Bonnay's imperative pumped a mild electric shock through the interior of the car.

Hayward responded, 'The piss is even running out of Paul's ears.'

'Keep your chat for the doll in the laundry – you'll need it all then,' returned Pestiaux.

Bonnay slowed and turned to Hayward. The Irishman was taken aback by the intensity in the leader's eyes. He appreciated

Bonnay's innate understanding that his own facetiousness was a cover-up for his inner tension.

'You okay?' Bonnay asked. 'It all depends on you, Burt, once we get inside there. You've got to fast-talk whoever we find there into giving us the security uniforms.'

'It's only a question of whether they're ready,' replied Hayward.

Kennet said from the back seat, 'We could still avoid all this elaborate hassle of heisting security uniforms and a security van here in Maseru by going straight to Katse Lodge and doing the snatch in our own time and in our own way.'

'We've been through all that before,' snapped Bonnay. 'The game's on now – okay? If it's not with you guys, say so now, before I pull up. Katse is tonight, the ambush before that.'

'Cut the crap,' said Hayward shortly. 'We're on our way. There are the four laundry vans – just the way we saw 'em parked early yesterday, ready for the day's work.'

'Good reconnaissance and good intelligence are vital to success,' observed Bonnay.

'You sound like a bloody British army textbook,' scoffed Hayward.

'Are you set to start one of them, John, if there are no ignition keys?' Bonnay asked Kennet.

'Kid's play,' replied Kennet. 'What worries me stiff, though, is starting one of the security vans, when and if we get inside the depot. They must have been standing around all night – in this weather. Could be problems.'

'Don't forget to put out our jumper leads for a battery in the laundry truck,' Bonnay told Pestiaux. 'It's all we can do, except push- start.'

Kennet's laugh jerked out. 'In front of security guards?'

'We'll meet our problems as and when we come across them,' answered Bonnay. He pulled in to the kerbside, ahead of a row of four light laundry delivery vans.

Hayward went on talking just for the sake of it. He indicated the sign on the front van. '"*The Flat Spin*" – seems someone has a sense of humour.'

'Irish, I hope,' retorted Bonnay. He cut the engine and got out. 'My oath, it's cold!'

Pestiaux said, 'That's why I keep my Makarov under my arm. Warmth keeps the oil mobile.'

'No guns, no shooting, understand, everyone – for the last time. This whole business is by surprise, stealth; no force, see?' Bonnay said tightly.

'What if . . .' began Pestiaux.

'Get the extra petrol for the security van and the grub for ourselves into the laundry van,' ordered Bonnay, cutting him short. 'Don't forget 'em. Come on, Burt!'

The two men started down the pavement, ducking against the icy wind.

Bonnay pushed open the laundry door for Hayward to enter first. It was make or break now. The ball was in Hayward's court.

Hayward headed for a young woman behind the counter: she was crowned with a diadem of notices behind her which read: 'Zips and Buttons'; 'Turn-ups Shortened'; 'Suede our Speciality'. The Irishman did a couple of dance steps as he approached and said in a music-hall voice, 'You put me in a flat spin, the moment I saw you.'

The woman addressed Bonnay, 'Is he always like this so early in the morning?'

Bonnay saw his opening. 'It's the prospect of action – it hypes him up. It makes us in the Force want to throw up.'

'Force? Action?' she asked.

Hayward leaned across the counter confidentially. 'You must hear a lot of things in here, honey.'

The girl laughed. 'You'd be surprised!'

Hayward beckoned her closer. His hamming act made Bonnay recoil inwardly. Still, he seemed to be making progress.

'Want to hear something right from the horse's mouth?'

The girl pretended to shy away. 'Depends what it is, mister. And what sort of horse.'

Hayward pretended contrition. 'It's nothing like that, I guarantee.'

'I ain't so sure.'

Hayward glanced round the empty shop conspiratorially and said in a stage whisper, 'There's a buzz on, that's what. That's why we're here, bright and early.'

'A buzz? What force are you talking about?'

Hayward dropped his voice further. 'Don't tell anyone – Security. That's what we're here for – our uniforms.'

It seemed to Bonnay that the woman became suspicious. 'What uniforms?'

'The batch that came in about eleven yesterday morning. Look, we've been drafted down from the north especially. "Clean uniforms," says the major. "You can't go out in the streets of Maseru with your gear all mussed up and crumpled."'

'Out on the streets?'

'That's what the major said, eh, Jules?'

'That's right.'

'We've got to be togged out before eight this morning. Spit and polish,' went on Hayward. 'Like I said, that's why we're here – to collect the uniforms.'

'They aren't ready. There wasn't any priority order with 'em yesterday.'

Hayward did a quick double-take. 'Of course they didn't mention priority – we're a security outfit, aren't we? They were just expecting the usual super Flat Spin service.'

His remark seemed to touch the woman's work-pride.

'I mean, not all of them are ready. About half.'

'That'll do meanwhile – about a dozen.'

'Where's the slip? I'll make a note on it.'

This was a moment both Hayward and Bonnay had antici-pated – and feared.

'Slip?' asked Hayward with an air of innocence. 'The major didn't give us a slip. He just said, go and collect 'em . . .'

'Sorry,' said the girl.

Hayward ran both his hands down his duffel coat. 'We can't go on parade in this civvy clobber.' He went on, and Bonnay turned cold, 'I'll give you the major's phone number, if you like but . . .' He winked knowingly. 'On a morning like this, I'd say he was still tucked up in bed, and not alone, either. Wouldn't you, if you had the chance?'

She laughed and said, 'You're a bad bastard, you are.'

Bonnay added, 'He's Irish.'

'Okay, I'll take your word for it,' she went on. 'Will you sign for the uniforms I give you – just for the record?'

'Sure, it's a pleasure,' replied Hayward. He meant it.

She disappeared and came back with a pile of dark green Security uniforms. 'Thirteen, to be exact – lucky number,' she said. 'You coming back to collect the rest?'

'Honey, I'll twist the major's arm so that it will be me. What time?'

'Not before eleven.'

'See you – and thanks. You won't mention the buzz, will you?' He winked again. 'But a man can trust certain people.'

'Good luck. See you, smoothie.'

When Bonnay took his share of the uniforms, he found that the palms of his hands were wet. Wetness condensed on his face, too, when they went out carrying the pile and walked towards the quartet of laundry vans.

'Nice work, Burt.' Bonnay's voice was muffled by the pile of uniforms up to his chin.

'Could half wish we were staying – I could have managed something with that tit in there,' replied Hayward.

Kennet got out of the gang's own car as Bonnay and Hayward drew level. His balaclava and heavy sheepskin jacket made him a sinister-looking figure in the dim light.

'Got one my size?' he asked.

'If you don't like the fit of what we've brought, you can always go back and change it yourself,' snapped Bonnay. 'Into the back of the laundry van – snap it about, man!'

Pestiaux also started to get out of the gang's car.

'Back!' Bonnay ordered. 'Don't turn the sidewalk into a bloody circus! If anyone comes along, they'll wonder what is happening . . .'

'I only wanted to know . . .'

'You have your orders,' retorted Bonnay. 'Follow this van with us in it across town. The depot is next to the prison.

You break away about half a kilometre short of that and wait. Clear?'

Pestiaux replied, chastened by Bonnay's tone, 'Okay. But if I hear shots, I'll be right along.'

'You won't – you stay right there at the rendezvous – whatever!' ordered Bonnay.

'Must we stand here jawing?' broke in Kennet.

'You fixed the ignition?' demanded Bonnay, indicating the van.

'Didn't have to – careless bastard left the keys in the lock. Or maybe it's standard practice, in this trusting town.'

'Into the rear, then – find something that fits. Sure to be. Bang on the partition when you're ready. Then I want the uniforms back in front.'

'What in hell's name for?' demanded Hayward.

'They could ask us at the gate to open up and check the rear,' replied Bonnay. 'The uniforms are our pass – right here on the seat between us.'

Kennet ducked into the back of the van. Bonnay threw an anxious look down the street towards the laundry. There was not a soul in sight.

'Weather's on our side,' he remarked. As if to disprove it, the van gave a series of jerks and sputters as he snicked home the gear and gunned the engine.

'Cold,' said Hayward. 'Take it easy – that's the secret.'

'No time for fancy driving,' snapped Bonnay. 'Either the bloody thing goes or – Is Pestiaux following?'

'On our tail.'

CHAPTER SIXTEEN

The gang's van threaded its way through the bleak, icy streets. They were all silent. They saw no one. It was only when they reached Kingsway, the big thoroughfare which divides Maseru roughly in half from east to west, that they sighted the first few cars and pedestrians hugging heavy coats against the penetrating wind.

The van had just crossed Kingsway and was heading down the main road towards the security van depot when Kennet thumped on the partition.

Bonnay pulled in to the side of the road.

Hayward said uneasily, 'Can't you go a bit further? There are those two police stations just up the road in Kingsway.'

'Too late now,' said Bonnay. 'Get those uniforms from Kennet – quick, man!'

Hayward opened his door. 'Pestiaux's behind – signalling.'

'Tell him to get on to the rendezvous – it's only just down the road – and *stay there!*' rapped out Bonnay. 'He's to keep away from the depot, whatever. See?'

Hayward sprinted back to the gang's own car, which then overtook the parked van as Hayward got its rear doors open.

In its dark interior, Kennet looked like a cartoon figure in his dark green camouflage uniform, sheepskin jacket and balaclava.

'Fits near enough,' he said laconically. 'Room enough to get at my gun.'

'Good luck,' said the Irishman. 'You'll need it.'

Bonnay was gunning the engine impatiently.

'Good luck is what you make it,' he said as Hayward dumped the pile of uniforms between them.

They had travelled only a few hundred metres further when Bonnay gestured ahead into the murk.

'Jeez!' exclaimed Hayward.

113

A vehicle, with flashing lights on its roof, was coming down the road towards them.

'Police! They couldn't have heard about the van so soon!'

It kept on coming; Bonnay kept on going.

Then – when the body of the approaching vehicle emerged white from the dim light, Hayward said shakily, 'Ambulance! I forgot the hospital's close to the police stations . . .'

Bonnay added, 'The hospital is our landmark for getting out of town, remember? Back route, avoids the police stations, that way.'

They drove further. Hayward said, 'There's Pestiaux.'

The gang's car was burning its sidelights and facing up the road towards them – the gang's escape route from the van depot.

Bonnay kept on. He did not respond to Pestiaux's dipped light signal.

But there was a signal ahead once the laundry van passed the prison on the right and the road dead-ended. A red signal. Danger.

The gate guard's brazier made a glowing red patch against the greyness of the morning. It was burning in front of a door which opened into a small room which formed an integral part of the gate complex, which in turn was part of a bigger structure behind. Further back, behind a six-foot security fence topped with razor-tape, a dozen or more security vans merged their grey-green camouflage with the morning's bleakness near some buildings which looked like barrack-blocks. The depot was sited on low ground towards the Caledon River; a light mist off the water contributed its share of murkiness to the ranks of parked vehicles.

'It's colder here by the river than up town,' Hayward observed.

Bonnay steered towards the brazier. 'You don't have to say it, Burt. If the van won't start for Kennet, it won't start for anyone.'

The laundry van came opposite the big security gate; Bonnay pulled across the road to it and flicked his lights.

'Guard door's open a little,' said Hayward in a low tone.

Bonnay revved the engine, flicked the lights again. 'I don't want to rouse them by blowing the hooter.'

'Perhaps the sentry's still asleep . . .'

He wasn't, although he looked like a sleepwalker. The man must have been breaking all regulations by being wrapped in a bright blue Basuto blanket. Like Kennet in the van's rear, his face was masked by a woollen balaclava.

Bonnay screwed down his window. The cold was numbing after the warmth of the heated cab.

'Uniforms,' he called cheerily. 'Good morning!'

The man started to unlock the security gate. 'The only good thing about it is that I'm going off in half an hour,' he responded.

Bonnay said sympathetically, 'Been on all night?'

'Yeah. For what? Do they expect anyone to be around on a night like this?'

'It's morning, friend.'

The man came to Bonnay's window. 'What brings you out so early, anyway?'

Bonnay slapped the pile of uniforms between himself and Hayward. 'Line of duty. Shall I put 'em in the usual place?'

'You know your way.'

'We'll be quick. Fire looks cosy.'

'Not allowed indoors,' grumbled the guard. 'Orders. Piddling electric heating's not the same.'

'Nothing like a good old blanket, eh?'

The man hunched himself and pulled open the gate. Bonnay drove through.

Hayward said quietly, 'Usual place? Where in hell is that?'

'Watch him through your side mirror,' snapped Bonnay. 'As soon as we're out of sight of the gate, I'll stop – over by those buildings – anywhere. We'll offload Kennet.'

The barrack-like red brick buildings formed a kind of open square; there were lights here and there in upper windows. No one seemed to be stirring below.

'Round the next corner,' said Hayward. 'That'll put us out of sight of the gate.'

'Sure?'

'Can't see the brazier any longer.'

They turned into a tarmaced square where security vans were huddled together in groups of twos and threes.

'One nearest the building could be easier to start – slightly warmer there,' suggested Hayward.

The vehicle halted. Hayward doubled out, taking the uniforms with him. He opened the back and waited for Kennet to emerge before pitching them in.

'Which van?'

'Take your pick,' Bonnay rapped out. 'Be quick, for God's sake! The gate guard's only firing on one cylinder still. We'll be on your tail.'

Kennet glanced at the heavy overcast sky, as if consulting the omens for starting. 'I hope so.'

Bonnay and Hayward sat, waiting. The van's door seemed to offer Kennet no problems – maybe it had been left unlocked, in the heart of an already tight security area.

They saw Kennet's balaclava-clad head disappear as he set to work on the ignition.

One minute.

Two minutes.

Four minutes.

Hayward said softly, 'All the time, the guy at the gate's waking up more.'

'Shut up! Kennet's the best . . .'

As if for an answer, the security van's starter gave a low groan, as if in pain. It turned over, reluctantly, like a sleeper trying to drag himself from a warm bed.

Bonnay asked tightly, 'Jumper leads?'

The van's starter turned over again, hesitatingly.

'That battery!' exclaimed Hayward in an agonised voice. 'May St Christopher give that battery guts!'

The starter spun suddenly, as if in reply to Hayward's invocation. Then it cut. Once, twice, half a dozen times. Silence.

'Why doesn't he keep it going!' whispered Hayward.

'See anyone around?' Bonnay's voice was as chilly as the morning.

Hayward took his eyes from the recalcitrant van and scanned

the buildings. 'Not yet, but there will be soon, with that damn noise.'

The starter sounded again. It had a new, confident, athletic note. Three, four times. The engine coughed, fired. A balloon of condensation leapt from the tail of the exhaust. The machine hesitated, finally picked up.

'Get moving!' urged Hayward. 'Get moving – out, out, out!'

But Kennet wasn't to be hurried. He coaxed the engine up in temperature for another full minute. Only when Bonnay heard the gear engage did he in turn start the laundry vehicle's engine.

Kennet rounded the barrack block and headed for the gate. He came to a standstill opposite the brazier, with Bonnay immediately behind.

Bonnay screwed down his window to hear what Kennet and the guard were saying.

'. . . reserved for officers,' the guard was telling him. 'A108, A109, and A110.'

'I'm sure it is,' replied Kennet. 'It's a VIP job to move the Eagle of Time up to Katse. Colonel said so.'

'Is it for him?'

'How do you think I got hold of the keys?'

The guard hesitated. 'You say you are taking the Eagle of Time . . .'

'It's been announced all over – special viewing for the workers at the dam site,' said Kennet.

'You're not going alone,' said the sentry, deliberately obtuse.

Kennet replied with a long-suffering note in his voice. 'I've been ordered to pick up three other guys at the Moshoeshoe statue at 7.45. Time's running out while we stand here and argue. Then all four of us go on to the bank strongroom.'

Bonnay nodded to Hayward and got out. Hayward felt in his pocket. His Colt butt was as cold as a corpse in a morgue.

Bonnay walked up behind the sentry, at Kennet's window. The man was taller than average, and his thick Basuto blanket and balaclava would make the blow to the back of his head with the Browning a tricky one. He kept his hand on his gun and took up position behind his victim. Kennet showed no flicker of recognition.

117

Bonnay broke into the exchange. 'Sorry – is there a problem? I can't get out with this van blocking the gate. I've got a mighty full day ahead – got to hurry.'

The guard checked his watch. 'In a quarter of an hour the day guard takes over . . .'

Kennet said, 'I've only got five minutes left to get to the Moshoeshoe statue in time.'

Bonnay decided to hit the man where a bulge in the woollen cap showed his right ear was. He moved closer.

'A109 is reserved for officers . . .' the man began again.

'I've told you,' said Kennet. Bonnay knew the Englishman well enough to recognise the slowing-down of his voice before he plunged into action.

The guard suddenly retreated from the window, so that he collided with Bonnay behind him. The gang leader's incipient blow was aborted by the unexpected move.

'Okay, okay,' he said. 'But if there's any comeback, you've got to do the explaining, see?'

Kennet said reassuringly, 'There won't be, fellah. You'll see.'

Turning to go to the laundry van, Bonnay said, 'I'll be right behind you – I'm going your way myself.'

Before the guard could change his mind, Kennet edged the security van through the gate when it was wide open enough only for it to scrape through; Bonnay crowded him from behind.

In tight formation, they headed for the rendezvous with Pestiaux.

There was no possibility of overshooting Pestiaux. The Frenchman was grinning and waving as Kennet pulled up, with Bonnay hard on his heels.

'Wonderful! You pulled it off!'

Bonnay jumped out angrily. 'Stop it, you bloody fool!' snarled Bonnay. 'Do you want to draw the attention of the whole town to us? Three vehicles all packed together and an arse clowning on the pavement!'

Kennet gunned his motor. 'Let's get the hell out of here – quick!'

'First the spare petrol and food into Kennet's van,' Bonnay ordered Pestiaux.

'What about the rest of the uniforms?' asked Hayward.

'We only want three, but we can't hang around seeing what will or won't fit,' responded Bonnay. 'Pitch 'em all in behind Kennet.'

'Now – the car and the laundry van . . .' began Bonnay.

'Leave 'em right here – save time,' said Kennet.

'No,' replied Bonnay. 'Paul, take our car up to the Moshoeshoe statue, park and lock it, as if everything was normal. We'll be along shortly to pick you up. Burt, into the laundry van with me. I'm going to dump it separately.'

'For Pete's sake, you're throwing away the headstart we've already got!' the Irishman objected.

'There's a hotel close by on the corner,' said Bonnay. 'We'll abandon it nearby – a laundry van parked near a hotel won't arouse any suspicions.'

Bonnay drove the laundry van back up their previous route. They saw no one, except a bread delivery truck at the hotel. They left the laundry van in the street, locked it, and jumped into the back of the security van.

'You're sticking out your neck – and ours,' said Kennet. 'We've now got to retrace our steps for half a kilometre back towards the depot to reach Moshoeshoe's statue. What if . . .'

But there was no if. Pestiaux was already out and waiting when the van, moving as fast through the streets as Kennet dared, pulled up and loaded him also into the back. Then, with Kennet alone in uniform at the wheel, the van shot away to skirt the hospital and miss the two police stations. It then followed back streets which finally brought it out at the big traffic circle at the end of Kingsway which marked their exit and escape to the north.

It was nearly eight o'clock.

They had 134 kilometres to go to the ambush site on the Bokong River.

CHAPTER SEVENTEEN

Beware the Bokong Crossing, Sholto. Beware, Grania.

'What a stroke of luck, having to go to Katse instead of Maseru!' exclaimed Grania.

'It means we can investigate the Bokong Crossing on our way – it's about twenty kilometres from Katse itself,' added Sholto.

'Let's hope the River Lily leads us to a hard clue which will convince General Mak,' said Grania.

Grania and Sholto had been finishing breakfast at 'Cherry Now' when a telephone call had come in from Dr Poortman at Katse Lodge to say that the pilot who had been due to fly him from Katse to Maseru that morning for their financial discussions had considered the Katse airfield unsafe because of the bad weather conditions. Dr Poortman had asked Sholto rather to motor to Katse for their deliberations. Sholto had jumped at the chance: he would be able immediately to follow up his clue of the River Lily which he had found embedded on the sole of Jonathan's boot.

'You'll need waterproof boots – we'll have to do some wading,' said Sholto, eyeing Grania's faded blue anorak and ski pants approvingly. 'It will also be much colder once we get the other side of the mountains.'

Grania gestured beyond the windows to the purple storm-cap over the far peaks.

'I thought it would have been snowing here already.'

'The altitude of the farm is too low, and we're also too far to the west,' said Sholto. 'Out there in the east is where the action is.'

Sholto and Grania were not to know that the snow had been in action already that morning in Maseru and had emptied the streets, like an ally for the Chunnel Gang's heist. Nor did they know, at the moment they were talking, that the stolen security van was hightailing in their direction up the main north to south road inside Lesotho as the gang sought to outstrip the setting-up of police road blocks which would follow as soon as the news of the theft became known.

'How far is Katse from the farm?' asked Grania.

'About ninety kilometres; it takes about an hour by car. The only bottleneck on the highway is the washed-out section at the causeway. We can leave right away.'

Grania got up from the table. 'Does that mean our kayak trip upriver this afternoon is off?'

'By no means,' replied Sholto. 'All the more reason to go, if we find some useful lead at Bokong. There's no reason for us to be back at a fixed time for a meal, seeing Mother's away.'

'Sholto, if Katse airfield is out of action, what happens to the plan to fly the Eagle of Time there from Maseru tomorrow?'

'Dr Poortman didn't say it was out of action. He said the pilot considered it risky with a VIP passenger. I guess he was playing it safe, just because of Dr Poortman's status. I myself feel certain that at this stage a helicopter could still use the airfield.' He shrugged. 'But that's tomorrow. Anything could happen.'

By the time they had left 'Cherry Now', crossed the Lesotho border at Ficksburg Gate (Sholto's ombudsman status gave him priority clearance), and headed for Leribe some twenty kilometres further on, their lead on the flying security van had been reduced to less than twenty-five kilometres. Nor had the gap been overtaken, although it had been narrowed further by the time Sholto slowed about sixteen kilometres on the Katse side of Leribe and indicated to Grania a gravel track leading off to the left.

'If we really wanted to have fun, that would be our route,' he said. 'It's the way to the Kao diamond diggings deep in the mountains. Some of the mines are still operating, some are disused. Some strange tales are told about them.'

'It looks pretty rough,' said Grania.

'Not as rough as the characters at the mines,' grinned Sholto.

They headed east, into the vast barrier of the Malutis. All around were the peaks, towering over 3000 metres high. Suddenly, a maverick sun struck through the overcast, which had reduced everything to a solid grey shadow and the landscape to a thing without depth. The ephemeral light flashed off the peaks flanking the road high above like a vast diamond, hard and variable as those taken from the shafts at Kao. They spotted tiny iced-up pools which had been invisible to them before, with outsize frozen tongues locked between the black rocks, reaching down at them like silent white fangs. A thousand colours, intolerable in intensity to the eye, flashed up from the ice and high snow, as if a space galaxy had been trapped in a net and was fighting to escape at a million sparkling points. The bright light held only a short while until they reached the summit where the road broke through the barrier of the Malutis, and they looked out across the 100-kilometre valley on the farther side where the Malibamatso River splits Lesotho in half for another 100 kilometres (the heart of the Highlands Project), assisted by its smaller and more western counterpart, the Bokong. With its peaks and stunning burden of snow suspended in cloud-blackness above while the ground below was stage-lighted by the passing sun, the immense terrain gave the impression of an ocean at once tempestuous and yet at the same time wholly still.

Then the light shut down; they glissaded down the remaining few kilometres to the Bokong Crossing.

Sholto stopped the car on the temporary gravel approach ramp which led to the ruins of the bridge. The inlet waterfall, the higher of the two, cavorted down the bush-covered slope with juvenile abandon; to their left, over the causeway itself, it widened into a quieter, wider stream which made its own waterfall as it tumbled over a deep, wide shelf of blue shale.

Sholto indicated the bushy slope. 'That's the sort of habitat the River Lily likes; it tucks itself away in tiny gullies and pockets alongside the water. You can sometimes walk right past and not spot it.'

'How do you know so much about it?' asked Grania, getting out of the car.

'Part of the Bokong above where it joins the Malibamatso to form Katse Dam was due to be flooded when the wall was built,' explained Sholto. 'It was a stretch which was rich in the River Lily and I and some other enthusiasts did a rescue operation before it was too late. That is why I recognised it at once on Jonathan's boot. The Bokong is one of its few natural habitats in Lesotho.'

'It's an endangered species, then?'

'Very much so. I didn't know, though, that it occurred as far up the headwaters of the river as we are now.'

'What makes you so sure about this being the spot?'

'I'm sure of nothing, Grania. It's all guesswork on my part. But where else Jonathan could have travelled in the time without a four-wheel drive, I don't know. The Bokong Crossing seems the obvious spot.'

'And if not?'

He shrugged. 'Let's start looking. I promised Dr Poortman I'd be there in good time.'

'What about footprints, or tyre marks?'

Sholto pointed at the road, which was intersected by innumerable muddy tyreprints. 'This is a main road. There's traffic all the time. It's hopeless to sort out tracks.'

They started ankle-deep into the water and worked their way along the river's bank past irregular, water-worn slabs which projected from the bush into the water. Each slab created a muddy pocket. They found nothing. Sholto was in the lead, about ten paces ahead of Grania.

Suddenly Grania gave an exclamation and pointed to a clump of shrubs, about four metres up the slope, in the direction of the incoming waterfall. 'Sholto! Look!'

A tiny strip of bright yellow was hooked on a branch. It drew attention to itself by stirring slightly in the wind as it funnelled down the gully.

Without waiting for him, she scrambled up to it.

'Sholto! Quick! It's a ribbon from Jonathan's boot!'

It was.

Sholto was at her side in a flash. 'That's what we've been looking for!'

'Your hunch was right, Sholto!'

'Don't touch anything – for the moment,' said Sholto. 'We've got to find the crushed River Lily next – there's nothing round about here – and the flower was trampled, remember!'

But they did find it, about half a dozen metres away, close to the waterfall. Several bushes had been crushed and the gound was disturbed and muddy. Then Sholto spotted a solitary leaf squashed deep in the mud – all that remained of the tell-tale River Lily.

'This is where he died, Grania.'

'What went on here?' asked Grania. 'What led him here in the first place, so far from Maseru? Can't you still recall anything from his conversation which would help?'

Sholto shook his head. 'No, but we've established something substantial now. Let's go on looking.'

Grania glanced at the threatening sky. 'Any further clues will disappear with the first heavy rain.'

'See any footmarks?'

'Nothing.'

The surface of the trampled spot was soft and, in places, semi-liquid. However, there was a badly defined line of disturbed bushes from the murder-spot past the bush on which the gay yellow ribbon fluttered forlornly, on down the slope to the water's edge. Sholto unhitched the ribbon and put it in his wallet.

'The murderer must have dragged him into the water in order to cover up his getaway route.'

'No,' answered Sholto. 'Jonathan's body was dry when we found it. The police made great play of the fact. It was an important negative clue in their opinion.'

In the gloomy storm-light the crossing itself withdrew, it seemed to Grania, into a score of lurking-places, each one cunning and malicious, where a would-be killer could be lurking and observing them.

She shivered, and Sholto said, 'I'm being squeezed for time because of my appointment with Dr Poortman. We won't have the opportunity to fine-comb the place now as I would have wished. I'll put a couple of marker-stones at the ribbon bush. On our way back we can make a more comprehensive search.'

'Be quick,' she urged him. 'I feel I'm being watched all the time by unseen eyes.'

Grania remained standing in the water while Sholto built a

small rough cairn as a marker, and then rejoined her. Together they splashed to the edge of the causeway where their car stood.

Grania said in a low voice, 'We could be repeating the killer's own movements – except that he would have been carrying Jonathan's body to his car.'

'We'll check out the secret crossing over the Caledon this afternoon and see what it yields.'

They did not, in fact.

Sholto's consultations with Dr Poortman gave the storm a vital two hours in which to thrust from the great ranges in the east across the valley of the Malibamatso, dump snow on the Malutis, and reach out even to the soft farmlands on the South African border. By the time Sholto and Grania left Katse to return to 'Cherry Now' a thin drizzle of sleet accompanied them.

'It makes me think longingly of all that wonderful skiing gear in the hut at Katse Lodge,' Grania told Sholto. She had spent a long time admiring the collection of skis, anti-snow clothing and equipment while Sholto had been occupied.

They gave up their plan to check out the Bokong Crossing when they saw the state of the place under the cold, driving rain. They realised that whatever clues there had been in the vicinity of the ribbon bush were now part of the liquid mud of the gully slope. The rain froze to snow as they climbed out of the Malibamatso Valley into the Malutis; on the western side, the side of the South African border, there were sleet scurries on a bitter, driving wind.

They left 'Cherry Now' almost immediately in Sholto's long fibre-glass kayak and pushed up the Caledon River. They wore wet suits and bright orange lifejackets, waterproof mittens and light crash helmets over balaclavas. Sholto realised at once that Grania knew more than she had admitted about managing a canoe.

Their moment of truth came, however, when they struck towards the first of the dramatic gorges which the river had cut over centuries through the sandstone cliffs. The wind pressed on their eye-lids like anaesthetic pads and the gloom was Avernal as they fought their way upriver against current and wind.

125

Sholto called, 'That's the first of the gorges. It's called Terugdraai. Turn back!'

However, they kept going for several more kilometres. Finally Sholto realised that the kayak was making almost no progress despite their all-out paddling.

'Grania!' he shouted above the wind. 'We're going round!'

'You're turning back?' she called.

'Yes. It's crazy to go on. We'll never make it.'

'That means our second lot of clues today has gone overboard.'

'Yes. But this is hopeless. Help me hold her so that the wind doesn't capsize us!'

Sholto judged his turn to a nicety, using an overhanging buttress as a partial windbreak to carry out the tricky manoeuvre.

The wind on their backs pushed them home in less than half the time it had taken to travel up.

It was four o'clock when they made the kayak fast to a small jetty not far from the sand-raft.

On the Kao track to the diamond diggings, Bonnay checked his watch.

He said to the half-frozen men waiting in the back of the security van, 'Four o'clock – get moving!'

CHAPTER EIGHTEEN

Beware the Bokong Crossing, Bonnay.

Bonnay seemed to be doing just that.

He was edging the security van down the gravel ramp towards the causeway with the caution of a jackal sniffing at a poisoned bait. So slow was his descent towards the water that the dark green camouflage of the van merged completely at moments with the dark green of the bush slope in the late afternoon light.

It was five o'clock.

When would the Maluti Rider's first volley come? *Would* it come?

The plop-plop of the engine overrun beat time with the drubbing of his heart as Bonnay's thoughts went board-sailing along. With a conscious effort he trimmed them down to the immediate task at hand. Forget that he was sitting in full view behind the windscreen (luckily mud-splashed and caked with snow), the target on which the ambusher's sights would naturally zero first. Forget that the moment the van reached the water and he had positioned it (he believed) so that it would constitute an unmissable target for a gunman emplaced in the bushes flanking the incoming waterfall, he would stop, get out and walk round to the rear engine compartment with no armoured glass or bullet-proof panels between himself and eternity. At the thought, the muscles in his lower abdomen rippled and gyrated. His only outward reaction to his inner stress, however, was that his hands clamped hard by reflex action on the steering. His voice was harsh as he called through the mesh partition to Hayward, Kennet and Pestiaux behind.

'We're here! When I hit the water, I'm going to stop!'

There was no reply. There was only the bright gleam of their eyes and the dull gleam of three gun barrels.

'Hear me?' Bonnay snapped. 'Put those bloody guns away – for the moment. I want him alive – alive, alive, see!'

The sharp orders cleared his fazed, racing mind. It was always this way with Bonnay once the action began. He perked his shoulders, gunned the engine, as if he found it hard to keep it going. He hoped the action would deceive the lurking gunman.

The gang had spent a miserable day holed up in the security van on the Kao diamond track. Its scenic wonders were every bit as fine as Sholto had told Grania, but to the four desperate men the grim peaks, blotted out at intervals by driving snow, were a funkhole from which they could not wait to escape in the afternoon. Their swift, professional job in Maseru on the security van had easily outrun the setting-up of police road blocks, and they were already clear of the small town of Leribe (the last of any consequence on their route) before the first news came over the radio of the van's heist.

There was also the cold. While they had been moving, the van's heater had kept the interior of the big vehicle tolerably warm; it froze progressively during the long hours they had to sit it out. Nor had they any proper food: shortly after stopping, they had devoured the handful of stale sandwiches and sausage rolls they had brought from the hotel. They had no hot coffee or tea; only a half-jack of brandy which Hayward found in his pocket.

Bonnay had said, taking a cautious drag at the bottle as it passed from hand to hand, 'You see what I mean about us needing a safe house for Poortman? If we grabbed him and went off into the mountains unequipped as we are now, neither he nor we would last more than a day or two.'

'You're not ratting on our agreement, are you, Jules?' Kennet had responded. 'If your Maluti Rider doesn't show up this afternoon, we still go on to Katse and snatch the banker – okay?'

'I'm not ratting, but you can see that we're up against other problems beyond the police,' he had replied.

'What are you trying to say?'

'That once we've got Poortman in our hands and we go for the contingency plan, priority number one is the Katse kitchen. Food. Drink. Some sort of portable stove to take along to make hot drinks.'

'Whadderyemean – contingency plan?'

Bonnay had replied levelly, 'I said, contingency. To me, the plan for us to sit out a siege in the control room at Katse is messy, full of loose ends. However, I said I'd go along with it, and I still will – reluctantly. Food is one of the loose ends. It'll be as cold as a morgue in the control room over 100 metres down, bottled up inside the concrete of the dam wall. You realise that?'

'We can make it work,' Kennet had responded sullenly.

'We've *got* to make it work,' retorted Bonnay. 'Our necks depend on it.'

'You don't know whether this Maluti Rider bastard has the least intention of attacking us at the Bokong Crossing,' Hayward had observed, knocking back a swig of brandy.

'Lay off that stuff,' ordered Bonnay. 'It doesn't really beat the cold – only makes you feel colder, in the end.'

The gang had spent more time than was really necessary – anything to kill the long waiting hours – drafting two ransom notes, using the van's logbook for paper. The one was designed to meet the situation if they decided to hole up in the control room, and the other if the Maluti Rider joined them and they used his hide-out for Dr Poortman.

Now they were at Bokong, now they would know.

The van's wheels hit the water. Bonnay worked the clutch, then the brake, achieving a realistic stall. The ambush was all a question of firing angles. Bonnay deliberately stopped short of a spot at which he calculated the ambusher would have the optimum angle to blast the van. It was also where the entire left-hand side of the van was masked from the ambusher's view. This was the side with the big sliding door. From it, once the firing started, the trio behind would slip out and – still hidden by the body of the vehicle – would sprint into the bush and jump him. *If* he did not spot them; *if* he did not hear them coming. The Chunnel three, to reach his hypothetical lair, had first to cross the stream below the incoming waterfall at about the level where Grania had found Jonathan's boot ribbon.

Bonnay was staking everything on his assumption of the site the ambusher would choose. The stake included his own life.

He called out softly, 'This is it!'

His next moves were all prearranged.

For a brief moment he paused with his hand on the driver's door catch. The sheet of armoured glass, tightly screwed to the maximum, was his life-shield, as was the armoured panel in the door. Bonnay knew that he must be in sight – perhaps not ideal sight yet – of the gunman out there in the bushes. At this range, the man couldn't miss, even if he had to find his way round with a blind-stick.

Bonnay snapped open the door, dropped down into the water.

Two things struck him – the paralysing cold of the water, and the soft chuckle of the two waterfalls in the silence.

Bonnay splashed to the rear engine compartment, turned his back. The gunman's sights must be homed between his shoulder-blades. He threw open the compartment's flap, ducked inside, as if he were adjusting something.

Was the gunman there at all?

Bonnay called out, as prearranged, 'Dunno what's biting this flippin' motor, you guys! Only hope it holds together for the next twenty kays to Katse, or else they're going to be in the shit tomorrow for the Eagle exhibition.'

He let the engine lid drop with what he hoped sounded like an exasperated thud, and started back to the cab.

The falling water made its own noise; the sleety wind made its own noise; the exhaust pipe contracting in the cold water made its own noise.

Then – there was another noise.

Bonnay knew that noise in a flash. There was no other noise like it in the world. That clunking kiss of metal in the breech.

It was an AK-47 being cocked!

Bonnay's inner triumph at having outguessed the ambusher was obliterated by the icy fear the AK-47 sound brought with it.

The cab door was perhaps five paces distant.

Bonnay knew that if he ran for it, he would never reach it alive – not a sudden break coming hard on the heels of that giveaway sound. The killer would realise he had heard. The man must be there, tracking him with sights trained on him – body? head? guts? – holding back just long enough for the ideal shot.

Bonnay's stomach seemed full of wandering muscles.

Yet, this was the way he had planned it. The stalker stalked.

Bonnay nerved himself, took one, two paces.

Three. One big lurch would take him to the door handle. But he'd never reach it. Would he hear the sound of the AK's volley before it ripped into him, or would the hot lead come first? The muscles in his right-hand rib-cage – the side facing the ambusher – rippled like a horse's under a switch.

He lifted his foot to make another step. It seemed weighted with eternity.

Four paces.

One to go!

The door handle was within reach. One measured pace – he was there!

By reflex action, it seemed, he whipped open the cab door, swung himself in, banged it shut.

He was alive!

He turned to address the trio in the rear. His words snagged on his contracted throat muscles. They came out hoarse, unnatural.

'He's there! He's got an AK-47! He won't be able to spot you from his position! Get out of the door under cover of the noise when I start the engine! I'll gun it as if something's still bugging it! Take the handcuffs and the rope – I want him *alive*! Now – get out!'

Bonnay fired the starter, threw in the gear, moved the van forward a few jerky paces, a chessmaster staking his all on a precisely calculated move.

Bonnay felt, more than heard, the big sliding door behind start to open.

'Shoot!' he whispered. 'For Chrissake, shoot!'

The uninhibited incantation of the Kalashnikov black mass filled the gully. Instant frost coated Bonnay's window in long stripes as the 7.62mm slugs spun off the armoured glass. Long white scores, like minute jet vapour trails, skidded across the windscreen before the lead whinged and whanged its way ricocheting off the wrecked bridge pillars and boulders. Bonnay fought a mad impulse to duck for the safety of the armoured door. But he knew he had to keep station – until his team was safely on its way.

He was aware, with a kind of heightened consciousness, of the loss of weight in the van as Kennet, Hayward and Pestiaux vaulted clear of the floorboards into the water.

Bonnay played his final card. He took a hand microphone from its hook on the dashboard, clicked on the loud-hailer on the roof, and screamed into the instrument.

'Stop! For God's sake, stop! This is Security. Stop! Stop!'

Almost derisively, the red-hot fusillade switched from the cab to the amplifier mounted on the roof. It vanished in a scatter of flying metal. Bonnay found himself yelling into a dead microphone.

How much longer could the armoured glass take it? What were Kennet, Hayward and Pestiaux up to? It seemed light years since they had left.

Then the sound cut.

Something round and hard, like a cricket ball, thumped against the side of the van behind him and splashed into the water.

Bonnay's mental computer was a split second faster than the concussion – grenade! The petrol tank!

The gully roared and echoed like a berserk soccer crowd to the crash of the detonation. A fountain of water – and shrapnel – rose alongside the van like war-time pictures of a bomb near-miss on a warship.

How much more could the van absorb? An incendiary grenade next time?

The ambusher sighted on the cab, using a single round as a marker, preparatory to unleashing another volley.

That shot pinpointed precisely to the gang trio, now across the waterfall among the bushes, where the gunman lay.

CHAPTER NINETEEN

In the pre-volley silence, a horse whinnied.

The legend said that the Maluti Rider used a horse. A popular myth had grown up around it – of a sure-footed mountain brute blessed with almost supernatural intelligence who always took his rider clear of pursuit.

If the marksman had been less intent on annihilating the van, he might have heeded that tell-tale whinny. The horse had been trained never to make a sound. Now he was warning his master of the presence of three men, frozen in a low crouch above and behind the ambusher's back so that they only had to drop down and slug him cold.

Kennet had led the attack from the causeway up through the bushes, over the waterfall outflow, and into the trio's present knock-down position. Despite his bulk, he moved soundlessly, with a swift deadliness of purpose.

Now he signalled the other two slightly behind him, with a backhand command: 'Spread out – me in the middle, one of you on either side, and we take him . . .'

Kennet found himself up to the gunman almost before he realised it. He was lying full-length with the AK-47 butt hard against his shoulder. He was blanket-shrouded, and his head was swathed in a strip of the same material. His camouflage was near-perfect.

But not perfect enough for the Chunnel Gang.

Kennet landed square in the middle of the gunman's back. He had pre-positioned his Scorpion at the outset of his leap so that it would clamp flush against the base of his victim's neck. Simultaneously, Hayward and Pestiaux came down on the man's arms with their full weight. One pistol barrel – Pestiaux's Makarov – was under the gunman's right armpit. The other, Hayward's colt, was into his left side next to his heart.

Three tough men – and three weapons – pinioning a man face

133

downwards to the ground would, anyone would have thought, been enough to give their victim second thoughts about fighting his way out of the trap.

But members of the *Koevoet* (Crowbar) anti-insurgency unit had not gained their formidable fighting reputation by pussy-footing their way out of no-escape situations. *Koevoet* was the name of a South African unit which operated on the Namibia-Angola border. The Maluti Rider had been a member before turning his talents to personal freelancing.

Now the Maluti Rider's brain and survival instincts acted together – and explosively. He had been hunted for so long that it was immaterial who the persons were who nailed him – police, security, private avengers. His reactions simply told him he had been nailed.

He sloughed the blanket like a honey-badger swivelling inside its own loose skin in order to slip from a lion's claws. Kennet found himself grasping merely a handful of wool; instead of arms, Hayward and Pestiaux were gripping handfuls of empty fabric.

As he slipped the blanket, the Rider lunged, so that he projected forward flat on his stomach. However, like a carrier jet taking off with not enough incline on the launch deck, he could not get himself airborne – and free.

For what seemed a minute in slowed-down time although it was no more than a second or two in reality, the gunman's back arced and jerked as his muscles tried to propel the rest of his body onto his knees. Perhaps if they had been less jarred by the weight of three heavy men falling on them out of the blue, they might have succeeded.

But the Chunnel Gang had not fought its way through a cordon of hundreds of police in the Marseilles bank raid without a trick or two of their own.

Kennet, also half on his knees, snatched the AK-47 and swung its butt at his victim's arcing neck. At the last fatal split second he changed his aim as he remembered Bonnay's order – bring the ambusher in alive! Instead of smashing his spine at the neck, Kennet caught him across the shoulders with a savage blow which pitch-forked him head-first into the icy mud.

134

Before the ambusher's break-out from his blanket, Hayward had been poised to snap on the handcuffs. Now with one handcuff safe on his own wrist, and with the jaws of the other outstretched like a pair of blind stainless steel crab's claws, he simply let himself fall forward. Then they were home! If the ambusher tried to break away now, he would have to drag Hayward, dead or alive, with him.

But the gunman wasn't beaten yet. He knew what the clamp of steel round his wrist meant – police!

He somehow found the strength to jerk upward. Hayward gave a yell of agony. The impetus of the thrust wrenched him half clear of the ground.

'Stop! Hold it, damn you!' screamed Kennet.

He wasn't yelling at the gunman. He was trying to get through to Pestiaux. Pestiaux's impetuosity was a byword amongst the gang. He would overstep all bounds of savagery and brutality – as he had indeed done the night of the gang's Marseilles break-out by braining a policeman far from the bank itself and not involved in the operation with a paving-stone.

Kennet saw what Pestiaux was about to do – ram his Makarov barrel into the gunman's eyes.

It is doubtful whether Pestiaux heard Kennet's yell, even from a metre or two away. He came to awareness with a grip of steel round his wrist, the same sort of snap of steel which a moment before had nailed the gang's victim himself.

It was Bonnay.

From the marooned van on the causeway, the gang leader had made a lightning assessment of the desperate mêlée, had grabbed another pair of handcuffs from the van, and raced to the fight.

As he hog-tied his own gang member, Bonnay kicked hard and low into the writhing, half-kneeling victim's stomach. With his free right forearm, he chopped down savagely onto the side of the gunman's neck.

The man didn't go out clean. He sagged forward, his survival instincts still holding him up, like a boxer who has taken a right cross and a full uppercut to the jaw, but still won't fall off the ropes.

135

But the one-two attack from a fresh quarter sapped his muscles and another pair of handcuffs snapped home; this time from Kennet. Bonnay wasn't finished with the man yet. He snatched up the short strip of blanket which had enveloped the gunman's head and corded it round his neck. The sagging figure started to choke and gasp.

Pestiaux was screaming, 'Let me kill the – ' He lunged at the half-conscious gunman with the steel handcuffs. Bonnay's Browning pulled him up in his tracks.

'Leave him! Get the blanket, quick!'

The order worked. Pestiaux turned away, grabbed the blanket awkwardly and, releasing the handcuffs, straitjacketed the gasping gunman into it. Hayward and Kennet then wrenched his arms behind his back with Bonnay standing clear with the Browning aimed between the man's eyes, rehandcuffed his wrists using Pestiaux's as an extra, then his ankles. The gunman was left kneeling and pinioned, like an executioner's victim about to receive the axe.

Bonnay whipped the strip from the man's throat, and signalled the other three back from the kneeling figure. His Browning was steady on the ambusher's head.

'All your guns on him – the AK too! This time, cut him in pieces if he tries anything funny!'

The captive's face sank slowly forward into the wet mud. But even before it reached the ground, Bonnay recognised him.

It was the casino brandy-buyer the tart in the Croupier's Arms had called Stefan du Preez.

CHAPTER TWENTY

'The Maluti Rider!'

The way Bonnay said it was condemnation in itself.

The fact that he had been identified was enough for the Maluti Rider's swimming senses to hook on to. He raised his head an inch or two, as if it had been weighted down with river-bed boulders. He aimed his shaky sight at Bonnay, who still had the Browning in a firing position. There was enough back-up firepower from the others to shoot the hill-slope full of holes.

His eyes had a strange, fanatical glimmer. 'I always swore you fuzz would never take me alive.'

'Do you want to change your mind?' snapped Bonnay.

Stefan made a kind of slumping move as if he were trying to get at the group again, but all he succeeded in doing was to fall face down.

Bonnay threw an anxious glance up and down the highway. One car's headlights would be enough to reveal the scene and ruin the night's onward plan.

'Quick! We've got to get the hell out of here! See anything coming?'

'Nothing.' It was Kennet. With the Scorpion thrust into his belt and his big hands pointing Stefan's own AK-47 at the prostrate figure, he was a broadside by himself.

'Hayward! Pestiaux! Give Kennet and me your guns! Pick that bastard up and carry him down to the van! Move! We've been here too long already!'

The two men moved cautiously in on Stefan, and grabbed him under the armpits to haul him up. But somehow he seemed to endow himself with a kind of negative buoyancy so that his legs and lower body clung to the ground.

Pestiaux kicked savagely at Stefan's ankles. It hardly seemed to help. It was going to be a long, tough haul down the bush-covered slope, past the waterfall, and then across the water itself to the van standing on the causeway.

'Wait!' Bonnay ordered, without any specific plan in mind.

Then, from the slope higher up, came the whinny and stamp of a horse.

Stefan had a thick, rough voice with a strong accent.

'My horse – he's up there tied to a tree. Cut him loose. He's got on a blanket. He can look after himself.'

Bonnay saw his chance. 'We'll look after him, all right,' he said harshly. 'Pestiaux, take the AK and shoot that animal.'

Stefan's strangled reaction was half-drowned in liquid mud. 'No! No!'

Bonnay went on, with a deliberate softening-up sneer, 'If the horse has wings like the media says, then shoot 'em off first. Shoot it! It hasn't any place where we're taking you.'

Stefan levered his face an inch or two out of the mud. 'You've got me – isn't that enough? What harm has the horse done?' he managed to get out.

Pestiaux relieved Kennet of the AK-47 and worked the breech as a pre-firing check.

'Get going!' Bonnay ordered Pestiaux. 'We can't go on hanging around here!'

Pestiaux turned to go. 'A full burst?'

'Any bloody way you like,' retorted Bonnay. 'But don't waste all the ammo. No, hold it. Single shots, rather. We may need the rest of the magazine ourselves. I don't want the whole country-side filled with the sound of gunfire either – just in case anyone is around.'

Stefan shifted his eyes from Bonnay to Pestiaux, and then on to Kennet and Hayward. Some last light was reflected in the corneas. Bonnay was grateful for the triple sets of handcuffs on the man.

'Listen,' he told Stefan, 'I'm offering you a deal. I couldn't give a stuff whether your magic horse lives or dies. Either you come under your own power to our van without playing the arse further or the horse dies. Okay?'

The words seemed squeezed from Stefan. 'Okay. But he can't stay all night tethered to a tree. Let him go free.'

'Pestiaux, you heard,' said Bonnay.

'Aw, shit!' grumbled the Frenchman. 'One moment you're telling me to shoot and the next not . . .'

'Get up the gully and free the horse – and leave the AK behind, just in case you are overcome with last-minute feelings, see?' ordered Bonnay.

Pestiaux moved up the higher ground at a trot; Stefan sank back into an untidy heap on the ground.

Bonnay repeated his question to Hayward and Kennet. 'Hear anything coming?'

'No.'

'We've got to get off the causeway and clear of the highway and talk to this bastard,' added Bonnay.

'What are you scared of? You'll be a lot of heroes, capturing me,' Stefan said in his harsh accent.

'Not yet, we aren't,' replied Bonnay enigmatically. 'Later, maybe, with your help.'

'Don't give me that soft sell, fuzz,' Stefan answered. 'Save your breath.'

Pestiaux came stumbling back through the bushes. 'I nearly decided to shoot the bastard after all with my pistol. Wild as hell. Tried to savage me, using his front hooves . . .'

'You set him loose?' Stefan broke in.

'He's gone, all right. Vanished into the night.'

'Good,' answered Stefan. 'I'll carry out my side of the deal now and walk to the van. First get these things off my ankles.'

Kennet and Hayward looked inquiringly at the gang leader. Bonnay nodded. He addressed Stefan. 'On the way down, these guys will stay as close to you as your vest. The only difference is, your vest isn't bullet-proof and their guns will be right against your heart.'

Kennet went to unlock the manacles round the Maluti Rider's ankles. He was wary of a kick. The others stood clear, in a tight circle. There seemed enough weaponry trained on Stefan to down an Exocet.

When the group reached the water, Stefan eyed the pitted, but not penetrated, side of the van and the long white scores across the windscreen – not enough to make driver vision impossible, only uncomfortable, depending on the angle of vision.

'You security guys certainly know how to protect your own backsides,' Stefan sneered. 'Armour-plating . . . Jeez, I never thought of that! I should have, what with the Eagle of Time on board.'

'We're not security,' answered Bonnay. 'That's what we want to talk to you about.'

'Don't give me that line of bull,' responded Stefan. 'Not security – in those uniforms? And driving this van?'

'That's what I said,' replied Bonnay. 'Now, in! John, get the manacles on his legs again.'

An access road for clearing the wreckage of the bridge and building the causeway had been constructed up the gully. When the gang had originally reconnoitred the crossing they had decided that this would be the ideal place to conceal the van while they persuaded Stefan to join them in the Poortman kidnap. Now, however, Bonnay was uneasy. It did not seem far enough away from passing headlights. Inwardly, Bonnay shrugged. They would have to browbeat Stefan quickly in time for the next business of the evening, the Poortman kidnap from Katse Lodge.

Bonnay drove to the head of the gully and pulled the van in hard against the small trees and bushes. In the back, the gang trio covered Stefan with their guns.

Stefan looked at Bonnay with eyes that refused to accept his capture. The interior light, weak and faintly yellow as it was, seemed to go right past the retinas; the casino tart had been right, Bonnay thought quickly, his eyes were the colour of piss. They were a killer's eyes. Bonnay was glad of his own gun, and the others' to back it up.

You must lie blackened in your grave with the revenge unfinished, Rali.

The captive's muscles jerked involuntarily so that the handcuffs jangled against the van's steel floor as if his past had taken command of his control reactions. If he had ever come to articulate it, Stefan would have told you that he had become a killer by circumstance, not choice.

Stefan du Preez was thirty-five. He was – or had been – a farmer on the South African side of the Lesotho border, along the beautiful and fertile banks of the north side of the Caledon River. More than a century and a half before, his ancestors, of French Huguenot descent, had trekked from the Cape into the border area. The region was then the scene of murder, pillage, brutality, mass killings – even cannibalism – as broken-up tribes, hounded and decimated by the regiments of Chaka, the Zulu Napoleon, fought for possession of its lovely valleys, fertile highlands, and rich watersheds.

The du Preez clan brought peace – through the barrel of a gun – to the area they occupied, which consisted of two great farms about twenty kilometres apart, one where the present Golden Gate national park is situated, and the other on the Ash River near the picturesque village of Clarens. The Ash River now forms the main outlet point into South Africa for the vast quantities of water stored by the Highlands Project and fed to it by an eighty-kilometre-long double pipeline driven under the mountains.

Stefan had been reared on family bitterness over land. Some thirty years before the scheduled opening of the Highlands Project, the state had expropriated about 5000 hectares (about 12,500 acres) of one du Preez family farm to convert this magnificent mountain area into a national park. A bitter court battle ensued, but finally the state won. For years, the loss of some of the finest land in the whole border area ate like acid into the du Preez clan.

Stefan inherited the second ancestral farm on the Ash River on his father's death. But not for long. The jinx which had dogged the du Preez clan struck again when the South African authorities decided to expropriate the major portion of the farm in order to provide an outlet – the Ash River – for the water which would flow from Lesotho into South Africa. Further abortive court proceedings only served to sharpen Stefan's hatred of the authorities – and the Highlands Project, in particular, as the focal point of the evil.

The strip of territory along the Caledon River has always been desperado country. Scottish Lowlanders had nothing on the cattle raiders from across the Lesotho border. In the early 1980s, when relations between Lesotho and South Africa were very strained, some dark deeds and equally dark counter-deeds were perpetrated.

During this time, Stefan did military service on the Namibia-Angola border with the crack and dreaded South African anti-insurgency unit named *Koevoet*. In his absence from the Ash River farm, a group of Basuto tribesmen from deep in the Maluti Mountains crossed the border, attacked his farm, and killed his young wife Rali and two small daughters by that most hideous of murder methods, 'the necklace'. This consists of putting a car tyre around the victim's neck, dousing him or her in petrol, and setting the unfortunate alight. It is a barbaric practice which gained world-wide notoriety during the South African township troubles in the 1980s.

Stefan returned and swore revenge against the clan, whom he believed he could identify by their use of an old-fashioned type of barbed wire with which they trussed Rali before setting her ablaze. Armed with Soviet weapons which he had brought back as loot from Angola, Stefan launched a series of one-man killing raids into the Maluti Mountains, 'the Mountains of Death'. In Stefan's hands, they lived up to their name. He became a legend of death.

With the start of the Highlands Project, Stefan had broadened the scope of his operations to take sporadic single-handed action against convoys transporting dam-building equipment and supplies through the mountains to the remote sites.

Soon he had gained his dreaded reputation as the Maluti Rider.

CHAPTER TWENTY-ONE

Now the legendary Maluti Rider lay trussed and twitching like a wild animal on the steel floor of the Chunnel Gang's stolen van.

Bonnay knew he would have his work cut out to enlist the cooperation of the man whose name was a by-word of terror and death.

Bonnay repeated, 'I said, we're not security.'

Stefan was derisive. His restricted gesture took in the van and pile of security uniforms. 'Then what?'

'Private enterprise, you could call us.'

'I like *sprokies* – fairy-stories. Go on.'

'If I told you the four of us hijacked this van from its depot in Maseru this morning after first grabbing ourselves this armful of uniforms from the laundry, would you believe me?'

'Interesting. No. I don't buy fantasy.'

'Did you listen to the police announcement on the news? General alert out for a missing security van and four dangerous armed men.'

'I don't have a radio installed on my horse.'

'Pity – for you, I mean, not for us. If you had, you would have recognised the van as it came spluttering onto the causeway. Deliberately, I might tell you – as a decoy, a bluff. You'd never have put your head into the trap – *our* trap.'

'You're lying all the way. You're trying to soften me up,' snarled Stefan in reply. 'You're a bunch of security shits. Why don't you get on with it and take me back to Maseru in triumph?'

'Because we wouldn't get past the first road block. They're up on all the main roads, the radio said,' answered Bonnay. 'I like risks, but not suicide.'

There was a tight silence.

'I said, private enterprise,' repeated Bonnay, and the trio nodded agreement. 'Get this clear, though. I may have to shoot you afterwards for what I'm about to tell you – it's up to you whether you want to listen to reason. If you don't, we could alternatively turn you in to the police, as you suggest.'

'And collect the reward of R25,000.'

'We're not interested in peanuts. We're interested in a million – in dollars. That's why we want you.'

'I have to listen, I haven't any option. Go on.'

'I said, if I go on, I will tell you things I may have to shoot you for knowing.'

Stefan shrugged, as best he could. 'This is all a load of security jaw-jaw. I don't know why you're going in for all this beating round the bush. It doesn't convince me.'

'Not even if we cut you in on a million – in dollars?'

'I said, I don't talk fantasy. You offer me a million, and I don't even know your name. You don't know mine.'

Bonnay regarded him. 'Stefan du Preez.'

There was a tense silence. Then Stefan said, 'If you know that, you know the rest.'

'Only that you are the Maluti Rider. That's enough.'

The revelation of his own name seemed to unleash the floodgates in the man. He spoke so quickly in a voice which became progressively hoarser and harsher as it charged with emotion, and with occasional Afrikaans words thrown in that the gang had difficulty at times in following.

'Rali!' he burst out, as if it were a physical relief to get rid of the name. 'Rali! Have you ever seen anyone – let alone a woman – who has been necklaced? She wasn't a woman any more, my Rali – the black hair was gone and . . . and . . .' He got a firm grip of himself and the four hard men drew back a little, keeping their guns aimed. 'Other things were gone, d'you hear! Can you understand? And my two little girls – ' He clanked the handcuffs as if his hands were trying to claw at the hideous memory which the burning tyres and petrol had branded on his mind. 'But I knew the killers, I knew where they were from, up there in the mountains. They made the mistake of bringing their own barbed wire with them – it was an old-fashioned sort of wire which went out years ago – I went back. By God, I went back!'

'The papers said, you shot down the women and kids as they

144

rushed out of their burning huts in the middle of the night,' said Bonnay.

'It wasn't enough – I didn't get them all!' Stefan raged on. 'I wanted every man, woman and child – didn't they take everything I had? And what was left the authorities took – they stole my farm, my ancestral land, for their filthy water project! And I made them pay for that too – but not enough!' He glanced round the interior of the truck and mouthed, 'Where is the Eagle of Time? *That* is what I wanted! The heart of the Highlands Project . . .'

Bonnay went forward and thrust the Browning into Stefan's face. 'Shut up! Pull yourself together! We're not carrying the Eagle of Time! You can still have your revenge – if you join us.'

Sanity seemed to flow back into the yellow eyes.

'How?' he jerked out.

'First, my name?' He drew back from Stefan and said with slow dramatic emphasis, as if it would recall something in the captive's mind: 'Bonnay.'

It didn't.

Bonnay added, 'Here are the others – Kennet, Hayward, Pestiaux.'

The only reaction from Stefan was a glare around the armed men.

Then he said, 'You can't prove I'm the Maluti Rider.'

'The authorities wouldn't need any proof once they saw what you did to the side of the van with your AK-47.'

Stefan said, with grudging admiration, 'You should have been cut to pieces. It took a lot of guts to stand up to that sort of fire.'

'It shows how badly I wanted you,' replied Bonnay. 'The others were under strict orders not to injure you, certainly not kill you. You were a sitting duck. There was nothing to stop them finishing you off, except my orders.'

'Except that you wanted to have a chat with me.'

'Correct.' Bonnay threw a quick glance round the trio on guard. Its unspoken message was, get ready to shoot if he stalls too long.

'Tonight, whether you join us or not, we intend kidnapping the Swiss banker Dr Hans Poortman at Katse Lodge where he's staying . . .' He glanced at his watch and laughed without much

145

humour. 'At this moment, he's probably having his dinner – the last square meal he's going to have for a while. We intend to demand a million American dollars ransom for him – and free passage for us to whatever destination we choose.'

'You're a load of nuts!' exclaimed Stefan. 'You'll never get away with it! A top Swiss banker!'

'We think we will. We intend to. Dr Poortman is one of the key figures in the gala opening of the Highlands Project in nine days' time. Neither Lesotho nor South Africa can afford to have a man of that status being held to ransom while the eyes of the world are on the opening ceremony.'

'I'll be damned!' exclaimed Stefan incredulously. 'I really think you mean it!'

'We do. To prove it, we've already drafted the ransom note. I can show it to you. It's here in the van.'

'You'll never get away with it!' repeated Stefan.

'Our chances are better if you join us.'

Stefan hesitated a long time before replying, testing the water, as it were.

Finally he rapped out: 'I don't believe a word of this yarn. You're trying to frame me in some clever way . . .'

'You don't need framing,' retorted Bonnay. 'You've got enough on your track record to hang you a dozen times over. And you know it.'

'You're a gang – I can see that,' went on Stefan. 'You're foreign . . .'

'French and British – yes, a gang. You may have heard of us.' He paused almost histrionically. 'The Chunnel Gang.'

Stefan's eyes went in stunned amazement round the hard circle of eyes which glinted in the low light of the van's interior: Pestiaux, the short-fuse impetuous gunman; Hayward, volatile and unpredictably Irish, yet the superlative explosives artist; Kennet, as single-track as a runaway bulldozer; Bonnay, the intellect of the bunch, and not the less ruthless killer because of it.

'The Chunnel Gang! You're the lot who tried to kill the British and French leaders!'

'The English make me puke!' Hayward interjected

146

irrelevantly. 'Pity we missed. I would have liked to have seen . . .'

'Okay, okay, Hayward, stow the IRA propaganda!' snapped Bonnay. 'We've got our hands full enough at the moment without it.'

'What the hell is the Chunnel Gang doing in Lesotho?' demanded Stefan. 'They vanished after they failed to blow up the Channel Tunnel.'

Bonnay lifted the Browning sights so that they rested on the centre of Stefan's forehead. He said thinly, 'That's another story, and it won't interest you now. But just knowing who we are means you have signed your own death warrant. Unless you come in with us on the Poortman operation.'

Stefan replied, with a little less of his previous truculence, 'Why do you want *me*? You've got it all worked out, the way you talk.'

At the change in the man's tone, Bonnay lowered the sights to his abdomen. He said, almost conversationally, 'Our scheme is good, but it has one big weak point. That is where you come in. Let me tell you our alternative scheme first. We intend snatching Poortman from his bungalow at Katse Lodge tonight. After that, we will force him to accompany us down the perimeter gallery of the Katse Dam wall to the control chambers from where they operate the sluices and the hydro-power. It's a good spot – I've recced it already. It's solid concrete, being part of the wall. It will stand up to any amount of small arms fire. Grenades also. The place has only one entrance and one exit – easily dominated by us.

'Still, it's vulnerable to tear gas. We could be caught like rats in a trap if they started to pump in gas. Nevertheless, we could stand a short siege and make our ransom demand while they were getting themselves organised. However, if they resorted to a long-term tactic and set about starving us out, we'd be in trouble. Before entering the perimeter gallery after we've grabbed Poortman, we'd have to ransack the Lodge kitchens. We'd need heat, too. That's what I meant when I said Poortman was probably having his last square meal in a while tonight.

147

'A couple of my guys favour this plan. I don't. I say that, to make the kidnap work, we need a funkhole for Poortman. A funkhole where the security forces don't know how to get at us and where we can keep the banker stashed away while we hold out and negotiate the ransom. Somewhere remote, with food and water and fire. I reckon you have just such a spot in the mountains where you hole up after your attacks.'

Stefan eyed each member of the gang in turn with a long stare. His eyes were frightening; theirs as hard as an Ak-47's breechblock.

Then he clanked his handcuffs as if to underscore his reply. 'It's a trap! You're trying to trap me – somehow! I know you security devils and your tricks – promise a man anything when he's on the spot, and when he comes out with what you're looking for, you say you never made any promise whatsoever! You say you want a cave in the mountains – I say, go and bloody well find one for yourselves!'

Bonnay checked the time and then deliberately worked the slide of his Browning.

'There isn't time, or we might do just that,' he answered levelly. 'We're working against two time factors – the opening ceremony in nine days, and tonight. It's a very tight schedule. If you don't care to join us, there is only one thing left – ' He lifted the gun again so that Stefan looked along the barrel into Bonnay's eyes. 'And you can be damn sure it won't worry me if I have to pull the trigger. The choice is yours – come in with us for a split of the million and show us your hide-out, or . . .'

'I don't buy this million story,' Stefan compromised. 'Who says Poortman is worth a million, anyway?'

'Maybe by himself he isn't,' replied Bonnay. 'Or maybe he is. It doesn't really matter. Lesotho and South Africa together can easily put it up. They can't afford not to. They can't let the kidnap drag on to the opening, or even near it . . .'

Bonnay let his sentence trail off: he had seen something in the Maluti Rider's eyes which gave him a surge of hope. Until now, the ugly glare in his eyes had been that of a trapped, dangerous animal; now, for a split second, there was a burst of light in them like a phosphorous flare being dropped. It was a glow from the dark heart of the force which had made Stefan into the most dangerous lone killer in Southern Africa.

'It would damage the Highlands Project, you say?'

'You don't have to be a genius to realise that.'

'Badly? I mean, real bad?'

Hayward interjected, 'Yeah, badly – almost as bad as if you blew up the wall of the Katse Dam – which I'd like to have a stab at.'

'These bloody IRA!' remarked Pestiaux without rancour.

Bonnay took a firm grip of the conversation again. 'That's behind our idea of asking a million dollars for Poortman. Both Lesotho and South Africa will have their backs against the wall, with the opening just around the corner. Otherwise, their tactics might be to wear us down. That's why the hide-out idea is good, and the control room alternative bad. We don't want a short, sharp action – we want a place which will give us time to play the kidnap off against the opening – in nine days.'

'You're banking on the fact that if the authorities don't choose to play along with your demands, they may even have to call off the opening ceremony?' asked Stefan.

'We make the opening our deadline date for meeting the million-dollar ransom. Either – or. That way, it throws the spotlight square on the opening ceremony.'

Stefan muttered, so softly that Kennet and Pestiaux, who were slightly further away to provide back-up fire for Bonnay and Hayward, did not hear his words. 'They did it to me, and by God, I'll do it to them!'

Bonnay indicated his watch with the Browning barrel.

'You've got just five minutes to make up your mind.'

Stefan extended his manacled wrists. 'Right now, I want that banker more than I want anything else in the world.'

'Does that mean yes?' asked Bonnay.

Stefan went on quickly, excitedly, as if the prospect of the kidnapping had pumped adrenalin into his veins. 'I've got a place in the mountains – you were right. No one will ever find it. We'll take Poortman there tonight. He won't starve or die of cold – there are plenty of supplies. It's a long way, and the snow will start coming thick in the mountains later on tonight.'

Stefan again stuck out his wrists and tinkled the steel, as if to draw unspoken attention to them while he talked.

Bonnay felt in his pocket for the key. The other three looked uneasy and kept their guns levelled.

'What time's the job tonight?' asked Stefan almost conversationally, as if the desperate struggle between himself and the gang had never taken place. He extended his handcuffed hands for Bonnay's key.

Bonnay also played it cool. He unlocked the double handcuffs almost nonchalantly and replied, '9.30.'

Stefan shoved his ankles forward to be freed. He spoke directly to Bonnay still, as if the other three guns trained on him did not exist.

'If Poortman puts up a fight, what do we do?'

'I don't want him hurt, if possible,' said Bonnay slowly. He thrust his key into the lock of the manacle round Stefan's one ankle and clicked it loose. 'We'll have to slug him if he hollers. Not too hard, though.'

Stefan drew up his legs and flexed them, still seated. The three guns tracked him. He went on, addressing only Bonnay. 'Who is "we"? I mean, what is the division of forces? There are five of us.'

'Five is a good number for the snatch,' replied Bonnay. 'You and I will go for Poortman. Hayward and Kennet will take the ski hut as their target. Pestiaux will be the getaway van driver.'

'Ski hut?' asked Stefan. 'What for?'

'Warm clothes,' answered Bonnay. 'If we hadn't received your, er, cooperation tonight, we would have had to hole up – as I told you – in the control chamber. It's as cold as a fridge. We have to have warm gear for ourselves and Poortman. The ski hut's packed with stuff – anoraks, gloves, balaclavas, even fur-lined boots. I know. I recced it myself.'

'Good,' said Stefan. 'It's a point I was going to raise myself. Where we're going tonight could kill an out-of-condition softie like a well-fed banker. The going will be tough. All of you will need warm gear too.'

The exchange died in its tracks. Gun-mouths aren't good conversationalists.

Finally, Stefan broke the silence, still speaking directly to Bonnay. 'I need my gun for this job. You've still got it, remember?'

This was the crunch Bonnay had been waiting for. It was the break-or-break (or life-and-death) moment of the whole deal. He wondered for a split second, whether Stefan had been too amenable, too willing to go along with the kidnap scheme simply in order to get his hands again on the AK-47, still with half its magazine unexpended? Would the Maluti Rider, a by-word for cunning and saving his own skin, gun them all down with a single burst?

Bonnay temporised. 'We're dealing with a harmless, middle-aged banker,' he said. 'A pistol should be enough; we don't need an AK-47.'

The sinister truculence they had all heard before scarred Stefan's voice again now. 'I like an AK. It's my weapon.'

'I reckon it will only get in our way. It's too big . . .' Bonnay started to say.

For the first time, Stefan looked straight at the three guns trained on him. 'Either – or,' he snapped.

Bonnay gave the trio an imperceptible nod. 'Take it, if you want. It's over there in the corner.'

'I'll check it over.'

He got up. The Chunnel Gang trio parted to let him through. His back was to Bonnay. If he had looked round, he would have seen the gang leader again produce his Browning. Once Stefan's hands were on his favourite AK-47, he could face about firing –how many would he get with a burst before they got him?

Stefan took up the automatic, turned to them. He sat down in a studied way on the floor, snapped open the breech. He then removed the magazine, checked its contents.

'Best weapon of 'em all,' he remarked. He indicated the bullet-clouded glass of the driver's window. 'Pity I had to waste ammo – getting harder to come by these days.'

With a swift, deft move, he snapped the magazine back into place. The sharp sound almost activated Pestiaux's trigger-happy fingers.

Bonnay restored his Browning to his pocket. He told himself, if you're going to work with this desperado, you've got to learn to live with his ways.

'Where'd you come by your supplies in the first place?' He was aware that his voice sounded stilted, dry.

'Long story – the sort of unit I served in picked up a lot of loot. No questions asked.'

'The grenades also?' asked Hayward. It was the first time one of the gun-trio had spoken. The fact that he had lowered his sights meant that the thaw had set in, reasoned Bonnay. Still, Stefan's manner could be a clever bluff to lure them all into a sense of false security, in which case it would all be over in seconds with that AK-47.

'Yes.'

Hayward went on, 'Between us we've got enough hardware to put up a show if they try and smoke us out of your hide-out once we've got Poortman.'

Stefan's pale eyes went round the men. 'Get this quite clear in your minds,' he said abrasively. 'My hide-out is *my* hide-out, Poortman or not. No one is ever going to find out where it is situated. That goes for all of you too. If the heat is turned on us, I know a backdoor way of slipping away. The hide-out is mine, mine, do you understand, and I intend keeping it that way. Is that clear?'

Bonnay checked himself from raising the nitty-gritty question of the ransom pay-out and split. Now was not the time. Stefan could turn ugly so quickly. He seemed now to be playing along – on his own terms. He hoped the truce would last.

Bonnay consulted his watch, but Stefan said, 'It's too early to set out for Katse Lodge – it's only twenty kilometres away. We don't want to have to hang around on the highway. The van is too distinctive and there's the alert out – we could be spotted. I know a place where we can wait until it's time to strike . . .'

CHAPTER TWENTY-TWO

Eight o'clock.

One and a half hours to go.

Stefan's jumping-off point for the sortie against Katse Lodge – he called it a *blaaskansieplek* (a breather-spot) – was a pull-in on a narrow service road which had been cut into the side of the Malibamatso gorge and which followed the river for about twenty kilometres upstream from the wall. This road's purpose had been overtaken by the construction of the big highway which crossed the Bokong; only an occasional official car used the road now.

The security van was parked about five kilometres from their target.

Hayward, who was in the back with Stefan and Kennet, said, 'It's getting damn cold.'

'It'll be a bloody sight colder before the night's out,' replied Stefan.

Hayward, who seemed to have warmed to the Maluti Rider in a way which the others had not, indicated the occasional snow-flakes drifting against the window. 'They say it gets warmer when it snows.'

'You can judge for yourself later,' answered Stefan. 'Where we're going is over 3200 metres.' He addressed Bonnay, who was in the passenger's seat next to Pestiaux, the driver.

'You sure about all that warm gear in the hut?'

'There's more than enough.'

'We want more than enough. We'll take the blankets off Poortman's bed also. Don't forget them.'

Bonnay bridled inwardly. He wasn't used to taking orders from anyone, and in the short time since the ambush Stefan seemed to have grabbed the reins. Although he sat in the command seat next to Pestiaux, Bonnay felt relegated to the back burner. He bit back a retort. It was self-evident that Stefan, who knew the route and the terrain, would have the

153

major say. Nevertheless, Bonnay felt less an associate than a subordinate.

Kennet entered the conversation, the first time he had really spoken out since the ambush. Perhaps he found it harder than the others to stomach what had gone on in that desperate hand-to-hand by the waterfall.

'There's plenty of heat from the van's heating system while we are moving. It's only when we stop . . .'

'We are ditching this van along the way,' Stefan interrupted.

'What!' exclaimed Bonnay. 'Do you expect – '

'I don't expect anything except you follow what I know is right,' retorted Stefan. 'This van is a liability. We'll use it to come back along this road after we've got Poortman. About twenty kilometres from the dam it intersects the road to the diamond diggings. That's the road we take – to start with.'

'I had my eye on it also,' said Bonnay. He again felt the initiative passing out of his hands. 'I rather fancied some disused digging to stash Poortman away.'

'You'd have been crazy,' replied Stefan. Bonnay did not care for his dogmatic certainty.

'Why?'

'I know 'em well. In fact, it's the disused diggings we're headed for after we pass the Kao fields, which are still in operation. They've been worked out years ago and abandoned. That's the place we ditch this van. They're a little over thirty kays beyond Kao. High in the mountains.'

'Where is your hide-out from there?' It was Pestiaux who asked the question.

Stefan brushed it off. 'About sixty or seventy kays from here – as the lammergeyer flies. But not that distance the way we're going.'

'You say, we ditch the van. What then?' asked Bonnay.

Stefan answered obliquely, 'Is there extra petrol in these jerry cans?'

'Yes.'

'Good. Then we won't have to drain the tank into the other vehicle.'

'Other vehicle?'

'It's waiting at the abandoned diggings,' said Stefan shortly. 'We transfer and carry on in it. This van is a millstone round our necks. The sooner we get rid of it, the better.'

'We carry on in this, ah, second vehicle, to your hide-out?' persisted Bonnay.

'You'll see.' Stefan was brief. 'You'll see.'

To Bonnay, the snow-covered mountains were as faraway and alien as extragalactic nebulae.

'If this place of yours is as remote as you say, how do we conduct ransom negotiations from it?' Bonnay went on.

'Get this absolutely clear,' said Stefan. 'No one – but no one – comes near my place. Not even for a million dollars. You must have worked out your own strategy for the ransom demand before I came on the scene.'

'We discussed it this morning,' replied Bonnay cautiously. 'We had the whole day to kill. Plenty of time. We know what we intend doing.'

'What?'

Hayward said, 'Pass me the van's logbook from the cubby, will you, Jules? I'll read out the ransom note I wrote.'

'Fingerprints!' warned Bonnay. 'Use gloves, man!'

Hayward pulled on a light pair and started to reach for a torch.

'Keep that light down!' Stefan snapped.

Without resorting to the flashlight, Hayward said, 'We decided on two notes – one if you joined up with us, and the other if we holed ourselves up in the control chamber.'

'That's of no interest to me,' said Stefan.

Bonnay felt needled by the man's assertive arrogance, but he kept his mouth shut.

'We used a page of the logbook because it was the only paper we could find . . .' began Hayward.

Pestiaux said unexpectedly from the wheel, 'You see, we forgot the crested notepaper at home.'

The effect of the remark on Stefan silenced the gang for a moment. 'Cut the crappish humour!' he snapped. 'Use the torch now. Start reading!'

Hayward began to read self-consciously, like a child at a school concert.

To whom it may concern . . .

'My oath!' burst out Stefan. 'Where do you expect to get with an opening like that? "*To whom it may concern.*" Sounds like a job reference! The first thing anyone coming across a shitty remark like that will do is to say it's a hoax!'

Bonnay rushed to Hayward's defence. 'Poortman's flying off to South Africa first thing tomorrow. When they come to call him, they'll find him missing and the note . . .'

Hayward said defensively, 'What do you suggest? Maybe you've had more experience than us of this sort of thing.'

'Less,' he answered equably. 'I usually shoot first before the talkie-talk begins. You want to be *specific*. Address it specifically to someone.'

'Who?' asked Hayward. 'We did think of General Mak, the security chief.'

'He's not the guy with the dollars,' retorted Stefan.

'You can't address it to the Lesotho or South African governments,' objected Hayward. 'It sounds too corny and too general.'

'The Swiss banks will have to foot the bill,' said Stefan. 'Why not address it to them? Better still, to their representative in Maseru.'

'The guy they call their ombudsman?' Bonnay asked. 'He was on the TV with the rest of the VIPs at the Eagle of Time unveiling.'

'His name is Sholto Banks,' said Stefan. 'Everyone knows him. He'll see the ransom note reaches his money bosses.'

'Okay,' said Hayward, deleting his opening sentence. 'Here we are:

"*To Mr Sholto Banks, ombudsman, the Swiss Banking Consortium in Lesotho . . .*"'

'Good,' approved Stefan. 'Good.'

'"*Dr Poortman is being held in a place of safety. He is safe and unharmed. He will be released on payment of one million US dollars at a rendezvous to be mutually determined and guarantees of safe conduct by air from Maseru to . . .*" It's something we still haven't worked out,' he added.

'Say, an international destination,' suggested Stefan.

'Does that include you?' asked Bonnay. 'We were writing the demand as coming from us, the Chunnel Gang.'

'You don't have to include me,' said Stefan. 'The Maluti Rider will simply fade away into the mountains after the kidnap, as he always has done.'

'Plus two hundred thousand dollars – in cash,' added Kennet.

'The deal is for an even-Stephen cut amongst the five of us,' said Stefan. 'If you don't like it, go and get stuffed. Find your own hide-out – if you can.'

Although Stefan's tone stuck in his throat, Bonnay said placatingly, 'You are free to do as you wish – afterwards.'

'Thanks!' he replied ironically.

'Read on, Burt,' ordered Bonnay.

'"*This demand must be met by midday on the day of the opening ceremony of the Lesotho Highlands Project. Failure to comply with our demands will result in the death of Dr Poortman.*"'

'That's what I like to hear!' exclaimed Stefan. 'By God, that'll teach them!'

'We still have a problem,' said Hayward. 'How does the consortium or the South African or Lesotho governments get in touch with us in your hide-out?'

'Tell them to broadcast on Radio Lesotho, just before the main news bulletins, at lunch and dinner,' said Stefan.

Hayward wrote and quoted: '"*Official communication with the kidnappers must be made immediately before the main news bulletins on Radio Lesotho. Signed, The Chunnel Gang, The Maluti Rider.*"'

Hayward asked, 'What about our response to them? How do we say we accept or whatever?'

'We'll make a plan – we'll play it by ear, once we're in the hide-out,' answered Bonnay.

Bonnay checked the time.

'Still too early,' said Stefan. 'What will we do if Poortman's not in his rondavel when we pitch up?'

'Wait,' replied Bonnay. 'But, as I see it, there's not much to keep him in the main block – no other VIPs to chat with.'

'Except a warm fire,' said Hayward.

'John and I haven't any problems about the ski hut,' said Hayward. 'But what's our briefing if we arrive with the gear and you're not around?'

Again, Stefan usurped the command. 'We'll fix a rendez-vous at the fence. If we're not there in ten minutes after the time we arrange, then you two get back to the van with the stuff.'

Kennet said, 'The longer we have to hang around at the Lodge or making our way back along the road to the van, the greater our chances are of being spotted. It's still the main road past the Lodge. The service road only forks further this side.'

'You can't plan everything,' Bonnay replied. 'If things start to go wrong, play it the best you can.'

He glanced again at his watch.

9.15.

'We're on our way,' he said.

CHAPTER TWENTY-THREE

'Stop!' ordered Bonnay.

Pestiaux cut the lights and the engine. A moment before, as the five gunmen approached the junction of the river road with the new main highway, the van's headlights shone across the water of the dam and picked out the great wall through the murk. The van was on an upgradient leading away from the river road; on their left was the cliff, at least fifty metres higher than the wall itself, on the top of which stood Katse Lodge with its commanding view of the huge stretch of water to the north.

The van halted about fifty metres from the road fork: to climb the Lodge cliff on foot, Bonnay, Stefan, Hayward and Kennet would have to walk about 100 metres along the highway – risking detection by any passing car – and then plunge into the tumble of boulders and bush on the hillside.

Stefan indicated the cliff-top lights.

'You know where you're headed?'

'Yes. The main road carries on past the foot of the cliff; there's a branch leading to the Lodge security gate with a signpost. We go over the wire instead. It's dead simple. It's a grid lay-out inside. Poortman's hut is on the side where we land – Number Fourteen.'

'Seems a hell of a lot of light. Are the paths between the huts lighted?' Stefan said, eyeing the clifftop.

'I don't know – I only saw it in daylight.' Bonnay turned to Kennet and Hayward. 'You two stick with us until we're over the wire. The ski hut is a cinch. It's bigger than the other huts, and not far from Poortman's.'

'Number Fourteen,' mused Stefan. 'That's good intelligence.'

'Any questions?'

Pestiaux asked, 'If anyone comes along and finds me sitting alone, what do I say?'

Hayward said derisively, 'Say your girl beat it when you tried the rough stuff.'

'Use your nut – I can't tell you what to say,' replied Bonnay. 'Only, no shooting, see?'

The four men dropped from the van into the roadway. The wind, after the warmth of the van's interior, took their breath away. Stefan, in his knee-length anorak, was the only one who was fully equipped for the weather. It also provided a shield for his AK-47.

Bonnay led, the others followed in Indian file. At the highway fork, Bonnay looked for headlights. There were none. Light snow, laced with sleet, spilled over the cliff-top, hooking itself on to the stunted trees, high grass and boulders of the slope.

'Any particular place to start climbing?' asked Stefan in a low voice.

'No. This is good enough here. I'll orientate myself once we hit the top.'

The slope was steep; the terrain rough and uneven. The four fanned out, Bonnay leading from the right flank, as it were. Within minutes they were warmer from the exertion, but the occasional gust of wind lanced down their throats and made them wince. The snow made the tall grass wet; they slipped and stumbled on hidden rocks and skirted those which were too big to clamber over. They floundered upwards, the Lodge lights growing stronger all the time.

'I hadn't bargained for so much light,' said Bonnay.

'Can they spot us from the security gate?' asked Stefan.

'Not unless we're unlucky.'

Almost without advance warning, a silver barrier rose across their path.

The security wire fence.

Stefan accelerated despite the steep slope, and grabbed a strand. He ran his hand along the wire, walking with it until he reached the nearest metal pole to which it was anchored.

'What gives?' demanded Bonnay when he got up to him.

Stefan's voice was hoarse and emotion-packed. 'I thought it was barbed wire.'

Barbed wire. Rali's necklace of barbed wire.

To lower the emotional temperature, Bonnay said, 'There isn't even any razor-tape along the top.'

160

They were not at the summit of the cliff yet, but about four or five metres below it, still amongst the boulders and steep, shrubby undergrowth. It was plain to Bonnay once again – as it had been on his reconnaissance – that the fence, lacking even razor-tape capping, was more a keep-out gesture than a serious threat to an intruder.

The Maluti Rider showed his contempt for it by jumping on top of a big boulder and vaulting over it. He dropped down in the undergrowth and waited for the others.

When they came, he whispered to Bonnay, 'Can you identify this place on the way back? It will be an easy ride for Poortman.'

'Yes.'

Now all five went up and on, on their bellies and elbows through the grass and rocks. When they reached the top, Bonnay and Stefan, crouched low so as not to break the skyline, edged into the lead.

'Over there.' Bonnay indicated a row of huts which occupied a grandstand seat to their right. In one a light burned.

'That it?' Stefan squirmed to make himself comfortable with the AK-47 under his anorak.

'If it's not, it's Poortman's neighbour.'

Kennet and Hayward joined the pair.

'Which is our ski hut?' breathed Kennet.

'See where the roadway passes the main block and cuts back again behind it? That hut there with the triangular roof.'

'We'll have to work our way round the back to reach it. We daren't go anywhere near the main building.'

'Where's the security gate?' asked Stefan.

'Where the most lights are, away on the other side. No problem.'

Bonnay gave his final orders. 'Be back with the warm gear in ten minutes. If we're not at the rendezvous, take everything you can and get back to Pestiaux.'

The two men slid away into the darkness to the left, away from the light, in the direction of the ski hut.

'Now – us,' said Bonnay to Stefan.

They made towards the lighted-up hut which they assumed to be Dr Poortman's at a half-run, half-crouch. Stefan had to jack the AK-47's barrel clear of the ground. It gave him a curious, crab-like stance.

Number Fourteen!

The hut number was on the wall above the lighted carport, which was separated from the bungalow proper by a chest-high wall. The two men ducked down behind it; Bonnay gestured at the number and gave the thumbs-up sign. The hut's curtains were drawn.

Stefan now communicated to Bonnay with hand-signs.

'Take the front door! Poortman's probably inside!'

The banker was.

In response to Bonnay's smart rat-tat, the door opened far more quickly than either kidnapper had expected, as if the banker had been expecting something to be delivered from the main block.

Stefan substituted the delivery with the AK-47.

He brushed past Dr Poortman as he opened the door, and he was inside with the automatic thrust into Poortman's back as Bonnay came from the front with the Browning aimed.

He kicked the door shut behind him.

The place was warm. Dr Poortman was dressed casually, with a thick sweater, Stefan noted with approval, and a woollen choker and scarf lay over the back of a chair.

'What!' he demanded. His voice was more outraged than scared.

'Shut up!' snapped Stefan from behind. 'You're coming with us. Keep your mouth shut and don't try and raise the alarm, and you won't get yourself hurt. Otherwise . . .' He came round into his full view with the AK. 'There's this.'

'*Go with you! Who are you!*'

'We'll explain that later,' rapped out Bonnay. 'Get on your jacket and scarf. You'll need it, where we're headed.'

'This is an outrage! Do you know who I am?' Dr Poortman got out angrily.

'Yes, we know. Dr Hans Poortman, the Swiss banker. You're just the guy we want.'

'What do you want from me . . .'

A telephone ring stopped the confrontation dead in its tracks.

162

It rang once, twice. Dr Poortman started towards the instrument which was on the far side of the room, but Stefan blocked him.

'If you answer or say a word, you're a dead man!'

As if it had overheard the threat, the ringing stopped.

Stefan rapped out, 'Get on your jacket, man!'

Poortman still showed no signs of fear, only of anger and affront.

'You'll pay for this outrage . . .' he began.

'We won't pay – someone else will.' Bonnay laughed at his own joke, thrust Dr Poortman's jacket at him, and clapped the scarf roughly round his neck. 'Now!'

Dr Poortman fumbled with the jacket. It may have been nerves, or he may have hoped to gain time in the hope that the phone would ring again. To the kidnappers, he was taking hours.

'Hat?' Bonnay asked Stefan.

'Forget it – balaclava's better,' replied Stefan. He prodded Dr Poortman towards the door with the AK-47. Bonnay went ahead to switch out the light as the door was opened.

'No noise, d'ye hear!' breathed Stefan. 'It's up to you whether you get hurt or not.'

Bonnay whipped open the door and snapped out the light-switch next to it in one lightning-fast movement. Another light, in an inner room, remained on.

Bonnay stopped as if a bullet had struck him.

'Jeez! I forgot the ransom note!'

Stefan clapped his hand round Dr Poortman's mouth and shoved the AK barrel hard against his ribs. Bonnay searched frantically in his pockets for a minute, and then found Hayward's ransom composition.

'Blankets also!' snapped Stefan.

Bonnay rushed back inside and put it on top of a scatter of documents and papers on which Dr Poortman had obviously been working before the break-in. He dived into the inner lighted room – the bedroom – and snatched the blankets off the bed. He rejoined Stefan, closing and locking the door silently behind him.

Stefan let go of Dr Poortman's mouth, after a further admonitory wave of the AK-47. Together they guided their hostage out of the muted light of Number Fourteen into the darkness of the unoccupied rows beyond, piloting him to the rendezvous with Hayward and Kennet.

CHAPTER TWENTY-FOUR

The whole operation, the stealth, the surprise, the surgical execution had gone just as he had planned it, thought Bonnay as he watched the last of the Chunnel Gang come over the wire. *Spetsnaz* – its ruthless criteria could not have been better fulfilled. Here was a million dollars standing next to him on the hoof, so to speak. Balloon men, all of them now, enveloped in the contents of the ski hut against the penetrating wind and fitful snow flurries. Dr Poortman had needed the anorak, the balaclava, the gloves and goggles they had plastered on his person. He had been shaking, perhaps from the cold, perhaps from delayed shock, while Bonnay and Stefan had to wait nearly five minutes at the rendezvous for Kennet and Hayward to arrive. When the pair appeared – they had loomed grotesquely through the murk under the mountain of stuff they had looted from the ski hut – they had quickly swapped Dr Poortman's blankets, which they had wrapped round him while they crouched by the fence, for proper anti-cold gear.

They were all so encumbered, and Dr Poortman so stiff from cold, that they had chosen to climb the wire for the return trip via one of the heavy steel posts, set in a concrete base, on which the structure was anchored.

Hayward reached the top of the post, and pitched over the last of the warm gear.

'Check that you don't leave anything behind, it could give away our escape route,' warned Bonnay. It had all been so easy – almost too easy. Everything had gone his way tonight, even the ambush of the Maluti Rider. There hadn't been a single alert.

The booming thud-thud of the alarm burst through the night.

The outlandish sound nailed Hayward to the summit of the post like a 66,000-volt high tension shock.

'We've triggered the alarm system!' exclaimed Kennet.

Hayward more fell than descended from his perch; Bonnay

165

and Kennet were already on the ground; Stefan dragged Dr Poortman down by his side and the clunk of the AK-47 snapping off safety was drowned by the racket.

The rolling thud-thud seemed to echo across the invisible water; it appeared to emanate from a small thatched structure slightly to the side of the main complex entrance. Stefan's sights were tracking its origin, although the light was too difficult for a random burst.

The drum roll turned to a flourish, as if the unseen drummer realised he had nailed the intruders.

'Keep down – keep quiet!' hissed Bonnay. 'Don't move, until I give the word. Then, down the hillside . . .'

Hayward whispered back, 'It's too fancy for an alarm. Someone's playing the arse!'

As if to answer him, the drum roll gave another elaborate flourish, and then died. The silence was eerie. There were no shouts, no lights, no running of security men. Stefan's eyes and sights were everywhere.

Dr Poortman spoke. The note of dry sarcasm in his voice showed that he was in less a state of shock than his captors might have suspected.

'It's the signal for lights-out in half an hour,' he said. 'African drums, to give an air of reality to the African setting.'

It was only then that Bonnay remembered the outsized thatched replica in the form of a Basuto hat near the main entrance where the Basuto crier had been the afternoon of the sluice-gates scare.

Stefan, however, was not amused. 'Good thing you warned us. If we have to do any shooting, you'll be the first to catch it. Get up!'

'Let's get the hell out of here,' said Hayward uneasily.

Dr Poortman managed the rough terrain down the hillside to the main road better than they had imagined. An AK-47 at your backside can be as effective as an abseil rope, under the right circumstances.

As the five Michelin man-like figures neared the fork, they spotted headlights approaching along the highway. They broke into a trot, but Dr Poortman could not keep up the pace. It was a warning for the night ahead. Stefan shook his head.

But they made it to the junction with the river road where the van was parked before the oncoming vehicle and moved at their best speed towards the van. Shortly before they reached it, the headlights cut a broad swathe through the darkness, but the group was already too far away to be spotted.

They came up to the van.

'I'm damn near dying of the cold,' Pestiaux complained.

'If that's all dying is, then you're well off,' retorted Stefan, at the driver's window. 'Into the back everyone – fix Dr Poortman up first. Fleece-lined boots – those light shoes of his are for the birds. He'll have frost-bite if he keeps 'em on.'

'Light?' asked Bonnay as they all piled into the van.

'Yes,' Stefan said. 'But for as short a time as possible. I'll start turning the van and stop once we're facing the right way.'

Bonnay again bit back his resentment at being ordered about by Stefan. However, he was the man who knew the way and the onward success of the kidnap was now entirely in his hands. It would, Bonnay assured himself, be different once the authorities started reacting.

Dr Poortman said nothing as the gang packed warm clothing on to him. The overclad, balaclava-helmeted figure, his eyes masked by snow goggles, might have been a dummy.

'Bonnay!' said Stefan. 'In here, with me in the front.'

'I thought I was driving . . .' said Pestiaux.

Stefan cut him short. 'Not where we're going. You will form the second line of defence guarding Poortman – sit behind him with your gun. Kennet and Hayward – one of you on each side of him – okay?'

They set off. Stefan seemed to know the route well. The road hugged the twisty course of the Malibamatso upstream. The headlights picked out the blue-mauve rocks of the canyon walls powdered with snow, a strange, bruised light; at times the snow clouds seemed to spill right down to the water's surface.

Stefan drove quickly and confidently. After a time he gave a grunt of satisfaction when three white-painted huts showed up on his left; there was also a bridge-like structure across the river with a concrete protruberance like a squat belly hanging down to water level.

167

'Monitoring weir,' said Stefan. 'In a moment we pass under the highway bridge, our own is a little further on. We leave the river there.'

Within minutes they passed under a fine concrete bridge carrying the main highway, and at twenty kilometres (Bonnay had been checking the distances on the odometer) Stefan turned right across the river over a much lower, more lightly constructed bridge and gunned the van up the western bank.

'She'll drink petrol all the way from here to the Kao diggings,' he said, changing into a lower gear and pushing the engine hard. 'Beyond that, it's up and down all the way to the abandoned diggings – and more up and down to follow that.'

Stefan's words prompted Dr Poortman into muffled speech from behind his balaclava. 'Where are you taking me? What do you hope to gain by all this? You won't get away with it!'

Bonnay vented his frustration over the leadership on Dr Poortman.

'If we don't, nor will you, so shut up! Play along, and you won't get hurt. Precisely, what we hope to gain is one million dollars. That's what you are worth to us, and that's why we are taking such good care of you.'

'Where?'

Bonnay swung round angrily and silenced him with a gesture from his Browning.

The gravel road they followed was a complete contrast to the tarmac surface they had just left. It was potholed, corrugated, and pitted with rocks and occasional small boulders. Slopes and rises followed one another in quick succession – all fuel-guzzling gear work – as they picked up altitude out of the great Malibamatso valley. And, with the altitude, the snow grew thicker.

About ten kilometres from the river, a glow – a man-made electric glow – appeared against the low cloud ceiling on their left.

'First of the diamond diggings,' explained Stefan. 'Fortunately, they are well away from our road. What we have to worry about are those – ' He indicated a glare starting to emerge on their right. 'That's Kao diggings. The road passes their front door, so to speak.'

It did. A stark scene – a series of grey prefabs of various shapes and sizes, plus a water tower, made starker by powerful flood-lights – showed up. The only softening effect was the snow, still heavier as the altitude increased.

Bonnay laid his pistol in his lap. 'Bright as bloody day. Why do they have to have all that light out here in these remote mountains?'

'More diamonds are stolen than ever reach the sorting-tables, they say,' said Stefan. His normally harsh voice took on a harsher edge. 'There may be a road block ahead – part of the security checking for stolen stones. They put checks down at odd times and make a snap search of traffic.'

The Chunnel Gang tightened their grip on their guns. Only Dr Poortman seemed aloof from what was going on.

Bonnay spotted it first. 'Barrier pole across the road!'

'I'm going to rush it. Use my AK, if you have to,' said Stefan.

He gunned the engine hard. The barrier had been cleverly sited near the summit of a steepish slope which automatically slowed approaching traffic. Under high revs and low gear, the van crawled at the checkpoint like an ant.

Bonnay, craning through the windscreen past the bullet-scores, said suddenly, 'Pole's up! It's unmanned!'

Then they were through.

'See anyone at all?' Stefan's was a rhetorical question.

'At this speed, it would have been a messy shoot-out,' observed Kennet from the rear.

'Perfect giveaway,' added Hayward, sitting on the other side of Dr Poortman.

'It didn't happen – and it can't happen now.' Stefan killed the discussion.

They pushed on in silence. The next thirty-five kilometres were a dark nightmare with white trappings. The surface of the road – if it could still go by that name – became execrable. At times the van's pace was down to that of a lame horse. The snow became thicker and thicker as they climbed up and up; the cold, despite the vehicle's warming system, seeped in until they were all grateful to wrap themselves in Dr Poortman's blankets.

169

At some undefined point in place and time the van slithered like a crab down the slippery side of a steep bank. At its foot was a river; the headlights showed white water foaming across stones in the bed.

Stefan gave it no name; no one cared. He piloted the van to the water's edge like a rider coaxing a reluctant horse to a jump. Water rose to the door sills; steam and condensing exhaust fumes poured from the van's rear like a mock-up comet.

A wild jolt threw Hayward almost into Dr Poortman's lap. If the banker had been smarter, or perhaps more wide awake, he might have capitalised on the jerk and grabbed Hayward's Colt. As it was, he seemed to reserve both hands for trying to hang on. Behind him, Pestiaux was rocketed from his seat and came down heavily on the steel floor. He dragged himself up again with an oath.

The steering wheel spun in Stefan's powerful grip this way and that from the impact of the boulders littering the crossing – then they were through, and went steaming up the far bank.

'Not far now, then we transfer,' commented Stefan.

It was, in fact, only several kilometres – no one could say how far, in those conditions – until Stefan slowed and indicated a track leading off to the right. The van bucked over more mini-boulders, more washed-out road surface; Stefan kept the lights on dip to spot the rocks close under the vehicle's nose. Suddenly, they were upon derelict buildings, wind-torn roofless sheds and shacks looming in the headlights.

Stefan made his way confidently between the ruined buildings; as the van passed one, a stray sheet of corrugated iron detached itself from somewhere and crashed down. Until it happened, no one in the van had realised the power of the wind. The snow had eased off; there was a coating of frozen sleet on the windscreen, mixing with the long cross-scores of Stefan's AK volley at the Bokong.

Stefan pulled up at a brick building. Part of the roof was missing. But it had doors; they were shut.

'In there – transfer vehicle,' said Stefan cryptically. 'Bring the jerry-cans. It'll take most of what we have.'

170

Hayward slid open the van's big side door. The men inside recoiled. The wind was like an icy dagger in their throats. They seemed hardly able to draw breath.

Stefan led the group – all except Dr Poortman – to the building, unhitched the wire round the clasp with which the doors were secured, and wrenched them open.

Inside was a white Toyota station wagon.

It had white upholstery.

Light from the van's headlights illuminated its registration plates.

Bonnay said, 'There's a police alert out for this vehicle also.'

Bonnay could not make out Stefan's pale eyes behind his goggles. He didn't have to. He could guess.

'So what?'

'Man called Jonathan stabbed to death, body found on the ombudsman's farm. Car missing. A white Toyota. Killed elsewhere, the police said.'

Stefan's reply seemed entangled in the wreath of frosty breath spilling from his mouth.

'You listen very hard to the radio news, don't you, my friend?'

'Yeah. There was an alert out for our van. So we stayed tuned in.'

'Then that makes two.' Stefan's words had a chill as piercing as the wind. 'If you don't want to ride on, you can always stay here and freeze to death.'

'I didn't say that.' Bonnay held himself in check. 'I was simply making an observation about the station wagon.'

'If you want to go on working with me, you'd better keep that sort of observation to yourself – see? Make up your mind. Are you coming?'

'I never said I wasn't.'

'Okay then, that's settled. Fetch Poortman. We're on our way once we've refuelled. Is he still in good shape?'

'Seems so. He can't get far, even if he ran.'

'Put any extra clobber you can on him.'

Bonnay went to summon Dr Poortman; the others busied themselves refuelling the station wagon and hefting all the heavy clothing and blankets from the van. Dr Poortman stood by,

171

watching. In his snow-goggles and swollen clothes, he looked like a cartoon of a king penguin. The Antarctic climate was certainly real.

When the transfer was complete, Stefan said, 'I'll bring the Toyota out. One of you can replace it with the van. Bring the keys afterwards – it'll make it more difficult for whoever finds it eventually.'

'Why not set it on fire?' asked Bonnay. 'There'd be no clues left.'

'No,' answered Stefan. 'These old diggings have a bad name with the tribesmen, and they never come here on their own. But the sight of a fire might attract someone. Otherwise the place will probably stay unvisited for weeks.'

'Which is what we want, isn't it?' said Bonnay.

'Nine days is all we want,' interjected Hayward. 'That's what it is to the opening – and Poortman's deadline.'

CHAPTER TWENTY-FIVE

They swapped the vehicles after Stefan had backed out the Toyota, and the six men were grateful to get out of the perishing wind and cram into the smaller station wagon.

Bonnay noticed dried blood on the white upholstery on the rear squab of the driver's seat; he wasn't squeamish, but nevertheless he exercised his status to occupy the front seat alongside Stefan, who drove.

Stefan started off again down the rough road. The Toyota's suspension was softer than the van's and its clearance lower, so that every so often the vehicle would bottom with a jarring crash. The windows fogged up with condensation; the car's heating and the men's own body heat kept the interior passable.

About five kilometres from the abandoned diggings, the track came to a T-junction. Stefan took the left-hand road – the surface seemed slightly better – and almost immediately they started to climb.

'Pass of Guns,' remarked Stefan. 'The road at the top goes through the clouds – over 3200 metres. There are two more passes to follow it, each about the same height.'

As if to underscore what he had said, the snow started up again. It grew heavier and heavier as Stefan pushed the overburdened vehicle up the pass, its wheels slipping and spinning, and its radiator temperature starting to soar, both from the pace and the altitude. The headlights revealed only an impenetrable curtain of white on either hand. The only way they had of telling that Stefan had surmounted the pass was that he was able to change into a higher gear.

They went on.

Now and again there would be a short hill up which Stefan pushed the Toyota at full bore. To Bonnay the drive was like a blind nightmare rally on a track on which anything could suddenly loom up and knock out the Toyota's sump and leave them with a steaming, useless hunk of metal in the middle of a killer-cold night. The two passes which followed would have made Bonnay sweat, if he could have sweated on a night like theirs.

If Stefan had meant to conceal his escape route, he certainly succeeded. They could have travelled any distance – it was, in fact, about thirty-five kilometres – along a track which seemed to head diabolically for almost every patch of non-negotiable basalt, up which the spinning wheels had to claw a way, filling the interior with the stink of singeing rubber. The snow was almost continuous now.

Then the station wagon's nose dipped, as if it were headed for a ravine or steep valley.

'Big danger ahead!' snapped Stefan. 'It's the Malibamatso River again, near its headwaters. Next to it is Oxbow Lodge, one of the best skiing centres in the country. It's probably full of visitors right now. Our road goes right past the door – there's no other way. Keep a gun in Poortman's ribs, in case he tries to attract attention. The place is always lit up . . .'

Oxbow Lodge looked unbelievably beautiful under snow, with powerful floodlights making the thatched chalets and buildings, designed to typify Lesotho architecture, glisten; the Lodge was backed by a cliffside with trees and shrubs which were a fairyland.

The road improved as they got in sight of Oxbow and Stefan speeded up. Their road by-passed by only a few metres the main entrance to the complex – a central triangular-roofed building flanked by two round ones.

The Toyota stormed past: through the big glass double doors Bonnay had a glimpse of men and women inside in a warm glow.

Then they were past.

'Think we were spotted?' Hayward asked.

Stefan countered with a question of his own. 'Did you see anyone look out?'

'Maybe, maybe not,' responded Bonnay. 'I saw people inside. We were past in a flash.'

'You can bet that later someone will remember that tonight a car went past at speed without stopping. On a night like this, that's something,' said Stefan.

The plunge into darkness beyond Oxbow's lights was almost palpable. The road improved, but visibility was worse. Stefan was forced down to almost a walking-pace.

They crossed a big river a few kilometres further on and almost immediately started up what seemed to be a sharp ridge. This was followed by a long haul (anything up to four or five kilometres, Bonnay guessed) with snow dumping itself out of the clouds so close above their heads that they could almost reach up and touch them. The engine was wheezing and near boiling point. Then they levelled out.

Stefan said abruptly, 'If it interests you, this is the highest point reached by ordinary vehicles in Southern Africa.' He braked to a halt. 'Now, out! We go on from here on foot.'

Hayward's exclamation put the question in all their minds.

'On foot? How far?'

'As far as I say,' retorted Stefan. 'And that's what I say.'

'What about the Toyota?' asked Bonnay.

'Get yourselves and all the clobber out before I release the handbrake.'

'Isn't there a chance that it could be spotted – I mean, once the snow clears?' Hayward persisted.

'You can't see the drop, or else it would turn your stomach over,' replied Stefan. 'It's about 800 metres. Anyone is welcome to look for a smashed-up load of junk at the bottom.'

If the wind had been remorseless before, it was merciless now. Even with their heavy protective clothing and goggles, they could hardly bear to face it head-on. Stefan wrapped a blanket round Dr Poortman. It wasn't a caring gesture.

'Stand clear!'

Stefan removed the ignition keys, snapped off the handbrake, and then jumped out. The rest of the group stood back, watching the Toyota run backwards, gather speed, and become one with the whirling snow as it vanished over the edge.

Not Dr Poortman.

The others had been so immersed in watching the demolition job on the station wagon that they did not notice the banker edge away from the group, turn, and start down the road in the direction of Oxbow Lodge. He shed the blanket, moving at an awkward shambling trot because of his snow boots and heavy clothes.

Stefan turned to the group, and saw their prisoner was missing. His reactions were lightning-fast.

'I'll get him!'

There was no race, really. Stefan was up with him in seconds, dodged purposefully right to the banker's right side – the side of the precipice – and threw an armlock round him above the elbow.

'Don't be bloody silly!' There was hardly any anger in Stefan's remark. 'There's a drop next to me here which will take you into eternity. You'd never get to Oxbow alive – you can't see where you're going!'

Dr Poortman tried to fend him off, but that was not the sort of thing to try on with the Maluti Rider. Stefan laughed and wheeled him round bodily, tightened his armhold, and marched him back to the group.

'Get his blanket, one of you.' Then he said tightly to Dr Poortman, 'Don't try anything funny again. Just keep going, and you'll be okay. That goes for everyone. Stick with the party, or else . . .'

He led the group up the road – Dr Poortman in the centre, flanked by two members of the gang on either side – for a couple of hundred metres, and then turned aside. They could not see where they were going in the murk. They stumbled down a rough slope following the Maluti Rider. After a further couple of hundred metres, Stefan stopped, and turned on his flashlight. In its limited light, there seemed to be a small rock overhang among stunted trees and bushes.

Stefan called out something, and a grotesque, blanketed figure came towards them. It was bigger than a man, smaller than a nightmare. A head and two hairy ears stood out.

'That's my girl!' exclaimed Stefan. The Basuto pony came and nudged its muzzle into his chest. 'She's one of my best,' he said to no one in particular. 'Not as good as Major down on the Bokong, but for sure-footedness she'll beat a mountain goat. Neither of them has ever let me down. She'd wait here all night in the snow for me to come.' He addressed Dr Poortman. 'Can you ride?'

'Yes. But it's a long time ago.'

176

'She doesn't have a saddle. The blanket doubles as one. She'll lead us home.'

Pestiaux said, 'None of us are mountaineers. How far is it?'

'If I told you, I'd have to shoot you to keep the secret,' was Stefan's curt response.

Stefan helped Dr Poortman on to the horse's back and then took the halter – she had no bridle or bit – in his gloved hand.

Stefan led, the others followed.

The snow, the snow!

Each soft flake seemed to become an object of lancing torment as the party, in single file behind Stefan and his horse, headed into the wind. It fell heavier; the cold became more intense.

Up, up, up! It was like walking into an indefinable wall of white: there was no dimension, no point of reference to judge the scale or the distance.

More and more snow. Bonnay's eyes began to ache, and he was in distress from a constant feeling of nausea which over-took him. He began to feel dizzy and breathless from the altitude. He tried to keep his eyes focused on the horse's tail, and the unreal white figure of the banker perched on its back. Whiteness flowed over his shoulders like a shawl.

Without warning, he walked into the rump of the animal. It had stopped. Stefan came round from the front, wiping the snow clear of his goggles.

'Are we there?' asked Bonnay.

'Food stop,' replied Stefan briefly. 'Fuel for the last leg.'

He addressed Dr Poortman, 'Down! I need to get at the saddlebags.'

But Dr Poortman remained oblivious to his words. Bonnay wondered whether he was dead.

He wasn't. Stefan manhandled him down; he stood like an automaton where he landed, but he ate the chocolate which Stefan handed out. They munched in silence; there was no-thing to drink, nothing hot.

The horse stood with her head in the group as if she belonged; she had her share of something Stefan took from a saddlebag for her.

Then Stefan took some *biltong* – dried cured strips of meat –

and handed them round. They were black and about as long as a man's boot. And as hard.

'Keep on chewing,' ordered Stefan. 'This will keep your strength up. There's one bad section, and then we're home.'

The sight of the *biltong* revolted Bonnay's sensitive stomach; he wanted to vomit. A bad section still to come! What had they already been through!

Dr Poortman remounted; they pushed on. It was after midnight.

Their pace was slower now, the upward slope was steeper. Bonnay concentrated on the horse's tail; it seemed the only part of her not covered in a fine armour of white.

As his body suffered more privation from the bitter cold and still rising altitude, his mind seemed to take flight from the present. Long forgotten incidents from his past floated up before him, but they were sterile and unreal, made more so by the snow and ice all round. There was nothing to be seen except a white wall into which they burrowed.

The snow grew deeper, the cold more vicious, the wind more remorseless. Bonnay's heart beat so violently that all he wanted to do was to lie down and merge himself with the soft snow. From behind he heard the sound of slightly hysterical keening – it was Hayward, intoning in a child-like voice to lost saints of childhood. Kennet was grunting like a bear *in extremis*; Pestiaux was sobbing and cursing in French.

Bonnay had no idea of when he started to hallucinate; he might have been stumbling on for one or a hundred kilometres. His mind was now as empty and foggy as the view. He was only dimly aware that the nature of the terrain had changed: it was now hard underfoot instead of softness at one stage and broken scree at the other.

He stumbled again into the horse's rear. It had halted; Stefan had given up the lead and had come to join him. He had thrown the halter over the mare's head.

'What?' he managed to say.

'She'll take us in.' Stefan's voice was thick, anxious. 'She doesn't need me. It's one hell of a drop on both sides. She knows the path better than I do.'

Bonnay for once was grateful for the anaesthetising effect of the altitude and the march. Height – risk – death – it didn't matter any more. Nothing mattered, any more.

Stefan called out something to the mare. She moved forward slowly, picking her way. Bonnay, thinking of Stefan's warning of a precipice, edged forward to take the horse's tail as a guide.

'Keep your hands off her!' snarled Stefan. 'Do you want her to slip and kill us all?'

She did slip.

It was Dr Poortman's fault.

Perhaps he blacked out, perhaps he fell asleep from oxygen starvation at the altitude.

He suddenly slumped sideways, to the left.

The horse's left hind hoof lost its goat-like grip on the icy slipperiness of the rock. It was off-camber; it must have been some kind of narrow whale-back bridge between peaks.

She gave a fart of fear, scrabbled for a hold with the unshod hoof; her entire body seemed to start moving slowly towards whatever fearsome drop there might be. She knew the danger: she gave a scream of fear which cut off in mid-breath.

Stefan threw his right shoulder against her left rear flank, propping her up momentarily while she fought for a foothold. At the same time, Stefan leaned up to the blanket-saddle and punched savagely at the banker with his left fist.

'Wake up, you bastard! Sit up straight, damn you! You're taking her over the edge!'

The message must have got through whatever was fogging Dr Poortman's mind. He swung upright; Stefan grabbed the kicking hoof and jammed it hard against the rock; she steadied herself and stood still in a clever instinctive way which had been bred into the genes of her mountain ancestors.

Stefan eased his shoulder away from propping her flank and picked his way carefully across the icy rock to join Bonnay at the mare's tail.

Bonnay, like the others, had simply stood still while Stefan made his lightning-fast rescue. Perhaps his brain, like theirs, was fazed through exhaustion and lack of oxygen. They would probably have all stood like that and watched horse, rider and Stefan go over the edge without an attempt to save them.

Stefan put his hand on the mare's flank and spoke to her in a language Bonnay did not understand. He kept his hand there until her kicking muscles subsided; then, of her own accord, she moved forward again into the thicket of snow.

In minutes it was all over.

They must have passed from the rock bridge into a cut in the mountainside; the uneasing fusillade of snow dropped away to a few isolated pellets; most merciful of all, the wind, which had generated a chill factor far below zero, stilled. By comparison with the past hours, it was almost warm; only the halo of spent breath round the mare's nostrils bore witness to her ordeal.

Stefan took over the halter again; they could not see the rock walls on either side, but it grew more protected and relatively warmer as they moved deeper into the cut.

Stefan shone his flashlight ahead. A wall of rock daubed with ochred Bushmen figures confronted them. There was no way through.

The way was up, up a rope ladder which hung from the cliff top out of sight above their heads. They climbed the rungs like zombies. Once they had scaled the cliff Stefan opened a trapdoor with a concealed ringbolt on the cliff top and lowered the rope ladder again into darkness.

'Down!' he ordered. 'You're safe. The hide-out!'

CHAPTER TWENTY-SIX

'Have you got a million dollars?'

The telephone spat out the question without preliminary. Not even a routine query to check who was answering.

But Sholto, taking the call at 'Cherry Now' next morning in the alcove off the breakfast-room where he and Grania had finished breakfast a short time before, recognised both the voice and style of the caller. It was General Mak.

'Not on me, General Mak, but just give me time to slip into town and cash a cheque,' Sholto answered. A preposterous question called for a flippant reply.

General Mak went on: 'I have here in my hand a note addressed to you demanding a million dollars.'

Sholto laughed, still not taking the conversation seriously. He felt good, despite the dark cloud of Jonathan's murder: although Grania seemed to be avoiding any confrontation with him regarding her incomprehensible attitude during her absence in Switzerland, she appeared to be drawing closer to him all the time. They had been planning to go to Maseru together that morning, which was Thursday. She had been standing, dressed in her favourite ski clothes against the cold day, close to the phone when General Mak's call had come through, so she could overhear part of the exchange.

'Is it a chain-letter?' went on Sholto in the same vein. 'You security guys must be pretty much on the ball to intercept my correspondence.'

'Perhaps it will interest you to know where I am speaking from, Sholto.'

'Maseru – from your headquarters, I guess.'

'Katse Lodge.'

The security chief's voice was flatter, more brittle, than before.

Sholto realised immediately from his tone that something was amiss. He could not think of a suitable response.

'Katse Lodge?' he echoed.

'I flew in here a short while ago after security at Katse Lodge phoned me – at home – about this note addressed to you.'

'Read it to me. Otherwise I'm in the dark about what you're trying to tell me.'

'Not over a phone which might have ears. I want you to get to Katse Lodge – right away.'

'I was just about to leave for Maseru with Grania . . .'

'I'm not asking you, it's an order. Get here as quick as you can.'

'What is this all about?'

'It's not an ordinary note. It's a demand for a ransom.'

'Ransom? Me? Someone must be out of their mind!'

'If I thought so, I wouldn't be sitting right here. I'm deadly serious, Sholto. They're not asking a million for you.'

'In heaven's name, for whom, then?'

'Dr Poortman.'

'*Dr Poortman*! You must be joking!'

'Get up here right away,' snapped General Mak. 'Bring along plenty to identify yourself. My security guys are pretty trigger-happy around Katse this morning – after the stable door has been closed.' His voice grated. 'Pity they hadn't been as wide awake last night. Anyway, that's not your problem.'

'Can I bring Grania?'

There was a moment's pause and then General Mak said, 'Yes, she's involved with Dr Poortman through the Eagle of Time. He's her father's friend also. Yes, she can come. I'll give orders for you to get priority clearance when you arrive. There's no knowing, however, what can happen at local level by some over-enthusiastic sonofabitch.'

General Mak's security net was certainly far-flung. It began as far away from Katse as the big highway bridge over the Malibamatso upstream from the dam (under which Stefan and the Chunnel Gang had passed the previous night) where there was a road block manned by armed men. Despite General Mak's orders, the men double-checked Sholto and Grania's documents and searched the car before allowing them through.

There was no enjoyment in the drive for either Sholto or

Grania even though the peaks of the Malutis were splendid under their previous night's coating of snow and their sides laced with unmelted runnels of silver ice.

'Where is Dr Poortman now?' asked Grania when Sholto outlined General Mak's message. 'Who is holding him to ransom?'

Sholto shook his head. 'He only told me enough to tantalise me. He wouldn't say who made the demand because he was afraid he might be overheard.'

'A million dollars! Why ask *you* for a million dollars?'

'General Mak left more unsaid than said. Why should I be the target?'

'Sholto,' said Grania quietly, 'you could ask yourself the same about Jonathan.' She leaned forward and put her hand on his driving hand. 'That worried me stiff. Now I'm scared out of my mind – for you.'

Now is your moment, Sholto, ask her what happened in Switzerland. Ask her why she did it to you.

He turned to her; she was looking fixedly ahead. He was sure of her in one way, desperately unsure of her in another. He wanted the sure way to go on for a while, like now, at least. He let it ride. They drove on in silence.

After they had traversed the summit of the road where it broke through the mountains and threw open the great view to the east, now stunningly august in purple and white, they dropped down towards the Bokong.

Grania said, 'Get across the Bokong as quickly as you can, Sholto. That place has bad vibes.'

'On our way back from Katse Lodge, I'd like to take another look,' replied Sholto. 'We may find some fresh clues in the better light.'

'I'll be like a cat on hot bricks all the time we're there.'

It was, however, General Mak who was like a cat on hot bricks when Sholto and Grania were ushered into his presence by two men armed with automatic rifles. He was chain-smoking in Dr Poortman's lounge-suite, the same room from which the banker had been snatched the night before. He had set up a kind of command headquarters in the hut; there seemed to be men everywhere.

'Out!' The security chief dismissed the guards and two officers with a jerk of the head. 'And tell the switchboard I don't want any further calls for the next half-hour,' he said harshly. ' – Unless Dr Poortman is located.'

When the men had gone, General Mak took a slip of paper from a folder on the table – Dr Poortman's documents were still there – and handed it to Sholto.

'It's already been checked for fingerprints,' he said. 'None. The kidnappers were professionals. Read it out.'

To Mr Sholto Banks, Ombudsman, the Swiss Banking Consortium in Lesotho:

Dr Poortman is being held in a place of safety. He is safe and unharmed. He will be released on payment of one million US dollars at a rendezvous to be mutually determined and guarantees of safe conduct by air from Maseru to an international destination. This demand must be met my midday on the day of the opening ceremony of the Lesotho Highlands Project. Failure to comply with our demands will result in the death of Dr Poortman. Official communication with the kidnappers must be made immediately before the main news bulletins on Radio Lesotho.

Signed,
       The Chunnel Gang
       The Maluti Rider

Sholto gave a long whistle. 'The Chunnel Gang! You know who they are, don't you?'

'I know.'

'What in heaven's name are they doing in Lesotho? They're an international gang. They disappeared after they failed to blow up the Chunnel Project . . .'

'I know, I know,' retorted General Mak. 'I've already contacted Interpol to try and find out if they know anything up-to-date about them.'

'Plus the Maluti Rider!' added Sholto. 'Is this note a hoax? If it isn't, it's a pretty formidable line-up.'

'That's what I intend finding out, and that someone's not trying to cash in on their notoriety.'

Grania intervened. 'We're in the dark about the whole affair. How and when was Dr Poortman abducted from here? Who discovered it?'

'Dr Poortman was due to fly to Johannesburg today at 9.30, you know that already. He was being flown to Maseru from Katse at 8.30. He arranged with the Lodge staff to be called for breakfast at 7.30. When he didn't show up, the manager came and knocked. He noticed that the bedroom light was on – blast it, what did he expect on a grey morning like today? It must have been burning half the night, maybe the whole night, for all we know! The manager couldn't get a reply, and tried Dr Poortman's phone. No reply, of course. He opened the suite with his master-key and found him missing.'

'Any signs of a struggle?'

'None. Odd, the blankets were missing from his bed, but not his pyjamas. Among the documents on this very table was that . . .' He gestured angrily at the note in Sholto's hands. 'He went straight to Security. They contacted me. I got up here by plane right away and took personal command of the search.'

'Have you found any clues?' asked Grania.

General Mak ground out his cigarette. 'No. It was a neat professional job – no break-in, no signs of escape, security wire intact, not a sound heard by the guards on duty or anyone else. Bah!'

'Does the media know?' asked Sholto.

'Not at this stage, praises be!' replied General Mak. 'But they will have to. You can't keep a thing like this in the dark.' General Mak's attitude suddenly hardened. 'Sit down, both of you. I want to ask you some questions.'

'Go ahead,' answered Sholto.

'Why should the ransom note be addressed to you, Sholto? With that sort of money involved, surely the more appropriate people would be the Lesotho and South African governments?'

General Mak's attitude was not suspicious, but it certainly was probing. 'I'm not involved, if that's what you're hinting at,' Sholto laughed briefly. 'Do you want an alibi for last night? Grania and I were together at "Cherry Now".'

185

General Mak ignored his assertion. 'The Chunnel Gang,' he mused. 'What the devil should the Chunnel Gang be doing in Lesotho? If that signature is kosher, how in hell did they get into Lesotho in the first place? You were involved with the Chunnel Project, weren't you, Sholto? How could the gang have known your position and status here? How did the gang trace you to Lesotho? Have you had any suspicious contacts recently from anyone?'

'No one has approached me recently,' replied Sholto levelly. 'The only strange thing I know was Jonathan's hint of an informer the night before his death . . .'

'Jonathan's killing and this business have nothing in common,' General Mak said brusquely. 'I know he was a friend of yours, but get any connection out of your head right away. Jonathan's was a simple case of stabbing. This kidnap has frightening implications for the Highlands Project. It's a bigger thing altogether. Too damn big, for my liking.'

'The Eagle of Time was involved in the Chunnel Project also,' Grania observed thoughtfully. 'The artist, Elie Kiefer, died, and I was given the job to finish it.'

'Don't whomp up connections where they don't exist,' replied General Mak tightly. 'What I am looking for is a strong lead, something hard to go on.'

CHAPTER TWENTY-SEVEN

The security chief lit yet another cigarette and waited for Sholto to answer his questions.

'I severed my connection with the Chunnel Project seven years ago in 1988, when my father died and I returned to the farm at Ficksburg,' Sholto replied. 'It was only in November 1992 that I was offered the job as ombudsman to the Highlands Project in Lesotho. As you know, the Eurotunnel was successfully opened two years ago in mid-1993.'

'And it damn near didn't open, thanks to the Chunnel Gang,' General Mak cut in. 'They were after the British and French heads of state, you no doubt remember. Scotland Yard found enough high explosive to have caused a minor tidal wave in the Channel had it gone off. And now these thugs have surfaced in Lesotho! How have they come to team up with a bandit like the Maluti Rider? He's always operated on his own; maybe that's why he's got away with it up to now. However, he's been turning on the heat recently – look at that shoot-up the other day. And now it's the Highlands Project itself.'

'He's been after the construction convoys for a long time now,' Sholto pointed out.

'You don't have to remind me,' snapped back General Mak.

'Apart from the Lodge staff and his pilot, you were one of the last people to speak to Dr Poortman,' the security chief went on. 'Did he give any hint of trouble?'

'None at all.'

'Were his blankets all that was stolen?' asked Grania.

'No,' replied General Mak. 'Oddly enough, the ski hut was ransacked and a lot of warm gear taken.'

'That could point to the mountains,' said Sholto.

'Of course it does – but where does it get me?' asked General Mak. 'There's not a trace round the Lodge of an escape route, and last night's snow would have provided the perfect cover.'

'It all presupposes local knowledge,' said Sholto. 'Without it, anyone who ventured out last night would be dead by now.'

'Maybe he is,' added General Mak. 'I'm asking the South Africans to lend me a helicopter for a mountain search this afternoon, just in case. You know the mountains better than anyone else, Sholto; will you fly with the chopper?'

'Yes. But I'm not hopeful. The peaks are still thick with snow. A body or bodies could be hidden all winter.'

'I know, I know!' retorted General Mak. 'But it's a routine precaution I must take.' He addressed Grania. 'Dr Poortman was a family friend; are you sure he said nothing – an aside perhaps – which might have a bearing on the kidnap?'

Grania shook her dark head. 'There was nothing of that sort. It was all on an official level. Dr Poortman seemed very pleased with the way everything had gone. The only thing which didn't please him was the thought of an extra security guard tagging along behind him; but you were there when he objected.'

'I wish now to high heaven that I had insisted!' exclaimed General Mak. 'I've got to get a lead quickly! Immediately I was given the news of Dr Poortman's kidnap, I phoned the Prime Minister.' The cigarette shook in his hand as if the premier's words were still blasting at him. 'Nothing, but nothing, must stand in the way of the Highlands Project opening. It's only eight days away – Friday afternoon next week!'

'That gives a little elbowroom, at any rate.' Sholto tried to cheer him.

'It doesn't,' snapped back the security chief. 'Not when the media and the government are sitting on your neck wanting results! Even if we knew where they were holed up with Dr Poortman, negotiations would take time . . .' He pulled himself up, as if he was admonishing himself inwardly for indulging his emotions. 'I have got to get a lead *today*! The first thing I want to know is, how long has the Chunnel Gang been in Lesotho? How'd they get here in the first place? Who let in a bunch of thugs like that? With their sort of track record, how did they get past our immigration authorities?'

'I'd say, still more important is how they managed to establish communication with a bandit like the Maluti Rider, who has never been anything more than a shadow,' said Sholto. 'How could there be a link between an international gang like them and a mountain desperado thousands of kilometres away in another continent?'

'You're the only connection with the Chunnel Project that I know of,' said General Mak. 'That is why I asked you here, apart from the fact that the ransom note is addressed to you.'

'I haven't the Maluti Rider's whereabouts in my address book,' laughed Sholto.

'You may have been used, without your knowing it,' said General Mak darkly. 'Go away and do a lot of thinking, man! If anything strikes you, phone me, however way-out it may seem.'

'There's Jonathan . . .' began Sholto, but General Mak cut him short.

'Forget it, I say again, Sholto. Don't go barking up that tree and lose sight of the hot potato on our plates. Concentrate on the Chunnel Gang.'

'What about the Maluti Rider?' Grania asked.

'He seems to have got away with his exploits for so long that one is inclined to think of him as infallible,' replied General Mak. 'If I knew where to begin on him, I would have done so long ago. He brings a hellish dimension to this whole business.'

'Do you think he would actually kill Dr Poortman as the note threatens if the demand is not met?' she persisted.

General Mak stood up and strode up and down before replying. Finally, he snapped, 'Yes, I do. Look at the way he slaughtered the men and children in the mountains after he'd set fire to their huts. It's probably lucky for the tribe that they were relocated because of the Highlands Project works in their area.'

'Could the Chunnel Gang be using the Maluti Rider as their hit man?' asked Sholto.

'I'd say they were quite capable of doing their own dirty work,' replied General Mak. 'What worries me is how two such notorious parties teamed up.'

'Have you been in touch with the banking consortium over the ransom demand?' asked Sholto.

General Mak smiled thinly. 'That's your baby, Sholto. You can break it to 'em. It's addressed to you, as their representative.'

'Can I use your phone?'

'No. There are too many ears which might be listening. Use your office in Maseru.'

'It's quicker to "Cherry Now". Grania and I will get back there right away.'

'The Lesotho and South African governments are in this thing right up to their necks,' went on General Mak. 'I'll also have to bring in South African Security, in a limited way, if I want their helicopter.'

'When and where do I meet it?' asked Sholto. 'What is your target search area?'

The security chief shrugged his broad shoulders. 'Your guess is as good as mine. Could be anywhere.'

'That ski gear gives us a clue. I'll go for the mountains, make a big sweep to the north and northeast. Okay?'

'The chopper will have to come from the nearest base in Bloemfontein – that's 150 kilometres away,' went on General Mak. 'To save time, I'll arrange for it to pick you up on your farm. Let's make a tentative ETA of 1.30 this afternoon. Suit you?'

'Fine. But don't expect too much of the search. That was a pretty heavy fall of snow last night.'

'I know, I know!' retorted the security chief. 'The odds are against us.'

'That's the way the Maluti Rider operates,' added Sholto.

'It's all so professional, so well thought out. That's why I think the signatures on the ransom note are genuine,' said General Mak. He dismissed Sholto and Grania with a glance at his watch. 'Let me know as soon as you have spoken to Switzerland.' He opened the door and spoke to a guard: 'See that these two get straight back to their car. Skip the searches. My orders, see?'

The number of guns in evidence round Katse Lodge could have shot the tops off the Maluti's peaks, thought Sholto. Eventually they found themselves safely in their car.

Sholto said, 'Grania, I'm stopping at the Bokong Crossing to take another look.'

'*What* are you looking for, Sholto?'

'I don't know, only I have this powerful hunch that Jonathan and the kidnapping are related.'

'In what way? You heard General Mak's opinion.'

'Dr Poortman's kidnap was a highly professional effort – not a single loose end, not a single clue. Jonathan is the one loose end – a messy killing.'

'*If* the two are connected.'

'Jonathan *knew* something that night when he came to me. If only he'd gone further!'

'Do you think he knew the kidnap was in train?'

'Grania, I don't know. If he did, I ask myself, would he have kept anything as big and important as that to himself without confiding in me?'

They crossed the Malibamatso by the fine new highway bridge. On the northern and northeastern horizon – where Sholto was bound in the helicopter – the mountains were a majestic and mysterious coronet against the sky.

Sholto gestured towards them. 'Dr Poortman and the kidnappers could be anywhere among that lot.'

When they reached the Bokong Crossing, Sholto noted the water level. 'It's deeper than it was when we were here this morning; snow's melting higher up. Let's find the River Lily spot and cast about from there.'

They made their way along the river bank and then up towards the waterfall. They reached the River Lily site.

Suddenly Grania burst out urgently, 'Sholto! Look! Over there, among the bushes, across the waterfall!'

'What is it?'

'It looks like the sun shining on a handful of coins . . .'

They had to make a detour to cross the waterfall to the place Grania had indicated. In a flash, Sholto dropped on his knees among the bright things scattered about.

'They aren't coins,' he said grimly. 'They're cartridge cases.'

He held out a palmful to her. 'Newly fired. Look how bright they are; the metal hasn't even had time to tarnish.'

'We cased all this area before,' said Grania. 'They weren't here then.'

Sholto indicated the firing-rim. 'Russian.'

'Look how the grass has been flattened,' said Grania.

'Something happened here. I mean to find out,' said Sholto.

'Maybe the kidnappers brought Dr Poortman here and shot him.'

'It doesn't require that amount of ammunition to shoot one man,' answered Sholto. 'Besides, Dr Poortman alive is worth a million to them; dead, he's worth nothing at all.'

'Let's try further and see what else we find.'

The patch of horse manure was there under a small tree and hooves had trampled the grass flat.

Grania eyed Sholto questioningly. 'A horse, a volley of automatic fire – it seems to have the stamp of a familiar scenario, Sholto.'

'What was the Maluti Rider doing here? Shooting up what? When at the same time he was kidnapping – or helping to kidnap – Dr Poortman? There are no reports of convoys or people being waylaid on this road yesterday.'

'Are you going to inform General Mak about this, Sholto?'

Sholto tossed a handful of shellcases thoughtfully in his hand. 'No, not at this stage. You saw how he reacted to my suggestion about Jonathan. He'll say I am trying to force a further connection between the two incidents.'

'But you think there is a connection nevertheless?'

'If I can find some further, firmer evidence I'll tell General Mak. We'll see what the helicopter sweep yields this afternoon.'

The Puma of the South African Air Force landed at lunchtime on the wide front lawn of 'Cherry Now' to collect Sholto with the punctuality of the Orient Express.

The slipstream pinned Grania's dark hair against her head as it lifted off and headed northeast into the Lesotho mountains. She stood immobile with her hand raised in a goodbye salute long after it had clattered away. Her sight stayed locked on it until it became a speck in the distance as if she were afraid to let it go. Her eyes were as empty as the sky, as if they had witnessed more things than any woman should have been called upon to witness.

CHAPTER TWENTY-EIGHT

'It's like looking for a flea under a polar bear's armpit.'

The Puma helicopter pilot, whose name was Major Len Badenhorst, gestured ahead. The machine had just left behind the Malibamatso River and had turned ninety degrees to follow the diamond track to Kao and the old abandoned diggings further on. The other three occupants of the aircraft – the pilot, his copilot McLachlan, and a security captain whom General Mak had designated to join the flight from Maseru – all looked to Sholto to take the lead and direct the operation. Inwardly, he agreed with the pilot's comment; for want of anywhere better, he had begun with Katse Lodge. From there, he had instinctively followed the course of the river northwards, inadvertently following the kidnap van's route.

'If only we knew what our flea looked like,' interjected the security man. He had an unpronounceable name derived from the mysterious rock pinnacle called Qiloane near Moshoeshoe's mountain fastness grave. 'Call me Phil,' he had told the search party. He had a face honed thin by cynicism and mistrust of his fellow humans; the poison had dripped into his voice, too, and left it caustic.

'Trouble is, we don't know what it looks like, except that there are six men together, one of them Dr Poortman.'

'They couldn't have fled on foot last night,' observed Len the pilot.

'If they did, then maybe we'll come upon their bodies,' added Phil with a ghoulish laugh.

Sholto said, 'General Mak links the theft of a security van in Maseru yesterday morning with the kidnap. If that is so, we are looking for a green camouflaged van.'

'Standard type,' added Phil. 'You can see 'em everywhere on the road today, ever since they set up road blocks yesterday. Is

194

there anything concrete to show that the party left Katse Lodge in such a stolen van last night?'

'No, except by putting two and two together,' answered Sholto. 'Equally, there is nothing to show that I am not heading on a totally wild goose chase. The kidnappers could have left Katse in an air-conditioned Mercedes and driven back to Maseru and at this moment could be sitting in front of a warm fire in a house in the city playing patience and waiting for reaction to their ransom demand.'

'While we grind our arses out looking at the snow,' said Phil.

The machine was following the rising trend of the terrain beyond the river, out of the great valley, and then on to the snowfields the storm had confected during the night.

'Here come two fleas now,' said Mac unexpectedly.

Phil leaned forward. 'They're heading the wrong way if they're searching for kidnappers.'

'Signal 'em?' asked Len. 'Or just drop down on them?'

'Those guys are probably trigger-happy. Don't try on anything out of the ordinary routine.'

'Then call 'em up, Mac – special search frequency,' ordered the pilot. 'Ask if they've found any clues.'

The two vans came bumbling along the track and the helicopter made a circle while Mac spoke.

'No dice,' he said when the conversation had finished. 'The guy down there says they've questioned people at the diggings far back from the road and also those at Kao. No one saw anything, not even a headlight.'

'How can they be certain?' asked Phil in his carping voice.

'Kao security had a road block operating last night. Not one vehicle after dark. It finally got so damn cold they shut it down at nine o'clock and went home.'

Sholto told the operator, 'Tell 'em we're following the track up past the old diggings. After that, we'll play it by ear.'

'What's the use of following the road?' demanded Phil. 'It's the last place they'd stick to.'

Sholto waved beyond the windscreen. 'You'll see for yourself soon. There's no place to hide, except the road. And I'm not so sure about that either.'

The snow had put such a cosmetic coating over the abandoned diggings further on that Sholto thought for a while that they had overshot. However, he spotted the turn-off by a lucky chance and showed Len.

'Let's have a look there for tracks, in case anyone came here . . .'

'Then they'd be crazy,' interjected Phil. 'What's the temperature outside, Len?'

'Minus fifteen degrees Celsius,' the pilot replied after checking his instruments. 'The cold's holding the snow together.'

'I guess it's also a sort of overspill from the two passes ahead,' said Sholto. 'Both are over 3000 metres.'

'Not a tyre track, not a footprint,' commented the pilot. 'But you wouldn't expect any – it's been snowing all night.'

'Let's take a look-see at the place itself,' said Sholto.

The derelict prefabs and rusted machinery cowered away in the snow like a down-and-out in a Salvation Army shelter.'

The pilot checked the dials in front of him. 'I'll go if you say, but I don't know what you've got in mind for afterwards. I gotta watch the fuel. We don't want to run short and have to ditch somewhere up there . . .' he waved at the formidable barrier of peaks and whiteness blocking their horizon to the north and east ' – and create another crisis.'

'One quick flyover should be enough,' said Sholto.

It was. The ruined diggings were as placid as a nun's face; the caved-in roof of the building in which Stefan had locked the security van had canted still further with the weight of the snow, so that it was all white to the sky above. Had the helicopter crew been specifically searching for it, they might have taken time to check one by one a dozen other buildings exactly like it. As it was, the machine's quick pass was as unyielding in its revelations as a magician's sleight-of-hand.

'Now?' asked Len, after they had cleared the diggings.

'Beyond the Pass of Guns – that's the next pass up the road – we'll strike away from the road. There's a bridle path running northwards from the pass to Mont-aux-Sources – that's the source of our three biggest rivers. We'll then head off on the leg of a triangle from there to Oxbow.'

196

Mac spotted the bridle path first; the pilot pointed the machine's nose north.

'Good grief!' he exclaimed softly, gesturing ahead with a gloved hand. 'What do you expect to find there?'

This was the true majesty of the Drakensberg, the Dragon Mountains. The peaks were white with haze and aeons of inaccessibility, high above the world and one with the eternal sky. The feathery mantle which overlaid them had nothing of softness; its name was death.

Phil summed it up in his cynical way. 'If they're out there, then all we're looking for is bodies.'

Nevertheless, they flew on for about a dozen kilometres, the scenery growing in immensity, and their chances of spotting anything diminishing in proportion.

Eventually, when they were within distant sight of Mont-aux-Sources and Len was starting to fuss over his fuel gauge, Sholto called off the search in that direction.

'Oxbow, turn west for Oxbow,' he told the pilot.

The helicopter was already within visual range of the road Stefan had followed from the Pass of Guns in Jonathan's station wagon, traversing a snow field which looked like an outsize attempt at whipped meringue, when Sholto saw something moving far below.

'There she blows!' he called, using the old whalerman's cry. 'Rightwards, moving right!'

Len banked to get the object in his vision.

'Tracks below,' added Sholto. He craned forward. At first he thought the blanket concealed a tribesman, but as they came closer he said, 'Horse! It's a horse with a blanket over it!'

When the animal heard the roar of the approaching rotors, it threw back its head and doubled away at a gallop.

'Look,' said Sholto. 'He's been travelling as straight as a train – those tracks look as if you'd drawn them with a ruler.'

'Shoot him up?' asked Len, banking and trying to keep above the startled animal. 'We could go on doing this until he drops.'

'I wish we'd left him to see where he intended to go,' replied Sholto. 'That horse is heading somewhere definite. And why the blanket?'

197

Phil interjected in a bored voice, 'You're making bricks without straw. That's the way the tribesmen always dress their horses when it's freezing. He's probably heading home, that's all. Basuto ponies are uncanny at finding their way.'

The horse had now stopped and was trying to locate the position of its tormentor in the sky.

'Northwest,' said Sholto half to himself. 'He was heading northwest.'

Len tapped the fuel gauge on the instrument panel as a reminder.

'There are lots of wild horses up here in these mountains,' Phil dismissed the subject.

'But they don't run in a dead straight line,' answered Sholto. 'My guess is that that horse knows where he's going.'

'One horse couldn't carry six men, if that is your thinking,' interrupted Phil. 'It's got nothing to do with the kidnapping. It's just another wild horse.'

'Okay,' said Sholto. 'But give me a heading of those tracks before we go, will you, Len?'

'North-northwest,' answered the pilot.

'Do you want me to follow the road into Oxbow?' asked the pilot.

'Our people will have looked after the road already,' said Phil.

'Head in from the north via one of the tributaries of the Malibamatso, which flows right past Oxbow Lodge,' said Sholto. 'Then follow the road back from the Moteng Pass to the Lodge itself.'

Approaching Oxbow from any other angle, Sholto would have missed seeing the crumpled object lodged, nose-down, on a crag jutting out of the precipice flanking the road over the Moteng Pass. As it was, the white paintwork hid the white Toyota against the snow; the black of its tyres were the real giveaway.

'Hold it, Len,' snapped Sholto. 'There's something down there below the pass. Could be a wreck.'

'I don't see anything,' began the pilot.

'There – on that shelf of rock – low down, amongst the rocks and bushes.'

The other three occupants craned in the direction of Sholto's pointing finger.

'It's a good sighting,' observed Len. 'I'll go in as close as I can and see if we can spot any survivors.'

He steered the Puma towards the formidable crags and jutting rocks. Hundreds of metres above, they could make out the line of the road where it crossed the summit of the pass.

'It's not the rocks which give me the willies,' said Len. 'It's the updraughts. You only need one to throw you a few metres off course and the rotors smash against the rocks . . .'

The Puma stood off the wreck like a wasp cautiously sniffing nectar. It looked like something that had managed to slip from the jaws of a scrapyard demolisher. All the vehicle's glass was gone, the hatchback swung crazily open; the doors were jammed shut and twisted by the cleft into which it had nose-dived.

But there was something which was recognisable and about which Sholto could make no mistake: the white upholstery. It was as individually vain as Jonathan's ornate snow-boots. He knew the station wagon was Jonathan's before he had checked the registration plate under the buckled metal.

'Len!' said Sholto urgently. 'I've got to get down and have a closer look!'

The pilot gave him a sharp glance and said, 'What more do you want to see? There's nothing there.'

Sholto addressed Phil. 'You people are also looking for that vehicle – Jonathan's. My assistant Jonathan, who was murdered.'

'It has nothing to do with the kidnapping,' he replied, echoing General Mak's line. 'It's the kidnapping we're busy on.'

'We don't know until we've looked.'

Sholto saw the same closed look in the security man's face as he had done in General Mak's when he had tried to suggest a link between the two events.

'We can get a ground party down there in due course,' added Phil. 'We can then make a plan to get the wreck out, if it is relevant.'

'No ground party will ever get up or down there,' he said.

'The only chance is from the air. Now, Len, will you go in close and lower me on the winch-wire?'

'And risk all our lives?' said Phil.

The pilot's glance at Sholto was half admiration, half doubt.

He laughed. 'We took a climber out of the mountains last winter from a spot like this – he'd been there three days. I guess it was only a shade less hairy than this situation. Okay. Know how to work the horse-collar? Mac here will winch you down.'

When he opened the rear door to go over the side – the machine made little lunges backwards and forward as the pilot held it away from the cliff – Sholto felt as if his lungs had been injected full of dry ice. The cold in itself was intolerable enough; the whirling rotors created a wind chill factor all their own.

The Puma hung about ten metres above the wrecked Toyota. Sholto chose the rear, where there was access via the smashed hatch. Keeping the horse-collar firm, he manoeuvred a foot on to the broken aperture, and then another. Over the precipice, the drop was terrifying.

Sholto managed to ease himself through the opening and, still gripping the horse-collar firmly round his shoulders, crawled forward into the rear seat – or, where the rear seat had been. It was a marvel to him that the vehicle had not caught fire, it was so pulverised. He crawled over the ruin of upholstery and seat.

Then he saw the bloodstains.

The driver's seat was canted drunkenly; on its rear squab was a tracery of red lines.

They were wavering and indistinct and irregular; Sholto thought at first they had been traced by water melting and coursing down the seat, taking blood with it.

Then he stopped short, galvanised.

It was writing – broken, contorted, the writing of a man *in extremis*.

Two words only.

And he had written it with a finger dipped in his own blood.

Jonathan!

CHAPTER TWENTY-NINE

'Jonathan didn't manage to finish the second word, but there is no doubt what he meant,' Sholto told Grania. 'The first was the figure "4" above. The second scrawl, below it, was a word – "Bushme . . .". In other words, Jonathan's message read, "Four Bushmen".'

Sholto and Grania were sitting together that night in front of the lounge fire at 'Cherry Now'. Grania was wearing dark pants and her jersey with the bold design across the breasts. Her eyes were quiet and in the present, as if she had managed to internalise her remote, agonised mood of the morning when Sholto had flown off.

'In his own blood – with a finger – it's too horrible,' she shuddered.

'It was the last act of a very brave man,' said Sholto. 'He even tried to push on beyond the end-point of his senses when he couldn't manage the last letter of "Bushmen" but all there were were a lot of incomprehensible squiggles and smears.'

'Somehow the message seems to bring home the murder even more than the sight of his body on the raft,' said Grania. 'A sort of last reaching-out of life – to you, Sholto.'

'Four Bushmen!' repeated Sholto almost to himself.

'What was he trying to communicate by that, Sholto? What does it *mean*? Why should the message be for you?'

'If it is what I think it is, the message was a continuation of the conversation we never finished,' replied Sholto slowly. 'I had pressed him very hard that last evening to tell me where he was going; he had refused to take me along. Four Bushmen is the local Sesotho name among the wild tribesmen for a virtually unknown, inaccessible foursome of peaks way up beyond Oxbow towards the South African border. I myself heard the name from some local tribesmen who were rounding up wild horses in the area. It's the only time I've ever heard it used.'

'Why Four Bushmen?' asked Grania. 'Where do Bushmen come into it?'

'I don't know. The peaks, from the little I've heard, are reputed to be unclimbable; there have been a couple of deaths among the climbers who have attempted them. I believe, though, they were scaled once many years ago by some intrepid old-timer. Apparently not only the peaks themselves but the approaches to them are very tough indeed, the story goes.'

'But why Four Bushmen?' persisted Grania.

'I don't know,' repeated Sholto. 'Maybe there's a Bushman cave or paintings hidden away there. It's a tribesmen's name, and they have always had a kind of respect – and fear – for Bushmen strongholds.'

'What did General Mak say when you told him about Jonathan's message?'

'As you know, I phoned him when I got back here a couple of hours ago,' said Sholto with a wry smile. 'He was pretty uptight. He's had a bad day, with everyone from the government to the public breathing down his neck.

'When I said I had located the wreck of Jonathan's car, he said, "So you're back on that tack again, are you, Sholto? I told you to leave it alone – it has no connection with the Poortman affair." I kept my cool and said it was the only thing the helicopter sweep had yielded. But he didn't want to know, Grania. He told me in no uncertain terms that he wasn't looking for a Toyota, either white, or blue, or bright pink. He wanted information on a green camouflaged security van and six men. Whatever else I spotted was of no interest to him. It was useless to tell him about the message. I merely said that the upholstery was bloodstained, and his reply was, "Well, what do you expect? The man was stabbed to death, wasn't he?" When I explained how the wreck was half-impaled on a high crag, he answered that if it was so difficult to get to, it wasn't worth wasting time on.'

'Did General Mak say whether there had been any further word from the kidnappers?'

'Nothing. They hold all the trumps. The ball is in the court of the Lesotho and South African governments, plus the banking consortium.'

'I listened to the main news bulletins, but there was no official reaction to the demand.'

'They're all wavering about what should be done next, General Mak said. Listen, Grania, I'm sure – intuitively, deep down, call it what you will, just as I had that hunch about Bokong – that Jonathan *knew*, or had some strong hint, either about the kidnapping itself or some momentous event that was about to happen. It has happened.'

'To an outsider, Sholto, your reasoning seems tenuous, if I may say so.'

He smiled. '*You* may say so, Grania. I can take it from you. Just as I don't expect you or anyone else to believe that that horse heading straight as a die through the snow wasn't bound for somewhere.'

'Somewhere?'

'I got the pilot to take a bearing – north-northwest.'

'It doesn't mean anything to me, I'm afraid.'

'It means those tracks were running straight in the direction of the Four Bushmen.'

'You only found that out later.'

'It doesn't invalidate the sighting. I'm not reading anything by hindsight into the situation.'

'But . . .' began Grania, but Sholto interrupted her.

'See here, Grania. The kidnappers' overwhelming advantage – physical as well as psychological – is that secret hide-out. They've got their man. They've launched their demand. All they have to do is to sit pretty. It was a masterstroke of strategy. The authorities can't *do* anything, can't even make a show of force. They're shadow-boxing. That goes for General Mak as well. General Mak has made a cookie-cutter approach of going through the motions – that's really what the chopper sweep amounted to. Just to say that it had been done. But he knew as well as anyone else that it was a waste of time searching those impossible snow- and ice fields.'

'Yet the sweep gave you something, Sholto – the Four Bushmen. What are you going to do about it?'

'I'm going to look for it. On my flat feet. Tomorrow.'

While Sholto had been talking, Grania had sat fingering her

right carnelian earring and letting her eyes slide along an imaginary line of sight, as if it were a beam leading to her thoughts.

Now she jumped up, her eyes aglow, and came close to Sholto at the fire.

'Wonderful!' she exclaimed. 'It'll be another climb like ours in Lammergeyer Land, Sholto! The only thing you'll have to find me is a suitable pair of climbing boots . . .'

Later, among the high snows, he told himself he had been a fool. He should have let her come; he should have taken her in his arms at the crest of that lovely moment.

Instead, he raised his hand almost by reflex and said, 'Not this time. I'm going alone.'

She looked sandbagged by his refusal.

'Alone, Sholto, alone?'

'Yes, I'm afraid so.'

'And me?'

'As you know, there is a great deal of information passing between Switzerland, General Mak, the Lesotho and South African governments, and the ombudsman's office. You're right in the picture. I thought you could act as my communications link while I'm gone.'

'Communications link!' Her heart pooled in her eyes. 'Communications link! What do you take me for? I am a woman!'

She was standing close to him; with the fire's warmth, the sweet woman-smell was about her like an aura.

She burst out, 'You ask me to stay here in comfort and safety while you go and trail your coat in front of five men whom any policeman would shoot down like rabid rodents! I'll bet you aren't even taking a gun with you! I'll tell you something that wild horses would not have otherwise dragged out of me: this morning, I watched your helicopter go off in the distance and I stood there – God knows how long – coming to terms with myself. Does that interest you? That was only a routine flight, with no active dangers attached to it! And now you propose putting your head alone into the lion's mouth and you ask me to stay behind and be – a communications link! I ask you again, what do you take me for?'

He replied gently, 'I would take you for a caring, wonderful, loving woman – except for one thing you've forgotten.'

'What is that?' There was fear in her eyes now.

'Your eighteen months of rejection and silence in Switzerland.'

Her eyes swept away from his face to a point mid-way on his chest, so that they would not reveal her secret.

'I can't answer that.'

'Why not?'

'Sholto . . .' There was desperation in her voice. 'I . . . I . . . simply can't explain. Not now. The moment is not right. Will you accept that?'

She still wouldn't look directly at him.

'Not any more, Grania. Do you know what it meant to me when you accepted my invitation to come and stay – to actually *see* me again – for the opening ceremony? To know that our sortie to Lammergeyer Land meant . . . meant . . .'

He stumbled, then rushed on. 'It wasn't as good as love, Grania, and it wasn't as good as hate, if I could ever have felt that for you, but it was something to put into the emptiness inside me – better than nothing at all. Can *you* accept that?'

She lifted her eyes, and he saw their torment. 'Yes, with all my heart, Sholto. That's why I want – must – go with you again tomorrow so that we can find another Lammergeyer Land.'

'It won't work a second time, Grania,' he replied. 'It would simply be papering over the gap – that traumatic, unexplained eighteen months' gap. Unless you can tell me.'

'No!' she cried out as if in pain. 'No, Sholto! You don't know what you're asking!'

'Until I hear I can't judge.'

'If I told you that one's world can collapse and hideous things surface which . . . which . . .' She broke off with a kind of dry sob. 'No, no, no! Don't ask me, Sholto! For God's sake, don't ask me. Not *you*, of all people, Sholto!'

The silence was broken only by the dry sound of the flames in the grate, like the sputter of a welder's torch.

Grania said suddenly in a controlled, flat voice, 'I'll do what you ask and stay and be your communications link, Sholto.

205

On one condition: you don't ask me about the time in Switzerland.'

'Does that mean never?'

Her voice rose, despite her tight control. 'Go out there into the mountains – alone. It may give you – us – something we can't envisage at this stage. I'll tell you afterwards – if I can.'

'If the time is right.'

She sat down and hid her face in her hands, as if he'd reached out and punched her in the solar plexus. 'Don't! Don't hit me with my own words!'

'You've given me a lot to think about in those mountains, Grania.'

'Don't take any risks because of my words! Rather remember . . .'

'You?'

'Yes, yes, me. But come back safe – come back safe, do you hear?'

He moved to take her in his arms, but she slid aside and said as matter-of-factly as she could, so that he dropped his arms by his side: 'How long will you be away?'

'About three days. I'm motoring up to Oxbow Lodge and striking out from there on foot.'

'You'll phone me from Oxbow?'

'If you want me to.'

She made a gesture of despair. 'I want to know you are safe every hour of every day you're away. Can you understand that?'

'No. Not in the full context of Grania.'

'Just leave it at a communications link, then,' she said brokenly, and turned away.

CHAPTER THIRTY

'Marzipan and nuts!'

Hayward sniffed appreciatively, like one of the specially trained Labrador dogs trained to detect the scent of plastic explosive used by terrorists.

'There's no smell like it in all the world – makes me feel at home on the turn,' he went on, casting about the cave hide-out like a sniffer hound itself, trying to locate the origin of the smell as dear to an IRA man's heart as Lanvin is to a society beauty.

It was mid-morning the day after Dr Poortman's kidnap, half a day before the helicopter sweep which that afternoon had, in fact, brought Sholto almost within long-distance sighting range of the peerless barrier of peaks barring Lesotho's northern frontier with South Africa, where the terrain then plunged thousands of metres away into the soft farmland of Natal. This barrier included the unknown, mysterious Four Bushmen quartet of free-standing pinnacle peaks.

Stefan's cave shrank back out of sight near the summit of one of these peaks.

The cave was roughly kidney-shaped, about twelve metres long from entrance to rear exit, and about half that width at its widest. It fronted onto a platform about fifteen metres long and three at its broadest. This shelf tapered, being about half a metre only at one end, and three at the other. It was a sun-lover's dream up here among the snow-covered peaks, with their tongues of ice salivating down striated, perpendicular cliff-faces. The roof of the cave was low towards the front – the summit structure must have collapsed at some remote time in the past, so that a man had to bend in order not to bump his head. Further in, however, the height increased dramatically, until at the rear beyond the central kidney-shaped turn, the basalt ceiling was about seven metres from the floor, and out of anyone's reach up the smooth rock walls.

When the roof had originally half-fallen and canted, it had formed three natural satellite chambers of irregular shape – one of them more a long slit than anything else, where the most upheaval had taken place – and the other two on the opposite side of the cave. Between these two, a spring dropped a steady flow of life-giving liquid. There must have been an intrusion of softer rock – dolerite, perhaps – into the iron-hard basalt because the cave had two more water-points. One was where the place finally dead-ended above the high roof, and the other was on the outside of the hide-out. This could only be reached by leaving the cave proper. Inside again, the spring at the terminal point of the cave found its way out through a crack in the corner; it was Stefan's homespun toilet.

Stefan had improved on the natural fortress in which at least one Bushman clan – whose paintings were on the walls – had resisted all attempts by tribesmen to exterminate them. Across the low doorway leading to the sun platform he had mounted a steel door. It was covered outside with a camouflage of rocks and pebbles so that it was indistinguishable, even at short range, from the surrounding cliff face. On the inside it was faced with asbestos, thus insulating it from the cold outside and retaining the heat inside.

At the cave's rear, high in the ceiling, the Bushmen had used a natural cleft to slip in and out; Stefan had thrown a counter-weighted trapdoor across it, as skilfully camouflaged and carefully insulated as the front entrance. Access was by means of a rope ladder, which he drew up behind him on leaving.

It was probably a waft of warm air from the sun platform which flooded into the interior when Stefan unlocked the entrance door and brushed the plastic explosive in passing which set Hayward's explosive-sensitive nose twitching.

'That's pretty smart of you,' observed Stefan. He indicated the slit-like chamber branching off the right-hand side of the interior. 'I keep the stuff in there.'

'His mother weaned him on liquid gelignite mixed with milk and the first words she taught him were IRA,' commented Bonnay ironically. 'He was also hipped on hi-tech technology before he could spell.'

Hayward ignored the gang leader's sally. Had he been more acute, he would have noted the growing resentment in Bonnay's tone at the way Stefan had assumed control of the entire operation. It was his hide-out, he was calling all the shots. It was he who decided when he would wake the group after their late sleep, and open the outer door to let in the welcome sunlight. By contrast, the more Stefan and Hayward saw of one another, the better they seemed to get on together.

'Like to see my collection?' asked Stefan.

'Sure I would,' replied Hayward.

Stefan brought a flashlight – the interior of the cave was lit by portable gas lights and heated by the same means – and shone it into the magazine.

'Jeez!' exclaimed Hayward as the beam fell on stacks of Soviet S-Z6 and S-Z3 demolition charges, a cluster of eight PMN anti-personnel mines, half a dozen booster charges for these mines, a cardboard box of MD-2 and RG-42 hand grenade detonators, and a number of gleaming AK-47 magazines.

'Where'd you get this stuff from, Stefan? The last lot like this I saw at IRA headquarters – a special shipment from Libya.'

Stefan directed the torch beam further. 'There's more I'd like you to see.'

Hayward went down on his knees and ran his fingers – like a child at a Christmas tree – through a collection of wires, electric detonators, miniaturised timers. One of the devices was a wiring diagram and electric cord attached to a stop-watch with a fixed conductible wire.

Hayward's voice was hushed with admiration. 'All you're lacking is an Agile Chimp,' he said.

Stefan was puzzled. 'Agile Chimp?'

'The British Army's secret weapon against hi-tech bombs in my part of the world,' he grinned. 'It's a device which scans high frequencies and emits radio waves and triggers off our bombs in advance, or jams the frequency our guys are using to set it off,' he explained. 'You have to hand it to those British bastards. They're pretty clued up. But never as smart as Gilbert McNamee.'

'Who was he?' asked Stefan.

Hayward looked shocked, as if one had asked who Margaret Thatcher was.

'The British nabbed Gilbert about eight years ago – 1987, I think it was. Jailed him for twenty-five years. He taught me my trade – a great guy, and a genius at booby-traps and hi-tech bombs.' Hayward laughed reminiscently. 'He rigged a petrol tanker and our boys left it near a border post in Ulster, but the British were suspicious. It took them five days to unsnarl Gilbert's handiwork. Five days!'

'I picked up most of this stuff when my anti-insurgency unit raided into Angola,' said Stefan with a touch of pride. 'I only know the basics, not the finer points.'

Hayward broke in with an exclamation. 'What's this? Where'd you get this, by all that's holy?'

He took from a small box a purple plastic case from which he slid out a tiny metal tube. He blew on it, half a sigh, half a blessing.

Stefan said, 'I looted it with some other circuitry. I don't know what it is.'

'Stefan boy,' replied Hayward dramatically, 'this sweet little thing is the most sophisticated timer-transmitter you could hope to find in a day's march. It works like this . . .'

'Don't start him off.' It was Bonnay who had joined Stefan at the entrance to the magazine and was eyeing the collection of terrorist weaponry. 'Once he gets started, you'll never stop him. When we were going for the Chunnel bombing, you never heard such a lot of bull on the state-of-the-art electrical circuits and switches.'

Hayward came out of the small chamber into the light of the cave proper. He still clutched the tiny tube and its purple plastic sleeve.

He shoved it at Stefan, as if he had been responsible for the gang's failure to kill the British and French heads of state at the Eurotunnel opening.

'This is the gadget I was going to use in conjunction with their fancy clock to trigger the bomb and blow them all to hell,' he said savagely. The Irish bomber seemed himself almost to have slipped on to an abnormal wavelength. He was talking faster and breathlessly, as if the sight and feel of the hi-tech equipment had triggered an explosion in his psyche.

'It's the same timepiece as they're going to use for the opening of the Highlands Project, only then it didn't have its top.' The words poured out. 'The pediment was to have been a rose which would have unfolded at the moment of the opening ceremony, but the guy died and it couldn't be ready in time. It was to have been called the Rose of Time. Now it's the Eagle of Time.'

'The Eagle of Time!' The last scraps of pigmentation seemed to vanish from Stefan's eyes. They were as distant as the outer nebulae. He stared so fixedly through Hayward that the IRA man repeated: 'I said, it's now the Eagle of Time.'

Stefan hauled himself back into the present. 'Let's go outside and get some sun,' he said in a harsh voice.

They went on to the sun platform and joined Pestiaux, Kennet and Dr Poortman. The banker looked tired, but in good shape after his ordeal of the night. He had slept well on a bracken bed in the cave, well warmed by a gas heater, and he was fortified with a good breakfast.

The sun platform was no more than a ledge on the cliff face which towered up hundreds of metres from it. The view on every side was stunning – row upon row of serrated, superb peaks and, nearer on the left, a trio of free-standing pinnacles arising from unknown depths of a mist-shrouded valley to form, along with the one where the cave was, the quartet known as the Four Bushmen.

There was no need to guard Dr Poortman: the sun platform fell away to a dizzy precipice at their feet; even a hang-glider would have thought twice about launching himself into those unnerving depths. The drop was broken, however, about seven metres below their feet by a narrow saw-edge ridge which skirted round the hide-out and disappeared round the left-hand side of the cliff. This was the icy, slippery whale-back over which Stefan's mare had picked her way so unerringly the night before. She had taken them round the corner of the cliff into a sheltered cleft, which was flanked on one side by a wall of rock and on the other by the outer wall of the cave. The cleft – which boasted the third of the cave's springs – was big enough to accommodate a squadron of horses; bracken and heather grew on its floor and wild plants in its sheltered rock crannies. The rope ladder which Stefan used for the trapdoor entrance served a double purpose as a means out of this otherwise unclimbable cul-de-sac.

Hayward was so carried away by the sight of Stefan's arsenal that he seemed to have missed the Maluti Rider's deep abstraction.

'The Rose of Time bomb would have been as sweet as sugar,' he was saying. 'This same sort of little baby – ' he tossed the minute timer in his palm ' – would have sent 'em all to hell. Instead, I had to improvise, use all kinds of conventional stuff the British were wise about from Belfast. The Rose would really have caught 'em with their pants down – combination clockwork timer working off the clock itself and radio transmitter to trigger the explosive. Not even Gilbert himself had developed such a simple, beautiful bomb. However, Scotland Yard was able to detect the makeshift and . . .'

'And sent us running across Europe with Interpol and every police force snapping at our arses,' added Kennet.

'Well, we got away, didn't we?' said Pestiaux. 'It was fun while it lasted. Better than rotting in Maseru for close on two years.'

Stefan's eyes seemed focused on the distant peaks.

Rali! The grand revenge, Rali! The masterstroke which will reverberate clean into your blackened grave!

The Rose of Time! With its new pediment, it had now become The Eagle of Time. It was to be the centrepiece, the very heart, of the Highlands Project opening! Strike at that, and you strike at the very kernel of the grandiose project, bigger and more daring in many ways than the Chunnel itself. What was a mere Swiss banker alongside the plan starting to avalanche through Stefan's burning brain? What was a million dollars, beside *this*?

A two-pronged vengeance!

Katse – Katse Dam!

Water! Untold millions of litres of water! Stored behind that massive wall like a short punch coiled ready to be thrown! And only fifteen kilometres below that wall were the nine hundred tribesmen, resettled from their mountain home because of the Highlands Project, who had throttled Rali with their old-fashioned barbed wire! He could wipe them out with the same blow as he struck at the Eagle of Time – hundreds of them, at least – with a killer flood from the Katse Dam!

Stefan got a grip on his reason as his thoughts unleashed themselves like a snowslip from one of the high peaks after a hard winter.

Not all the resources of his arsenal put together could blow a hole in the Katse wall. That would need hundreds of kilograms of high explosive, expertly sited, and then its success was doubtful. But – Bonnay himself had reconnoitred the control chamber as a possible hole-up site for Poortman and had noted the one desk-sized console, the switches of which, operated by one man, controlled the great Katse sluices. Jam the switches open with a bomb, a bomb triggered by the Eagle of Time, and release a killer flood at the tribesmen – Rali's murderers. He had here right next to him the most sophisticated terrorist bomb-maker loose in the world today whose killer motives were activated not by his own blood-lust but by hi-tech electronics. Hayward was his man! Hayward could arm the Eagle of Time with that tiny lethal sliver of tubing he still held in his hand in its distinctive purple plastic case. It was the sort of intricate job Hayward would revel in; he had already admitted that about the aborted Chunnel bomb. Stefan relegated Poortman and his kidnap on to the back burner in his mind; the Bomb was the thing!

Stefan stared out from the sun platform. He heard nothing of the Chunnel Gang's boasting of their near-misses while on the run across Europe and their notorious escape down a Marseilles sewer to safety, and Lesotho. The great view was as blank to him as the black paper which master-bombers of the IRA use to mask the photo-electric cells of their hellish devices so that sunlight cannot fall on their killer eyes prematurely and trigger a blast. He heard nothing either of their animated discussion on

213

the reaction they could expect on the lunch time news from Radio Maseru about Dr Poortman's snatch.

The Eagle of Time! He had to get his hands on the Eagle of Time . . .

CHAPTER THIRTY-ONE

'Sholto, the Eagle of Time has been hijacked, stolen!'

Grania's agitation smacked down the telephone like a grenade-burst to Sholto at the other end of the line. She could scarcely hold the instrument steady. She had been poised at the phone at 'Cherry Now' waiting for Sholto's promised call from Oxbow. She had pounced on the instrument before it even had had time to give one full ring.

It was Friday, the day following their confrontation over his refusal to take her with him in his search for the Four Bushmen, two days after Dr Poortman's kidnap.

They had had a strangely silent, early breakfast together before he went off in his pick-up truck, into the back of which he had loaded his climbing gear. Grania had been unable to bring herself to help him get together his kit – scarlet lightweight climbing tent, nylon climbing ropes, sleeping bag, aluminium stove, food, and all the other paraphernalia of the skilled high climber. She had hung around on the fringes of his packing, as miserable as a dog watching its master's luggage, knowing it will be left behind.

Her eyes were opaque with misery and lack of sleep until he drove off; then for a moment they had flared with an intensity which belied the controlled tone she had used all morning, an intensity fuelled also by the inner secret she could not confide to him.

Now, as she took Sholto's call from Oxbow, her voice was agonised, stunned.

'*What did you say, Grania*? The line's bad . . .'

'Unfortunately you're hearing right, Sholto. General Mak phoned about half an hour ago wanting you. Then he told me the news.'

'The Eagle of Time – *your* Eagle of Time!' exclaimed Sholto in disbelief. 'How? When?'

'It's just happened,' Grania went on. 'I can't get a grip of the idea myself, Sholto, my thoughts are all numb. It's like trying to rip my way through an opaque film which is wrapping me round, telling me it didn't – couldn't – happen . . .'

'It's yours – *your* masterpiece! It can't be!'

'That's what everyone says, including General Mak. But it's happened, Sholto. It has – and it's gone!'

'Tell me what happened, Grania! What did General Mak say?'

'He was shaken right back on his heels,' replied Grania. 'He wanted you to pass on the news to the consortium in Switzerland. But when I told him where you were, he decided to inform them himself because apparently Maseru is humming with the story and he wanted the consortium to hear it officially rather than from public rumour. Radio Maseru has already broken into its programmes to broadcast it and a description of the man.'

'*One* man, Grania? Did *one* man steal it? How?'

'The TV monitors got a picture of him, and that'll be on TV as soon as the station opens. In fact, General Mak wants it telecast as soon as possible so that the public can assist in trying to pick him up before the scent goes cold. But the Maluti Rider is armed and dangerous . . .'

'*The Maluti Rider*! What are you saying, Grania?'

'I'm saying what everyone in Maseru is saying, that it was the Maluti Rider who hijacked the Eagle from clean under the nose of the guard at the Exhibition Centre.'

'They know exactly who to look for if the TV monitors got his picture.'

'General Mak says it's not that good. It still could be anyone in a crowd – except that he was stocky and looked powerful. He was wearing a long snow jacket and balaclava and he walked out with the Eagle in his hand . . .'

'Start at the beginning,' said Sholto.

'Quite a short while after the Eagle went on show at the centre this morning, this man in a threequarter snow jacket came in . . .'

'For Pete's sake, what were the guards at the entrance doing?'

'The usual two at the entrance had been withdrawn – General Mak has put every available man on the road to try and find Dr

Poortman,' Grania resumed. 'He also cut the usual two men guarding the Eagle down to one for the same reason. So the previous close search as visitors went in wasn't operating. Maybe the Maluti Rider knew this, maybe he didn't and took a chance. But whatever it was, it had all the hallmarks of his handiwork.'

'You keep saying, the Maluti Rider. What has General Mak to back that up with?'

'Less than anyone cares to admit. The man's made Security look a fool twice in two days. Because of the raid's daring and ruthlessness, everyone says it must be the Maluti Rider.'

'Ruthlessness? Did he kill anyone?'

'The guard he hit with the AK-47 he had hidden under his snow jacket is in the intensive care unit at the hospital with a fractured skull. The TV monitors picked up the raider first as he strode towards the dais with a balaclava on and pulling out the AK-47 from under his jacket. The guard never stood a chance. It was too sudden, too brutal. He walked straight up to him and without warning smashed him across the head with it. He then turned and pointed the AK-47 at the crowd. Being so early, there were only a handful of sightseers. They were terrified. He then spoke his only word during the raid: "Down!" General Mak said they dropped like ninepins on the floor. The Maluti Rider then lifted the glass case off the Eagle of Time, dropped the timepiece into a shopping bag he had with him, and walked out carrying it as if he'd just come from a supermarket. The cameras got their best shots of him then.'

'What did General Mak say he looked like?'

'He was wearing a balaclava. His face was hidden, except for his eyes.'

'Was he a Basuto, does he think?'

'Apparently there is no way of telling whether the figure on the monitors is black or white. He was wearing gloves and the balaclava hid his features – except, as I said, for the eyes, and they were well back in the folds of the balaclava.'

'What happened then?'

'He simply walked out as bold as brass into the street. No one there seems to have noticed a man carrying a shopping bag. He just merged into the sidewalk crowd. He must have got rid of the balaclava as he left the centre.'

'Surely there must be eye-witnesses!'

'Everyone who saw it happen was so electrified that each has a different version. General Mak says that a member of the public outside in the street even claims he saw a masked man emerge and ride away on a black horse.'

'People's imaginations run riot when something like this happens,' said Sholto.

'General Mak doesn't seem very hopeful that the guard will be able to help either – if he ever recovers. At this moment, he's deeply unconscious,' went on Grania. 'Apparently it was a terrible blow with the barrel of the gun. There was no preliminary. The Maluti Rider simply went straight up to him and clobbered him to within an inch of death.'

Grania heard something over the phone. She stiffened and exclaimed, 'Sholto, what's that noise? It sounds like a gun being cocked!'

'Sorry, I'm fiddling with the karabiner clip on the end of my climbing rope.'

'Something seems to rip inside me every time I hear an unusual noise – ever since General Mak's call.'

'Did you tell him why I wasn't at home?'

'No. All I said was that you had motored up to Oxbow and were due to phone me when you got there.'

'Good. In the light of this latest happening, General Mak will be less inclined than ever to listen to anything connected with Jonathan. Has there been any ransom demand for the Eagle of Time yet?'

'No. It was all so swift, so deadly, so clinical. The possible ransom is something General Mak wants to discuss with you, but I expect by now he has already got the consortium's views on it.'

'It's another body-blow for the grand opening in a week's time,' went on Sholto. 'First Dr Poortman, and now the Eagle of Time. The two together could pull the mat from under the opening. Did General Mak say anything about postponing it?'

'Not in those terms. He merely said that he had spoken to the

Prime Minister about it when he informed him of the theft of the Eagle of Time. It's not a decision for one man – it'll have to be taken at the highest level, in consultation with South Africa, the consortium, and . . . and . . .'

'It makes me cold,' broke in Sholto. 'All the VIP invitations have gone out, of course; they can't be recalled. You can't stop a major thing like that in its tracks, not at this late stage.'

'Not at this late stage,' she echoed.

'Listen, Grania,' went on Sholto, and his words tumbled out over the line, 'all this is true, but it's the outward aspect of the picture. The inward, and more important aspect, is what stands on top of the Eagle of Time – your masterpiece, the lammergeyer. We found it together, you created something right from the heart of you to match. I want you to know that it is more important for me to get that back than anything else in the world.'

'Anything. Does that mean, anyone also, Sholto?' Her voice went very quiet.

'You yourself said, the time is not right. I have to accept that. That is all I can say at the moment.'

The uneven, higher timbre of her voice underscored the evidence he had seen in her face that morning of the pressures mounting inside her.

'This business in Maseru this morning and its bearing on you are like a landmine of foreboding to me for your road home,' she hurried on. 'For God's sake, look after yourself, Sholto! There seem to be hidden forces at work everywhere!'

Sholto heard the news on Radio Maseru as he raced back to 'Cherry Now' from Oxbow; at the farm itself Grania heard it also, and saw on the TV screen the blow-ups of Stefan striking down the guard with the deadly callousness of a mamba; then striding out in his snow coat and balaclava carrying a plastic supermarket shopping bag. The scene had the remote quality of a TV drama roughhouse; nor could she relate herself to the contents of the bag the helmeted figure carried loosely in one hand, or the poised and cocked AK-47 he carried in the other.

No screen producer, however, would have tolerated the foggy outline of the raider as he raced across the Exhibition Centre from dais to entrance. His face was completely hidden by the balaclava;

the gloved hands barred any sight of the pigmentation of his hands. He was slightly below average height, but by contrast broader in proportion. He kept his face half-averted from the cameras as he hurried out; he knew they were recording him.

The news bulletin said:

No trace has yet been found of the kidnapped Swiss banker, Dr Hans Poortman, who was forcibly removed from his chalet at Katse Lodge the night before last, according to an official announcement from the office of the Prime Minister. He is, according to his captors, being held in a secret hiding-place pending the Government's response to a ransom demand for one million American dollars and safe passage for the kidnappers out of the country. The Lesotho Cabinet has been meeting in secret session to formulate a reply to the kidnappers' demands; it is hoped that a suitable intermediary, acceptable to both sides, will be found. At this stage the Lesotho government, in close consultation with the South African authorities and the Swiss banking consortium which Dr Poortman heads, has not taken a stand on the matter as it could jeopardise the ceremonial opening of the Highlands Project in a week's time.

The ransom demand was signed by the Chunnel Gang, which Lesotho security experts consider an attempt to add notoriety to the demand. Further attempts at notoriety were made by adding the name of the Maluti Rider, Lesotho's most-wanted bandit, to the list of signatories.

Until today, security experts considered that this signature was spurious. But this morning, a masked man, armed with an AK-47 automatic rifle, entered the Exhibition Centre in the middle of Maseru, knocked the guard unconscious, and escaped with one of the world's great art-jewellery masterpieces, the Eagle of Time, which is to form the centrepiece of the Highlands Project opening ceremony. The man – who seems to be associated in the public mind with the Maluti Rider without any evidence to substantiate such an exaggerated claim – was caught by television monitors in the act of bearing away the priceless masterpiece.

This picture will be shown throughout today on all TV stations and anyone with any information is asked to contact their nearest police station. In the meantime, the Lesotho Chief of Security,

General Makoanyane, has said in an interview that several important leads are being followed up . . .

'Leads!' snorted General Mak at Sholto and Grania. 'Leads! I haven't a solitary firm lead, in spite of what the news bulletin said. That was only flannel, in the hope that the kidnappers will make a slip and give themselves away, which isn't very likely. Leads! All that there is is flak, and more flak!'

Sholto and Grania were sitting in the security chief's Maseru headquarters that afternoon. He had summoned Sholto, via Grania, to Maseru as soon as he returned from Oxbow.

He snapped at Sholto, 'I suppose you haven't anything for me to work on?'

For a moment Sholto hesitated. Mention of the cryptic, bloodstained message would only draw derision from the security man in his present harassed frame of mind.

'No.'

General Mak hardly waited for his reply before addressing Grania. 'The theft of your masterpiece is a great blow not only to us but to you,' he said. 'The Prime Minister phoned me before lunch and, when he heard you were coming here this afternoon, asked me to pass on his and the country's profound regrets that such a thing should have occurred.'

'I hardly know what to reply – I still can't believe it,' said Grania. 'Do you think the gang will make a ransom demand for it as well?'

'Anything can happen,' rejoined General Mak. 'The major decision-making has been taken out of my hands. It's a matter for the Cabinet – our Cabinet and the South African Cabinet – and the acting head of the consortium in Switzerland now. The big decision they're trying to reach is whether or not to negotiate with the kidnappers. You perhaps noticed the let-out in the news bulletin about "a suitable intermediary". Both you and I are kind of fifth wheels on the wagon at the moment, Sholto. Certainly there's nothing much for you to do around here.'

'If we only knew where to begin to look,' said Sholto.

'That unknown hide-out was a psychological masterstroke,' said General Mak grimly. 'I can't *do* anything, and while I can't, the kidnappers' image grows in the public mind – ' His voice turned to an angry abrasiveness. 'And the nerve of that Maluti Rider this morning! Heavens, I mean to get my hands on that bastard! The bloody cheek of walking away like that with a priceless masterpiece in a shopping bag – an ordinary plastic supermarket bag!'

The shopping bag lay among half a dozen identical bags on the pick-up's front seat next to Stefan. There was nothing to show that it did not contain the same miscellaneous collection of groceries, vegetables and fruit as the others did; Stefan had gone shopping for the occupants of the hide-out before his daring raid into the Exhibition Centre.

He grinned to himself; he, too, heard the radio news bulletin on his vehicle's radio. He had nothing to fear – he had beaten the hue and cry by making straight from the Exhibition Centre for the border post on the outskirts of Maseru, only a few kilometres away. He'd used his special clearance at the border, a clearance which had been issued to him as a privileged person by virtue of his landowning which had been taken over for the outlet point of the Highlands Project water. He'd even joked with the border guards about the growing cost of living, indicating the cluster of supermarket bags on the vehicle's seat, in one of which was the Eagle of Time.

Now he was safe, travelling fast towards his farm on the road which followed the border on the South African side. From there on, he'd follow his secret backdoor route to the cave hide-out in the mountains . . .

In the hide-out, Bonnay, Kennet, Hayward and Pestiaux sat on the sun platform with Dr Poortman apart to one side and heard the news bulletin on the radio.

Their easy, relaxed confidence at the first part of the bulletin was blown apart when the announcer gave the news of the heist of the Eagle of Time.

Bonnay stared round the stunned group. 'Stefan!' he burst out. 'The Maluti Rider – Stefan! He must have gone out of his bloody mind!'

CHAPTER THIRTY-TWO

'I'm out of my mind, am I?'

Stefan stood at the open door of the cave, eyeing the Chunnel Gang. They and Dr Poortman were sunning themselves on the sun platform. The panorama across the precipice towards the other Three Bushmen was stupendous. Although it was still mid-afternoon, the purples and violets were pre-empting the sunset and creeping in between the serried and serrated agglomeration of peaks, plateaus and precipices on every side.

Stefan held his AK-47 in one hand and a shopping bag in the other.

Bonnay got off the fisherman's stool on which he sat and faced the Maluti Rider. He gestured towards Dr Poortman.

'How to balls up the perfect kidnap operation; go and do the same again like an encore for a useless bit of jewellery that you couldn't flog anywhere! Especially now that the heat is on.' His tone became gratingly sarcastic. 'Look at me, the great Maluti Rider! Couldn't give a damn for your security or your guards! I walk in, slug a defenceless guy half-dead, and walk out under the eye of the cameras! Finesse! Bah! You must be suffering from delusions of grandeur!'

'Is that so?'

Bonnay was too angry to notice the harsh menace come into the Maluti Rider's voice, but his almost involuntary movement towards the AK trigger was not lost on Pestiaux. It was Pestiaux who had come crawling in the first place to Bonnay in Calais on the run from his commando unit with only his ultra-sharp trigger reflexes as a recommendation. Now his hand moved towards his left armpit as if seeking the source of a sudden itch.

'And I suppose that is the shopping bag which is hitting the headlines?' The gang leader indicated the container in Stefan's hand.

'It is.' He put it down carefully. 'There are half a dozen

223

replicas back there in the cave, filled with genuine shopping. Had 'em next to me on the seat as I went through the border check.'

Stefan wasn't boasting; his conversation was to gain time to heft the AK-47 surreptitiously to the ready – in case.

Bonnay went on heatedly: 'The guys and I discussed lifting the Eagle ourselves, but it wasn't on. And the reasons are exactly the same for you – even more so now. What in hell do you intend to do with it? What's it worth? Damn-all! No fence or shady dealer will look at a fancy thing like that. The only price you could get would be to melt down the gold.' He gestured at Dr Poortman as if he were an ox standing ready for the abattoirs. 'He's worth a lot more – a whole million. That's why we went for him. He's negotiable, in money terms. And that's what we're in this for – money. A million.' He gave an angry shrug, and said in an almost schoolmasterish tone, 'In this game you've got to get the right configurations planned before the shooting starts. The configurations are all wrong. You've blown the operation.'

'You're talking about the kidnap.'

'My oath, what else?' demanded Bonnay.

Stefan looked past Bonnay at Hayward in particular, at the same time silencing Dr Poortman with a curt gesture – the banker seemed about to intervene in the discussion.

Stefan pulled back the white plastic shopping bag and the banker half-started forward. The bright sun up among the peaks was right for the glory of Grania's lammergeyer: it looked set to take off at any moment. The sun was also right for each one of the sixteen modules of the timepiece under the pediment, and struck back in points of fire from the artwork, the jewels, the miniaturised carillon.

All this seemed to pass the Maluti Rider by. 'You missed the chance of a lifetime with this timepiece over the Chunnel blast, didn't you, Hayward?'

'What's that got to do with what's going on now?' asked the Irishman sulkily.

'I'm giving you another chance.'

'I don't know what you are talking about.'

224

Stefan said to Dr Poortman, 'I don't suppose it makes much difference whether you hear what I am going to say or not. Your life's in the balance anyway.'

'Forget about my life – just don't do anything to the Eagle of Time,' Dr Poortman answered. 'It is one of the world's great masterpieces . . .'

'Okay, okay, we've heard all that bull before,' snapped Stefan. 'Its only use to me is functional. That's where you come in, Hayward.'

'What's this second chance?' demanded Hayward.

'You said you missed out using the original Rose of Time for a timer for a bomb which would have killed the British and French heads of state and flooded the Channel tunnel because the artist died and the top couldn't be finished. So you had to improvise and it went sour.'

Hayward continued to look puzzled. Bonnay started to say something, but Stefan silenced him with a gesture.

'That's right.'

'Here it is now – the Eagle of Time, complete with new and different pediment. You've got my hi-tech timer in the purple case inside the magazine there. Get busy. Wire it up – or whatever you do. Make a timer out of the Eagle of Time.'

'Saints in heaven!' exclaimed Hayward. He went forward and dropped on his knees. It may have been an act of perverted worship; it may have been to examine the pediment fitting more closely.

Bonnay felt the leadership ground now totally slipping away from under his feet. Any moment, he'd simply be taking orders as Stefan's crackpot scheme was thrust down their throats.

'Now, wait a moment . . .' he began.

'There's no time to wait,' retorted Stefan. 'That miniaturised timer of mine – it's okay, is it?'

Hayward looked up like a man in a dream. 'It's everything I want – couldn't be better. Hell's teeth! What I would have done to the British if only I'd had this!'

'You're jumping the gun, you're indulging in fantasy!' Bonnay intervened. 'Timer! You can't have a timer without a bomb – and where's the bomb? What's it all about . . .'

There was an ugly rasp in Stefan's voice. Bonnay didn't care for it any more than the wildcat scheme which was being thrown undigested at him; it chilled Kennet; Pestiaux's itching fingers moved a little closer to the butt of his Makarov inside his shoulder holster.

'There is a bomb. It's back in the cave there with the other stuff,' said Stefan. 'One of those S-Z3s or S-Z6s or the plastic explosive should be enough. Hayward will decide – he's the expert.'

'Depends what you mean to do,' replied Hayward.

'It's meant to wreck the sluices control console of the Katse Dam and jam them open, the very moment this – ' he indicated the Eagle of Time ' – opens its wings at the climax of the opening ceremony in a week's time.'

'The sluices!' burst out Bonnay incredulously.

'You can't do this – it's madness – you'll kill . . .' exclaimed Dr Poortman, starting forward. Stefan half-lifted the automatic. 'Stay away from me! That's what I mean to do – kill!'

'Who?' demanded Bonnay. 'The VIPs . . .?'

'VIPs – bah! I'm not interested in VIPs, only as far as they are part of the Highlands Project! My bomb won't get them – they'll be way on top of the wall, and the blast will be deep down in the control chamber. The amount of explosive we'll use won't even blow chips off that concrete wall, let alone make a hole in it!'

'Then who?' repeated Bonnay. He stopped short. Stefan's eyes frightened him. They were so pale – he remembered the casino comparison – that the whiteness of the snow-capped peaks was reflected in them. Stefan's voice changed gear too.

'They killed her,' he got out. 'They killed her – necklaced her. They first half-strangled her with old barbed wire from one of their fences. Rali! And my two little girls also. I only got some of them, back there in the mountains. They moved them because of the Project. Now I've got them in the hollow of my hand.'

It was the calm tone of the banker which brought a measure of normalcy into the nerve-stretched conversation.

'Who are you talking about? Who was Rali?'

226

'Rali was my wife. I'm talking about the tribe which burned her to death. They moved them from the mountains to land about fifteen kilometres below the wall of the Katse Dam, land right alongside the river itself, flat land for growing crops. The bomb will jam open the sluices; the water will do the rest.'

He looked aggressively round the men on the sun platform staring at him. 'That's what the Eagle of Time is all about – for me. Hayward will fuse it up, we'll plant it, and then at the supreme moment of their gala ceremony, I will strike right at the heart of the Project! That's why I went and brought out the Eagle this morning. Nothing to do with its value, or anything else.'

'The perfect timer!' breathed Hayward. 'Perfect, perfect!'

'Hold it!' interrupted Bonnay. 'This sort of off-the-cuff improvisation won't work! We haven't even begun to think the plan through. The configurations . . .'

'Configurations!' Stefan's tone was ugly. 'Is that another way of saying you won't come in with me?'

The AK-47 came up to his hip. He seemed to be watching every one of them. Pestiaux realised he would not reach the Makarov butt before he was cut in half by a burst from the automatic.

Bonnay saw, too, the raw threat staring him in the face.

'An operation like this has to be worked out and discussed – you can't just go in boots and all,' he temporised. 'You haven't even said how you intend putting the Eagle of Time in position for the opening ceremony. No one will be such a sucker as just to say, look guys, those nice kidnappers have given it back for the ceremony and we'll go right ahead, complete with primed timer.'

'Cut out the humour and the sarcasm,' Stefan retorted roughly. 'The Eagle does go back, as soon as Hayward has armed it with the hi-tech primer. I'll take it myself.'

Kennet joined the conversation for the first time. 'Jules is right – the whole plan needs a lot more thought and working out.'

'And you?' Stefan barked the question so suddenly that Pestiaux almost involuntarily snatched at his Makarov.

He said, hesitatingly, watching the AK-47, 'Maybe we need more discussion.' It was a lame contribution.

There was no need to question Hayward. His head was down, peering under the plinth of the pediment where it joined the main body of the timepiece. 'This will have to come off,' he muttered, half to himself.

'So,' Stefan said. 'Non-cooperation from three of you?'

Bonnay made an attempt to recapture his leadership. 'You want to launch one operation, we are right in the middle of another,' he said with an air of compromise. 'There is no reason why cooperation can't be double-ended, with no clash of interest. You want a bomb at the opening, we want a million dollars.'

'Cut the double-talk,' snapped Stefan. 'Either you are for me, or against me. Which is it?'

Kennet voiced Bonnay and Pestiaux's views in the tight silence which followed. Hayward squatted apart, his mind blown on a hi-tech high.

'If we don't go along with you?'

Stefan answered without hesitation. 'I have several options. I can become a public hero and inform the authorities who you are and where you are holding Poortman. I can add that it was you who hijacked the Eagle of Time, and that in the public interest I have decided to tell all and turn you in . . .'

'You wouldn't dare!' broke in Kennet.

'Wouldn't I? Wouldn't I?' retorted Stefan. 'My other option is simply to shoot you all – except Hayward – and then push you over the cliff. No one will ever find the bodies.'

Bonnay's reply was a tacit concession that Stefan had won – for the moment.

'About the logistics of the bomb – I speak for the others when I say we feel we're being crowded. How, for instance, do you propose to restore the Eagle of Time once Hayward has armed it?'

'Simple,' replied Stefan. He relaxed a little, but his eyes remained wary. 'I take the Eagle back to Maseru – in the same shopping bag which everyone knows by now. I casually put it somewhere where it is certain to be discovered – at

Moshoeshoe's statue, for example, right in the middle of the city. There will be a note attached expressing apologies and saying that in view of the uniqueness of the art masterpiece, it is being returned undamaged – as it will be. Hayward's primer will be hidden away under the pediment. Unless they strip it, it won't be seen. The clock will be going too, just as it was when it disappeared. The authorities will be so relieved to have one hot potato off their plate that my bet is they'll put it on display for the opening ceremony, just as scheduled.'

Hayward broke in from his scrutiny. 'The transmitter won't be one hundred per cent effective over a distance of more than half a kilometre.'

'It's nothing like that distance from the top of the wall where the opening dais will be to the control chamber down below,' replied Stefan.

'You've first got to plant the bomb there,' observed Bonnay.

Stefan eyed him suspiciously. How much obstruction was there in that doubting tone?

'You will brief Hayward on every detail. You've recced the place, you said so yourself,' replied Stefan. 'The console operating the sluice controls is only the size of an ordinary office desk – again, you said so yourself.'

'He'll never get past the security net at Katse, ever since . . .' he jerked his head at Dr Poortman '. . . we snatched him.'

'You'll give him your Pony Card – it's the way you got there in the first place, isn't it?' retorted Stefan. 'That's a free pass anywhere, just like my special border clearance because . . .' his laughter jarred '. . . because they stole my land for their outlet works. Landowning priority! Landowner gent! They'll see what I mean when that bomb goes off at the big moment of their blasted opening ceremony!'

'This could be the biggest thing since Enniskillen!' interjected Hayward happily. He addressed Stefan. 'A second chance, after the Chunnel, thanks to you!'

His effusiveness made Bonnay feel sick.

'What was Enniskillen?' asked Stefan.

Bonnay answered quickly in the Irishman's place. 'It was a massacre of eleven civilians by the IRA on Poppy Day 1987 in the town of Enniskillen with a radio-controlled bomb . . .'

'Massacre be damned!' interrupted Hayward. 'It was a bomb intended for the British, but their army set it off with high frequency radio waves.'

'If it's got nothing to do with Katse, I couldn't care less,' snapped Stefan. 'Burt – ' Bonnay noted the sudden use of the bomber's Christian name and chalked it up for future reference ' – get going on priming the Eagle of Time. There are tools in the magazine. Use anything you want. You'd better work out here, where the light is good. The rest of you, get inside. It's a tricky job, and he mustn't have any distractions.'

Orders, more orders! At gunpoint, or nearly so. Bonnay seethed inwardly with anger. Outwardly, he inclined his head towards Kennet and Pestiaux, who followed him inside, with Dr Poortman bringing up the rear. Once or twice, it seemed, Dr Poortman had been about to break into the acrimonious discussion, but now he was silent.

Hayward, with Stefan's help, found a collection of specialised detonator tools and sat on a fisherman's stool in front of a low table in the sun with the Eagle of Time scintillating in front of him. Stefan spent a little time with him, and then he, too, went indoors, still carrying the AK-47.

In a little over an hour, Hayward also came inside.

'What's wrong?' rapped out Stefan, when he saw the Irishman's face. All the excitement and exhilaration had gone out of it and in its place was a greyness, like that of a man who has had news of a sudden death.

'It can't be done!' he said huskily.

Stefan towered over him. 'What can't be done?' he yelled. 'What is it, man? I thought you were the best . . .'

'I can't remove the pediment without damaging the clockwork mechanism of the timepiece proper,' he replied hoarsely. 'And that's vital to activate the radio signal which is transmitted to the bomb. It's as intricate as hell – I've never seen anything like it before. It must also be connected to the mechanism opening the bird's wings. It needs an expert who's worked on it.'

Dr Poortman gave a soft ironical laugh; Stefan rounded on

him as if he meant to smash the AK down on the banker's head, and then stopped.

'Thanks, Dr Poortman,' he said with a sneer. 'Thanks for drawing attention to yourself. They say you found the girl to sculpt the Eagle; she's here, right here in Lesotho! She'll know how to shift the pediment! I'll have the girl!'

CHAPTER THIRTY-THREE

'You'll have the girl!' echoed Bonnay sarcastically. 'Just like that! I suppose you'll go along to her carrying the Eagle of Time in its now famous shopping bag and say, please Miss Grania Yeats, will you remove the pediment you made so that my IRA pal Burt Hayward can insert a radio trigger to set off a bomb at the opening ceremony of the Highlands Project next Friday . . .'

'You can keep the shit to yourself, I don't need it,' snapped Stefan. 'I said I'll have the girl, and I mean it. I'll go and get her and bring her here with this – ' He made a lunging movement with the AK-47.

'Another kidnapping!' exclaimed Bonnay. 'You really mean you're going to kidnap her too?'

Stefan rocked backwards and forwards on the balls of his feet. The way he did it made a simple movement full of menace. 'Unless you have any other bright ideas on how to make her come here.'

Kennet said, more as an aside than a contribution to the conversation, 'None of us knows how to get in and out of here anyway.'

Bonnay formulated into his reply the thoughts which he had been trying to pinion ever since the arrival of Stefan with the horological masterpiece. He avoided Stefan's raking stare and chose his words so as not to provoke the Maluti Rider.

'You've already turned our Poortman kidnapping into something very different from what it was to have been at the outset,' he stated levelly. 'In fact, it's now become a sideshow. The Bomb's the thing.'

'Go on,' said Stefan. They talked over Dr Poortman's head, as doctors do over a near-dead patient, as if he didn't hear any more.

'Now, by kidnapping a second person, this girl, you're

introducing a still more dangerous element into a razor-edged situation. You're sticking your neck out – and with it all of ours – so far that all of them must get chopped off. You – we – can't handle all these elements. You've stacked the odds so high against us that nothing can possibly succeed. It's simply wishful thinking, this new idea of kidnapping Grania Yeats. She's a top VIP, like Poortman here, and now the security beehive has been set by the ears you won't stand a chance of getting her.'

'She's staying at Sholto Banks' farm, you said so yourself,' retorted Stefan. 'She's not under security surveillance like Maseru. It's a piece of cake.'

'You're blinding yourself to the realities of the situation,' went on Bonnay, trying not to provoke Stefan and keep the discussion on a commonsense footing. 'Forget about the bombing, and admit it can't be done. Forget about kidnapping Grania Yeats. Put the Eagle back, like you said. It will count as a plus point in our favour. Concentrate on the Poortman ransom. Let's start negotiating.'

'Is that all you have to say?' Stefan was searingly contemptuous. 'No wonder your Channel plan aborted! A lot of scared old women, seeing shadows everywhere! The only one of you who has any guts is Burt here! He and I will show you; we'll go and fetch the girl and bring her back here!'

Bonnay made a last attempt to bring sense into Stefan.

'What is the plan?' he asked with as much self-restraint as he could. He had already thrown a cautionary glance at Kennet and Pestiaux not to do anything rash.

'I don't need a bunch of lily-livered wets to stuff up my plan,' he retorted scathingly. 'Burt, coming? Got a gun?'

Hayward nodded. He was as far away in his dream as a Mexican sorcerer on a mescalin high. 'We've got to get her and fix the timepiece,' he repeated anxiously. 'They'll remember me in the record books along with Gilbert McNamee for this.'

Bonnay made a last attempt with Stefan. 'You're rushing off on a plan which will go off at half-cock and ditch us all. Why not stay here tonight and talk it over and we'll work out something which will work?'

'Take it or leave it,' replied Stefan in a hectoring voice. 'I don't need you – any of you three – see? You're part of your own Poortman plan, and I don't need that either.'

Bonnay played for time. 'How long will you be away?'

Stefan misread the question; he thought it was directed at his plan – or lack of it – to kidnap Grania. 'Ask the horses,' he answered.

He really meant it. A trio of goat-footed Basuto ponies was the key to the hide-out's back door. They were quite separate from the team which could pick their way across the saw-edged ice ridge below the sun platform into the shelter adjoining the cave. To reach the trio, the first part of the way was via the trapdoor exit. The trapdoor gave entry to a long – half a kilometre or more – diagonally sloping crack in the mountain, so narrow in places that it scarcely permitted the passage of a broad-shouldered man like Stefan. The crack had enabled the small-boned Bushmen to live on in their sanctuary long after their fellow clans had been wiped out. From a narrow platform where the cleft ended, a profound gulf opened up. The place was apparently inaccessible, but with a climber's skill it could be mastered quite quickly if one could stand the terrifying drop to two great rivers which tumbled over the edge of the escarpment. From the foot of this cliff, it was downhill all the way to Stefan's farm – 'Rali's Rest' – across the border. A kilometre or two away from the cliff Stefan kept his Basuto ponies, which ran wild in a sheltered radius where they could be rounded up. Stefan used them as an intermediate means of transport to where he holed up his pick-up on the South African side of the frontier on what had been his ancestral farm. There was no border fence or frontier post. Stefan had roamed here since boyhood: he knew every remote track – and the routes which had no tracks.

Now Stefan turned and went with Hayward to the trapdoor. He drew up the rope ladder behind them and snapped the exit shut.

'You're as much captives as I am.'

It was Dr Poortman. It was one of the longer sentences he had uttered since leaving Katse Lodge. Bonnay, Kennet and Pestiaux all turned to the banker in surprise.

'There's no pathway the way they went – and only an eagle wouldn't be daunted by what's over the edge of the sun platform.'

The banker's air of total withdrawal had vanished; his tone was almost conciliatory.

'We've got our guns,' said Pestiaux.

'He's got more firepower than all of you put together,' went on Dr Poortman. He got up from his camp stool; he seemed to rise also in mental stature with the movement. He faced the three members of the gang, with his hands behind his back.

'He doesn't need any of you three any more,' he continued. He gave a deprecating little shrug. 'He doesn't need me any more either. Nor the million dollars. He's gone overboard on the bomb idea.'

He quirked his eyebrows at Bonnay. Until now, the gang leader had regarded Dr Poortman merely as a million dollars wrapped in an ill-fitting ski suit; now he was becoming strikingly human. And – Bonnay would hardly have admitted it – rather a likeable one. Dr Poortman was, in fact, formulating what Bonnay himself had been thinking.

'He could come back and pick you off one by one with single shots, or with one volley from his automatic rifle,' Dr Poortman said. 'You're supernumeraries in his grand scheme.'

'What does supernumeraries mean?' asked Pestiaux uneasily.

'Odd men out – fifth wheel on the wagon,' responded Dr Poortman with a smile. 'He could just as well push you over the cliff, as he says.'

'I can appreciate his grudge about losing his land – the same thing happened to me,' said Kennet unexpectedly; Dr Poortman's calm, matter-of-fact statements seemed to have the effect of throwing the spotlight on each man's basic motivations. 'They built a huge highway to serve the Channel tunnel across my farm – the Kennets have been there in Kent since Roman times. That's one of the things which brought me into the Chunnel bomb scheme.'

'And the others?' Even Bonnay had never heard Kennet open up like this before; he had always viewed him as a taciturn, private person.

'They paid me out for my land, but so what?' he went on, looking down at his feet. 'I hadn't a son any more. He was part of the shitty deal life dished out to me, after the wife was killed in a car crash.'

'Where is your son?' Dr Poortman was exploiting the gang's uncertainty; it was a skilful softening-up for what, in his mind, was to come. Kennet's life story was relevant only to that.

'I can also understand Stefan's hatred against the tribesmen,' Kennet said with unexpected heat. 'That's the way I hate the Channel. It drove me to Jules' outfit. It took my son away from me.'

'How?'

'The Channel ferry disaster. 1987. *The Herald of Free Enterprise*. Drowned. Trapped below decks.'

Bonnay quickly resumed the reins of leadership. 'Are you trying to say that you'd rather go along with Stefan?'

Kennet's reply was unhesitating. 'No, no way. It's plain crazy. It won't work. You know that too, Jules. You told him so.'

Dr Poortman assumed his board-of-directors air. 'So, you three gentlemen simply intend to sit here and wait for Stefan to come back and pressure you into something for which you have no stomach?'

'What else can we do?' asked Pestiaux. 'We can't jump off the cliff.'

Dr Poortman addressed Bonnay. 'There's me.'

'What are you trying to say, Dr Poortman?'

'I – on behalf of my banking consortium – will offer you 100,000 American dollars each to set me free.'

'You must be joking!' exclaimed Bonnay. 'One hundred thousand – why, you're worth a million to us!'

'Not to you three – to five of you, including Stefan,' replied Dr Poortman. 'That means a five-way split of the million – 200,000 dollars each. Right?'

'A drop of one hundred thousand each . . .'

'If – and the if gets bigger all the time – if you live to see the million,' went on Dr Poortman. 'Accept my offer, and I won't press charges against you. I will also exert all my influence to see that you are given safe passage out of Lesotho. In other words, all the things you are demanding in your ransom, without the risks.'

Bonnay shook his head. 'These are a lot of fine words. You won't say the same, once you're out and free.'

'I am a banker, and in my game millions are exchanged on the basis of a man's word – sometimes even over a telephone,' he said quietly. 'If I say I will give you 100,000 dollars each, you can be sure you will get it.'

'You're asking us to cut our price – and cut our losses.' Kennet gave no indication what he was thinking about the offer.

'The losses include your loss of freedom – if you go along with Stefan's crazy scheme to kidnap Grania Yeats and plant a bomb in the Katse control chamber. You are men of action, and you yourselves know it won't work. It's a dead-end which means either death or capture. I'm offering you something positive and constructive.'

'Say, for the sake of argument, that we accept your offer,' said Bonnay tentatively. 'How do you think we get out of here? What do we do about Stefan?'

'And Hayward,' added Kennet. 'He's gone overboard on the bomb – he's besotted on hi-tech bombs, for the sake of hi-tech. It's a wonder he ever deserted the IRA.'

'It was only because the Chunnel bomb gave him the opportunity to strike directly at the heart of the British. He'd have been an IRA hero forever after,' said Bonnay. 'He couldn't go back – he's been on the run with us ever since.'

'True, you can't get out of here – now,' said Dr Poortman. 'But Hayward now knows the way because Stefan took him along. You can force him to show you – at gunpoint.'

'And Stefan?'

'You three jump him the moment he comes back down the rope ladder – you've all got guns. He won't be expecting an ambush. After that, it's over to you to handle the situation.'

'What about Grania Yeats?' asked Bonnay further.

'First, I don't think any of you believe he'll be able to kidnap her, do you? If he does, by handing her over unharmed to the authorities, you'll earn yourselves another plus point.' Dr

237

Poortman unexpectedly addressed Pestiaux. 'The other two have spoken up – what about you?'

Pestiaux looked embarrassed and muttered, 'I go along with Jules, whatever. My gun's his.'

'The question of charges against us . . . I'm not too happy about it,' said Kennet. 'How can you be sure that someone like General Mak won't take the whole matter out of your hands and put us under lock and key?'

'The Highlands Project is costing over four billion and my consortium has contributed directly and indirectly a major share of that sum,' said Dr Poortman. 'Its influence – and mine – are accordingly immense. I can only say that if I ask for something, it is most likely to be done.'

He looked round the trio. 'Well?' he asked after a silence.

Kennet said, 'Are you prepared to put your proposal on paper?'

'If you wish.'

Bonnay said slowly, 'It's a way out of a growingly impossible situation. I, for one, will buy it.'

Kennet's answer was a long time in coming. 'That goes for me too.'

Pestiaux added, 'I said, my gun is for Jules – whatever.'

Dr Poortman smiled. 'Good. Then we'll await Stefan's return – on red alert.'

CHAPTER THIRTY-FOUR

'These maps are useless!' exclaimed Sholto in disgust. 'Look – here's a whole area of at least 150 square kilometres without so much as the name of a peak or a river!'

'Is that what makes you think the Four Bushmen are there?' asked Grania in a small voice.

'It's the general area all right,' went on Sholto. 'But specifically where?'

Grania and Sholto were together in the big lounge at 'Cherry Now.' It was late Friday afternoon, after their interview with General Mak. Spread out on the large table were a number of maps, weighted down with books. It was beginning to grow dark; the lights were on; but far in the east the last sun still picked out the sombre line of the Malutis with snow cloudbanks starting to spill over them.

'Sholto!' said Grania. 'Must you go? And alone? Wouldn't a helicopter serve the same purpose? I'm sure that if you asked General Mak he'd arrange another sweep for you where you want to go.'

Her eyes travelled over his face and the hard, tough body with the wide shoulders and narrow waist of the dedicated canoeist and climber. The power-to-weight ratio of the man was phenomenal. Also, his face seemed harder; resolved would have been a better word.

Sholto laughed wryly and slapped the map with the back of his hand. 'Where? That would be General Mak's first question. What could I tell him? Somewhere west or south of the Namahadi Pass, or maybe not, maybe where the map simply says, "sponge-unmapped"?'

'It would be quicker, safer . . .' replied Grania rather helplessly.

'And noisier,' added Sholto. 'You can hear a helicopter's rotors kilometres away, especially with the echo from the

239

mountains. Plenty of time to hide away all the tell-tale traces –
including Dr Poortman.'

'Sholto, tell me before you set off tomorrow, what do you
hope to achieve even if you do locate the Four Bushmen?'

'Jonathan didn't write that last message – in his own blood –
without some desperate purpose. I see it as the key to all the
incredible events that have happened over the past few days.'

'Even to the awful hijacking this morning? It seems like light
years away now.'

Sholto put down the protractor and ruler with which he was
working on the maps. 'Yes, Grania. General Mak sees the
kidnapping of Dr Poortman, Jonathan's murder, and the heist
of the Eagle of Time as separate, unrelated events. I believe
there is a connecting thread running through them, if only we
could find it.'

'And you hope to find that at the Four Bushmen?'

'I don't know what I am looking for there,' he replied slowly.
'But I know that if I can find it, I'll be right on target, and it'll
yield clues we are all looking for.'

'If it's a hide-out for the gang and the Maluti Rider, do you
intend going in there all by yourself?'

'It's a reconnaissance – a reconnaissance by stealth,' said
Sholto. 'We – that includes General Mak – can take it from there
afterwards. To know *where* they are holed up would in itself be
invaluable information.'

'For all you know, they could be sitting tight in Maseru.'

'I might think that if I hadn't had this bond with Jonathan. He
didn't write that message for nothing.'

The telephone rang in the hall; Sholto went to answer.

Grania eyed the collection of maps sightlessly, miserably. It
was clear that Sholto regarded his journey next day – Saturday –
merely as a continuation of his trip interrupted by the news of
the Eagle of Time's theft and not as a different venture. So the
arrangements stood: it was tacitly accepted that she would stay
and act as 'communications link' at 'Cherry Now' for the next
three days while he was away. He had not repeated his request to
her to explain about Switzerland; without clarification, it was
plain, there would be no invitation to join him. This was the way

it would always be now between them – no shared intimacies – if she continued to hide her secret from him. She knew that she loved him and wanted him; without her inner unburdening, their relationship would – could – never be what they both wanted.

A wave of guilt and revulsion swept over her. She could not tell him – it was too big, too horrible! She could not suddenly spring it on anyone who was unprepared! The trauma of it all required the presence of an equal trauma to expurgate its horror; now was not the time! Would it ever be right? Could she ever go to him and reveal what had happened to her?

She heard him still talking on the phone; she looked panic-stricken round the big table. She could blurt it all out now when he returned, ask him to try and understand the un-understand-able. No! She couldn't do it! The far mountains glowed like blood against the dark sky, like her own blood, when she had surfaced in the cool hospital bed, so calm and clinical after the heat and horror of what had happened.

They could go on, Sholto and she, and they could love – in a kind of way – and perhaps be happy, in a kind of way – but her secret would always lie between them, by day, and between them in her bed at night.

From his voice, she assumed that the phone conversation must be ending. If she told him now, would she lose him? Would he turn his back and walk away in disgust? Most likely. She could not take the risk of losing him; yet unless she told him, she would never have him – not the way she had when he grabbed her from certain death as she toppled over the lammergeyer precipice. Keep talking, Sholto, let me think! Silent anguish swept over her like one of the avalanches in the remote high Maluti peaks which brushes away half a mountain without a witness to its convulsions. Was not the time now? They were together; they would be together until the opening ceremonies began and then they would be engulfed by the public appearances, the meetings with dignitaries, the dinners and the luncheons . . .

She heard Sholto put down the phone. No! The time was not right!

Sholto came in. 'Are you all right, Grania? You look very pale.'

'It must be the light. I'm perfectly all right.'

He continued to eye her curiously, but added, 'That was General Mak.'

'Have there been any developments?' Anything, anything to lead away from the abyss which yawned at her feet while he had been busy talking.

'Nothing. All he wanted to tell me was that the Cabinet, and the South Africans and consortium together, have decided to play along with the kidnappers – for the moment, anyway. They will propose a neutral mediator – probably an ambassador in Maseru – in a message before the main lunch time news bulletin tomorrow. That's the method the kidnappers asked for communications to be made. I'm taking my small transistor radio along; I'll listen with interest.'

'Are they climbing down, then? Are they willing to pay the ransom?'

'Certainly not. It's more a plot to win elbow-room. General Mak admits frankly that the kidnappers have a knife at their throats – especially after the heist of the Eagle of Time.'

'Any word from the Maluti Rider about that?'

'Nothing. In fact, General Mak is, so to speak, down on his knees taking the mandatory count. I'm glad he phoned. It gave me the chance to tell him I'd be away for the next three days.'

'What did he say to that?'

'He hardly bothered to ask. He thought . . .' he looked at her keenly, '. . . that we were going off somewhere together.'

She let her eyes slide down that imaginary line-of-sight along her right cheek.

'It's a logical deduction.'

The silence fell between them.

Finally, she said, 'I'll see you off in the morning.'

'It'll be very early. About six. It'll still be dark and cold.'

'I'll see you off, Sholto.'

Had things been otherwise she could have fussed over his food, his equipment, checked his gear, let him know in a hundred small ways that she loved him. But the reserve between

242

them forbade all that: it left only the stilted, polite phrases on the surface, and the heartbreak beneath.

'Are you taking your gun along?'

He shook his head. 'Not this time – it was simply a nuisance before, even for such a short time. Kept banging around in my anorak pocket, the sort of thing which would throw one completely off balance of a stiff rock-face climb.'

'So you're heading into the lion's den unarmed?'

He grinned a little. 'No, I've got this.' He fished from a small canvas bag on the table a wicked, foot-long saw-edged survival knife with a razor-sharp blade. He pulled it from its sheath.

'Everything a man needs in the field – plus! There's even a compass here in the haft, and a tiny cable-saw and fishing-line and hooks.'

'You'll phone me from Oxbow again?'

She realised from the way he framed his reply that even in the short space of a day – had it been because he had been on his own and had had time to think things over? – their relationship was not quite the same.

'If you want. It'll still be very early, though. Nothing much could have happened.'

'I want, Sholto.'

'Very well, I will then.'

That was not the way she wanted it! Was his sortie into the mountains in fact also a sortie into himself, to reorient himself towards her, as well as its stated purpose, to find the kidnappers' hide-out? Would she lose him – forever – among the same high peaks where they had found one another to begin with?

Her eyes were full of shadows.

Her eyes were full of shadows the following morning too, from a sleepless night when she stood in her dressing gown on the terrace at 'Cherry Now' in the cold grey light and raised her hand in salute as he got into his light pick-up to drive away. A raised hand – that was all.

Go and tell him your secret, Grania! You may never see him alive again!

CHAPTER THIRTY-FIVE

There were two phone calls to Grania that morning. One was from Sholto at Oxbow a few hours later – and the other was the call that never was.

She both welcomed and half-dreaded Sholto's call. Its metallic ring cut through the big, empty house – Sholto's mother was still away until the following Wednesday, two days before the opening ceremony. Grania could not hold herself still as the inordinate inner pressures built up inside her mind. They seemed to rip her apart in opposite directions. She half-hoped Sholto would cue her in on what she should do, but in the event the call might have been a prosaic one from a mountaineer to his base camp: the weather was sunny, although it had snowed on the high peaks overnight. Base camp, that was as she saw herself – unless and until she could unmask her secret. She put down the phone and wandered unhappily through the house.

The other call might have followed soon after, had it not been for the information Sholto's office in Maseru gave to the inquirer with the soft Irish accent and pleasant voice. He was, he said, a fellow canoeing enthusiast from Natal who had brought Sholto some spares for his kayak.

With his free hand Hayward gave a triumphant power sign at Sholto's secretary's words – the sort of gesture a golfer makes when he has killed the opposition with an eagle putt. There was hardly room in the public phone booth for both Hayward and Stefan. They were at Ficksburg, less than half a dozen kilometres away from 'Cherry Now' – and Grania.

'I'm sorry – but he'll be away for the next three days,' the woman told Hayward. 'But if you wish a message to be passed on, you can contact Miss Grania Yeats on his farm outside the town. We have been instructed to redirect any calls to her there.'

Hayward kept his voice calm, while his eyes blazed with inner excitement at Stefan.

'Have you the number handy?'

The secretary gave it to him, and added, 'I'm sure Miss Yeats won't mind if you drop the spares off at the farm. You can call her there first and check, if you like.'

'I'll do that.'

Hayward put down the instrument and smacked his palms together. 'Played right into our hands – couldn't be better – ' He gave Stefan an outline of the message.

'Let's get out there right away,' he added. 'It's a piece of cake. All we have to do now is persuade the lady to join us.'

'No,' said Stefan. 'We'll wait. Today would be premature. The secretary said Banks only left today, didn't she?'

'This morning.'

'Grania Yeats could smell a rat if we come up with our cover story so soon today,' went on Stefan.

'The secretary didn't say where he'd gone,' answered Hayward. 'But if we strike while the iron is hot . . .'

'This is a case where the iron is still too hot to strike,' replied Stefan. 'Let Banks get well clear, wherever he's gone, and then we'll spring the story on her. Also, tomorrow will be Sunday. A good day for what we have in mind – not many people around, especially at the farm.'

'Aren't we crowding our schedule by leaving the kidnap another day?' asked Hayward doubtfully. 'How long will she take to fix the pediment? We've got to get the bomb planted at Katse as well. It will all take time.'

'We've still six days left,' answered Stefan.

'We've also got to restore the Eagle . . .'

'That's the quickest and easiest job of the lot,' replied Stefan confidently. 'Now we'll get back to "Rali's Rest" and stay overnight at the farm. We don't want to hike up to the cave unnecessarily – the climb takes it out of the horses, all the up-and-down mountain work.'

Hayward glanced at the Maluti Rider. Maybe horses were the only thing he had ever loved – since the necklacing.

They moved out of the phone booth into the street between fine sandstone buildings.

Stefan asked, 'You've got her number safe?' Hayward

nodded. 'We'll make the call tomorrow – from here, it's easy and close to the heart of the operation.'

At lunch time, Sholto heard the authorities' compromise offer to the kidnappers over his small transistor radio as he halted in a rock-strewn gully which led to the snow-bound peaks to the northwest.

The announcer said:

'*Here is an important announcement. The Lesotho government, in consultation with South Africa and the Swiss banking consortium involved in the Highlands Project, have decided to make an approach to the kidnappers of Dr Hans Poortman, who was abducted from Katse Lodge last Wednesday, using the services of a neutral intermediary. So far there has been no direct communication from Dr Poortman's captors, and it is not known whether Dr Poortman is uninjured or in good health.*

Dr Johann Dietz, West German ambassador in Lesotho, has agreed to act as intermediary between the authorities and the kidnappers, who are asked to telephone Maseru 050–31–2121. This is a special number which has been installed for the purpose, and the confidentiality of any information will be strictly respected, as well as the identity and whereabouts of any caller. The Lesotho government has also given assurances that no attempt will be made to trace the origin of calls made to this number, in order to facilitate the establishment of a link for negotiations between the parties concerned . . .'

Grania would have heard the bulletin too, Sholto told himself. He could not dissociate his thoughts from her and what she might be doing at 'Cherry Now' – he'd been through all that a hundred times since he had started out from Oxbow and crossed the tributaries which fed the upper Malibamatso, heading towards the great peaks where he knew he must go. Now, as he turned his face more west than north, he was aware in himself of the uncontrollable compulsion which had underlain his decision to set out, and exclude even Grania. No, it was not to exclude her, he told himself now as the wind came up icy at his back, it was to try and come to terms with her, a flight further and

246

further away from the past, into the future, a flight of the heart, as well as of the body . . .

By sunset he was in a strange, nondescript world of iced-up boulders rearing out of sponges overlain by treacherous crusts of dirty ice; the purity of snow, up ahead where the Four Bushmen hid their prehistoric heads among other peerless peaks, was yet to come.

Grania. He pitched his tiny scarlet pup-tent behind a huge boulder to protect it from the wind and looked into the cold blue flame of his gas burner, the way he and she had done together while searching for the lammergeyer eyrie. He sat staring – time had no meaning up here in the high peaks. It was a world of neutral time, and Grania was behind, in the past, but also in front, in the future. His route to her seemed as uncertain as that which lay before his feet tomorrow.

Grania!

The ringing bell cut through the still homestead like an alarm to action stations.

It was just after nine o'clock next morning, Sunday.

Grania sprinted from the terrace to the hall and the telephone. Her immediate thought was that it was Sholto; but she would have even welcomed a disc jockey's gag call to break the emptiness and isolation of 'Cherry Now'. She had tried to pass the interminable weekend by reading Sholto's scrapbook of press cuttings of his canoeing successes; she even checked his silver cups one by one and correlated them with the accounts of his achievements. But nothing helped. It all came back to square one: tell him, or else!

'Is that Miss Grania Yeats?'

There was an accent, a shade of inflexion which revealed to Grania that the caller was Irish.

'Yes.'

'Before I go on, I must ask you to regard the contents of this call as strictly confidential, and for your ears alone. Is that clear?'

Grania felt a cold shiver of apprehension go down her spine. The man seemed to be talking under stress.

247

'Until I know who you are and what it is all about, I cannot give such an undertaking.'

'I think we saw one another briefly at General Mak's headquarters. I am one of his aides. Captain Hedley.'

'I'm afraid I don't remember.'

The voice may have relaxed a little, or it may have been the inrush of Irish charm. 'No matter then. But I hope we are to have the pleasure of another meeting very soon.'

Grania did not reply. The man went on. 'General Mak has asked me to phone you. You see, we have found the Eagle of Time.'

'*What!*'

'This is the reason for the utmost secrecy – for the moment.'

'Did Sholto – I mean, Mr Banks – have anything to do with it?'

Grania was not to know that the slight variation in tone meant that Hayward saw his chance to improvise on this piece of news.

'I am happy to say, yes.'

'But – he promised to phone me from Oxbow if . . .'

Hayward also chalked up this piece of information for future reference.

'As you can appreciate, he's right up to his neck in things arising out of the recovery.'

For the first time since the conversation began, Grania sounded doubtful.

'Strange.'

'But we also have a small problem, Miss Yeats.'

'He's not hurt? I mean, is that why he's not phoning himself?'

To Hayward himself, his laugh sounded reassuring, avuncular.

'Not at all, not at all, Miss Yeats. We need your services urgently – this morning.'

'What are you trying to say, Captain Hedley?'

'The Eagle of Time has been slightly damaged. I cannot go into the circumstances now. You can understand that we cannot allow such a priceless masterpiece to go on show again showing any signs of damage – it would boost the image of the thieves in the public's eyes.'

'Thieves?' asked Grania. 'I thought only one man was involved – the Maluti Rider.'

Hayward backtracked on his slip of the tongue. 'It is an involved story, which we will tell you as soon as we see you. Are you free to come right away?'

'Yes – but where?'

'We understand you have your tools with you?'

'Yes, but . . .'

'Bring them along. It is only a small thing, but it needs your expert attention.'

'Where is it damaged?' asked Grania quickly. 'Where – and to what extent? Is it in the clockwork, or the pediment, or where?'

'You'll see for yourself.' Hayward felt it was time to land the fish rather than go on playing it – at the end of a telephone line where one slip could prove fatal.

He said in a formal tone, 'The greatest security surrounds all this, Miss Yeats – do you understand?'

'Yes, but there is so much I don't know.'

'In order to avoid any possibility of the Eagle being seen prematurely in its damaged state, we want you to meet us at a secret rendezvous close to the town of Ficksburg . . .'

'Us? Who is us? You mean you and Sholto?'

'No. Unfortunately he is still at the scene of operations. I have with me Captain Bresler of South African Security.'

'The Eagle was recovered *outside* Lesotho then?'

Hayward was sweating in the phone booth. 'Yes – and no,' he replied judicially. 'It's a very delicate question of localities, which we will explain to you personally. What we are asking you right away is to meet us at ten o'clock. The place we propose is a landmark about five or six kilometres from Ficksburg, on the main road running along the Lesotho border. It's a strange-looking conical hill close to the road. You can't miss it, if you don't know it already. There's also a railway siding right opposite the hill, and a big main road junction on your left a couple of kilometres before you reach the hill from the Ficksburg side.'

'I remember passing the hill on my way here.'

'Good. Then we will meet you there at ten? We are in a yellow Datsun pick-up. You can't mistake it. What will you be driving?'

Grania's mind was racing. 'I'll use Sholto's car – he took his farm pick-up to Oxbow and parked it there. I don't know much about makes of cars. It's an ordinary grey medium-sized saloon.'

Then Grania said suddenly, 'Why all this undercover business of a rendezvous, Captain Hedley? Why don't you come straight here to "Cherry Now"? There's no one here except a servant or two, and I could work on the Eagle here in ideal surroundings. I am sure Sholto would be only too pleased.'

The fish had slipped off the hook! Hayward swallowed and said, 'I'm afraid you do not understand the security implications, Miss Yeats. It may sound somewhat cloak-and-dagger, but I assure you the precautions are essential, if we don't want the masterpiece to slip through our fingers again.'

'I don't understand.'

'Be at the rendezvous at ten, and Captain Bresler and I will explain everything.'

The explanation was self-evident the moment Grania pulled up alongside the pick-up parked by the side of the road near the rendezvous hill – a Colt and an AK-47.

Hayward had her passenger's door opened almost before the car's wheels stopped turning; he flopped down in the seat and thrust the Colt against Grania's left side. Grania didn't have time to react to her surge of fear at her photographic impression of the man coming at her from the other side – it was the same swift, sidling movement she had seen on the TV monitors. A hard, potent stocky body moving across the road like a sidewinder closing on its prey. Then the door was open, the ignition keys whipped out of the still idling engine, and the AK-47 in her right side, low down, so that it was hidden from any chance passing motorist.

She was looking into pigmentless eyes, down a tunnel unterminated by compassion. She noted his bristles from a bad shave; he smelt of horse sweat and gun oil

The identity of the man crashed home on Grania. 'The Maluti Rider!'

'If you realise that, keep it to yourself for your own good!' snapped Stefan.

He addressed Hayward. 'Hold her like that, Burt. I'll fix one of the tyres.'

Bonnay would have admired the attention to fine detail of the operation: Stefan whipped a valve-screw from his pocket, and dropped on his knees by the right front tyre. The air escaped in one gasp like a spirit rocketing to salvation.

Stefan was back at Grania's door in a flash. 'Out – into my truck! Don't try any games if anyone comes past!' He started to move aside for her to pass and then rapped out, 'Your tools – where are they?'

Grania indicated the dashboard shelf. They were wrapped in a soft leather roll about a foot long.

'Bring 'em, Burt. Now!' He half-jostled Grania towards the pick-up on the other side of the tarmac. 'If any nosey motorist wonders about your car, he'll see the flat. Owner hitched a lift to town to get help, he'll say, it's so close.'

They reached the truck. 'In between us,' ordered Stefan. 'Don't try anything funny, I warn you, like interfering with my driving. Burt will take care of you if you do.'

Grania was sandwiched in between the two men. The butt of Hayward's Colt balanced on the seat next to her. It would blast away her kidneys if he pulled the trigger.

Grania managed to stammer out as Stefan gunned the engine hard, made a swift U-turn, and accelerated away down the road, 'What have you done with Sholto?'

'Nothing.'

There was an edge of fear in Grania's voice. 'You're lying! You're the Irishman on the phone! You said Sholto had asked . . .'

'The name's not Hedley but Hayward,' retorted Hayward. 'As for your Sholto, we haven't seen him. Nor do we want to. You're the one we want.'

'You said . . .'

'Shut up!' snarled Stefan.

'And the Eagle – what have you done to the Eagle of Time?'

'Put a sock in it, or I will,' rapped out Hayward. 'And remember the warning about trying to attract attention, see?'

Stefan slingshotted the truck round the tight bends and

sweeping undulations of the beautiful border road for the next eighty kilometres. Grania had travelled this same road with Sholto from the Golden Gate to 'Cherry Now'. Here and there from among the sandstone hills or the tops of innumerable small passes there were great views eastward towards Lesotho – and, beyond, the magic Malutis. Somewhere out there among those distant peaks, Grania told herself, Sholto must be trying to locate the Four Bushmen.

Suddenly, with no exchange of words beforehand, Stefan braked hard to a standstill. Like a rehearsed performance, Hayward withdrew the Colt from Grania's side and tied a blindfold round her eyes. It was so deftly done that she had not even time to protest. Then Stefan raced off again. After a while, the truck slowed, Hayward got out to open a gate (she heard it squeak) and then they set off again along a bumpy gravel track. There was no knowing how far, or in what direction, they went.

Then Grania was aware, when they stopped, of the smell of horses and of the moist vegetation one gets among the countless streams and willow-lined rivers of the Golden Gate region.

'Can you ride?'

It was the only thing Stefan or Hayward had said to her for the past half an hour or more. She nodded.

'Give me your foot.'

Stefan cradled her sandal in his hand – she could feel the power of it – guided it into a stirrup, and hefted her into a saddle. Then she heard the clink and chomp of other horses and Stefan took her rein and led. Hayward followed.

After a time, the pony's gait became short and economical and the saddle leaned back at her on the upward slope as the animal picked its way towards the high peaks – and Stefan's hide-out.

CHAPTER THIRTY-SIX

Pestiaux's bullet should have killed Stefan.

There was nothing wrong with his aim: the target was the Maluti Rider's head. It was a difficult upward-angle shot, from the floor of the cave into the dim light of the roof. But Pestiaux was a deadly artist with his favourite Makarov; moreover, the opening of the trapdoor to allow Grania, Hayward and Stefan to enter provided a silhouette.

Stefan, with his animal-like instinct for self-preservation, had sent Grania first down the rope ladder into the cave. He had no reason to suspect that the other members of the Chunnel Gang were lying in wait to jump him as he entered.

It was Grania really who saved his life. She had gone down the swaying rungs uncertainly; it may have been the effects of the blindfold on her eyes all afternoon up the mountain ascent from 'Rali's Rest', combined with the dimness of the cave. Whatever it was, she half-tripped a metre or so from the bottom, jumped unhandily from the ladder, and in doing so kicked the ladder clear of her.

Stefan had just put his feet on the rungs via the trapdoor. His head snapped into view in Pestiaux's sights; the ladder jerked backwards from Grania's lurch.

Pestiaux fired.

The flash and crash in the confined space might have been that of a 155mm howitzer. It stunned Grania into immobility on her hands and knees. It took both Bonnay and Kennet completely by surprise; the leader's orders to the others had been to stand about apparently nonchalantly with guns concealed and to seize Stefan when he reached the cave floor.

Pestiaux, always impetuous, and eager to assert his standing in Bonnay's eyes as the faithful and fearless gunhand, decided to improve upon Bonnay's orders. He alone would bring the game back and lay it at his master's feet. When Stefan's head showed and Grania at the same moment fell off the ladder, he whipped out his Makarov and fired.

The slug chipped the rock next to Stefan's temple and ricocheted away screaming.

If you are dropped once behind the wicket with a killer like the Maluti Rider, you don't get a second chance.

The swift, deadly response might have been rehearsed. He notched a knee round the topmost rung of the rope ladder and threw the AK-47 to hip-level. It wasn't a single shot which caught Pestiaux in the chest; it was a whole volley. It mule-kicked him back across Grania's recumbent figure and against the cave wall. Perhaps he was dead before he smashed into the rock.

Grania felt as if the flames from the AK-47 had lanced into her eyes, blinding her, and into her ears, paralysing them. She sank down flat, her arms outflung across her head. She had a momentary glimpse of Dr Poortman falling, too. Was he a victim also of the AK-47, or was he dropping down for cover?

She heard a startled oath from nearby and the rasp of frenzied shoe-leather against the cave floor. Stefan heard – and saw – Kennet dive at a low crouch for the magazine on the right-hand side of the cave, dragging his machine-pistol from his pocket. If he could put the line of the cave between himself and the ladder, Stefan's line-of-sight would be blocked by the wall . . .

Stefan fired a single shot.

Kennet didn't drop; his running knees kept going. But above them his torso bucked and jerked convulsively and the Scorpion went spinning out of his grasp from nerves and muscles severed somewhere in his upper spine area. Grania jerked up her head at the sound of a thin, animalistic scream coming from the Man of Kent as he plucked his way along the wall, blindly, towards the entrance to the sun platform.

Bonnay never even had time to grab his Browning.

Stefan was above him on the rungs, at head-level. The barrel of the automatic was almost in his face. He could smell the stench of hot cordite.

'Burt!' yelled Stefan to Hayward above, who was leaning head-and-shoulders through the trapdoor gap now. 'Watch him! Shoot him if he tries anything!'

Stefan sprang from the rungs and across Grania. Then, in a low, killer crouch he went after the jerking, bleeding figure clawing in agony at the rock wall.

Stefan grabbed Kennet from behind by the collar, threw him bodily through the cave entrance. Even in his desperation, there must have been some realisation left in Kennet as to what Stefan intended to do. He fell, squirmed back, grabbed Stefan round the ankle.

Grania saw the AK go up.

'No, no!' She had not meant to scream; her vocal chords were acting on some other level of impulse.

Stefan kicked the clutching hands free with a shove which sent Kennet towards the edge of the precipice. It was not quite strong enough to project Kennet over; the punch of a new burst of slugs did that. Seconds later, there was a dull thumping noise. Grania remembered the whale-back ridge, on which a body must fall and bounce clear. She rammed her face against the rock and gagged.

She heard, but did not see, Bonnay's execution. A sense of total unreality, coupled with terror, wrapped her round like a plastic body shroud. She might have been hearing from inside her coffin the scuff of boots, the tight angry words, the harsh shrill denials, and the final march out to the sun platform. Then the final two-shot obsequies of the AK-47. She plugged her ears with her cupped hands. Then the silence.

It was broken by Stefan's voice. 'Hell's teeth, is she all right? Did that bastard get her with his first shot?'

'I don't see any blood,' Hayward answered.

'If he tagged her, it's the end of the Eagle – you can't fix it yourself.'

Stefan – she knew it was Stefan from the power of his hands – rolled her over on to her back. She managed to bring her vision up from beneath that awful opaque cover and opened her eyes. She wasn't sure which was worse – the blankness, or the close-up of those colourless eyes, which even the killings had failed to ignite.

Stefan propped her up. 'Get some water!' he ordered Hayward.

It tasted of rock and mountain vegetation.

'You weren't hit, you're all right?'

She had seen Stefan go after Kennet like a wounded buck to finish him off; she half-gagged into the brown water. Those solicitous words could mean nothing but his own self-interest.

She threw a glance round the cave, as if trying to relate it in her shocked mind with what she knew had just taken place. All she saw was Dr Poortman sitting with his back to the wall near the entrance to the magazine. Kennet's chase must have gone right over him. The banker was deadly pale, but he lifted a hand in salute when he saw Grania look round.

'Is that what you brought me here to see?' she demanded in a shaky voice.

Stefan said to Hayward, 'Get the Eagle. It may make her feel better.'

Hayward went to the stores chamber on the opposite side from the magazine. He came back, knelt down next to Grania, and pulled the plastic shopping bag clear. The bright gas light made points of fire of the jewels, and an otherworldly gold of the lammergeyer's wings.

The sight of it cleared Grania's head. 'It isn't damaged; there's not a mark on it!'

She got to her knees and turned it round and round, as if to convince herself. 'The clock's even going – the right time!' she went on.

Stefan also got to his feet. His bulk had hidden the object which brought a rush of horror to Grania's stomach so that she thought she would vomit without being able to control herself.

A big chunk of Pestiaux's chest was missing; where it had been was a bloodied mess. There was a pool of blood under the body which, to Grania's overheated susceptibilities, seemed to be spreading.

Stefan followed her glance and reaction.

'Burt, we can't talk with that about. Give me a hand, will you?'

They were careless about their guns: Stefan propped the AK-47 against the cave wall and Hayward thrust his pistol into his pocket. It would have been the time to jump them – if the thought had crossed either Grania or Dr Poortman's minds. Perhaps Stefan realised that they were still out for the count from shock.

He shocked them further. He and Hayward each took an arm and a leg, hauled the body through the entrance, and pitched it over the precipice. Their only other witness was a trail of blood.

'Clean it up, get a bucket,' ordered Stefan. Minutes later, he picked up the Eagle of Time as the water swirled close. 'Nothing must happen to this.'

'What are you trying to tell me?' Grania found it better to talk than stand silently by. Dr Poortman was also on his feet now.

'Why did you bring me here if the timepiece is all right?'

'I'll tell you. You can get busy on it tonight. Right away, if you're okay.'

'Hold it,' said Hayward. 'Apart from anything else, the gas light isn't good enough to work by. We'll have to wait until morning for sunlight.'

'That means valuable time lost,' replied Stefan. 'We can't afford it.'

'It's not only a question of removing the pediment, but also seeing that the clockwork activates the detonator – and it's far too tricky to risk by artificial light.'

'Detonator? What in heaven's name are you talking about?' demanded Grania.

Stefan came closer. She could smell what the killing had done for him. He had a stale, off-putting aura, like spent cordite.

'Let me spell it out so that there won't be any chance of a misunderstanding,' he said. 'I – we – kidnapped you today for a specific purpose – something beyond Burt's skill here.'

'Skill? Are you a clockmaker?'

Hayward grinned. 'Lady, my pals in the IRA would certainly like to hear that!'

Stefan cut in, 'He's a hi-tech bombmaker, one of the best in the world. I intend using the Eagle of Time as a piece of ultra-sophisticated circuitry to set off a bomb. Burt, go and get the

257

radio-trigger and show her what she has to do rather than jaw-jaw.'

Grania threw an anguished glance at Dr Poortman. 'You kidnapped Dr Poortman for a million dollars. What has he got to do with a bomb?'

'Nothing,' retorted Stefan. 'He was Bonnay's idea. Poortman has nothing to do with my plan.'

'Plan? What plan? What are you talking about, for heaven's sake?'

'You have to know so that Burt can prime the Eagle. But it's also your death warrant if you should somehow blab about it before next Friday's opening of the Highlands Project.'

'You're talking in riddles. You must be crazy.'

'See this little beauty?' He took the tiny timer from its purple plastic case and extended it in his palm to Grania. 'This is a radio trigger which sets off a bomb. That's putting it simply – Burt here can fill you in with the technicalities. I can't understand them myself. The bomb will be planted in the sluice-gate control chamber of the Katse Dam. I don't have to tell you that at the moment of the opening, the lammergeyer will spread its wings and the carillon will chime – yes?'

Grania nodded.

'Burt will fix it – with your prior co-operation – so that the clockwork will also activate the radio timer at that precise moment.'

Grania stared at him in disbelief. 'You are a monster – a cold-blooded monster!'

'Rali . . .' he began to reply heatedly, but cut himself short. 'No, that story is for another time – it's my reason. You will work under Burt tomorrow in order that he can insert the timer under the pediment where it can't be seen.'

'My answer is, no! Never! Never!'

Stefan hardly raised his voice. 'Never?' He reached for the AK-47, cocked it, and went to Dr Poortman. He pointed it at his face.

'You must realise by now that I mean what I say. Another life means nothing to me. It's your decision. Co-operate or – ' He raised the automatic to a firing position.

Grania stared desperately at Dr Poortman. Some of the colour which had come back into his face after the shooting drained away.

She said thickly, 'I'll do it. You leave me no choice.'

Stefan went on, 'I'll be watching you all the way. Don't try on any technical tricks. If you do – ' He nodded towards the banker. Then he addressed Hayward. 'Burt, there's something else we must do. Help me get all the explosives out of the cave – outside, up through the trapdoor. Get more lamps lit. We don't want anyone having bright ideas about escaping. We've got to have the decks clear for tomorrow.'

For Sholto there was no tomorrow. He squinted into the last light of the sun, trying desperately to locate what he knew must be the quadruple peaks of the Four Bushmen. It seemed hopeless. The terrible, limitless splendour of it all quivered slate-blue into the sunset. A light haze confused the issue further: anywhere, anywhere, lurking in the staggering wall of mountains which dramatised the horizon, could be his objective.

If he could get there.

He had spent hours casting about trying to find a pathway through the total desolation of the great sponge capping the plateau on which he now stood. It was an agglomeration of pools veneered over with a coating of dirty ice, whose treachery he had experienced several times during the afternoon when he thought he had found a through-route and had sunk up to his knees in the freezing muck. Wild scraggly sedges and wiry-leaved plants added to the confusion. He had tried a detour, but the deadly sponge stretched, as far as he could judge, right to the escarpment's edge where it plunged over thousands of metres into the Natal Drakensberg. On the other flank his route onward was blocked by a clutter of peaks, any of which would take a week in itself to scale – if it could be done at all. The wind on the exposed plateau was bitter; he was over 3500 metres up in the sky. If he could not progress next day, he would have to turn back.

Sholto pitched his tent in the lee of a big rock and turned on his small radio. It was almost time for the six o'clock news.

The announcer said:

'Events in the kidnapping drama of the Swiss banker and the disappearance of the Eagle of Time took a dramatic turn today with the disappearance of another key figure connected with next Friday's grand opening of the Highlands Project. Miss Grania Yeats, the artist responsible for the unique pediment of the Eagle of Time, disappeared today without trace from the farm "Cherry Now" where she has been staying as the guest of Mr Sholto Banks, ombudsman for the Swiss banking consortium in Lesotho. Mr Banks was away at the time . . .'

Grania! Sholto sat paralysed from shock. He screwed the sound volume up to its maximum, as if that would help. Grania!

'A car in which Miss Yeats is believed to have left the farm early this morning was found abandoned a few kilometres outside Ficksburg by the side of the main road after it had been reported to the South African police in the town. General Makoanyane, head of Lesotho's Security Branch, has assigned a team of top detectives to investigate this latest development, and is heading the search personally, in closest co-operation with the South African authorities. Although there were no signs of a struggle in the abandoned vehicle, fears are being expressed for the safety of Miss Yeats in the light of recent events. General Makoanyane has appealed to Mr Banks to contact him immediately. His present whereabouts are unknown. General Makoanyane also reports that there have been no attempts by Dr Poortman's kidnappers to communicate with Dr Dietz, the German ambassador and special intermediary nominated by the Lesotho government, in regard to the ransom demand for one million dollars . . .'

Sholto's mind felt as numb as his hands did from the wind sweeping across the ice plateau. Grania! He cursed himself inwardly for having left her; but who could have guessed she would be next on the kidnappers' hit list? There was no decision left any more about his quest for the Four Bushmen: he'd have to get back in the morning. Maybe the search had only been wishful thinking of a kind; General Mak had been right, one needed facts to go on. He had held out against all the odds that

260

that blood-scrawled message in Jonathan's car was a fact, meant for him.

Sholto was so overwhelmed by the news that he did not notice that darkness had come, except for a star out among the peaks he had scanned earlier for any sign of the Four Bushmen.

Sholto did not move; the star did not move. Just that point of light among the peaks.

At length, he reached to light his stove, and his eye caught sight of the star which stared at him from its fixed position.

The thought crashed home to him: stars aren't static! That pinpoint of light had been in exactly the same position for – he tried to reckon rapidly – over an hour, at least! It wasn't a star! It was a light! A light from a cave, up there among those unknown peaks!

The kidnappers' hide-out!

The Four Bushmen!

Sholto tore open his backpack for his binoculars. They hardly helped, they weren't night glasses, but the image was better: it was a light all right! Sholto found his compass also and, shielding his flashlight for fear that it might by some chance be spotted from that distant light, checked the bearings and wrote them down.

It was the bearings which gave him the key at first light next day when he went – a final sortie – to try and find a way across the ice sponge. All the previous afternoon he had concentrated on and scoured the area on the escarpment flank; now, on the opposite fringe where the great peaks were, the bearings showed how wrong he'd been.

A row of horse's hooves picked a passage through the sedges and ice along the line of his bearings, heading for the Four Bushmen.

That blanketed wild pony he had spotted from the helicopter had been heading home! To the Maluti Rider's hide-out! To the Four Bushmen! It had been his horse!

Sholto plunged in after the hoof-trail.

261

CHAPTER THIRTY-SEVEN

Tap-tap.

Grania stirred uneasily. She had slept on a hair-trigger, or had, at least, attempted to sleep. She had jerked awake time and again, trying to come to terms with the crushing, overwhelming sense of guilt which split her brain apart, like lightning does the thunder-clouds among the peaks. Nine hundred: the expertise in her fingers had sentenced nine hundred unsuspecting men, women and children of the resettled mountain tribe below the Katse wall to an engulfing, watery death.

But, she kept telling herself, it was a choice of either working on the Eagle of Time with Hayward, or seeing Dr Poortman's head blasted away by Stefan's AK-47. Had she herself not witnessed his sickening butchery of Pestiaux, Kennet and Bonnay, she might have tried to call the Maluti Rider's bluff. However, she knew he wasn't bluffing. He'd have done the same to Dr Poortman without a qualm, if she had refused her skill for the Eagle of Time.

Tap-tap.

Grania sat up in her sleeping bag, tried to shake the noises out of her head. They would be there, would haunt her, to the end of time, perhaps finally drive her over the edge into insanity. She was sleeping in the stores chamber, while the men slept in the general area of the cave. It was bitterly cold inside the hide-out, and dark: both exits were locked. She had slept in an outsize anorak they had given her, plus felt boots.

Tap-tap-tap.

All the previous day, Monday, after her arrival late on Sunday afternoon, she and Hayward had worked on the Eagle of Time in the warmth and light of the sun platform. As Hayward watched her fingers go to work, first to remove the pediment, and then on to the time mechanism which governed the spreading of the wings, his cool professionalism turned to admiration, and he became an almost genial companion. Stefan prowled about the platform like a jailer, the AK-47 under his arm, continually demanding to know of what progress she had made. Dr Poortman sat on a fisherman's stool in the sun, unspeaking, as withdrawn as an autistic.

Grania had played the card she had held back as she lifted the lammergeyer from its pediment.

She indicated the complex tracery of cogwheels and wires which made their way past what looked like an outsize golden golf ball.

'You can't do it,' she said flatly. 'You can see for yourself, there is no space for the detonator.'

Stefan's shadow fell across her. He said in a rasping voice, 'What did you say?'

'I said, there is no room for your detonator. It can't fit in. It can't be done.'

He grabbed her by the shoulder, so that she winced away.

'Don't give me that!' he snarled. 'By God, you're here to fix it the way I say, and you'll do it!'

'It's a masterpiece of miniaturisation,' Hayward said. 'It could be the sweetest trigger device ever conceived. But we could mess up the whole thing at the wrong touch of a screwdriver.'

'Cut the crap – how do you get past what she says?' He jabbed his finger at the round, golden object. 'What is this for?'

Grania hesitated. He was indicating the secret capsule which contained her three miniature art masterpieces – the silver chalice pouring the symbolic water, the dinosaur embryo, and Moshoeshoe's grave with its mysterious red sand dune.

'Answer me, damn you! What is this for?' Stefan shouted.

'It's a secret capsule containing three miniature artworks of mine.'

'I asked, what is it *for*!'

'After the lammergeyer has spread its wings, the capsule will in turn unfold automatically. It can be viewed through the open side here where there is this tiny window which will also open and reveal the artworks. Normally the window is opaque glass.'

263

'At the same moment the mechanism activates the bird's wings?' Hayward demanded.

'Yes.'

Hayward laughed, a strange, unnatural laugh.

'Does it, by heavens, does it? Enniskillen and Hyde Park have nothing on the Eagle of Time! Get that capsule out, d'ye hear? My detonator will fit nice and neatly into the same space with a shade to spare. Eh, Stefan boy?'

Grania, sitting up in her sleeping bag, felt sick at the recollection, sick at how her fingers – her own fingers which had crafted that capsule as secret as her love for Sholto – had followed orders and removed it to yield place to the crazy genius of Hayward's bomber hands. She didn't follow the display of hi-tech expertise he indulged in over the next couple of hours, but when he had done, he grinned and ordered her, 'Now you can put back the pediment into place, and Stefan can restore the Eagle of Time.'

Today! Stefan was returning to Maseru today, Tuesday, casually to deposit the Eagle in its shopping bag at the foot of Moshoeshoe's statue in central Maseru with a note to say the kidnappers were returning the masterpiece out of consideration for its priceless uniqueness! As Hayward had mouthed in his off-beat way, the prettiest bomb an Irishman had ever confected. Literally, a time bomb, calibrated for next Friday's opening ceremony!

Tap-tap-tap!

It wasn't noises in her head.

There is only one sound like that. And the rock wall next to her head relayed it faintly from outside.

It was the clink of steel on steel. It was a mountaineer's hammer tapping home a piton into the rock-face.

Stefan heard it too.

Sholto and Stefan arrived on the sun platform together. Stefan fired in reflex. But a man descending from above in an abseil down a vertical cliff, so fast that the rope was singeing through the karabiners in Sholto's belt, makes a difficult target. Especially when firing into the sun after the total darkness of the cave.

Stefan missed.

Sholto missed his aim also.

264

His target had been the cave mouth – he had seen light the previous night from far below and had pinpointed it as best he could in the dark against the cliff face. A more gruesome beacon had been two mangled bodies, one with most of the chest shot away, and the other with a gunshot wound at the base of the neck. Their mutilated states indicated that they had crashed down the precipice. Sholto was not to know there had been a third body. Of Bonnay there was no sign.

It was only when Stefan flung open the cave's camouflaged door that Sholto was able to distinguish the mouth against the surrounding rocks. By then, it was too late.

He plumped on the sun platform's narrow end on all fours, snapped himself free of the rope, and snatched the survival knife from his belt. Stefan was upon him. He swung the AK like a club at Sholto's head. Sholto shifted, and let the barrel go by. Sholto flicked the knife, slashing the wrist of his gun hand. The automatic fell on to the rock. Stefan backed away, going into a fighting crouch. Sholto advanced, with the point of the knife upwards, kicked the gun clear of the fight.

Stefan moved in, fast. Too fast for the knife-point to find his jugular. His arms looped over Sholto's head, hugging him, and lifting him. His quick, adenoidal breathing beat into Sholto's right ear. Sholto kneed him, lunged sideways, trying to force his head against the rock face. But Stefan retained hold, his hands locked at the back of Sholto's neck.

Sholto got close to the rock-face, rapped Stefan's head. For a moment Stefan went soft, slackened his grip. Sholto hit him with a short left hook to the stomach. The knife would do the rest.

But Stefan wasn't out. He projected himself. The knife-point went past his shoulder, and Sholto's face was sticky with the blood from his wrist-wound. Sholto felt the Maluti Rider's leg go behind his to trip him. From a vertical position one moment, he found himself horizontal, looking into the sun which blinded him, to the man on top of him. He tried, with all his muscle-power, to hold his head clear of the rock, but Stefan slowly forced it back. There was nothing between the back of his head and a drop to the bottom where there were two mutilated bodies.

He tried to roll aside, inwards, towards the rock face. It gave Stefan the chance to disarm him. Sholto saw the saw-edge of his own knife start to come at him.

'Stop!'

It was Grania.

She stood on the extreme lip of the platform; her toes might even have been over the edge of the hideous drop. Her hands were raised above her head.

The new day's sun sparked and jostled off a thousand light points of the Eagle of Time.

'Stop!'

The word got through to Stefan. The knife held back.

'Leave him! Let him go! Or this goes over the edge!'

She was out of reach of his hands, had he tried to grab her ankles and pull her back. She spoke across Stefan to Hayward. The IRA man had dropped into a firing crouch at the open door: he couldn't miss.

'The force of the bullet will take me over the edge – and this with me!'

'You bitch, you little bitch!' he mouthed.

Grania moved her toes slightly. It was only a mountaineer who could have stood like that on the edge of a drop about a thousand metres sheer.

'Get back!' Grania told Stefan. 'Let Sholto get up. Stay away from that gun!'

Stefan raised himself slowly, watching Grania all the way.

'The knife,' she said. 'Drop it – right there!'

Sholto gathered it up as Stefan got to his feet. He joined her, the karabiners on his belt clinking in triumph.

'Now!' she told Stefan and Hayward (she could see Dr Poortman at the back of the entrance). 'Listen! In return for my not throwing the Eagle over the cliff, you will let Sholto, Dr Poortman and myself go free . . .'

Stefan broke in, 'You can't go on standing there on the edge of the cliff indefinitely.'

'The sooner I fall, the worse it will be for you,' she retorted. She threw a quick glance at Sholto. Never, she told herself inwardly, while he looks at me like that.

266

'You will give us free passage out of here and show us the way to safety,' she went on.

'And the Eagle?' asked Stefan.

'Comes with us.'

'What about Burt and me?'

'The time we take to get back to civilisation and report will give you plenty of time to make your getaway. What happens to you after that isn't our concern.'

You have too many trumps in your hands, Grania. You can't play them all. And your arms are getting tired.

Grania could feel the polished smoothness of the cut crystal of the base of the Eagle of Time in her fingers, and above it the still smoother octagonal 'skirt' where the modules began – the bottom eight were separated from the top by a 'waist' in the structure. She would have to shift her grip soon, to be able to carry on holding the timepiece.

'We'd need guarantees.'

'So would we.' It was the first time Sholto had spoken. 'Guarantees that we would be certain could be carried out – and would be.'

Stefan was watching Grania like a black eagle of the peaks.

'So would we.'

'There's Dr Poortman. It's his neck you've put a noose around – for a million dollars.'

Hayward started to interrupt, but Stefan silenced him. 'We are easy about Dr Poortman.'

Grania felt her toes cramping up on the rough edge. Soon, she'd have to move.

'You knew the whereabouts of my cave – how?' Stefan asked Sholto. He was watching Grania, although addressing Sholto. Killing time.

'Your horse showed me. All I had to do was to follow his trail.'

'I must remember that for the future.'

The Eagle seemed to be becoming as heavy as the mountain. Grania knew she could not go on holding it high much longer.

She said incisively, 'Do you, or don't you, agree to my plan?'

If Stefan's eyes had been capable of taking colour, they would have glowed now.

'There's a great deal still to be discussed.'

Grania suddenly started to lower the Eagle towards breast-level and draw back her cramping toes. 'Sholto!' she called frantically.

Neither of them was quick enough.

Stefan moved like a striking cobra. Before her arms were half down – Sholto's eyes diverted to her – Stefan moved in. With his right hand he clamped her body to him hard, so that she could not go over the edge. With his left, he grabbed the Eagle by the base before it could slip out of Grania's grasp. She was against him, arms held high, like a reluctant lover. He pushed himself backwards hard, so that he staggered clear of the edge to where Hayward crouched with his pistol.

'Shoot him, if he moves!' he snapped, indicating Sholto.

As he regained his balance, he tossed Grania away from him so that she came down heavily on the rock near the entrance.

'Her too – she can go over the edge now – she doesn't matter any more!'

Grania didn't look up. She was gasping and gagging. The force of the fall had knocked the breath out of her.

Stefan clasped the Eagle and addressed Sholto. 'So you were very smart and tracked me here, did you? It's not the sort of knowledge I allow anyone to go around making public – come here!'

Sholto advanced warily. Hayward's aim followed him all the way.

'Turn round!'

There was a moment's pause. Sholto realised afterwards that it must have been while Stefan exchanged the Eagle for Hayward's gun.

There was a strangled cry from Grania. 'No!'

The blow on the back of his neck chilled Sholto the length of his spine. The last thing he remembered was pitching into the dark cave mouth of insensibility.

CHAPTER THIRTY-EIGHT

The arch of light which was the cave mouth took on sharp focus, dissolved again into an amorphous mess of watery shimmering, then took on form again. Sholto rose to consciousness reluctantly, unwilling to run the gauntlet of the surge of nausea which he knew was lying in wait for him. He had tried it earlier; he preferred to sink back into the soothing blackness of oblivion. The pain in his neck was like fire; his rib cage felt as if he had failed to take a rapid and had hit a rock.

Then there was water on his lips, and more cooling water being applied to his neck.

He opened his eyes. He was lying inside the dimness of the cave. Grania was kneeling next to him with the water. The silence was cracked only by some radio music.

He pulled himself up onto one elbow, but the on-off focus trick of the light forced him again onto his back.

'Take it easy, Sholto,' said Grania. 'You'll be all right.'

'What happened?' he began.

'Stefan hit you with the barrel of a pistol,' she said. 'You were out cold for quite a time. And woozy long after that.' She leant down so that her face was close to his. 'I was beginning to wonder whether you would come right back.'

Sholto felt his rib cage tenderly. 'A pistol barrel didn't do this.'

'No. Stefan seemed to go beserk once you fell. He cut loose with his fists and boots as if he meant to kill you. For some reason, he suddenly stopped. I don't know why.'

'How long ago was that?'

'I've spent hours picking up the pieces.' She was near enough for him to see the ragged pain in her eyes. 'A lifetime, maybe. You came to, and then went off again. I prayed it was sleep.'

'I'm all right.'

'You're not. Stay where you are.' She pushed him back gently on to the padded sleeping bag.

'Where is Stefan now? Why is everything so quiet?'

'Stefan went off alone to restore the Eagle of Time in Maseru . . .'

'What!'

'Of course, you don't know. How could you?'

'And Hayward?'

'Don't speak too loudly. He's outside, on the sun platform. He's got a gun. He's very nervous, even of Dr Poortman, who is too shocked to threaten even a fly.'

The force of what she had said about the Eagle seemed to project him up onto his elbow again. 'Tell me, what is this about returning the Eagle?'

She sat down cross-legged next to him. 'It's the reason behind my being kidnapped.' She told him about the snatch, Stefan's plan to use the Eagle as a timer for a bomb in the Katse sluice control chamber, and Hayward's need of her expertise to work on the pediment mechanism.

Her account cleared his brain like a wonder drug. Before she had finished, he was sitting fully upright.

'I can't believe it!' he exclaimed. 'The hellishness of it all!'

'Quiet!' she cautioned. 'Remember Hayward. He still has the other half of the job to do – to arm a limpet mine. Apparently that's a minor undertaking, though. I think he's waiting for Stefan to come back before he starts on it so that he doesn't have to divert his attention from guarding you – us.'

'Stefan must be crazy – he'll never get away with it!' went on Sholto. 'We must make certain that he doesn't!'

She put her hand on his arm to silence him. Hayward had turned up his radio.

It said:

'*We interrupt this programme to make a special announcement. The Eagle of Time has been found! A special bulletin from General Makoanyane's headquarters states that the priceless masterpiece was spotted by a passer-by a short time ago on the steps of the Moshoeshoe statue in central Maseru. The woman saw what appeared to be an abandoned shopping bag and investigated. Inside was the timepiece*

270

which was snatched by an armed man last Friday morning from the Exhibition Centre in Maseru. The woman, who has not been identified, was so shocked by her discovery that she left the bag where it was and ran up the road to the nearest police station in Kingsway. Within minutes, police had cordoned off the statue and the public was cleared from the area in case of a bomb threat. General Makoanyane was notified at his nearby headquarters building, and a team of bomb disposal experts rushed to the scene.

'Attached to the shopping bag was a note purportedly signed by the Maluti Rider saying that in view of the unique value of the masterpiece, he had decided to return it undamaged. The note also stated that Dr Hans Poortman and the other kidnap victim, Miss Grania Yeats, the artist responsible for the pediment of the Eagle of Time, were safe and unharmed. No mention was made of ransom negotiations, as had been proposed earlier by the authorities. Examination of the timepiece, which reflected the correct time, revealed no damage at all.

'In the light of the kidnappers' conciliatory gesture, General Makoanyane has expressed the view that negotiations for the release of the two hostages now stand a better chance of success, and has once again appealed to them to make contact through the official intermediary, the German ambassador Dr Dietz.

'The Eagle of Time is now being held at an unspecified venue under heavy guard. However, the Prime Minister has stated, according to General Makoanyane's announcement, that the Eagle will still take its place as the centrepiece of Friday's gala opening ceremony of the Highlands Project at Katse Dam.'

Hayward rushed in to where Grania and Sholto were, grinning ironically and giving the thumbs-up sign.

'D'ye hear that, eh?' he demanded, brandishing his pistol at them. 'Stefan pulled it off! Nothing's going to stop us now!'

Nothing stopped the radio either from trumpeting the news all afternoon, as if the recovery of the Eagle had been a personal triumph for General Mak's security. Sholto missed much of it. He slept, and awoke feeling better. Hayward still occupied the sun platform – he would not allow the others out – with his gun and a case of nerves.

It was beginning to get dark when the trapdoor opened.

Sholto had not seen it in operation. The rope ladder had been withdrawn by Stefan that morning.

The first thing to appear was the barrel of Stefan's AK-47.

'Burt! Burt! Is everything all right?'

Hayward went through, motioning Grania, Sholto and Dr Poortman aside with his pistol; he stood facing them when he positioned himself under the trapdoor.

'Fine, Stefan. You're hellishly late. I was getting the heebie-jeebies alone here by myself.'

Stefan descended with his automatic still at the ready.

'Any trouble?'

'No, but you were so long . . .'

Stefan laughed. It made him almost human, thought Grania.

'Just doing a little shopping on your behalf!' he mimicked Hayward. 'Natty gent's suit for the opening cere-mony, plus suitcase.' He grinned. 'Not for clothes, though. You guess what.'

Hayward started to expand under the shadow of Stefan's protection.

'I didn't work on the limpet mine – not on my own with three captives,' he said.

'How could you? It's outside the trapdoor.' Stefan jollied him.

Hayward joined in the laugh against himself. 'Jeez, what a nerve!' he said in admiration. 'Just dumping that damn Eagle right there in the middle of the crowds.'

'I had a bad moment when I went through the border on the way in,' said Stefan. He eyed Sholto. 'You are hearing things you have no right to hear. Each word equals a bullet.'

Sholto measured him up. Stefan was strong, very strong, and the AK seemed an extension of his hands. 'What you've already done is enough to put a noose round your neck,' he responded.

Stefan shrugged and addressed Hayward again. 'They had a new man on the border post. Most of the others know me well, and I just show my special privileged pass and go through. But this one eyed me. I could see the TV description going through his mind – broad-shouldered, stocky, all the rest of that bull. "Do you mind getting out for a moment?" he asked, full of politeness. But he was suspicious, I could see. Just then, as luck would have it, one of the regulars came along and he said, "Good morning, Mister du Preez. How's the inflation going today?" and pointed to a couple of shopping bags on the seat of the pick-up. One of them contained the Eagle. "Bad," I said. "It's up since you saw me the other day." "You know this guy?" asked the new guard. "Of course, no problems. He's absolutely kosher, I can vouch for that."'

'I'll bet you wet yourself,' said Hayward.

'We'll have to watch it, going in on Thursday,' said Stefan. 'I'd hate them to open up that beautiful new suitcase and find our bomb. It's even got travel stickers on it, for good measure.'

Hayward indicated Sholto, Grania and Dr Poortman. 'What are you going to do about these three?' he asked.

'They're a messy complication. I'm all for getting rid of 'em.'

'They could be very useful insurance back here at the cave if anything goes wrong on Friday,' Hayward said.

In a flash Stefan's mood turned ugly. 'Do you expect it to? What can, eh? Tell me!'

'It's just an "if" nagging at the back of my mind.'

'We'll work it out in the morning.'

Later, after they had had hot food and coffee and Grania and Sholto were sitting together on their sleeping bags in the storeroom, Sholto said, 'He's bluffing. He's simply trying to scare us.'

Grania dropped her voice, indicating Stefan in the distance in the main body of the cave sitting on a fisherman's stool with the AK-47 across his knees.

'He's not, Sholto. I saw him with my own eyes murder three men. Our lives are hanging in the balance. Neither of us may see tomorrow night.'

'Lights out!' called Stefan harshly. 'All lights out, except mine and Burt's!'

Grania was first to the light, and turned it off. The storeroom was dark, except for a muted reflection from Stefan's light.

Sholto did not see, but only felt, Grania come and lie against him.

There was a long pause, and then he turned to take her lips to his, but she held him back. He tensed.

'Sholto,' she said softly. 'Listen. Don't kiss me – not yet, not until you have heard what I have to tell you.'

He did not reply. She went on, 'We may never come out of this alive, and I want with all my heart for you to know. If you can take it.'

'Go on.'

She was both glad and sorry she could not distinguish his face.

'It has to be autobiographical, of course.'

'Of course.'

'My emotional life is inextricably bound up with my sculpting and painting.'

'Yes. Switzerland.'

'The time is right tonight, Sholto. It's right now for the first time. It needs the situation we face for me to be able to tell it.'

He stirred, and she put her head against his cheek.

'The time is right, now,' she repeated. 'Before, when you asked me, it wasn't. I was afraid – mortally afraid – of losing you. I still am.'

'Go on, Grania.'

'I was educated both in Switzerland and in England,' she replied. 'I studied the fine arts – they were my natural bent. I took degrees in them in both those countries. I think I was a slightly above-average performer, no more. I gave a couple of one-woman shows in Zurich before I was twenty-one. I see now that what I executed then lacked the sort of touch which might have set me apart from the herd.'

'No Holy Grail,' he said.

She did not reply for a while, and he wondered whether his interjection had inhibited her. He felt her go very tense and she drew away from him.

'Six years ago, when I was twenty-two, I went to an art seminar in Geneva. There I met a man named Boris Reimer. He was a French-born Swiss. He had great personal charm, and I fell madly in love with him. Meanwhile, he was living at a commune for artistic types in the city; my father's banking world was poison to him. At that stage, I never asked much about the source of his – or the commune's – income, both of which were pretty hazy.

'Boris despised my world with irresistible charm. The real world, he told me, was where freedom, love and dreams have no chains. I believed him, and went to live with him at the commune, to my parents' distress and heartbreak.

'My own heartbreak was to follow. The wraps were soon off Boris. Apart from anything else, I found out he was a druggie, a main-liner. Under the influence of drugs, he seemed to change personality completely, and become a maniac.'

Grania started to pull away still further from Sholto, as if she was having difficulty in going on. He reached out – the same way he had done up there on the lammergeyer shelf when he had saved her life – and held her.

Her voice choked. 'I didn't recognise him when he came at me. He was on a high. Most of all it was his eyes – eyes out of a nightmare, Sholto – like those sort of grotesque images you see in the sketches of madmen. I wonder if you can understand the horror of not being able to *communicate* with an out-of-control being to whom you have given your love, your body, before? A maniac came after me – a maniac raped me. Not once, but many times, until I couldn't scream any more. They took me to hospital to patch me up – I was there for a week. I was physically and mentally shattered.

'I returned to my family in Zurich. I knew I had to do something to get myself out of the trauma of Boris' rape. I'd heard that in Tokyo jewel-making is undertaken as a kind of therapy. With my parents' blessing, I went to Tokyo. The therapy assumed major proportions for me. I became fired at, and caught up in, the renaissance of the artist-jeweller movement which was taking place in Japan.

'I entered the Tokyo University of Art and was further inspired by meeting the legendary Yasuki Hiramatse. He was starting to get old then, but his work still possessed the miraculous grace of Japanese calligraphy, plus all the delicacy and sophistication of his gold crafting.

'I sat at his feet – and learned, and learned. It was as if Boris' assault had had a cathartic effect on me – it fined the dross out of

275

my spirit and left it transformed. People said my work had an otherworldly quality all of its own; the critics ranked me as world-class.

'You know my story, after that. Towards the end of 1992 the Swiss banking consortium offered me the commission to restructure the pediment of the Rose of Time after the death of Elie Kiefer; it's to Dr Poortman that I owe so much. He was the family friend who mentioned my name.

'But it was you – you alone, Sholto – who gave me the lammergeyer. You were also the inspiration behind the miniature art works in the secret capsule . . .' He heard her fumbling in her pocket. 'I have the capsule here; I had to remove it to make room for Hayward's detonator. I want you to see them tomorrow – the silver chalice pouring water, the embryo dinosaur, and the Moshoeshoe's grave.'

'You still haven't answered my question, why you refused to see me in Switzerland, and why you kept silent so long,' he said very quietly, and the hurt cauterised his words.

'You remember the night after we found the lammergeyer's eyrie, Sholto? That wonderful, wonderful day, and we camped back on that little plateau so high and remote that we could have reached up and touched the face of the stars?'

'That is what I kept remembering, when you wouldn't see me.'

'I wanted to make love to you that night, that is when I should have made love to you. Everything was right for it. I was happy, really happy for the first time in my life.'

She squirmed aside from his grasp and she seemed to be doing something to her wrist.

'What is it, Grania?'

'I'm rubbing the face of my good-luck god Hotei on my watch strap,' she murmured. 'Sorry, but I need the luck. I wanted you, my body cried out for you. But I was so happy – even when we didn't. I knew I was in love with you, Sholto, as I have never been with anyone else. Or will be, I think.'

Sholto waited, and she continued, 'I made the mistake of going back to Switzerland, leaving unfinished business behind me. When I arrived home, the trauma, the old trauma, hit me afresh, amongst all the familiar sights and places.

'Suddenly, there were two of me. I wanted you desperately, but my body didn't – couldn't. It kept remembering the way it had been shamed and ripped by Boris. My body wanted to repeat the loving – but not the performance. Can you understand? I didn't know whether I'd ever sort myself out. The lammergeyer pediment was born of that. As I fashioned and moulded the gold, my heart said, the way its golden wings open is the way my heart opens and takes you in, and shows you my secret treasures deep down, like the capsule. Then the agony would come back, the agony of Boris, in a great tidal wave. The Eagle pediment and the capsule are the embodiment of that time of silence, Sholto. I even thought of not coming to the ceremonial opening. But I came, and I am glad.'

There was a long silence, and she said, 'Do you still want me, Sholto?'

He took her close and kissed her, deeply, longingly. He said very gently and seriously, 'This is all we may ever know of our love – you realise that, don't you, Grania?'

'Stefan's out-of-touch eyes frighten me, Sholto – the way Boris' did. I hardly knew what I was doing when I saw him rush out with his gun when he spotted you on the rope. The place may take our world away, but it has also given us our world, our love.'

'We have got to get out of here somehow, Grania!'

She said, very softly, 'Yes – somehow. We must escape and make our love a reality. I learned something in Japan which was like a beacon in all the psychological darkness I experienced there. It is an ancient samurai martial teaching which also applied to my personal problems – it applies here, too. It's a strategy the warriors called "hold down a shadow". It means you must find out the enemy's plan of attack and then out-manoeuvre him with courage and timing.'

'"Hold down a shadow",' echoed Sholto. He felt her body trembling and shaking next to his.

'You're cold,' he said.

'Reaction,' she answered softly. 'But it's easily remedied.'

She took off her felt boots and outsize anorak and slipped into the sleeping bag next to him.

CHAPTER THIRTY-NINE

'When you hear the news that the bomb has gone off, you'll know that you too have reached the end of the line,' said Stefan.

He handed Sholto the portable radio. 'Stay tuned for 3.30 tomorrow afternoon and the grand opening,' he sneered. 'You'll know your fate then.'

It was Thursday morning, about 8.30. Stefan and Hayward were about to leave the hide-out. The door onto the sun platform was open; when Stefan locked it within the next few minutes, the light would be shut off and Sholto, Grania and Dr Poortman would be locked in darkness – until Stefan and Hayward chose to return from their Katse bombing mission. Glancing out at the snow-covered peaks, Grania found it hard to credit that this might be the last time she would ever see the sun.

Perhaps the same thought was in Sholto's mind. 'Listen . . .' he began to Stefan.

'There's no more listening,' snapped Stefan. 'Burt, have you checked everything? There's nothing left they could use . . .?'

Hayward nonchalantly swung a grey cylindrical object from a fabric strap attached to his right wrist. At one end was an ugly snout fitted with several threaded screws which held a tube in place.

It was a Soviet limpet mine.

The ex-IRA masterbomber had spent most of the previous day on the sun platform deciding which was the best type of explosive for the 'console job', as he called it. He had sun in the warmth surrounded by a formidable array of weaponry from Stefan's arsenal – he had toyed, like an expert wine-taster surrounded by vintage bottles, with this and that while Stefan sat on a canvas stool with the AK-47 across his knees. The platform had been declared out of bounds to the three captives.

Hayward had been animated, discussing the respective merits of an SZ-6 demolition mine against its 'little brother', the SZ-3.

The six kilograms of the SZ-6 were probably too much to demolish a mere control console, while the SZ-3 with its three kilograms was just about right, although he didn't much care for its shape. It was dilettante talk; Stefan listened and watched; there was nothing else to do to pass the time.

Hayward had even produced a TM-57 landmine and a much smaller PMN anti-personnel mine to join in the merit stakes, as well as three variously-shaped hand grenades.

Hayward moved these deadly weapons round and round, and finally left his choice between a standard Soviet limpet mine and its mini version, discarding plastic explosive in their favour. From inside, Sholto and Grania could smell the strange, lethal smell of the plastic explosive, like marzipan. Dr Poortman moved about, still silent, like a man stunned into speechlessness.

After that, Hayward had spent hours calibrating and inserting the detonator which would receive the signal from the radio trigger inside the Eagle of Time.

Now Sholto cast round for something further to say, something to try and delay what seemed inevitable. He nodded at the limpet mine swinging from the Irishman's wrist.

'You'll never get anywhere near with that.'

'No?' Stefan replied for him. 'He's got a Pony Pass and what would be more natural than a VIP going round with his camera and camera case photographing the wonders of the Katse Dam? Who's to know it contains a limpet mine?'

'There are two of you – and only one pass,' Sholto went on.

Stefan laughed, quite genuinely. 'You don't have to start worrying about us, *ou maat*, old pal. You've got enough worry over yourself. If you're really concerned, my special clearance as a landowner involved in the Highlands Project is the open sesame to anything to do with the Project. How do you think I've moved in and out of the border posts?'

Grania asked, 'You'll be watching the bomb?'

Stefan froze suddenly. 'I'll be – around.'

Hayward added, a little plaintively, 'He won't even tell me where he's going to be at the big moment.'

'Our rendezvous afterwards is all you have to know,' Stefan

snapped. 'At the parking ground exit. We'll take what offers in the way of parked cars for ourselves. We'll collect my truck down the Malibamatso River road, as we fixed. After that . . .' He shrugged and eyed Sholto, Grania and Dr Poortman. 'I've got several options. The easiest is for me not to do anything. There's enough food and gas here to last you till the weekend. If I simply didn't come back for another week . . .' He laughed harshly and added, 'You'd all be dead inside the cave. Saves me the hassle of shooting you one by one.'

'They're still a good backstop, I say, if anything slips,' said Hayward.

'That's why I'd rather get rid of 'em beforehand,' replied Stefan. 'If you've got insurance, it makes you soft.'

Hayward inclined his chin towards Dr Poortman. 'He's still worth a million, even after the bomb.'

'Cut the crap – we're wasting time,' said Stefan shortly. 'Let's get going.'

He herded Sholto, Grania and Dr Poortman into the store-room while he locked the sun platform door and pocketed the key. Then he and Hayward climbed the rope ladder to the trapdoor, Hayward standing guard at the top while Stefan ascended last. The ladder was withdrawn; the trap slammed shut. The cave went dark, except for a single light.

Grania was in Sholto's arms. 'I'm scared, my darling. Maybe because the sun's gone. Perhaps it really was the last time we saw it.'

'Our first task is to fine-comb the cave and see if there is anything we can possibly use to escape.'

It was Dr Poortman who spoke. Sholto and Grania turned to him in surprise.

'Well!' exclaimed Sholto. 'We thought the events of the past few days had had an effect on your mind.'

The banker smiled a little wryly. 'I think I still have a guilt feeling about those three of the gang he shot. It was to do with my suggestion, after all.'

'*Your* suggestion?'

'Yes. I offered them 100,000 dollars each to grab Stefan and set me free. Unfortunately, the plan misfired. After that, I felt the best thing to do was to keep my mouth shut so that even a chance remark would not bring coals of fire upon my – your – heads. That is why I haven't spoken.'

Sholto nodded in appreciation at the banker. 'Let's start looking then.'

Dr Poortman held the light. They went first to the door to the sun platform. It looked as solid as a medieval fortress.

Sholto slipped off his boot and tapped it with the heel.

'Solid,' he remarked. 'Not a chink. Stefan did a wonderful job with this door. You simply can't spot it from the outside because of the camouflage. He must have carted this rock up here to build the entrance to hang the door – it's not the same as the cliff, which is basalt, and much harder to work. This is sandstone – the sort of stuff we use at "Cherry Now".' He ran his finger along a mortar joint. 'Stefan really meant this to be a permanent funkhole.'

'All the bombs and weapons were in the magazine chamber – they might have overlooked something there,' observed Dr Poortman.

But they hadn't. Then Grania asked, 'What about the two springs? How does the water flow out?'

Centuries of seepage, predating the Bushmen inhabitants of the cave, had created little cracks in the rock at both springs, through which the water escaped. At the one adjoining the stores chamber it formed a tiny dam; the other at the rear flowed clean away. Sholto knelt down at this latter water-point.

He said flatly, 'There's air coming in here all right – but even a bulldozer wouldn't shift this rock.'

'And the trapdoor?' asked Dr Poortman further.

The ceiling of the cave was out of sight, high above in the shadows.

'I can't see anything I could hitch a rope to,' said Sholto.

'If we had a rope,' added Dr Poortman.

'What did they do with my climbing rope after I landed on the sun platform?' went on Sholto.

'It could still be in position,' said Dr Poortman. 'I didn't notice them bring in any rope.'

'I came in from the side, not directly from overhead,' added

281

Sholto. 'The rope probably swung back on its anchoring pitons. Anyway, what's the use of it? To use the rope we'd have to get out first, and that looks impossible.'

'Our chances are nil, nil, nil,' said Grania helplessly.

Nil. Nil. Nil.

The words, with the hours as hammers, slugged through their brains as they waited in the cold. There was nothing to do. Things became worse when they decided to turn off the heater and light in order to economise on the gas. They relied on a weakening flashlight for incidental light.

They tried the radio as a diversion: they could not stand the bright chatter of the disc jockeys and the endless deep-beat music. They finally switched that off, too, and reverted to the dark.

The lunch time news bulletin came after what seemed to be years of waiting.

It said:

'All preparations are in train for the gala opening tomorrow afternoon at 3.30 of the giant Lesotho Highlands Project at Katse Dam, and foreign and overseas VIPs have started to arrive in Maseru for the occasion. The South African Head of State, who will be accompanied by the Foreign Minister and Minister of Water Affairs, as well as other dignitaries, will arrive tomorrow by helicopter from a nearby air force base. He and Lesotho's own Head of State will jointly perform the opening ceremony by pressing a button on a special dais which has been erected on the wall of Katse Dam. This will activate the dam's giant sluice-gates and a short symbolic flow of water will be released as a spectacular for the capacity crowd which will witness the event.

'The Lesotho government, in consultation with South Africa, has decided to go ahead with the opening ceremony as planned, despite the threat of the kidnappers of Dr Hans Poortman, head of the Swiss banking consortium, to kill him if a ransom demand of one million dollars is not met by the time of the opening ceremony. Dr Poortman's place as one of the leading figures in tomorrow's ceremony will be taken by his deputy, Dr Adolf Becker, who has already arrived in Lesotho. His present whereabouts are being withheld for security reasons.

'There has still been no reaction from Dr Poortman's kidnappers regarding the Lesotho offer of an intermediary. Fears are also being expressed for the safety of Miss Grania Yeats, sculptress of the pediment of the Eagle of Time, which was returned so dramatically by the kidnappers on Tuesday, and will still take its place – as scheduled – on the dais at the ceremonial opening tomorrow.

'No trace has been found either, despite an intensive police search, of Mr Sholto Banks, ombudsman in Lesotho for the Swiss consortium, whose light truck was found by Security personnel abandoned near Oxbow Lodge. The Lesotho government has issued a last-minute appeal to the kidnappers to come forward and open negotiations, under guarantee of a temporary amnesty . . .'

'That must make Stefan laugh,' observed Dr Poortman.

'There's only way to stop his madness – to get out of here,' said Sholto.

Never. Never. Never.

That was the thought in the mind of all three as they sat in the dark all that interminable afternoon.

Towards evening – there was nothing to show except their watches whether it was midday or midnight – Dr Poortman said:

'Why are we conserving the gas? Aren't we simply prolonging our agony? What if Stefan decides not to come back?'

They did not reply.

They used the gas sparingly – there was one cylinder for the light, and one for the heater-cooker – to cook hot food and coffee. It did not help. They sat about miserably. They had nothing to say.

Afterwards they took to their sleeping bags.

Grania lay next to Sholto.

'Your lips are cold,' he told her. He held her. All they could hear was the monotonous tinkle-drip of the spring outside the stores chamber entrance.

'Our situation's like that water,' she said. 'It drips, and drips. And the dark and the silence wear you away.'

'We've only had one day of it,' Sholto reminded her.

'We'll go out of our minds after a few days more,' she said. 'Did you hear the crack in Dr Poortman's voice when he asked why we were conserving the gas?'

She felt him nod, and she said, 'Sholto darling, I had no idea everything would end like this.'

'I'm glad you told me about yourself, Grania. It makes everything right.'

She moved still closer and murmured, 'I wanted it for "Cherry Now" really, but it wasn't to be – could not be – not then. It was like seeing all those lovely things on the farm under an eclipse. How I loved it all! I knew, deep down inside me, that I loved you – but how to tell you, ever?' She laughed low in her throat. 'It made me sentimental about even the tiniest of things . . . You know what? Even that little gift of gunpowder the old stonemason gave me I tucked away safely inside my toolkit satchel – as if gunpowder had anything to do with love!'

'Grania! What did you say? Gunpowder! Your tool satchel!' He sat upright. 'Is that the toolkit they made you bring here for the Eagle?'

'Yes, it's here – amongst my things – right here . . .'

'Gunpowder! Do you know what you are saying, Grania! It can get us out of here! Gunpowder!'

'It's only a small quantity . . .'

'It's enough! Don't you see! The door to the sun platform – it's set in *sandstone*! That's the stone our masons shatter with gunpowder, that primitive gunpowder of theirs! They use it because it's low-powered and shatters and cracks; modern explosives are too powerful and destructive . . .'

Grania was on her knees now, fumbling by torchlight for matches to light the lamp.

The words avalanched from Sholto. 'We can shatter the rock with your gunpowder charge! We can crack the rock, and then dig our way out – get clear – '

Grania found the soft leather satchel and spread it out in the light.

There it was – a glass container of gunpowder!

'Surely Stefan and Hayward must have seen this container?'

'Hayward did. He asked me what it was, and I said emery powder for polishing metal. I didn't want him to touch it, for sentimental reasons.'

'Dr Poortman,' yelled Sholto. 'Wake up! Come here! We've found the answer! We can get out!'

The banker hadn't been sleeping. He came in at a shuffling run.

'Gunpowder!' Sholto held out the glass bottle to him. 'We've got it! We've found the way to get out!'

'Heavens above – gunpowder!' Dr Poortman exclaimed. 'Are you sure it's enough?'

'If you're thinking in terms of an explosion which will blast a whole block of Stefan's sandstone out of the way, no,' Sholto went on excitedly. 'It doesn't work that way! I only intend to do what Old Moho would have done – shatter the rock, crack it! We'll have to do the rest ourselves, after that!'

'How? With what?' demanded Dr Poortman.

Grania indicated her tool pack. 'That.'

'The cherry de-pipper!' exclaimed Sholto. 'It's got a special hardened steel point!'

'Use any other of my tools as well – it doesn't matter about them any more . . .'

'There are also the knives they left us for eating,' added Dr Poortman.

'Your tools look very fragile,' Sholto hurried on. 'If we can blast a toehold, so to speak, we'll then heat the sandstone with the gas flame, and then throw cold water over it. It's the classic way our masons split up the rock.'

'Do you think it will work?' asked Dr Poortman.

'I'll try anything, simply to get out,' replied Sholto.

'I'll go along with that,' added Dr Poortman.

They took the flashlight and the gas light and went to the entrance door.

Sholto concentrated on the side opposite the lock where the hinges had been sunk into the sandstone.

He shone the torch and ran his fingers along an unseen line. He then held the light closer.

'As I thought,' he exclaimed excitedly. 'There are already hairline cracks – sandstone always does that when you drill it. This is where we start operations. The metal flange for the hinge has been anchored here also – it means that the rock is weakest in this area.'

'How do you place the charge?' asked Dr Poortman.

'We've got a lot of hard elbow-work before we can even think of the charge,' Sholto replied. 'We have to fashion a hole to take it. Then the gunpowder must be tamped into the hole. It's simply no good firing a charge against a flat surface. All the force of the explosion will be dissipated into the air. Get the gas burner, will you, Grania? It'll have to serve as a light as well – we are going to need a lot of gas before the night is out. Dr Poortman, will you fill our little bucket from the spring?'

Grania and Dr Poortman watched, fascinated, as Sholto started to heat the rock round the area of the hairline cracks. It meant holding the cylinder and pressing the burner against the sandstone, and then moving on to the spot immediately adjacent to it.

'Won't the rock at your starting-point be cold by the time you've done even a small area round it?' asked Dr Poortman.

'Unfortunately, yes. Five centimetres square must be about the effective limit of the burner.'

The rock began to darken from Sholto's flame.

'When I pull back the burner, pitch the water as quickly as you can over the hot section,' he said. 'Now!'

No damp squib could have been damper. All that took place was a faint sizzle from the hot rock.

'Is that all?' asked Grania in a small voice.

'The stonemasons usually use an old tyre; it burns slow and long and hot,' he replied. 'Let's try again.'

They did, a tedious, time-consuming process, for about ten minutes. After the water had again drenched the hot rock, Sholto took off his boot – it had steel studs for climbing – and smacked the heel against the rock. A chip about the size of a child's hand fell off.

They carried on. Sholto's progress was like an orthodontist fiddling with a dinosaur's tooth. The cavity grew, chip by chip. Grania and Dr Poortman also took turns at the rock-face.

At the end of two hours they had a cavity deep enough, Sholto reckoned, to be the minimum for an effective explosion. They could make out the black spur of the hinge's metal flange where it split through the sandstone like an errant nerve.

'That flange can be of great service to us,' said Sholto. 'If we can tamp home the gunpowder behind the flange, it will direct the force of the explosion inwards – the way we want.'

They started the gas-and-water routine again. This time Sholto followed a mortar line which ran close to the flange. The hole was too small for the heel of his boot; now, after dousing, he employed the cherry de-pipper and the boot's heel as hammer and chisel, painstakingly prising out the mortar.

It was 11.30 when the hole was ready for the charge.

In his off-duty stints from working at the rock-face, Sholto had prepared the charge, plus a crude fuse he had concocted from newspaper he found in the storeroom.

The moment of truth arrived.

He thrust the charge behind the flange, and tamped it home with stone chips, loose debris, and more newspaper.

'Here goes!'

He lit the fuse and the three of them retreated into the storeroom. Grania thought the fuse had gone out, it took so long to burn. Then suddenly there was a heavy thud, and the end of the cave was filled with smoke.

Grania headed the rush for the rock-face. She had somehow expected to see a hole to the outside. What she made out through the smoke by yellow torchlight stopped her short.

'Sholto, it hasn't done anything!'

Dr Poortman was also staring at the place in disappointed silence. Only Sholto seemed unworried. He examined his handiwork.

'The charge has done its job,' he announced. 'It's cracked the rock. The rest is up to us.'

Taking it in relays, they picked away at the rock with the cherry de-pipper and table knives, whittling out tiny fragments at first, and then working their way round the bigger pieces to dislodge them. It was disheartening, finger-blistering work. They resorted to ski gloves to protect their hands.

'What we need is a four-pound hammer to make short work

287

of this,' said Sholto. But the best they could do was the pitiful thumping away with the heel of his boot.

At one o'clock in the morning, they got their first big break. Quite unexpectedly, a chunk of sandstone about the size of a Rugby ball detached itself from the line of mortar – the gunpowder had previously shaken it free – and fell down.

'This is what we need!'

Sholto grabbed it and attacked the cracked rock with it. The hole grew. They could now work with their shoulders full-width in the aperture; before they had to peck away at an awkward, half side-on angle.

'How thick is the wall?' asked Grania. It was the first time any of them had spoken for over an hour. They looked like zombies in the gaslight, with face and hair powdered with dust.

'There's no way of telling,' replied Sholto. 'We can only keep going.'

It was Grania's shift. She was working with her eyes half-closed against the dust, thumping and banging with the sandstone 'hammer'. She felt the face give, shut her eyes, and presumed it was yet another loosened chip. Somehow, however, the thump of the debris sounded different as it fell.

She opened her eyes.

She saw the morning star.

For a stunned moment, the brilliant object emblazoned against the snow-capped peaks in earliest dawn-horizon light did not register.

Then she yelled, 'Sholto! Dr Poortman! We're through! We're through!'

CHAPTER FORTY

Six a.m.

Friday.

Nine-and-a-half hours to the gala opening of the Lesotho Highlands Project.

It had taken them another hour after Grania had sighted the morning star to widen the gap through the sandstone sufficiently for them to crawl through.

Now they stood together on the sun platform in the growing light, hardly able to credit their senses and believe that they were clear of their death-trap. All round were the august peaks, the highest taking the sun's first flush.

'It's wonderful, wonderful!' exclaimed Grania. 'I can't believe we've escaped! We're free! Free!'

'We're only one step on the road to freedom, Grania,' said Dr Poortman sombrely. 'We've still got to get away from here.' He turned to Sholto and said quietly, gesturing at the drop over the precipice's edge a few metres away, 'Where do we go from here?'

'Down on to the whale-back ridge,' responded Sholto. 'Then we follow the horse trail to and across the sponge . . .'

'You're jumping the gun,' said Dr Poortman. 'You've forgotten one factor.'

'What is that?'

'Me.'

'What do you mean, Dr Poortman.'

'I'm not an athlete or a mountaineer. I'm an unfit, middle-aged banker. For a start, there is no way I can climb down to that ridge. Then you talk about negotiating the sponge – I'd never manage it either. You and Grania could – yes.'

'What are you trying to say, Dr Poortman?'

'Leave me here. You and Grania go.'

'Never!' said Grania. 'Do you expect us to save our skins and leave you here at the mercy of Stefan and Hayward later?'

'Never!' repeated Sholto. 'You will come with us – under any circumstances.'

Dr Poortman inclined his head in appreciation. 'Thank you, but you are being totally unrealistic. I am only an encumbrance. Leave me. I'll take my chance. You've got to stop that bomb going off this afternoon – that's more important than me. Sholto, I don't know what is in your mind about that.'

'Oxbow,' replied Sholto decisively. 'We get to Oxbow as quick as we can. From there I'll telephone General Mak.'

'How far is Oxbow?' asked Dr Poortman. He had about him an air of willing martyrdom.

'As the lammergeyer flies – ' Grania smiled at him for the allusion ' – I'd say, about eighteen to twenty kilometres. I came that way on foot, but the direct way is the tough way.'

'Eighteen to twenty kilometres!' echoed Dr Poortman incredulously. 'You expect *me* to cover that distance over *that*!' He waved a hand at the serried masses in the direction of Oxbow.

'No,' replied Sholto. 'I don't. We three will go round – and no rough stuff on the route, except perhaps a little at the beginning. The smooth way. Water.'

'What are you driving at, Sholto?'

'I know now the geographical location of the Four Bushmen, and I'm acquainted with the country on the other side of the sponge,' he said. 'The Malibamatso River itself rises out there and flows past Oxbow Lodge on its way to Katse. I keep a kayak with some supplies and climbing gear in the headwaters of one of the tributaries called the Tsehlanyane.' He smiled at Grania. 'Grania will remember. We used it as a base to strike out into what we call Lammergeyer Land. We'll use that same kayak to get downriver to Oxbow. We can be there in a few hours' time.'

'How many is the kayak designed to carry?'

Sholto looked uncomfortable. 'Two.'

'So that part of your plan wouldn't work for three. Listen, Sholto, do as I say. Leave me. You and Grania make your way to the nearest point where you can set the wheels in motion to stop the bomb.' He went on urgently. 'We're wasting time here talking. Get going!'

'Not without you.'

'We've got this far – don't spoil everything now,' argued Dr Poortman. 'Face it, there's no way I can get down to the ridge, is there?'

Sholto indicated the rock face. 'There's my climbing rope still hanging there.'

'It's out of reach,' said Dr Poortman. 'How do you propose to get to it?'

'Climb – if I can.'

'You'll break your neck.'

'Sholto, Dr Poortman!' Grania broke in. 'There's another way. Let's make a rope out of blankets. It will reach to the ridge.'

'Good girl!' exclaimed Sholto. 'That's that, then.'

'I'll only hold you back,' went on Dr Poortman. 'The journey here half-killed me – and then I was on horseback.'

'I'll do a deal with you,' Sholto said suddenly. 'I'll agree – halfway.'

'Explain what you mean before I agree.'

'My pup tent and stove and some iron rations are down there where I left them before I climbed up to the cave,' he said. 'We'll go and collect them. You come with us safely out of range of the cave – maybe as far as the edge of the sponge. We'll leave you there in the tent. You'll be safe and snug, with food, water and fire. I'll arrange with General Mak for a helicopter to pick you up before nightfall today. The tent is scarlet – like a marker from the air – that is what it is meant for. Grania and I will get on to Oxbow by kayak – okay?'

'I agree, but I still think you are better off without me. There's only one thing I want.'

'What's that?'

'The radio. I want to listen in and make sure the opening goes off without any trouble.'

'That's easy,' grinned Sholto.

They made a rope of blankets, anchoring it securely on the door flange. Sholto went down first, and guided Dr Poortman safely on to the ridge. Grania came down last, bringing the radio, her tool satchel, a bottle of water, and some extra food. They picked their way clear of the iced-up saw-edge ridge.

291

It was after seven a.m. when they reached the edge of the sponge nearest the Four Bushmen.

Dr Poortman looked as though another few kilometres would precipitate a heart attack in him. Sholto pitched the tiny scarlet tent in the lee of a big boulder where it could not be missed from the air. They said a brief goodbye to the banker.

Sholto took the lead from Grania across the sponge, in the horse's tracks. The treacherous soft-going slowed them down; Sholto kept looking anxiously at his watch. Finally they got clear and made their way to the tributary of the Malibamatso and found the double-seater kayak which Sholto used as his 'base camp'. They set off for Oxbow. They made excellent time down the narrow river under Sholto's strong, rhythmic strokes. The only delay was a portage round a series of small waterfalls before the tributary finally joined the river they were looking for.

'Malibamatso!' called Sholto, as the craft swept into the wider water. 'All the way to Oxbow – and Katse!'

They made a fast, trouble-free run to their objective: the river passed close by to Oxbow Lodge itself. Sholto pulled the kayak in to the bank, and he and Grania set off at the double along a well-marked tourist trail to the Lodge proper. It was not yet nine o'clock.

Oxbow was a smaller replica of Katse Lodge, and they approached from the rear, among similar-type thatched huts.

'It all seems very quiet,' remarked Grania.

They made their way through the chalets, round to the front.

There was not a human, not a car, in sight. The entrance was deserted, the glass doors closed.

Then a deep voice said, '*Lumela* – good morning!'

It came from under a Basuto hat which topped a coloured blanket in a chair on the verandah.

'*Lumela!*' Sholto spoke to the man in Sesotho. 'Where is everybody?'

The man got up from his chair. He carried a spear under his blanket. 'I am guarding the place. Who are you?' He eyed the two grimy figures suspiciously.

'We come from the mountains. I have to make a telephone call – urgently. *Where is everybody?*'

'You must have been in the mountains a long time if you don't know today is Lesotho's big day. It is a public holiday. The Water – ' he gave the word its full value ' – starts today. Everyone has gone to Katse to see it start to flow this afternoon. Oxbow is closed for the day.'

Sholto said desperately, 'I have to make a telephone call. It . . . it . . . is about the Water.'

The watchman eyed him warily. 'What has a telephone call to do with the Water?'

Sholto went on urgently, 'My friend, I can't explain, but it has. But what would all Lesotho say if they knew that something happened to stop the Water because you would not let me make a telephone call?'

'Very well, then,' said the man, finding his keys. 'You must pay for it. There is no public phone. You must also write the number down so that the management will know you have not cheated them.'

'Let's go in,' said Sholto.

The watchman stood by as he checked the number and dialled.

'Security Headquarters?'

'Wait.'

There was a series of snaps and clicks. Sholto put his hand over the mouthpiece and remarked to Grania, 'Being bugged.'

The voice came on again abruptly. 'State your name and business.'

'My name is Sholto Banks . . .'

'Spell that.'

'S-h-o-l-t-o B-a-n-k-s.'

'Proceed.'

'My business is with General Makoanyane. I must speak to him urgently – personally.'

'He is unavailable.'

It was like talking to a pre-set answering machine.

'Listen,' said Sholto as patiently as he could. 'General Makoanyane is a personal friend of mine. Tell him Sholto Banks . . .'

'No personal calls are permitted at Security Headquarters.'

Sholto bit back his reply at the man's obtuseness.

293

'If you won't put me through to General Makoanyane, then I must speak to the duty officer.'

'I am on duty. Everyone else is at Katse.'

'General Makoanyane also?'

'We do not disclose the movements of security personnel.'

'I must speak to the General, d'ye hear?' said Sholto impatiently. 'It has to do with Dr Poortman, who was kidnapped.'

'Give your telephone number and locality so that it can be checked.'

'Oxbow Lodge. The number is– ' Sholto found the number on the instrument and gave it.

'Any information will be treated confidentially.'

'For crying out loud!' burst out Sholto. 'What do you think I want to speak to General Makoanyane for? What is his number at Katse?'

'The whereabouts of security personnel are not disclosed . . .'

Sholto slammed down the phone. 'We are simply going round in circles – and getting nowhere. But he did let on that General Mak is at Katse. I'll phone him there and perhaps get some sense out of *him*.'

The watchman came forward. 'You asked for one telephone call. Now you want to make another? You must write it down . . .'

Sholto gestured helplessly to Grania, who noted the number.

He dialled Katse Lodge, and then held the instrument out for Grania to overhear. 'Out of order,' he said briefly. 'They've cut it off.'

He put down the phone and paid the watchman. The size of the tip made the man look more suspicious than ever. He failed even to give the traditional Basuto goodbye.

Sholto led Grania out of earshot.

'We've got to get to Katse ourselves,' he said.

'How?' she asked. 'There's not a car here.'

'Even if there were, I doubt whether we'd make it by 3.30,' he replied. He turned to her so that she faced him. 'Grania, would you be prepared to give the river a go?'

'Meaning, Sholto?'

294

His words came quickly. 'The kayak. I reckon it is something under forty kilometres from here to Katse. We can do it – we've got about six-and-a-half hours. I've made as good time as that racing, and it's a smooth passage all the way. We can raise the alarm ourselves.'

'Is there no communications point between there and the dam?'

'No. Oxbow is the nearest. It'll be a close-run thing, but there's no alternative. Give it a go?'

'I'll do my best. But I'm not a racing kayaker.'

She found that out after they had been going for about an hour. She kept her eyes fixed on Sholto's back – he had stripped off his shirt and it glistened with sweat – and tried to keep pace with the long, powerful racing stroke which had carried him to so many river victories. They made good time; then the muscles in her shoulders cramped and she caught a crab, slewing the craft across the waterway.

'Five minutes' rest – and give me your shoulders,' he said.

She leaned across the seat, resting her breasts on his shoulders, and he massaged her paddling muscles expertly.

'I'm okay, Sholto.'

They went on.

The countryside changed: the fast-flowing, rock-strewn streams backdropped by the snow-touched peaks of the high mountains softened into the wide gorge of the Malibamatso; green began to appear on the tablelands on either side of the blue-slate cleft which sliced its way through fossil-bearing beds.

Grania felt Sholto deliberately slow his stroke for her to keep up. The Malibamatso valley widened and deepened as they lost altitude; the sun struck down on Grania's head and neck; her arms were working blindly, painfully, trying to match Sholto's in front. As the river widened too, the current slackened its helping thrust under the kayak. It was the time when they needed it most.

Time!

Twelve noon.

Three-and-a-half hours to go!

Sholto pulled the craft into the shallows.

He asked briefly, 'Is ten minutes enough?'

She took a long pull at the water bottle. 'Yes, if you want, that is.'

'We're not halfway yet, Grania. There are only three-and-a-half hours left – maybe only three, if you allow us enough time for us to get through to General Mak. If that man at security headquarters is any example, every security guard at Katse will be as obstructive.'

She passed him the water. 'When you're ready.'

They saved themselves five minutes, and again began the rhythmic, shoulder-burning torture. The gorge twisted and darkened in colour; it grew hotter where it narrowed in places. Grania wondered how long she could go on taking it.

One p.m.

Two-and-a-half hours to go.

Grania's mind was numb; her arms and shoulders were numb; her lungs were numb, gasping in air which tasted like fire. Her arms were no longer beating time with Sholto's; they flagged, faltered, flailing instead of gripping the water. She knew she was beyond the limit. Yet she kept going for another hour; she did not realise that she was able to manage only because Sholto's pace was flagging too.

Without warning, Sholto doubled over, shipped his paddle.

Two p.m.

An hour-and-a-half to go.

He knew they would never make it.

CHAPTER FORTY-ONE

'What is it! Sholto, what is wrong?'

The kayak's nose grounded on the shaley bank.

Sholto clenched the back of his head with one hand. 'Where Stefan hit me – it's playing up. So is my rib cage. Here, wet my handkerchief and hold it against my neck.'

Grania did so. There was no need for her to ask to locate the spot – the ugly welt stood out against his sun-tanned flesh.

She dared not look at her watch. The minutes ticked by.

Then Sholto said, 'That's easier. Now, a quick stretch ashore and we'll push on.'

They both checked their watches.

Grania asked in a small voice, 'We won't make it, will we, Sholto? How far to go?'

'About twelve kilometres.'

They eased their tense leg muscles along a flat stretch by the water's edge. The grey-blue walls of the gorge seemed to press in on them. If they could only *see* Katse!

Grania took up her position again behind him in the rear seat.

As they pushed off from the bank and he took up the stroke, Sholto remarked, 'So near, Grania, and yet so far.'

'Do you know exactly where we are, Sholto?'

'Yes. Round this next bend we'll pass the inlet tower for the eighty kilometre tunnel which feeds Katse water under the mountains to South Africa,' he answered tonelessly. 'That's ten kilometres from Katse.'

'Maybe we'll see something there to help.'

They rounded the river's bend. The tower stood out like a monument to isolation.

'Look!' burst out Grania. 'Look, Sholto! There's a truck parked near the bank!'

Her words were like a shot of adrenalin to his arms. She felt the new power of his paddle-thrust.

'If there's a truck, there must be someone around . . .'

There wasn't. The spot was as deserted as the river's surface. Sholto headed the craft towards the bank and the vehicle.

'Sholto! I know that truck! It's Stefan's!'

'Stefan's! Watch out, then – where is he?'

Grania went on excitedly, 'There's no one! Remember what Stefan said? He arranged for him and Hayward to rendezvous and steal a car from the parking ground after the bomb and then make their way to his own vehicle on the river road! This is the place!'

'You're right, Grania! I remember now too! But how do you know it's Stefan's?'

'It's the one he and Hayward kidnapped me in.'

'It also happens to be the same make as my farm truck. Come on!'

Their exhaustion was forgotten as they sprinted up the bank to the parked pick-up.

'It's Stefan's all right!' exclaimed Grania. 'Those are his registration plates! And look at this!' She pointed to the windscreen. There was Stefan's special blue VIP sticker giving him priority clearance.

'This truck is our salvation – you know what it means, Grania? We'll hijack it, we've still got just over an hour to reach Katse before 3.30 – '

'Sholto,' broke in Grania, 'what about starting it? It's probably locked also.'

'I said, it's the same model as mine – I know how it works!' rejoined Sholto animatedly. 'No problem shorting the ignition wires. As for the door . . .'

He grabbed a chunk of rock. 'Stand back!' he said, and smashed the driver's window.

'Now – ' It was a matter of a minute or two before he had, with the help of a pair of pliers taken from Stefan's toolbox behind the front seat, fixed the wires and had the engine running.

'Wait, Sholto – I must fetch my tool satchel for the Eagle – it's in the kayak.'

'The rope and pitons too,' added Sholto.

Grania was back within minutes, breathless from the scramble, the climbing rope looped round her shoulders.

298

She pitched them into the front seat, and followed. Sholto did a U-turn – the truck was facing up-river, away from Katse – and gunned the engine hard.

'What do you want the rope for?' Grania asked.

For a reply, Sholto tapped his watch face. 'Grania, we're going to get there in time now – just. It'll take about half an hour to reach Katse. That leaves us another half an hour before the bomb is due.'

'My Eagle job won't take long.'

'There are thousands of people and hundreds of cars to block our way. If we do it the straightforward way, we'll have first to get into the parking area, and then make our way to the dais on the wall itself where the VIPs and the Eagle are. We're not going to get a smooth or quick passage – if at all – from nervous security personnel. There are sure to be endless questions and hold-ups. We've also got to run the gauntlet of all the ambassadors, dignitaries, special guests and the two heads of state on the dais itself. The way we look won't be conducive to an easy ride either. Also, you've got to have time to fix that pediment.'

Grania looked anxiously at her watch. 'Sholto, I'll never get the pediment off in time now. I'm going to change tactics. Instead of the pediment, I'm going to smash the tiny viewing window which was meant to open simultaneously with the secret capsule. It's opaque – you can't see Hayward's detonator inside. From there, I'll cut the wires leading to the timepiece itself – it won't interfere with the clock's working. That means, no radio signal.'

'Wonderful!' Sholto exclaimed. 'We'll still be hard pushed, though. I'm also changing tactics. We're heading for the dais via the dam's back door, so to speak. That's what I want the rope for.'

'Back door?'

'The outlets. The tunnels from the sluices into the river. You remember, that passage where we all had such a scare when the sluices stuck? That tunnel leads back to the control chamber, as you know. We can first alert the operator on duty, and then go unhindered to the top of the wall itself and the dais via the

299

perimeter gallery. I'd guess the security personnel will be concentrated on the wall itself and round the podium.'

'We can only hope for the best, Sholto. The place will be packed.'

It was.

Two-fifty p.m.

The crag which formed the anchor-point of the 168-metre high wall and on which also stood Katse Lodge on the upstream side, looked as if it had been spray-painted with cars. The massed effect was heightened by the natural layers which the terrain formed progressively to the summit, so that the vehicles looked as if they had been stacked, layer upon layer, from the flat concrete apron flanking the river to the raw black basalt at the summit.

The similarity to a bees' nest was not lost on the TV cameraman aiming from a helicopter hovering above the crag. The crowd was concentrated at the spot where the end of the wall joined the crag. There were flags and bunting everywhere.

The cameraman was already starting to focus on this concentration, the focal point from which the opening ceremony would shortly be conducted. Here the dais stood on the wall. The structure was novel enough in itself to provide unique television material. A tunnel borer, which looked like an old-fashioned tram even to its curved iron roof – it had been employed on the massive eighty kilometre pipeline under the mountains – stood on temporary rails on the top of the wall. It was close to the perimeter gallery entrance, which, in its turn, led deep down to the sluices control chamber. The 'tram' had a massive circular snout (its cutting edge) at one end and was open at the other. Wooden steps provided a way up for the two heads of state, who sat on big chairs in the centre of the strange vehicle. Immediately above them ran a ventilation pipe, thick as a man's body, which provided fresh air during underground drilling.

As a general establishing shot of the scene, the TV camera had shown viewers the way the cliff was scored from summit to base by five encircling 'walls' of weathered basalt. These 'walls' were high – twice to three times the height of a man – through which at intervals there were ragged gateways, especially on the outlets side immediately below the dam wall.

Of no interest to the cameraman, however, was the plume of dust thrown up by a speeding pick-up which came racing towards the parking area from the service road along the river. Near the entrance, however, it turned aside into a construction road which skirted the entire crag area on the side away from the dam.

'We're almost there!' Sholto told Grania. 'Once we get round the shoulder of the cliff, we'll be all set. We'll go on foot from there.'

'Won't we be spotted, Sholto?'

'Those basalt walls are ideal cover. We can dodge along behind them to reach the water's edge and the outlets. I'm sure the security cordon doesn't extend that far.'

Sholto rounded the cliff, slipped through one of the natural gateways where the rock had crumbled, and then braked to a standstill behind another wall, the third in number leading up from the water's edge. The bed of the river below them was dry; within less than half an hour, if Stefan had his way, it would be a boiling, murderous torrent.

'Now! There the outlets are!'

Sholto and Grania crouched against the basalt wall. Through another natural gateway Grania could make out two shovel-shaped concrete outlets at the extremity of the discharge tunnels projecting into the dry river bed.

'That's going to be our tricky bit,' said Sholto, and pointed. From their present vantage point to the lowermost wall, almost on the river bank, was a gap of about eighty metres. It was downhill, rough ground which had been used as a dumping-spot for junked machinery and other clutter left over from the construction of the coffer dam and diversion weir during the early stages of building the wall.

Sholto glanced apprehensively upwards and rightwards in the direction of the dais and the crowd.

'We'll just have to risk it,' he told Grania. 'If there is wide awake security up there, they could spot us crossing the open ground. But we haven't any other option. Got that tool satchel safe? Okay! Let's go!'

They broke cover at a sprint. Sholto's bright blue canoeing

windcheater stood out against the black terrain; the pitons from the rope around his shoulders clinked as he ran. Grania's jacket was red. A sharpshooter on the wall would have had no worries about tracking them as his targets.

It wasn't a sharpshooter who spotted them, however.

It was one of General Mak's aides, standing behind the security chief, who sat amongst the small select band of top VIPs next to the two heads of state. The aide leant down quickly, indicated. General Mak caught only a glimpse of a red jacket vanishing behind a junked truck.

He spoke briefly and rapidly to a VIP on his right, gave a half-bow towards the heads of state, left his chair, and along with the aide started for the entrance to the perimeter gallery – and the control chamber.

While General Mak was moving, Sholto jinked behind a yellow, half-rusted mechanical excavator, and stumbled downhill over the rough ground towards the final wall which would shelter them for the run-in to the outlets.

They were again lost to sight as they slipped behind the cover of the last wall on the river bank itself. They raced along it. Suddenly their feet were on concrete. They turned sharp right and found themselves in the dark bell-mouthed entrance, twice the height of a man, of the nearest of the two discharge tunnels.

Three p.m.

Half an hour to go.

'Catch your breath for a moment,' said Sholto. 'It's not far now.'

'How far?'

'I'd say about 200 metres up the tunnel to the control chamber, as I recall from our visit.'

'And then?'

'About half that distance from there to the top of the wall.' He checked his watch. 'We'll make it still.'

'Let's get on.'

They went in further; the walls were smooth; the roof rose higher; they came upon the railed catwalk where the VIP party had sheltered from the flood.

Sholto unhitched the rope from his shoulders and pitched it over the railing as an anchor-point to climb up.

The snake-like action of the rope drew a figure out of the catwalk's shadows.

It was Stefan.

Sholto moved like lightning. He was already halfway up the rope when Stefan came at it. A knife-blade stuck out of his fist. Sholto whipped a piton from his belt. Its thin pointed steel looked like a stiletto. Stefan switched his aim from the rope to the piton. He swung at Sholto's face. Sholto went back hard. The knife singed his cheek. Now Sholto had one leg over the railing. Stefan came again at him with the knife, but Sholto ducked down and lunged the piton at him. It must have gone home somewhere, for the Maluti Rider gave a grunt and did not complete the stroke.

Sholto went fully over the rail, moved in hard on Stefan's knife hand and threw an armlock on it. Stefan tried to jerk free. As he did so, something blue-black and metallic fell out of his pocket on to the floor of the outlet below. Grania gathered up the Makarov and started up the rope. Stefan wrenched himself free. Sholto went in under the knife and put all his weight behind the blow to the solar plexus. He fell back. Grania passed Sholto the Makarov. Stefan came at him to crowd him out of the shot. Sholto reversed his grip from butt to barrel. It smacked against Stefan's head. He sagged half to his knees, reaching for the railing to hold himself up. Sholto completed the knock-out.

'Is he – dead?' Grania was shaking.

'No,' panted Sholto. 'Out, well out – but not dead. It could sink everything, if he gets loose. Here, the rope – help me!'

Sholto lashed the Maluti Rider to the railings.

Three-twelve.

Eighteen minutes to go!

A voice said out of the darkness ahead: 'Hold it! Don't move!'

They didn't. The blue mouth of the pistol came first, and then General Mak. Then a shadow from the shadows, the lynx-eyed aide.

'What is going on here? We spotted you from the wall. Who is this?'

303

'The Maluti Rider,' Sholto snapped back. 'There's a bomb due to go off in eighteen minutes' time . . .' Sholto poured out an explanation. 'For God's sake, we must hurry!'

Grania didn't wait for him to finish or the security men to lower their guns. She used the slack of the rope holding Stefan to abseil down to the outlet floor and collect her tool satchel.

General Mak eyed her. 'You're either very brave or very foolish.'

On the railings, Stefan's breath came and went like a deflating hot-air balloon.

'Hurry!' rapped out Sholto. 'If you don't believe me, you can see the limpet for yourself under the control console!'

Three-fourteen.

General Mak threw a glance at Stefan's unconscious figure. 'He's safe enough for the moment; we'll come back for him.'

'Out for the count,' added Sholto. 'Let's go!'

General Mak, still carrying his gun, sent them first along the dog-leg branch of the railed-off gallery, which was a sideshoot of the main perimeter gallery. He put the weapon in his pocket as they entered the control chamber.

'What's going on?' demanded the console operator.

'What's your name?'

'Frank.'

'Okay, Frank. This man – ' he indicated Sholto and the way he said it reflected his doubts ' – says there is a limpet mine under your console. Put your hand under it and see . . .'

Frank's smirk showed what he, too, thought of the story. He reached down with a hand. His face went deadly pale.

'There's something hard here . . .'

There was no need to demonstrate it. Hayward's gun and his face verified the story. He stood with his Colt aimed on the five. Not bog-whiskey or mescalin could have bestowed on him a high like the Eagle. His smile was as seraphic as a child's or an idiot's.

'I saw you run across the open ground,' he said. 'I knew you would come here. Where's Stefan?'

'Out for the count,' Sholto answered.

'Ah, well.'

304

He addressed General Mak, and his voice became more Irish than Grania had ever heard the brogue.

'It's a bomb, all right, under the console,' he went on. 'With that trigger up top there inside the Eagle, it's the sweetest little darling you ever saw. I'm sort of glad now the Chunnel bomb aborted.'

He waved the gun. The security men had theirs in their pockets still.

'Backs against the wall,' he ordered. 'Now when I've checked this, I'll check you over too . . .' He reached under the console and smiled. 'That's my baby!'

From the wall facing the console, there was a sound like a Second World War naval firing gong.

The buzz of the alarm warned the operator – ten minutes to zero!

Hayward's startled eyes went to the buzzer. You don't take your eyes off the ball with a man like General Mak around.

The heavy .38 service bullet took Hayward in the head and threw him across the room. The Colt went every way.

'What in hell was that alarm?' demanded General Mak.

'That's the ten-minute signal to me,' replied Frank. His voice was shaky. 'There's another one due in five minutes. Then one at one minute, and the final when the heads of state press the button.'

'Get back to your post,' snapped General Mak. 'We can't do anything about that bomb under the console, but we can stop it from up above. Is that clear?'

'Clear, but . . .'

'Get moving!' went on the security chief. 'Time's running out!'

The concrete tunnel to the surface was lit by naked electric bulbs. The floor was uphill all the way to the top, to the dais. Beyond the hydropower chamber, it made a ninety-degree turn and finally debouched close to where the 'tram' stood on its rails.

Three twenty-five.

General Mak, Sholto and Grania burst on to the wall. The tunnel exit was at the snout end of the 'tram'.

305

A narrow pathway, railed off with ornamental chains, led round the entire front of the 'tram' where the two heads of state and a handful of top VIPs sat facing the huge crowd. The entrance to the vehicle, about as high as a man's waist off the ground, was on the far side via a short flight of wooden steps. A row of flags and bunting flapped. Immediately in front of the heads of state was a lectern with a microphone.

But it was the glowing object on a purple velvet cushion on top of a small podium which held the public eye.

A spotlight, concealed in the 'tram's' roof, threw a thousand lances of light in every direction from the sixteen jewelled modules of the Eagle of Time. Crowning all was the golden lammergeyer, poised now to spread his golden wings – and trigger the death-dealing bomb clinging to the console in the control chamber underground.

The five-minute signal buzzed on the wall opposite Frank, the operator.

His wet hands were on the switches. He was sitting in a pool of sweat. Would the one-minute buzzer sound at all?

Up above on the wall, General Mak rapped out: 'Follow me!'

The armed security guards gaped at the sight of their chief as he pushed past. Without him, Sholto realised in passing, he and Grania would never have got near the podium.

Equally startled was the Master of Ceremonies who was occupying the central microphone. However, he went on with his set speech as the trio approached.

'Ladies and gentlemen, we are now coming to the highpoint of the day's proceedings . . .' He glanced down as General Mak, followed closely by Grania and Sholto, passed in front of him. 'In a few minutes, at 3.30 to be exact, the two heads of state will come to the podium here – ' he gestured at the Eagle of Time ' – and await the exact moment when the clock shows 3.30. At that precise moment, you will hear the clock's carillon start to chime, and the Eagle of Time will begin to spread its wings.

'That will be the signal for the two heads of state to jointly press the button on the podium and open the sluice-gates, from which a token flow of water will be released for about ten minutes. The public is warned, however, that there will be a slight time-lag of several minutes between the pressing of the button and the actual release of the water, due to the time factor involved in the mechanism of opening the sluice-gates . . .'

General Mak raced up the 'tram's' steps. He halted Sholto with a gesture. He then led Grania by the arm towards the podium and the Master of Ceremonies, who glanced aside from his notes, half puzzled, half angry. General Mak went on, bending low. He stopped behind the Lesotho Head of State, said something rapidly, and indicated Grania. A look of startled surprise crossed his face; he nodded quickly. General Mak hardly needed to convey the approval to Grania.

Three twenty-seven.

Grania dropped on her knees next to the Eagle of Time, and hastily unrolled her tool satchel. She drew out a pair of long-nosed pliers. As she did so, a second spotlight came on, as if to highlight the drama. She smartly cracked the tiny opaque glass window at the base of the pediment – the window designed to view the secret capsule when it opened in conjunction with the spreading of the lammergeyer's wings. Little fragments of glass spilt onto the velvet cushion.

The second spotlight helped her. She could see clearly inside the timepiece. The concentrated light reflected off two wires, one red and the other yellow. They led from the clock's mechanism to Hayward's detonator.

The Master of Ceremonies was saying, 'It is now time for the heads of state to move to the podium and set the water in motion by jointly pressing the button which will activate the sluice-gates . . .'

Three twenty-eight.

Grania thrust the long slender nose of the pliers through the window gap. She felt for a moment. Then she cut.

She withdrew the tool, checked, thrust it in again, cut the second wire.

Sholto, watching from the steps, prayed that Hayward had not booby-trapped the timer with a trembler fuse. It looked too tiny for that.

The two heads of state moved on the podium.

Thousands of eyes were on them. And on Grania. The silence was intense. She got to her feet, uncertain, embarrassed. She gave a brief all-clear signal with her hand to General Mak.

Three twenty-nine.

In the control chamber, Frank had to steady his wrist with his other hand in order to read the minute-hand of his watch.

The buzzer rang on the wall.

One minute to go!

Everything was fine up above!

Ridiculously, he kept his knee clear of the limpet mine under the console, as if that would help.

On the dais, Grania found herself face to face with the two heads of state. There was no way of escape.

She reached into her pocket, held out to them what looked like an outsize golf ball.

'It opens,' she stammered. 'It comes – belongs – inside there –'

She thrust it into the hands of the Lesotho head of state, and edged past, to General Mak's side.

The hush became palpable.

The hands of the Eagle of Time touched 3.30.

The clear angel voice of the carillon sang through the expectant silence. At that same moment there was a movement from the lammergeyer and its golden wings started to spread wide. The spotlights made the gold almost transparent.

The great crowd seemed to sigh. The two heads of state put their hands together on the button, faced the crowd, and again together spoke the traditional Basuto words used to end major ceremonial occasions:

'*Khotso, Pula, Nala!* – Peace, Rain, Prosperity!'

General Mak paused only as long as protocol demanded. Then he snapped at Sholto and Grania, 'The Maluti Rider – we've got to get him, quick!'

He led them via the front of the 'tram' – the heads of state were still shaking hands – past the snout end of the vehicle where the guards were. He ordered the lynx-eyed aide who had previously spotted Sholto and Grania, 'Bring four men – guns. Quick!'

The concrete perimeter gallery seemed twice as long to Grania going down as when they had raced up it. They burst into the control chamber. Frank was sitting at the console. He stared at them, glassy-eyed.

He saw the guns and the guards.

'I've done my job – the sluices are open – I'm getting the hell out . . .'

'Anyone come through here?' General Mak indicated the door to the railed-off gallery.

'Dunno – if you'd sat on top of a limpet mine, you wouldn't have noticed anything else . . .'

He drew back from the console.

'It's stone dead now,' retorted General Mak. 'Stay here! We'll defuse the damn thing later. Come on!'

The Maluti Rider had beaten them to it. The only evidence that he had been lashed there was an end of rope hitched to the railing. Stefan himself was using the rest of the rope. He was wading shakily through the knee-deep advance guard of the sluice-gates water towards the bell-mouthed outlets, steadying himself with it.

'Look! Dear God, look!' Grania screamed.

A wall of brown, topped and laced with foam, filled the tunnel running from the sluices. Its thunder pulsed ahead of it.

'Stefan! You fool! Come back . . .!'

Stefan heard Sholto's yell. He heard the thunder of the flood, too. The flood he had meant to be unleashed for his revenge.

He swung round. The triumph in his expression turned to terror. One moment a man's figure stood in knee-deep water, the next there was nothing. The water boiled up to the catwalk. Grania buried her face against Sholto.

The crowd saw the great spurt of water foam from the outlets, and cheered.

High on the wall above, the Eagle of Time folded his golden wings.